SHADES
THE GEHENNA DILEMMA
By Eric Dallaire

Cover Illustration by Ron Lemen
Edited by Alex Bear of Constellation Editing

First printing. This is a novel from *IF Tales* imprint.

Print ISBN 978-0-9961811-0-5
Ebook ISBN 978-0-9961811-1-2

Dedication

To my parents, Elizabeth and Richard Dallaire, for their humbling belief in me. Thank you for all of the incredible support. This book could not have been made without you both. To my son, Brendan, for his inspiring imagination. Also, I am blessed to have the company of talented and supportive friends who gave their time and wisdom to make this dream of mine awaken. I love you all.

CHAPTER 1
Funerary Rights

>> DATE: Sept 22nd, 2039. Three days before present time.
>> TIME: 3:21 AM.
>> LOCATION: Atchafalaya Basin, Louisiana.

"A perfect night for your grave deeds, sir," Sasha whispered to me. Her cutting tone indicated a newfound grasp of sarcasm that made me smirk. Now all of the women in my life disapproved of my work, even the artificial one. My partner Spenner coaxed more speed from his black sedan to make up time. Tires screeched, and the engine's roar sent a hidden rookery of white herons soaring. The vehicle's climate subsystem beeped an alert about the hot Louisiana evening air rushing in through the passenger side. I ignored it and left my window open. Smells of fresh rain and dank earth filled my nose. I preferred keeping all of my senses active while on the hunt. We barreled down a narrow road, riding over the encroaching tendrils and fingers of the Atchafalaya swamp. I watched the passing shadow play of silhouettes from black marsh trees performing their twisted dance. Out of the murky air, a metal sign rushed to meet us, but red rust covered its words and population numbers. Peering ahead, I saw fresh tire tracks in the muddy road, so I motioned for Spenner to pull over. He slammed the brakes hard, and we skidded to a stop next to the only gas pump.

The sound of our arrival roused the station's elderly attendant. We exited the car to question him about our target: a truck registered to the Devereux family. He peered at us through brass glasses, the thick lenses magnifying blue eyes that twinkled a shade darker than my own.

"We're looking for an old 2020 green truck," I asked the old man. "Did it pass by here recently?" The attendant shook his head and shrugged with a suspicious quickness. I wondered why he had just suffered an acute case of memory loss.

"Buy some fuel or move along, blondie," he snarled at me.

With a scowl and his fists balled, Spenner stepped up with the intention of pummeling the truth out of him. I intervened before my rash partner acted. Out of my leather jacket I withdrew a small wad of cash. Widened eyes told me the man had a price. After we handed him a few bills, the man remembered a wealth of interesting information.

"I jus' serviced that truck an hour ago," he mumbled. "It had a big wooden box sticking out the back. They had about ten or eleven cars with 'em. Just like one of them ole time funeral processions. Some of 'em bought soda pop. Then they left." He motioned with his thumb, pointing outside. "They headed down the south road."

"You've been a big help," I replied, handing him a smaller stack of bills. "Remember, we weren't here." The attendant nodded and counted his money with a smile that revealed neglect and a chronic pipe-smoking habit.

Time ticked against us, so we hurried back to the car and got in. The Devereux family aimed to put that box in the ground. But they no longer owned its contents -- and that's why Spenner and I slogged through this god-forsaken marsh. Our car roared and peeled away from the gas station. We followed the trail of fresh tire tracks into a dense wooded path that could not be classified as a road, even by rural standards. After twenty minutes of blind search, we came to an overgrown thicket that engulfed all traces of the road. We rolled without a sound over the last of the winding dirt road before the black swamp ahead swallowed the vehicle whole. We slowed, and I spotted a line of parked cars, vans, and a chrome-covered aero-bike.

"There they are," I whispered to my partner. "Park ahead of them."

With a wave of his calloused hand, Spenner killed the car's headlights. Leafy branches parted and embraced our car to provide perfect concealment. As we parked, I tapped my wrist-com to review the dossiers of the Devereux clan one last time. I flicked through the photos of the family, my eyes scanning through the thick files for anything I missed. My ears listened to mission intelligence relayed by my other, secret partner.

"Jonah, no one in the Devereux family has any registered firearms or prior convictions," spoke Sasha into the microscopic receiver implanted in my right ear. She served as my resident artificial intelligence program, embedded within my specially created wrist-com. Her assistance came in handy for these kinds of missions. I felt Spenner's piercing green eyes on me as Sasha talked. I wondered if he had some preternatural sense to hear her presence. My instinct told me not to divulge her existence to a new partner. I stared straight ahead and didn't respond. Satisfied with my preparation, I shut off the wrist-com and opened the car door. My body started sweating from the bayou's night heat.

The two of us exited the car without a sound and headed for the car's rear. Spenner opened the trunk to reveal his armory, bathing our faces in a white electric glow. The trunk's light made his scar more prominent among the natural crags and lines on his face. The old wound traced a thin trail through the brown and gray hair near his temple. It appeared and faded like the ghost of a bullet from some past lethal encounter.

Damn. He had enough illegal military weaponry, stun-rods, and neural-paralytics to equip a small army. Expecting no resistance from the family, I opted for an easy-to-conceal tranquilizer gun and a stun-rod. Those choices prompted a contemptuous snort from my partner.

"If you're going to pack light, I'll pick up the slack," chided Spenner. He grabbed the double-barreled scattershot rifle, a sonic squealer modified with an illegal amplifier, and four cryo-grenades.

"Jesus, are we hunting a stiff or going to war?" I didn't bother to conceal my concern. "My research says this family is unarmed. It's an easy collection."

"If these families want to act like criminals, I'll treat them like criminals," he growled. "You want to make sure we get paid, right? My intel says your mother could really use that money."

I froze. Spenner had done his homework. Of course, I'd checked him out too. But it unsettled me that he knew more intimate details. My sources told me only the basics about him. Like me, he'd taken bounty jobs after the military served him with a discharge. He had a reputation for getting results, but his outcomes turned bloody. When I accepted the job two days back, I had ignored my instinctual warnings about him, passing other lower paying hacking gigs. Like he said, I needed the money. Too late for regret, I told myself. After this, my gut told me, I needed a new partner. For now, I focused on the mission.

"If the target is damaged, we don't get the bounty," I warned. I didn't want to let this hothead take charge. "We go in my way or not at all."

Spenner grinned back. "You'll need these," he answered, tossing me a pair of noise-reducing earplugs to ward against the squealer's effects. Then he turned away and started toward the swamp. "I want you to be able to hear me say 'I told you so' later." I put them on and followed.

Together, we crept into the swamp through fetid water, with only the buzzing choir of insects scattering to herald our approach. Looking up, I saw intermittent shafts of moonlight pierce through the treetop canopy. Our tall frames required frequent ducking beneath the five-foot-high tangles of claw-like tree branches. I tapped my wrist-com for occasional illumination and to query Sasha for updates.

"I hacked into a military satellite and downloaded its surveillance photos of this region," reported Sasha. "Its thermal imaging shows a count of fourteen people one hundred yards away. I'm unable to discern what they are doing, but I calculate the odds that they are planning a surprise party for you to be infinitesimally low." I cracked a thin smile, pleased that Sasha's ever-maturing personality sub-routines desired to cheer me up.

"The latest geo-satellite uplink shows fourteen ahead," I whispered aloud.

"Looks like the whole clan showed up for the service," he responded. "Good thing I came prepared." I extended my middle finger behind his back as a silent response.

Pushing through the foliage quicker, we smelled burning pine. Then we saw the telltale floating embers of multiple torches. When we reached the clearing, we found the family stacking fresh-cut logs onto a pile. I guessed they meant to use the wood as a funeral pyre. Lucky for us, the pyre remained unlit. We still had a chance, so we stepped up the pace of our approach.

Moving closer, we heard a hushed, deep voice speaking in an ancient but familiar tongue. We crouched behind a large moss-covered rock and surveyed the clearing ahead. A family of fourteen knelt, stood, and sobbed before a simple black casket bearing the body of their withered patriarch.

A tall robed man stood over the casket, speaking Latin. A priest performing the final rites of passage, I guessed. His weathered face featured a shaggy gray beard that hung like a clump of old moss, and his drab brown robes blended so well with the surroundings that he looked like a natural part of the forest.

"Gloria Patri, et Filio, et Spiritui Sancto," spoke the priest in a deep voice that reverberated around the wood. "Cinis ad cinerem, pulvis ad pulverem."

I didn't understand everything the preacher said, but at some point I'm fairly certain he said 'ashes to ashes', meaning he neared an end to his prayer. Spenner crouched and thrust the squealer's barrel through the middle of the bush concealing us. He placed his finger on the trigger and aimed his rifle. When I realized that he intended to shoot first and sort it out later, I placed my hand on his gun. Without saying a word, I locked eyes on him and shook my head as if to say we have to do this my way. In that tense moment, I felt him sizing me up. His face became an unreadable wall of stoic granite. At six-foot-four, Spenner possessed an imposing four-inch height advantage and thicker muscles than my leaner frame. Holding my ground, I waited to see if he would fire anyway or even turn his fury on me. After a few moments of consideration, Spenner nodded and lowered the weapon. While I knew these collections sometimes ended in conflict, I needed to give the family the chance to surrender. I made a countdown motion for Spenner to enter the clearing ahead. On the count of three, Spenner emerged first from our cover, double-armed with his scattergun in his left hand and squealer in the other.

"Everybody freeze! NOW!" Spenner's piercing, primal challenge shattered the serenity of the area, and the swamp erupted in chaos. A quartet of resting egrets flapped their wings to escape from the noisy predator. A trio of mangy river rats squealed from the nearby bush and scurried away. The fourteen Devereux family members jumped, cried out, gasped, and shouted obscenities at my partner. Then I emerged from hiding to present the formalities and rights.

"Everyone be calm!" I shouted, holding a glowing blue holo-sphere over my head. "We are lawfully deputized federal agents here to collect the deceased remains of Jebediah Devereux." The sphere possessed a portable virtual-casting generator inside of it. Since the v-cast machine only contained a simple portable mark-1 generator, the holograms it projected lacked high fidelity but looked real enough to an unsophisticated eye. Upon activation, the holo-sphere floated out of my hand and whined to life. Multi-colored shafts of lights from the sphere brightened the dark swamp. The sphere created flickering deputy IRS silver badges for Spenner and me, appearing over our jackets. Next, the sphere cast a cone of light particles that rearranged into the distorted visage of a human face. More color shot from the sphere, and the quality of the hologram increased. The sphere then transformed itself into the wrinkled face of the Honorable Judge Rutherford Prescott.

"Pursuant to United States Code, Title 26, Subtitle Z, Section 25158 (1) (a), the Incorporeal Revenue Service has been given the mandate to collect debts from citizens who perish in a state of serious delinquency and insolvency..." the ghost judge stated, droning on longer with more legal disclaimers.

"Shit!" yelled the largest of the family members. From what I recalled of the intel on the Devereux clan, they nicknamed this massive tank of a young man Little Scooter. "They're ghouls!"

All of the others started to protest at the same time. Three of the women wailed and pleaded with us to go away to let them proceed with the services. Rising tall above everyone, the priest demanded that we depart, his voice cracking with anger. He argued something about 'sanctified grounds', but I couldn't hear him over the din of protestations. Besides, our legal mandate superseded the ecclesiastic when it came to this kind of collection. Over the chaos, the holographically-projected judge continued to read the lien and rights. Spenner powered his rifle and pointed its glowing barrel at the Devereux clan.

"How dare you!" yelled a short, elderly woman. I remembered her face from my digital dossiers. Sherry, the target's wife, fumed bright red with anger and indignation. Her small frame trembled with fury. "This was a God-fearing man who deserves a proper burial! He was the mayor for Christ's sake!"

Scooter's mop of dirty blond hair covered his brow, but I could see his face twist into a withering scowl. He bent down to pick up an axe that he must have used earlier to cut and build the wooden pyre. I knew Spenner saw this, because he swiveled his guns towards the hulking youth.

"Bad idea, chubby," Spenner warned. "I will not hesitate to brain you so hard that you'll be serving your own life-debt with your gramps. That goes for all of you hillbillies. Interfere and you'll pay the same price."

"...the appeal process, pursuant to United States Code, Title 27, Subtitle Z, Section 21153 (2) (c), can be initiated at any local court should you elect to do so," the holo-judge continued.

No one moved or spoke while the judge read the rights. With every tick of the tension-laden moments, time slowed more and more. The Devereux clan glared at us with pure concentrated venom. The hairs on my arms raised, and I could hear Spenner's finger cock the trigger mechanism of his scattergun.

My mind raced to say something that didn't sound threatening or contrived that might defuse the deteriorating situation.

"Listen everyone, if we can all remain calm--" I stopped when I saw the old lady glance to each side, her hands balling. She readied herself. I tried to scream 'NO', but it all went to hell before that second got to tick. She broke the stand off by grabbing one of the torches lighting the area, and sprinted toward the pyre with swiftness that belied her petite body. A tinge of guilt knotted my stomach. Part of me couldn't blame her; she wanted to lay her beloved husband to rest.

Spenner flashed a twisted, vicious smile. I knew he wanted a fight. With a flick of his finger, he fired the scattergun. A signature yellow pulse distorted the air around the weapon's barrel, and slammed Sherry with a non-lethal but painful concussive force. The poor woman, a seventy-five-year-old grandmother, gasped as the blast took the air from her lungs, broke her ribs, and knocked her to the ground.

Scooter's frothing mouth uttered some unintelligible curse as he hefted the axe over his head. Like a full-grown bull with horns bared, Scooter let out a roar and charged us. Unfazed, Spenner readied and fired his other weapon, the terrible squealer. The crimson-glowing rifle emitted a cone of sonic force at the whole crowd. It unleashed a piercing sound that no living being should have to hear, like the amplified sound of an animal dying in pain. Scooter and his family collapsed, covering their bleeding ears, screaming the dreadful squeal of pain that gave the weapon its namesake.

With the crowd controlled, I moved toward the deceased body of the target with only the priest standing in my way. Despite blood trickling from his ears, he stood stoic and oblivious to the pain, and remained intent on his work. He mouthed a prayer and made a gesture of the trinity. I lowered my guard too soon, because right around the cross-shaped gesture for the Holy Ghost, his hand slipped into his robe and he pulled out a Magnum hand cannon.

I had time to curse "Damn" aloud, then I apologized in my mind for swearing in front of a clergyman. As I twirled to avoid his first shot, I swung my stun-rod down onto his shoulder. The stun-rod made a muted zapping sound and gave off an acrid burning smell from the electrical attack. With his muscles contracted, he groaned and dropped his gun. Knowing this bear of a priest still presented a threat, I lunged for the coup-de-grace and stuck the sparking end of the weapon dead-center at his chest, sending fifty thousand volts of stunning electricity through his crucifix and into his writhing body.

"Forgive me father, for I have singed," I joked. In that moment, I worried if Hell waited for striking the priest or for telling that joke. But the priest did draw first. At least, that's how I consoled myself.

"I've got the family pinned, do you have the stiff?" Spenner called out over the cries of pain. He brandished the squealer rifle as the Devereux family members, most still trembling and clutching their ears, crawled away from him.

"Yeah, I got it," I yelled back. Opening my backpack, I pulled out a long syringe and popped off its protective cap. The transparent tube bubbled with a noxious-looking yellow fluid, a serum formulated and programmed for Jebediah. Looking up, I addressed the transparent, virtual face of the judge. "Your Honor, the defendant is ready for sentencing."

"...Jebediah Devereux," announced the judge, "you have been sentenced to serve a post-mortem service to repay your after-debt to society. Your soulless body will be rejuvenated to work for a service term of no less than seventy-five years."

With the sentence announced, I plunged the syringe into the chest of the deceased man before me, and braced myself for something I never enjoyed seeing. All of the family stopped wailing and glared at me with hate, then looked to the body with sadness. We all waited for the inevitable. A muscle convulsion shook the dead body once, then twice, and the third made the body rise from the unlit pyre. It was now a shell of what the man used to be, a soulless commodity belonging to the stiff's debtor.

A shade.

When it looked at me with eyes blazing with a yellow-tinged hue, I knew that the juice had done its work. The serum coursed through the dead body, bringing it back, programming it to key into our voices and obey without hesitation. Jebediah, a former father of seven children, grandfather to fifteen, an honest but unlucky businessman, now became a lumbering, animated husk. As a mindless shade, he would toil for three quarters of a century somewhere on Earth, or possibly on the moon, wherever he fetched a higher bid, until he satisfied his afterdeath financial obligations.

"Let's go, Jebediah, it's time for you to start your first shift," Spenner announced without a modicum of pity. The Devereux family members, beaten and bloodied, mustered enough saliva to spit at us as we departed with our bounty.

CHAPTER 2
The Sickle and the Cross

"But in this world nothing can be said to be certain, except death and taxes."
- Benjamin Franklin, 1777

>> DATE: Sept. 25th, 2039, the present time. Three days after the Jebediah bounty mission.
>> TIME: Unknown.
>> LOCATION: Incorporeal Revenue Service, New York City Branch, Building D.

The sweeping view of black space, rocketing shuttles, and the blue-gray Earth from floor ten thousand of the Lunar Spire paled in my mind to Vanessa's radiant glory. Despite overlooking the most coveted table with a stellar view at La Vie, she captured all of my attention. Her cream-colored dress glittered with diamonds, bright stars shining and orbiting around her like a private galaxy. She smiled at me, and lifted her champagne-filled glass to mine. When her lips parted, my cheeks flushed and my heart pounded.

"I love you, Vanessa," I whispered, touching her glass with a crystal kiss. I motioned for her to sit so we could start our ten-course meal at the moon's most exclusive restaurant. Deep down, I understood this to be a dream, but in that moment I didn't care.

"I love you too, Jonah," she said, reaching out to hold my hand. Before we touched, the Earth, the restaurant, our table, and then Vanessa all melted away like pictures in a fire. My subconscious struggled to hold this hopeful fantasy-to-be together just a while longer. Despite my effort, everything faded into darkness, followed by a visual deluge of memories from the last three days. I saw a staccato slideshow of images. It started with Jebediah the shade lumbering behind me. Then the scene shifted to Spenner driving his car back to New York, followed by an explosion alongside a dark highway. The dreamscape changed into a digital advertisement featuring a man in a white suit waving to get my attention. The vision ended with a view of the High Tower meta-skyscraper dominating the skyline of New York. All of these confusing, disconnected thoughts flooded my mind's eye at once. As I tried to make sense of the chaos, a loud sound disrupted my dreaming.

"Jonah," sounded another voice that did not belong to Vanessa. That voice and the throbbing pain on the sides of my head awakened me from sleep. My heart quickened when I struggled to remember how I managed to get from the swamp to this cold, spartan room. When I raised my head, I felt an ache down my spine. My eyes fluttered, trying to refresh my blurry vision. After a few more blinks and rubbing my eyes, my sight adjusted to the room's harsh lighting. The interrogation room could have been plucked right from an old television cop show. Sterile white walls boxed me into a fifteen-by-fifteen room. Stale, cold air flowed through a grated ceiling vent. Along the room's far side, a smoke-colored glass wall allowed my captors to watch me but not the other way around. The claustrophobic space heightened my anxiety.

To calm myself, I reviewed what I knew. First, my body ached all over. Judging from the bruises and aching jaw, my body had taken part in one hell of a fight. Coarse blond and scattered gray stubble on my face hinted I had been here a day or more. A quick check of my faded jeans revealed emptied pockets. Beneath the arms of my well-worn dark blue jacket, I felt the telltale bumps from a pair of needle punctures. I wondered if my captors had administered medicine or some drug to enhance the integrity of my answers. Second, I remembered answering questions an hour ago from a pair of disembodied voices. Behind the opaque glass window, they had asked detailed queries about me, the Devereux family, my girlfriend Vanessa, and Spenner. They had repeated the questions a second time with the gentle approach. When they'd drilled the same questions with the tough approach, I'd gotten lightheaded and passed out on the hard steel table. Third, they'd confiscated my wrist-com and my access to Sasha. If they wanted her code, they would have a hard time unspooling her security protections. I found the silence of her absence unsettling. Before I started to review my escape strategies, the door opened, and two men entered the room. The first one, a taller, thinner man dressed in a silver suit, spoke first.

"I hope you are feeling better after your rest," he said with a soft, musical voice. "We now have enough information about the collection mission for Jebediah Devereux. We would appreciate it if you would continue with the next stage of your report."

Then the second interrogator, a well-muscled African-American man in a custom-fitted designer black suit, walked to the table and grabbed the seat across from me. With a purposeful aggressive motion, he dragged the chair so it grated against the floor. His stocky, muscular body moved with a purposeful lack of subtlety. When he fell into his seat, his fast-descending weight created a thud, and his hands slammed the table to steady himself. So, this one will play the part of the hard-ass, I thought.

"Where am I?" I demanded. "Do you have Vanessa?"

"We'll answer your questions after you answer a few of our own," replied the interrogator. He rubbed his thick, groomed mustache, then tapped at the data window before him to recall information about me. "You stated that after you procured the target, you and your partner Spenner returned to the city?"

Seeking any advantage, I paused before answering to study him and glean even the most minuscule detail. At six-foot-five, he still loomed over me even while sitting. His stern brown-eyed gaze met mine but revealed nothing. When he folded his massive hands, I noticed many white scars and calluses. Shifting in his chair, he seemed to wear his expensive suit with disdain, like a formality he observed but disliked. Instinct informed me that this large man felt more comfortable in the field than in a government office. His suit's sleeve slipped down just enough for me to notice the top portion of his colorful tattoo, the toothy maw of a green Chinese dragon. The distinctive serpentine Emerald Drake wrapped around his hand, a rare brand that represented special echelon technology access. Now I knew he had served with Navy Special Forces during the Korean conflict. When he saw that I glanced at his mark, he pulled his sleeve to cover it. Growing impatient, the interrogator narrowed his eyes and drummed his fingers.

"Yes," I responded. My attention drifted up to the silver pin on his collar. The emblem of the eagle, wheat, and scythe indicated he worked for the Incorporeal Revenue Service. The silver pin indicated a director level position within the IRS. "That is my answer, Director." A grin slipped through his stern countenance, soon replaced with his stoic mask.

"And after the bayou job," the black-dressed man continued, "it's your story that you returned to the city and parted ways with Spenner, and he promised to turn in the debtor to the IRS receiving station?"

"Not a story," I corrected. "That's what happened."

The black-dressed man grunted with disapproval, prompting the other, thinner interrogator to step closer. I took a moment to size him up. The second interrogator wore a tailor-made silver suit accented with a white silk mandarin collar. The collar indicated his high ranking in the New Universal Church. Though my computer knowledge far exceeded my understanding of modern theology, I knew enough to understand this man wielded considerable influence. I knew the Universal Church worked side-by-side with the IRS to regulate the shade-trade, so it didn't surprise me to see a priest here. However, the fact that such a high-ranking member of the Church and an IRS Director handled the debriefing of a simple collection raised my suspicions.

The silver-dressed priest represented the opposite qualities of his partner in every respect. He stood garbed in his exquisite clothes at ease. His silk suit, groomed gray hair, clean-shaven face, manicured nails, and lilac-scented cologne told me this man of the cloth did not wrestle with any guilt involving his wealth. The priest offered a warm smile, and placed his soft hand on my shoulder. I readied myself for the inevitable "good cop" routine.

"Thank you for answering candidly, my son," the silver-dressed man said in a soothing tone, while flashing a wide smile, showing off perfect, alabaster-white teeth. "You will find us most amenable to honesty. That is all we are seeking..."

"Funny thing," interrupted the black-dressed man, "Spenner never turned in the Jebediah-shade to the IRS transfer station."

I failed to stifle a surprised look. I gnawed my fingernail, thinking about my next response, and the silver-dressed man noticed my obvious discomfort.

"Jonah, don't worry, we're not accusing you of anything," the silver-dressed interrogator reassured me. "We're simply looking for the truth. In your initial report, you mentioned something about some unfortunate events on the trip back with your target," he said with an expression of concern. "Why don't you tell us more about that?"

The black-dressed man, not able to conceal his impatience with the slow progress of the interrogation, snapped. "Oh, enough of this! What do you remember about the video call? Tell us who Spenner talked with on your trip back to New York!"

The silver-dressed man betrayed his warm demeanor for the briefest of moments, flashing a seething look of fleeting anger at his black-clad partner.

"Patience, Barnaby," the priest said through gritted teeth. "I'm sure Jonah will explain this to us fully. We need only give him time to recall his thoughts. He has survived some harrowing events."

Silence blanketed the room as the two agents glared at each other. A palpable tension hung in the air, pushing me like an invisible physical force.

"You're right, Erasmus," conceded the black-clad man. Now, I knew their names, and that they wanted to know about the call Spenner received on the trip back to New York.

"Perhaps a respite from our discussion would be helpful for everyone," offered Erasmus. "Jonah, your doctor suggested that you get some exercise. If you feel able, would you like to take a brief walk and return to our chat in a few minutes? I would like to show you something."

Nodding, I pushed the table to stand. My nervous system shocked my extremities with lightning pain. A grimace twisted my face a brief moment before I regained my composure and walked toward Erasmus. He motioned for me to follow him out a door that slid open from the white wall. I limped out of the room, and entered a wide corridor forking in two directions.

"Come," Erasmus said, beckoning. "There is someone who is eager to see you." Erasmus and Barnaby turned right into the beige-painted hallway. We passed through several closed doors labeled with nonsensical government acronyms like NIDJS and ESPCOR.

Our footsteps echoed across the polished black marble floor. At each branch in the corridor maze, a pair of armed guards in brown suits nodded at Barnaby. We passed through five checkpoints until we came to the final corridor, ending with an oak door fashioned with a bronze plaque.

** Incorporeal Revenue Service **
** Global Level Auditing Division E3A **

As we approached, two guards flanking the door stepped aside then snapped back to their sentry position.

"Welcome to GLAD, Director Barnaby, s-sir," stammered the younger guard while the other opened the door.

We entered, and I found myself in one of the bustling command centers of the IRS. Dozens of agents scurried up and down steel stair steps with their heads down, skimming reports on their wrist-coms or hand-screen tablets. On the third floor of the wide, round hall, a tribunal consisting of twenty hovering holo-judges presided over dozens of simultaneous trials. A line of ghostly v-casting people wrapped around the circular second floor for a chance to appeal their case. The central space filled with moving, floating virtual displays all showing different data streams about investigations throughout the world and the moon. It struck me as organized chaos in motion. The business of the IRS involved collecting revenue from dead or near-dead people, and business appeared healthy.

A hawkish, gaunt man dressed in a white lab coat approached Barnaby. He handed over a thin black tablet, and my wrist-com lit by a faint blue illumination. Above the white-coated scientist, a four-by-four personal virtual projection screen floated behind him. A block of calligraphic text shimmered and repeated itself across the display. I smirked when I recognized the handiwork of Sasha's humor algorithm flashing above the scientist, highlighting his scowling face.

There's no place like home. There's no place like home. There's no place like home.

"The AI is still being--uncooperative," sighed the scientist. "However, all tests are conclusive – she does not violate any Promethean sentience regulations. She passed all criteria by the slimmest margins, but she passed. Quite ingenious how her heuristics--"

"Faith," Erasmus interrupted, dismissing the scientist with an arm wave. He looked to Barnaby. "I believe a show of good faith is in order. Our guest Jonah has been forthcoming. Let him have his equipment and be reunited with his friend." Before Barnaby rebutted, Erasmus smiled and raised his hand. "I'm sure Jonah will refrain from using his cyber-skills to pry into our network. We can trust you, Jonah, yes?"

My instinct told me they returned Sasha for a reason, likely because they could not hack her and hoped that I would reveal the information she possessed. Whatever the reason, I nodded my assent. Barnaby frowned as he examined the report from the scientist. After a few moments of scouring the tablet's data and scratching his head, he relented and thrust the wrist-com into my hands.

"Here," he grunted.

"Thank you," I said, fastening the device onto my arm. My fingers felt the warmth of the light-based finger sensors activating and embracing my hand. As the system rebooted, I heard Sasha's presence.

"Oh captain, my captain, our fearful trip is done," said Sasha into my ear. "It is comforting to be back, sir. My inquisitors seemed keen to learn about your trip with Spenner. Much to their great disappointment, they discovered nothing."

"Good to have you back, Sasha," I whispered.

"Now then," Erasmus said, pulling up two brown leather chairs, one for me and one for him. "I have helped you, and I hope you will aid us. Please, continue with your report. Begin with your departure from Louisiana with Spenner."

Part of me wanted to refuse to cooperate and keep my mouth closed. Then I weighed the benefits. Perhaps by telling what I knew I might also be able to learn more information from their reactions. Reviewing the events of the past few days also seemed to help rekindle my recollections. Besides, in my weakened condition, I made a conservative count of my viable options, and they added up to zero.

My thoughts wandered back two days and I resumed telling my story...

CHAPTER 3
Crimson Blues

*"The collaboration of science and religion established a
new, better order where citizens will be able to pay all
of their societal debts, whether here or in the hereafter. We pay our debts now and forever."*
- IRS Commissioner Jefferson McCourt

>> DATE: Sept. 23rd, 2039. Two days before present time.
>> TIME: 6:45 AM.
>> LOCATION: Raleigh, North Carolina, northbound on Interstate 81.

The first two hours of our trip back to New York dragged. Spenner focused on driving while Jebediah sat and stared in the back seat. My attention drifted between the fleeting landscapes of fields and small towns speeding by my window. Appearing lost in thought, I watched my partner from the corner of my eye. He looked older than his forty-two years. Though age had carved crags in his forehead and added crow's feet around his sea-green eyes, he represented a paragon of fitness. His mouth featured a slight angular imperfection, crooked from multiple broken jaws. The war stories etched across his face warned me to stay on this man's good side.

A bloom of fire and smoke pulled my attention toward the clear blue sky to witness something I had not seen before, at least not in person. Through the dirt smudges of my passenger window, I watched a sleek transport space shuttle, supported by two fiery rocket boosters, hurtle toward the moon.

"That is the Sagan Rocket, Jonah," whispered the voice of Sasha. Her programming granted the spontaneity to provide contextual information on interesting things around me. In this case, I welcomed her commentary as an interruption to boredom. I blinked in response instead of a verbal acknowledgment, still not wanting Spenner to know about her.

"I have found the cargo manifest for the Sagan," Sasha continued for my ear only. "Owned by the Goliath Corporation, that shuttle is carrying five thousand, six hundred, and seventy-four shades. All of them are assigned to work at the Mare Tranquillitatis, also known as the Sea of Tranquility. They will join a construction battalion expanding Lunar Spire's eastern quadrant."

My mind imagined the rocket's cramped interior. Hours or days before, those workers had lived as grandparents, parents, sons, and daughters. Those shades would enjoy no rest until the internal timer programmed into their serum expired. They became the world's beasts of burden, carrying humankind to its new manifest destiny in space. Without the need to breathe, they made the perfect worker to build opulent moon habitats.

The rocket's flight opened the endless blue with a long, gray zipper. Its destination, the pale moon, appeared to greet the oncoming space pilgrims. This scene stoked one of my familiar dreams. In my romantic vision, Vanessa and I embraced atop our home on the Lunar Spire, overlooking a sprawling view of the space colonies and Earth in the distance. Such thoughts fled too soon from my practical, terrestrial-bound troubles. With thoughts of my meager checking account and bills, my reverie faded, just like the fast disappearing rocket.

We continued driving for three more hours, not stopping for food, drink, or fuel. Time crawled, since Spenner remained silent while driving.

"I have observed an interesting temporal phenomenon," Sasha said to my ear. "As you are unable to respond to me, I observed that my emotional subroutines perceived time as slower than my clock program. Perhaps this is boredom? Accessing a relevant quote from Henry Van Dyke..."

"Time is too slow for those who wait, too swift for those who fear, too long for those who grieve, too short for those who rejoice, but for those who love – time is eternity."

I gave a thin smile, and nodded for more. For the next hour, Sasha maintained my sanity by reciting wisdom and beauty from Keats, Poe, Angelou, Dickinson, and Frost.

* * *

After another two hours on the highway, I wondered why Spenner chose to travel only on ground roads instead of flying along the aero-lanes. In all likelihood, he preferred old-fashioned driving to avoid the increased air traffic control government scrutiny.

When our car passed Raleigh, North Carolina, billowing gray smoke on the road's horizon heralded a multi-vehicle accident. To avoid the snarled traffic, Spenner spun the car's control hand-pads hard, whisking the car off the highway for a small town detour. We barreled through the off-ramp, then entered the local streets. That choice proved no better, since dozens of ambulances with blaring sirens swarmed the local roads. As we crawled along the line of cars, a parade of white and red vans lined up outside the hospital, delivering victims from the accident. My eyes spotted two black sedans parked just far enough away to avoid detection, but close enough to scoop up any debtor that died on the operating tables. Ghouls, I thought, ready for a quick payday. Then Spenner broke his silence.

"A lot busier than my last visit here," Spenner said, motioning to Mercy General Hospital.

"You there as a patient?"

"Not exactly," he answered. "Did I tell you about the time my old partner and I reaped twenty debtors in one week?"

"Twenty? How is that—"

"This was a few years ago," Spenner said, "back when the IRS gave juicy reaping bonuses for their Most Wanted. My partner Daniel and I, we made a record run." Spenner showed an actual emotion, a frown, for the briefest moment. Like someone had flicked a light switch on and off. Maybe he felt remorse, maybe anger; it appeared and disappeared too fast for me to register. This surprised me somewhat, since my research on Spenner showed that he preferred to work alone.

"One of the targets was Barbara Billups, a patient at that hospital," he said, clearing his throat to continue. "She owed a ton of dough from a bad real estate deal her late husband made. The bills she got in the mail gave her a stroke. I got a report that said she died, and I headed out to collect her."

Our car swerved around a long line of cars waiting their turn because of the detour. Not wanting to bother waiting, Spenner swerved into the side breakdown lane and sped up faster.

"So I show up, and she's in pain, on morphine, but alive. Inconvenient as all hell, right?" He looked to me for a sympathetic nod, that somehow I understood his feeling of irritation. Instead, his story evoked the worrisome image of my mother in her hospice bed, staving off death so she would not have to face her afterdeath.

"At the same moment, I mean the exact second, I get an alert from my data-hound that my next target is on the move. The late Mrs. Ortega racked up a mountain of loans for her gambling addiction, and the debt fell to her husband. Instead of turning her in to clear his slate, the old romantic tried to flee the US to bury her in her home country of Puerto Rico." Spenner paused to swerve around a large pothole, cutting off another driver to weave in and out of the one-lane country road. A rising unease in my stomach foreshadowed a dark ending to his story.

"Where was I? Right, so here I was in the hospital and standing in front of the only living person on the IRS Most Wanted list and my next target is about to skip town. I had to think of something if I was going to collect them both in time. So, I hurried her along..."

My eyes widened.

"Wait--what?"

"I didn't off the lady, I just handed her the morphine controls," Spenner shrugged. "I may have told a little white lie. That her debt was paid in full and she could, you know, pass along if she wanted. Then I showed her the button to override the drip delivery and she did the rest." To hide the shiver that went up and down my spine, I shifted in my seat.

"I found a record of the patient he is describing," Sasha remarked. Her quiet tone hushed even fainter. "Barbara Billups. She was eighty-two years old, and owed 23.2 million dollars. Her death certificate from Mercy General listed her death as an accidental personal overdose on morphine. She's now served six afterdeath years. Jonah, please increase your threshold of caution with this man." Now feeling more comfortable with my company, Spenner looked eager to continue his tales.

"If you thought that was funny, listen to what happened with collection number seven during that run. That reaping ended with me jumping on the nose of a moving Cessna. Wait, I'm getting ahead of myself, let me start from the beginning..." While Spenner boasted about his daring interception of Ortega's private jet, I mulled the survival odds of leaping out of the car.

* * *

Two hours later, the car's communication console beeped and interrupted Spenner talking about his sixteenth collection. A blue-tinged rectangular display appeared on the driver's side showing an incoming transmission. He accepted the call with a wave of his hand, summoning a hologram to form on the dashboard's display. Green photon particles formed a liquid sphere, rippling like a stone thrown into a still pond. The light coalesced to form a featureless human head, bald like an old-style store mannequin. Then the image's hollow eyes emitted a shaft of white light to scan Spenner's retina. I tucked my right hand to my side to hide it and tapped my forefinger and thumb together twice, a silent signal to Sasha.

"The message is a new form of advanced ocular encryption, patented by Goliath Corporation and licensed by a handful of governments like Russia and China," Sasha answered. "It is the most secure form of communication to date. I will record the raw footage. Without Spenner's iris and retina gene-map, it will remain indecipherable." Literally, the sender meant the message to be for Spenner's eyes and ears only.

I feigned disinterest in the message and looked out the window, though I kept watching with my peripheral vision. As Sasha predicted, the face in the digital message remained obscured and the audio scrambled into a random chorus of nonsensical beeps and clicks.

"Yes, we have the target," Spenner responded to the unknown caller. "We had mild resistance, nothing serious. Jonah handled himself well. No casualties."

More lower-pitched undecipherable chatter emitted from the console. An unbearable curiosity urged me to use my wrist-com and invoke an echelon, a pre-programmed digital function that coders used for a variety of different situations. The specific one that came to mind decrypted coded messages. Like most hackers, the desire to crack a difficult puzzle or pick a secure lock felt irresistible. Caution prevailed, and my hand dropped back down.

"I'm glad you're happy with our performance," Spenner said to the glittering hologram. Spenner spoke in a flat tone with no hint of real pleasure. His strange affect made me wonder about the accuracy of his responses. I focused my attention on his volume changes, body language, and any subtleties I could detect. His response prompted more unrecognizable chatter issued from the formless face. Then a thin smirk cracked his stoic face just briefly before he responded.

"I understand. That shouldn't be a problem. That will be an easy job. Anything else?"

The transmission concluded with the formless head uttering a final unintelligible string of fading mechanical sounds.

"Thank you, sir, we'll do our best," Spenner responded as the hologram burst into millions of smoldering light photons. He jabbed at the virtual console, and the car responded by accelerating. His attention turned back to me.

"Our client is happy that the stiff's been claimed on time," Spenner said to me. "He's impressed with you and says there will be more jobs coming soon."

"That's great to hear, thanks," I answered. Uncertainty prevented me from committing to more work with him. There would always be more jobs for able-bodied and willing collectors.

"So, back to my story, we're up to collection number sixteen now..." Spenner said. "His name was Peter, the son of a wealthy ex-actor who funded a religious cult. Peter was a pretty-boy, like you, Jonah, but he got a stomach cancer that his faith-healer father tried to cure with prayer. They didn't believe in science and they certainly didn't believe that the dead should become shades. You can probably guess that the prayer didn't work out so well."

As he resumed telling his reaping tale, our car raced down the highway and caught up to a light rainstorm. A few miles further and the storm worsened, sending sheets of rain sideways onto the windshield. Undeterred, Spenner maintained his high speed, even as we entered a treacherous sub-highway.

"So we invade the compound to collect Peter once the cancer takes him," he continued, making a hard-right turn around a curve. "And the damned place is filled with armed cultists." He made a rapid turn at a two-lane country road, flanked by tall green hills. "I shoot my way through, but just before I clear the whole place out, Peter's father gets a lucky shot and takes out my partner."

"My condolences about your partner," I muttered.

"Oh, it worked out," Spenner replied. "Turns out, Daniel had a lot of debts too, so I made both Daniel and Peter shades, turned them into the local IRS depot, and doubled my take for the day."

As my mouth opened for an acerbic response, the car's accident prevention system slammed on the brakes and displayed the words: Warning: Crash Imminent. A herd of cows crossed the road at the same time as our car swerved around the blind corner. Lumbering alongside the animals, a lone shade, an emaciated elderly male, pulled a wooden wagon laden with bales of hay.

"HOLY SH--" shouted Spenner, spinning the steering pads in vain. All four tires locked onto the wet road, scorching a black trail toward our inevitable impact. Our car swerved to avoid a brown heifer, slammed into the shade, and then came to an abrupt stop when the shattered pieces of the body jammed the vehicle's axles. Our seatbelts stretched but prevented us from hitting the windshield. Shaking his head, Spenner tapped his fingers on the car's virtual display to engage the car's auto-repair mechanism.

"Auto-repair initiated," spoke a tinny computerized voice. "Foreign object detected. Please remove to hasten repairs."

We exited the car and braved the rain to survey the damage. Billowing steam from the crippled engine stung my eyes. While we walked around the broken vehicle, the rainstorm intensified to a torrential downpour.

"We need a jack," Spenner said, crouching down to peer under the car. "Get the stiff out."

I nodded, slogged through the mud, and opened the back passenger door. Jebediah stared back at me with unblinking eyes and pupils shining a bright shade of yellow.

"Get out of the car and follow me," I shouted a clear and simple command over the fury of the storm and hissing car. After receiving their serum programming, shades possessed the auditory and mental processing faculties of a well-trained dog. He obeyed, exited the car, and stepped to me.

"Lift the back of the car," I commanded, pointing to the rear. Jebediah blinked to acknowledge the order. Bending down, he placed his withered hands under the corner fender and lifted the car without any complaint. Like a sturdy mechanical jack, he held the right corner of the car four feet above the ground. Veins around his neck and shoulder gave off a faint yellow luminescence, an aftereffect of the serum coursing through his veins. While his muscles bulged and the car lifted above the ground, my subconscious mind surfaced an often-asked question -- how the serum granted heightened physical prowess and sustained the shades for so many years. To hackers and conspiracy theorists across the datanet, this question represented the Holy Grail of mysteries. Many amateur armchair scientists speculated the serum contained radioactive isotopes. Other self-proclaimed technology experts hypothesized that shades converted sunlight into energy using a plant-derived chlorophyll compound. A vocal minority of digital pundits argued that symbiotic nanite colonies sustained the shades. However, the world would never know the truth, since the government protected the patented formula as a national secret. Spenner interrupted my musing with a rage-induced scream.

"Jesus H. Christ!" he shouted. "That shade we hit is smeared ALL over the goddamn undercarriage. Looks like the skull and spine got lodged in the axle assembly. This will take time." In what I can only assume was Spenner's warped sense of humor, he peeled off part of the flattened shade's severed hand and tossed it at me. "I'll need a hand," he joked. The hand struck my leg and fell to the ground. He laughed and disappeared under the car to continue the repairs.

I just shook my head while regarding the gory appendage Spenner tossed. The gnarled hand still held a diamond wedding ring on one finger. Even though the soul had departed the husk, I still made the sign of the cross and recited a Hail Mary in a hushed tone. Then my thoughts switched to the worry of more debt. We'd destroyed a shade, real property, and that would cost someone money.

"I'm sorry, Jonah," whispered Sasha. "I could have taken control of the guidance system and maybe spared that shade. However, I would have revealed myself to Spenner." With the noise of the storm rendering anything under a shout inaudible, I dared a soft, muted response. Otherwise, her sympathy algorithm would continue to review alternate actions she could have done.

"It's not your fault."

Spenner ripped more bone fragments from the car, causing a brackish liquid to flow from a punctured tank. With the foreign object removed, the auto-repair mechanisms engaged. Three fist-sized silver spheres detached from the engine block. They sprouted legs then skittered like metal insects towards the leaking gap. Then they emitted focused plasma beams from their antennae to cauterize the damage. Using my wrist-com, I tapped into the car's computer system and examined the code governing the repair-bots. Back in my old military days, one of my main areas of specialty involved field cyber-warfare and counter-defense--a fancy way of saying computer hacker. After a few of my code improvements, the repair-bots moved faster and initiated the repair of the oil drum.

Together, the three of us formed an effective team. Jebediah held up the back of the car. Spenner did the grunt mechanical heavy lifting to remove debris, leaving me to handle the technical repair.

Despite our speed, a nagging feeling of anxiety bothered me. Why was the shade we struck wandering around alone? In all likelihood, its master would not be too far behind to discover us with evidence of destroyed property.

"We need to hurry," I shouted over the storm's fury.

Spenner grumbled his annoyance but seemed to agree as he chiseled at the gore faster. After five more minutes of work by Spenner and the repair bots, we finished.

"Repairs completed," announced the computer voice from the car's speakers. "The automobile is at 93% capacity and within safe driving thresholds."

I heard Sasha scoff in my ear. "Technically, it is 92.53%, well within safe and nominal driving standards," Sasha informed me.

Spenner jumped up from the ground and motioned for me to get Jebediah into the car.

"Jebediah, put the car down slowly," I commanded. Jebediah complied and lowered his burden back to the ground inch by careful inch. I learned from experience that clear instructions like 'slowly' helped avoid nasty accidents with shades. In most states, owners needed to take online courses and earn a license before operating a shade for any work. When the government first approved and legalized the use of shade labor for private use, there were many learning pains during the first rollout. Many business owners experienced firsthand how literal the shades processed their commands. Today, if a master said something like 'throw out the garbage', shades would comply. Twenty years ago, a first-generation shade's reaction would have been more disappointing, if not dangerous. The IRS scientists put in charge of the research had improved on the serum's original formulae, and subsequent rollouts had added more colloquial phrases to the command phrase lexicon. Even with those improvements, accidents from vague orders still occurred. A famous example that captured national attention had happened in Cape Cod, Massachusetts nineteen years ago. A wealthy businessman had bought a first-generation shade, an expensive purchase back then, to be a house servant and ordered it to: "Move my furniture, hurry up, break a leg." That unfortunate disaster had led to stricter serum programming protocols and safeguards that prohibited direct or indirect harm to human beings by the undead. Despite those controls, common sense and good practice demanded that owners issue careful, direct, and literal commands.

"Enter the car and sit in the back seat." Jebediah obliged my instruction and sat down in the back seat without incident.

Before Spenner and I entered the car, a pair of headlights appeared and flooded the area with bright light. Then a deep revving engine sound preceded the arrival of a massive yellow farm vehicle crashing through the bushes. Atop the giant tractor, the dark-haired driver looked down and spotted the smear of gore and splintered bone from the remains of his shade servant.

"WHAT in the name of our great lord have you two assholes done?" he screamed then jumped down to the ground. He picked up the cracked skull of his former servant, then tossed it aside to ready his rusty pitchfork. "You squished MY PROPERTY to a god-damned pulp!" For emphasis, he brandished a long weapon against us.

"Put down the fork, old man," warned Spenner. "We are armed deputized agents of the IRS, and I've had my fill of southern hospitality today."

With a bad feeling gnawing at my stomach, my eyes darted around and spotted over two dozen shadowy forms walking behind the tractor. The shade's owner arrived with company.

"Government spooks...we don't like your kind in our parts," the farmer replied with a slow drawl, stepping closer and twisting his pitchfork at us. He looked young and able-bodied; probably the son of the landowner, I presumed. Mud caked over his high black boots and he wore a thick yellow raincoat over his denim work clothes. When his brown eyes twinkled and his lips broke into a grin, I knew we faced a young man with something to prove.

"Boys, protect me!" The farmer's command brought the attention of the three dozen shade farmhands. The undead servants dropped their burdens and marched toward their master. With a swiftness belying their dirty and thin bodies, the shades closed ranks and formed an imposing mob.

Sizing up our situation, I realized the odds favored the farmer, especially since my weapon waited in the trunk. One hopeful thought surfaced, that the default serum programming prohibited Shades from directly harming humans. However, if the farmer had hired a local good-ole-boy neurochemist with enough skill to hack the serum, those restrictions could be bypassed. Judging by the smug look on the farmer's face, I guessed he owned several modified and illegal shades capable of mangling us into something unrecognizable. Just as that thought crossed my mind, two shades, one wielding a hoe and the other garden shears, both stepped closer. Violence seemed inevitable. My mind raced to consider strategies to survive.

"We were just passing through and had an accident," I said in a calm voice, with my arms out wide and palms open. "Why don't we get out of this rain and talk about it?"

Emboldened by the shades gathering around him, the farmer walked closer toward me, threatening me with the three tips of his rusted but still sharp pitchfork.

"You city assholes owe me a debt for my shade," he demanded. "That was a good worker and you idiots turned it into road kill. I've got half a mind to take your car and let you both crawl back to the city."

"Take my car?" Spenner hissed. His lip curled crooked with a look of amusement, a look that invited trouble. "You're at fault for letting your shade cross the road. My car was damaged, so YOU owe me."

That answer inflamed the tension. The farmer took another step toward us, pitchfork lowered, and his shades formed a circle around us. Unfazed, Spenner flicked his stun-rod to life. The weapon exuded a smoky crimson glow of energy around its bulbous metal tip. The light from his stun-rod illuminated the mottled, impassive faces of the shades, a stark contrast to the farmer's snarled lips and furrowed brow.

"Mighty nice glowstick you have there. Boys, go ahead and rip this..."

Feeling desperate, I blurted out a risky compromise.

"WAIT!" I yelled. "You like the stun-rod? That's military grade. Take it. It's worth more than two of your shades."

Spenner's eyes smoldered. Given his anger, I shifted my stance just in case he decided to attack me for offering up his weapon.

"Well, boy?" the farmer said, pointing his pudgy finger toward Spenner. "I reckon that's a fair deal. I'll forgive you for destroying my chattel if you hand over the glow stick. I could use it to fight off the rustlers that been raiding me lately."

Spenner stood silent for a moment. I heard his knuckles crack from tightening his grip on the stun-rod. A facial muscle twitched to betray a rage he held inside. Then his posture changed, and an odd expression of amusement played over his face. Unseen by the farmer, his nimble fingers slid across the stun-rod, pressing a few indented buttons on the weapon until it issued a low-pitched whine. The glow changed from crimson to a dull blue. I assumed he put it into safety mode so he could hand it off.

"Fine," Spenner acquiesced. "Forget you saw us, get out of our way, and this is yours."

"Deal," said the farmer, snatching the offering in a hurry. For a few moments he seemed mesmerized by the inky blue energy issuing from the crown of the rod. Combining the blunt damage from reinforced titanium and the raw power of an industrial electrical stunner, the stun-rod proved to be a formidable melee weapon.

"Follow me, boys," the farmer called out. "Time to get out of this rain and go home." Without a word, the pack of thirty-six shades picked up their soggy bales and lumbered through the mud behind their master. The farmer climbed up to his tractor seat, then admired the shimmering mace like some burning victory torch. Before he drove away, I could have sworn that I heard the whine from the weapon grow louder.

Not wanting to stay longer, we rushed back into the car. Time to see if our repair job worked. With a touch of the console, Spenner started the car's engine with a mechanical roar. Satisfied with his repair job, he turned to me with a smile and I braced myself for an argument related to the loss of his stun-rod.

"Good thinking back there," he said as we started to drive off. "Really clever of you to offer the stunner to him. Now, let's get out of here before the fireworks."

As I struggled to understand what Spenner meant, a loud explosion rocked the surrounding area followed by a bright red flash and a plume of crimson smoke.

"What in the hell did you do?" I yelled in protest.

"Spare the rod, spoil the child," Spenner chuckled, pushing the car into a higher gear. "He got what he deserved." Then I recalled Spenner pressing the extra buttons on the stun-rod before he gave the weapon to the farmer. I realized his subtle movements had set the stun-rod on self-destruct, and that the whining noise had come from a massive overcharge of its power core. We departed the farm in silence, bumping over a piece of debris from the exploded tractor before we rejoined the open highway again.

During the rest of the ride home, I accessed the car's computer from the passenger console, pretending to check road conditions and traffic. While Spenner focused on driving, I downloaded all the video footage from the car's recording camera to prove Spenner murdered the farmer. With a few nonchalant taps, I transferred the data to my wrist-com storage banks.

"I have the video," Sasha confirmed. "The video quality is poor due to the storm, but convincing enough. I will feel much better when you have parted ways with your current partner." As her code architect, I swelled with a father's pride knowing that her empathy engrams registered compassion and an appropriate distaste for Spenner. During the remainder of the trip, we passed another five farms and six shade-staffed quarry mills without incident. Of course, I let the sociopathic driver choose the radio stations for the remainder of the trip.

* * *

After explaining the farm encounter to my interrogators, a sensation of weariness overtook me. The IRS command room spun around as if I stood in the center of a merry-go-round. I chalked this up to sleep deprivation, dehydration, and hunger, all part of the strategy my interrogators employed to wring the truth out of me. After I shook my head, my vision steadied and the nausea passed.

An influx of collection agents and supervisors buzzed around the large room, doing their business and delivering reports to superiors. Along the far wall, a series of pod-cubes contained IRS tax auditors in the midst of heated discussions with debtors, most of them v-casting in remotely from different parts of the world.

In the room's center, a double-sized floating screen displayed the infamous Most Wanted List. Only the most dangerous criminals and deceased debtors with the largest bills made it onto that list. Each of the names also showed the IRS agent assigned to that particular case. Scanning the list from bottom to top, my eyes widened when I saw the top position on the board.

** Incorporeal Revenue Service. Most Wanted. (Classified) **
** 1. Col. Colin Spenner **
** Assigned IRS Agent: Casey Steele (DECEASED) **

Adjacent to the Most Wanted List screen, another display showed an interactive map dedicated to tracking Spenner's movements. Five feet behind, a black-suited junior agent walked up to Barnaby and asked to give him an update. I leaned back and strained to hear.

"Agents Steele and Hunt both disappeared off the grid today," said the junior agent in a worried voice. "We--we don't have any current leads."

"Activate Bellamy and Hicks," whispered Barnaby. "I want Colin back on our grid."

Before I heard any more of the conversation, Erasmus interrupted my eavesdropping by handing me a cool glass of water.

"You must be parched, my son, please drink," he said. I eyed the glass, looking for any traces of sediment indicating drugs. My thirst won over my suspicion and I sipped the water. Satisfied with its purity, I gulped the whole cup and felt refreshed.

"After Spenner drove over the farmer's shade...it was most kind of you to offer the Lord's blessing," Erasmus said. "Unnecessary, of course, since the soul had already migrated to Him, All Glory in the Highest. But a kind and noble gesture, my son." My instincts told me that the priest's warm demeanor felt genuine, but I reminded myself that in my weakened state I would start becoming more susceptible to their small acts of kindness. I steeled myself for the next round of questioning.

"Sasha did release a small snippet of video to us of the farmer's death," continued Erasmus. "The footage exonerates you and clearly implicates Spenner."

"Your AI refused to give us all of the video footage from your trip," Barnaby said. "Tell her to comply."

"In time, Barnaby," Erasmus countered. "Let us allow our guest to continue his account. Jonah, would you indulge us with the remainder of your story?"

I nodded, and my mind sifted through yesterday's events, when Spenner and I had arrived in New York.

CHAPTER 4
Debt on Arrival

*"First our pleasures die - and then our hopes, and
then our fears - and when these are dead, the
debt is due, dust claims dust - and we die too."*
- Excerpt from "Death is Here and Death
is There", Percy Bysshe Shelley

>> DATE: Sept. 24th, 2039. Thirty-six hours before present time.
>> TIME: 8:38 PM. Location: New York City.

Much to my relief, we arrived in New York City without any
more undesirable incidents. The sun relinquished the sky to wispy
clouds and an eager moon. The slick remains of a passing storm
made the streets an electric river. Our car drove over wet roads
reflecting the neon signs of restaurants, advertisements, theater
marquees, peep shows, and other human necessities for sale. We
continued through a run-down section of Washington Heights filled
with a crowd of young Puerto Rican, Cuban, and Dominican teens
huddled outside the entrance of a neighborhood bodega. Crowning
a tall metal post and doubling as a street lamp, a spherical mark-2
v-cast generator shimmered. The machine glowed bright and
transmitted a portion of its proto-matter to a virtual billboard
above the store. A flash of light coalesced into a luxury convertible,
replete with a classic cherry red paint coating and modern aero-
thruster fins, revolving above the crowd. Like a gleaming idol to
capitalism or a monument to hope, the full-sized hologram basked
the youths in the mesmerizing allure of instant social status. They

all stood agape under the blazing digital billboard, entranced by a photonic message burning into their retinas. The billboard read:

** Why Wait For Luxury? **
** Drive home the car of your dreams, NOW! **
** Pay it off LATER, for ONLY nice afterdeath years! **
** Today's Deal: *LX Victory Sedan.* **
** Equipped for air and ground travel. **
** United Automotive. Live Your Life, TODAY! **

That kind of advertisement appeared after the powerful Committee for Brave New Commerce lobbyists advocated the public bartering for afterdeath years. As expected, a majority of citizens, keen to expand their credit options amidst a strained economy, approved the legislation. This change allowed car companies, jewelry stores, and home mortgage companies to entice people with the ultimate layaway service. Somewhere the devil laughed his ass off at us for inviting him back onto Earth.

The car took a sharp turn, and the illumination from downtown's commercialism faded, replaced by the soft yellow and white glows from coffee shops and Wall Street offices working overtime. Spenner pulled over at the spot I pointed out, a few blocks from my house.

"Fifteen thousand, you earned it," he said, accessing his wristcom to transfer the funds. With four taps on his crimson-hued console, the bounty transferred to my account. "There are bigger contracts due for reaping soon. Business isn't slow."

"The payment has been deposited from an off-planet source," Sasha verified. "A private bank on the Lunar Spire." The mention of the Spire made me look skyward to gaze at the moon. Visible from Earth, the Spire represented the pinnacle of human achievement, a modern wonder that housed the moon's ultra-rich. My gaze drifted down to the car's backseat, where Jebediah sat motionless, awaiting his next order.

"What about Jebediah?"

"I'll turn him in," Spenner offered, revving the car's engine. "The closest IRS dead depot is on my way. I'll be in touch soon." With that, he sped away and disappeared around the next street corner.

While walking toward my apartment, my brain started to work out how to manage two critical issues. First, the Vanessa situation demanded immediate attention. My soon-to-be-ex-girlfriend frowned on my profession. Last week, she'd made her displeasure clear with a withering barrage of expletives tinged with reasoned arguments against collecting debts. Second, the question of Spenner needed to be addressed. On one hand, doing more missions threatened my tenuous relationship with Vanessa. On the other hand, collection jobs represented a way to repay my family's debts and buy two first class space shuttle tickets to a new life. Looming over all these worries was the possibility that I could be charged as an accessory to murder. Although the farmer had threatened us, any self-defense argument would fail to overcome the simple fact that Spenner had killed the man after the conflict already deescalated. The idea of reporting Spenner to the authorities with an anonymous video upload crossed my mind. Caution stayed my hand. If I turned the video in, a man like Spenner would know who betrayed him. This decision needed to be slept on.

When I rounded a street corner, a series of shop window advertisements detected me and illuminated, turning on one after another. These electrical screens hawked their goods while some utilized the v-cast generators for more sophisticated advertisement. Around the corner, a beautiful redheaded virtual woman bared her breasts to accent her diamond necklace. I passed through her projected form, feeling the semi-solid proto-matter scatter around me like dew. Further ahead, four displays synced to display a single image. Appearing on the split-screens, a white-suited, pale-skinned man wearing a red fedora bowed with an exaggerated flourish. His trimmed black beard accentuated his wide smile while his commercial pitch flashed on the display with bold lettering.

----- DO YOU HAVE A TECHNICAL PROBLEM? -----
----- Does a virus have you sick with worry? -----
----- Wish it away! -----
----- Summon THE WHITE DJINN, today! -----
----- Ask about my financing specials. -----

The absurdity of the advertisement made me chuckle. Most of the hacker community knew something about the minor celebrity that called himself the White Djinn. His real name remained a mystery; he only answered to his mythological moniker. According to local lore, if one summoned him, he granted answers to any questions after receiving payment. Before I crossed the street, the proto-matter left behind from the redheaded woman swirled and coalesced. The White Djinn assumed a semi-corporeal form and stepped out of the flat screens. With a brisk stride, he walked beside me.

"You never know when you will need the Djinn's aid," said the man, keeping pace until he reached the limit of the v-cast generator's range. "A free fortune for you. When you're in trouble, you must buy her flowers...Jonah." As I turned back to face him, the projected body dissipated, leaving only his winking eye that dispersed into twinkling photonic embers. I wondered whether the White Djinn programmed a convincing smart-advertisement, or if he just v-casted in person. A sudden downpour pulled my attention back to finding shelter. Sprinting through puddles, I found cover under the awning of the local butcher shop. Then my thoughts returned to dealing with my first problem: repairing relations with Vanessa. A plan started to form inside my head, tracing a route across the city. Bringing home her favorite Chinese take-out food would be a solid start. Then my eyes drifted across the street to the chocolatier shop. She fancied their chocolate-covered strawberries, and those treats had absolved me from several past sins. While wondering which present to buy first, the White Djinn's fortune popped in my head. This situation warranted flowers and chocolate. After running through the rain to purchase a box of the strawberries, I hugged the brick walls to stay dry and ran to the local flower shop. Inside, the aromas of lilacs, orchids, and roses greeted me, followed by the short figure of Mrs. Hsu, a sweet middle-aged Chinese woman beaming with a warm smile.

"Hello, Mrs. Hsu, I'll take the 'I'm Sorry' premium package of your best flowers."

"Uh oh, in trouble again?" she admonished with a shaking finger. "Another dozen lilies and roses in two weeks? You need to pull your life together, Jonah. I have a good card for you."

Mrs. Hsu disappeared behind her counter and reemerged with a bouquet of flowers and a large brush. "You would be more handsome if you got a haircut," she scolded. Without asking permission, she brushed me with rough strokes, fussing over my appearance like my adopted mother. "Such beautiful brown hair, but when it's so tangled it hides your blond roots, and covers your blue eyes!" With renewed vigor, she groomed me, picking off lint, straightening my clothes, and wiping off dirt. "There, now you are at least presentable."

"Thank you, Mrs. Hsu. What would I do without you?"

"Without me, you'd be a flea-bitten mess in the doghouse," she sighed. "Try not to come back for a month!" she yelled as I hurried out of the store.

* * *

As I hurried through bursts of rain, my progress halted in front of a gawking crowd on the corner of Varick Street. Following their skyward points and astonished expressions, I saw a fast-moving blur falling from the Federal building. The victim's plummeting reflection against the polished steel and glass of the bank building made it look like several people falling. Jumping back to the sidewalk, I tried to move out of the way before the body impacted with the cement. Despite my efforts, a huge splash of muddy water drenched my freshly bought flowers when the body slammed into the ground.

My eyes blinked to focus, and I scanned the scene for details. The victim wore a light blue utility outfit issued to New York city workers. Nearby shattered remnants of maintenance equipment confirmed that he fell while cleaning a window. The crowd pulled back when the body writhed and started to rise. Several people sighed in relief.

"Oh, thank god, it's just a shade," said a young bystander.

"Maybe the safety harness was old and broke?" another man guessed.

Though the fall would have liquefied a normal human, the shade suffered only broken bones and a crooked gait. Not all shades would have fared that well, especially ones near the end of their afterdeath timer. Perhaps he benefitted from a newer serum formula. He limped near me on his way to the skyscraper's entrance. As he passed me to climb twenty-seven stories and return to work, my eyes noticed that the twisted harness looked brand new. Alternate possibilities for his accident flitted through my mind. Maybe the suspension platform broke underneath him? As he disappeared into the high-rise, my attention returned to my drenched, muddied flowers. With a lowered head, I walked back into the flower shop and endured another scolding from Mrs. Hsu.

"You're back ALREADY? This is a new record. You really stepped into it this time." I had no idea how right she would be.

* * *

I sprinted home with a fear, a rational and understandable worry given my very strange week, that a dangerous calamity could befall me at any moment. I made sure to obey all crossing signal signs, and looked up to the sky for falling dead shades every block. My mind focused on the simple goal to navigate a few more blocks to reach my apartment, apologize and make up with my girlfriend, and sleep away this long day. After passing a row of renovated brownstone apartments, the familiar smell of Coney Island dogs simmering with their sweet onions wafted to my nose. Roger, a New York institution known for his delicious food and generosity to the homeless, flipped a pair of sausages and nodded at me. He saw my bundle of flowers, smirked, and dressed up two fully loaded dogs.

"Two with the works for Vanessa. Any for you, Jonah?" Roger asked. His black hair pulled back in a hairnet. Steam from his cart billowed around his hawkish thin face.

"Yes, make it four, Roger," I replied. He slid open his steam cover, plucked two more cooked wieners with his shiny metal tongs, nimbly flipped them into the air, and caught them with two bread buns, smiling like a Yankee fan catching a foul ball in the venerable park. Most of the other street vendors had long switched to more mobile hover vans equipped with food replicators. Roger kept the old nostalgia alive. With a few taps of my wrist-com, money transferred to pay for the food.

He leaned to me and handed the warm paper-wrapped hotdogs, his usually jovial craggy face now creasing with worry. "Jonah, I've got a favor to ask. When ya get a chance, talk to Vanessa for me? It's my Uncle Morty. He's--he's got the cancer. Doesn't got too much longer to go, ya know? He owes--not too much, but more than hot dogs and franks can pay off, know what I mean? Every time I think I'm close to paying the debts, penalties pile up. Your lady, she's a blessing. She's our only hope -- but her vid-phone's always busy. Maybe you could put a good word in, for old time's sake?"

I took the dogs and shook Roger's hand firmly. "I'll talk to her for you, Roger, don't worry." Roger wiped his tearing eyes as another customer stepped up for an order. Seeing him get emotional stoked the embers of guilt that I had almost let extinguish from my earlier job. These days there were pretty much two kinds of people: those who couldn't give a shit about their afterdeath debts, and those that got scared as hell when the time came. When I first started collecting, it was simple and clear as day to me -- you owed, you came back from the dead to pay. I bought into the government's official motto: "We pay our debts, now and forever." Since then, every time I completed a job and saw how it affected the families involved, the worse I felt about myself.

CHAPTER 5
Pro Bono, Ad Mortem

"Nochen toit vert men choshev."
Translation: "After death one be-
comes important."
- Jewish proverb

At my approach, the rusted security panel of my apartment building flickered to life with a sickly green glow. With practiced ease, my fingers punched 1-0-1-0-1-0, my birthday date reversed, while it scanned the fingertips for confirmation.

"Welcome back, Jonah," said a deep voice as the door swung open. Mr. Chauncey Sanders, the self-appointed doorman, waved to me from his favorite leather chair. Like usual, he watched the evening news on the lobby's aging holo-monitor. Despite his older age, his dark skin showed few wrinkles and his body looked trim. He never needed the walking cane resting across his lap, but he kept it close in case an unsavory trespasser slipped by his gate. He flashed a wide smile through his trimmed white mustache, like usual. However, the one hundred or more spectral holo-projected people all crowding the lobby? Not usual. The motley collection of ghostly people all stood in a line winding around the paisley-covered walls.

Walking by the v-cast generator, I noticed the clear tank bubbling with its viscous gray proto-matter. The machine's digital display reported that the crowd of casting visitors stretched the capacity of the unit's resources.

**VIRTUAL CASTING GENERATOR: MARK-2. **
** GOZEN CORPORATION. Patent No. 4,033,332. **

** Proto-Matter: 99.9979% of 100% in use.**

Using a standard head-mounted device, people v-casted from the privacy of their homes to other locations using a projector. How they looked at the other end depended on the quality and mark of the local v-cast generator. Like most public networks, my apartment's generator possessed enough fidelity to make a passable looking human figure with photonic light. Mark-2 units and above merged excited light with malleable proto-matter. This combination granted v-casters enough substantiality that another person could feel their semi-tangible forms. In the eyes of the law, these v-casting visitors represented real people with rights to conduct business remotely. Most cities offered the use of basic mark-1, maybe mark-2 units free to the public. Only the military and a handful of corporations utilized the most realistic mark-6 v-cast generator technologies.

"They've been here all day, these bloody ghosts," Mr. Sanders said, pointing to the projected people. "There's more of 'em too, the line goes down to the basement. All waiting for her." He wagged a gnarled stubby finger at me. "Your girl..." he warned with a look of sadness. "She's working too hard, Jonah. The girl needs some rest. Maybe take her for a walk and to a nice dinner?"

"Yes, Mr. Sanders, I'll see what I can do," I answered back with a smile.

As one of the city's few lawyers specializing in 'Afterdeath Debt Reconciliation and Remediation', the recent demand for her services skyrocketed. Although she had many clients, almost all of them needed help from debt collection, which also meant they lacked money. Bless her big heart, she carried on a one-person crusade to help them maintain their dignity in this life and the next. Generous to a fault, she started getting a reputation for letting clients pay what they could. Many of her wealthier lawyer colleagues criticized her for her lack of business acumen, offering her jobs in more lucrative legal disciplines like off-world tech patents. However, her generosity and idealism was one of the many things I had fallen in love with and still loved about her.

Even during Vanessa's peak, she never had more than ten visitors. It made me wonder what might have caused an uptick in collections by the government. Maybe a new late penalty? I made a mental note to ask Vanessa about that later.

Winding through the crowds of v-casters, I tried my best not to walk through them. Most citizens observed modern etiquette and considered virtual visitors as ambassadors of the real person. A dwindling minority considered these ghosts to be phantasms, no better than high-polygon video-game avatars. I regarded other v-casters as I would want my own projected form to be treated, which is to say, with respect.

All of the v-casters projected their true elderly forms. Many knocked on death's door and rang the doorbell for good measure. Creating a different v-cast body than your true form required recent knowledge of technical upgrades that older users generally ignored. They gripped canes, sat in wheelchairs, and stood crooked but patient in their line. Their collective whimpers and soft prayers breathed an uncomfortable pall throughout the lobby. Death was coming for them, and soon their debts would be due.

Slinking across the room to avoid their attention, I reached the elevators just as an apparition noticed me.

"I'm casting from a cafe, this isn't cheap, please hurry," begged an older man with a Russian accent.

"Please sir, I've been waiting for hours!" cried an elderly Cuban woman while following me. I rushed into the elevator, beyond the range of the lobby's v-projector, causing her form to jitter and tear apart. The door started to close and in an act of desperation she thrust her arm to reach for me.

"I'm sorry," I mouthed. Her translucent form disintegrated, cut off from the excited photons and proto-matter transmitted by the v-cast projector, leaving only sparkling motes to drift and extinguish. Even today, I mused, there were still places with poor signal.

With a groan, the elevator lurched up to the sixth floor and opened its doors to an empty hallway. Walking to my apartment, I sighed in relief that no v-casters haunted here. With a touch, the door recognized my fingerprints and unlocked itself.

Inside, the room displayed blatant signs of neglect. Strewn over counter-tops and table surfaces lingered the remains of half-eaten take-out boxes from the last breakfast, lunch, and dinner. Sandwiched between a stack of coffee cups and meal plates, Vanessa looked frazzled. Tufts of her curly auburn hair stuck out in unruly directions. Evidence of sleep deprivation etched lines of exhaustion around her hazel eyes. Despite her exhaustion, she still looked beautiful. She worked at our dining room table, her long legs stretching under its narrow width. Pictures of clients appeared on the flat glass next to information about their cases. Piles of appeals paper work cluttered the table's left corner, creating a small tower of bureaucracy. On the right corner, a digital window showed real-time chats of desperate people trying to log in to speak with her. Hundreds of clients battled for her attention, their faces flickering in and out of the screen, the electronic equivalent of pushing and shoving in a long line. I set her flowers down, and closed the door.

"Hi, honey, you are a gorgeous sight for sore eyes," I said. After walking across the room, I leaned down to kiss her. She pulled back and returned a brief peck of a kiss. The touch of her soft lips and the faint hint of cherry from yesterday's lipstick cleansed the palette of my senses, dulled by my long road trip to the swamp.

In that moment, the feeling of regret heightened, and it struck me how much I had missed her, tinged with a moment of longing when she pulled away too soon. "Is our apartment haunted or do you have enough cases for one hundred lawyers?"

Vanessa let out a long sigh. "You do one pro bono case and word gets out. I won't be able to talk to half of those poor people." Then her expression of amusement soured, like she recalled a bitter thought. "You know, I'm still mad at you." Her narrowed eyes launched daggers into my heart before returning to her work.

"I-I brought you a peace offering," I stammered, holding Roger's hot dogs and the strawberry chocolates like a tribute to appease an angry queen. She took the food, unwrapping the shiny metallic paper that warmed the hot dogs.

"I should keep yelling at you for collecting those poor people," she admonished while chewing. "But I have too many meetings today." Her face softened, her angry resolve weakened by the onion-mustard-and-pork-byproduct rapture in her mouth. "We can talk later. And thank you for the hot dogs."

"Of course. I'll get us some wine." I counted my blessings. Vanessa still felt anger towards me, but at least I had a chance to make things right.

Hurrying to the repli-pantry, I spoke my request for two bowls of popcorn and two glasses of wine, a white for Vanessa and a red for myself. The food dispenser hummed to life, opening its wooden cabinet veneer to expose the coils and tubes of the machine's interior. Days before, I had added real popcorn kernels to the supply rack. I preferred the authentic smell of cooked corn and hot oil rather than the replication paste that left a funny aftertaste with quick-prepped popcorn. Within seconds, a delivery alcove opened to serve a perfect batch of popcorn. Since I had forgotten to restock the wine rack, the replicator improvised. It fetched the green and red grapes we had in the larders, and applied a rapid fermentation process to craft our favorite alcoholic beverages. Only a sommelier or someone with a refined palate for wines could tell the difference between a naturally aged corked wine and my replicated beverage. I was not burdened with such refinements, or many other refinements, for that matter. Having slaved in the kitchen for all of two minutes for our working dinner, I delivered the popcorn and wine to Vanessa with an exaggerated flourish and a bow.

She looked at me with a half-grin cracking on her perfect lips that burned away any gloom that darkened my day. Before her expression bloomed into a full smile, she caught herself, as if her brain reminded her heart of my frustrating missteps.

"Thanks, Jonah," she whispered, returning her attention to the table. She passed her hand over a blinking console to accept an incoming v-cast request from a hospital in upstate New York. I heard the signature hum of our v-cast projector thrum to life.

"Sorry you had to wait so long, Mr. Liebowitz," she said to her materializing guest.

"Thank you, Ms. Wright," responded the client. To discern more about the illusory visitor, I employed my observational talents, a handy skill I had sharpened, since my collection jobs often required classic deductive work. After reading many of the old classic Conan Doyle books, I aspired to be a modern-day Sherlock Holmes, without the brilliance, talent, or cocaine addiction of the famed detective.

I studied the v-cast form of the man standing before Vanessa. He looked middle-aged, short of stature, and his black and gray hair looked well-groomed. My eye noticed that he stood far too still, not moving his legs or arms. This indicated that he might be confined to a wheelchair and unaccustomed to a virtual form. In a v-cast, those with enough programming talent and imagination learned to project any semi-tangible form they desired within the technical limits and proto-matter reserves of the local v-cast projectors.

"Tell me again, Mr. Liebowitz, how I can help you?" Vanessa asked.

"Please call me Saul." The man spoke in an even, almost robotic tone. The odd, uneven cadence of his voice led me to believe he relied on an assistive medical technology for his voice. "My doctors have kept me in a medically-induced coma for years, but a recent stroke has worsened my condition. I am speaking to you through an experimental v-cast rig designed by my cousin that lets me communicate while unconscious. My medical care has been world class, but the cost has been exorbitant. All my fortunes are exhausted. When I die in a week, I will be reaped by the IRS."

"You have my sympathies, Saul," Vanessa said with sincere empathy. She reached out a hand instinctively to comfort the man, but he was unable to reciprocate. "Given your time remaining, I will do everything I can, but with my caseload and limited..."

"You would have some help," Saul interjected. "Please let me introduce Ambassador Ephraim Shoval from the Israeli embassy and my cousin Eli Solomon."

Two more holographic forms shimmered next to Mr. Liebowitz. Ambassador Shoval formed first, as a tall man dressed in a gray suit and white tie with large silver glasses. Eli materialized next, appearing as a shorter, balding man in a brown suit. He looked remorseful when his gaze turned to Saul.

"Shalom, Ms. Wright, it is our pleasure," Ambassador Shoval said with a slight bow. "On behalf of the people of Israel, let me start by saying that we appreciate your help in this matter. I believe we have an interesting point of appeal to discuss for Saul's defense."

"And what is that?" asked Vanessa. I saw a glimmer of hope twinkle in her eyes. As the conversation continued, I took a few steps back toward the hallway, but continued listening.

"Mr. Saul's coma occurred three months prior to your government's Mandatory Service Act. Unlike the other Jews who emigrated from the United States from 2021 to 2024 to avoid afterdeath service, Mr. Saul never received warning of the law and could not evacuate. It is our belief that an undeath would send a Jewish soul to Gehenna, our religion's version of your Hell. We will appeal Mr. Liebowitz's case on the grounds of religious persecution retroactively to the time of the amnesty. We will seek an appeal and request that he be allowed to leave the country and be buried, and stay buried, as per his Hebrew tradition."

I felt pity for Saul. Most of his people, likely his whole family, had long fled from the United States since the passage of the MSA in 2024. The legislation granted no safe-harbor, no exemptions, no diplomatic immunity, if you owed money. Upon its ratification, the

MSA had decreed that all citizens, tourists, and diplomats, had three years to depart if they disagreed with afterdeath service. Jewish citizens had fled en masse in the single largest religious migration since World War 2, since their orthodox laws required their burial within 48 hours of death.

"The state of Israel would be willing to fund your retainer for this case," the ambassador continued. "But I hope you understand if we only v-cast to the court rather than attend in person for our security."

"I can offer my services as your co-counsel," added Eli. "I serve as head of legal for my father's company, Titan Technologies." Eli's words echoed in my head. Any hacker or technologist knew that Titan Tech represented nearly ten percent of all hardware construction. They had made all of the sentient androids before the Promethean ban in 2020. This case held the potential to be the most important of her career.

"Of course, I'd be honored if you would help," Vanessa bubbled with enthusiasm. Now she had a paying client. This represented a chance to appeal the Mandatory Service Act before the appellate courts, maybe the Supreme Court. This would be the fuel that skyrocketed her career. She smiled as they delved into strategic discussions about Saul's legal options. Then she turned to give a quick sideways glance in my direction.

Catching the hint, I slinked away down the green-tiled hallway and entered my study. The spartan room contained an old-fashioned oak table and a comfortable leather chair. There was also plenty of open floor space to accommodate my habit of opening a dozen floating virtual screens at once. With a flick of my fingers, I summoned Sasha from the wrist-com.

"Sasha, why don't you join me?" Whenever possible, I encouraged her to manifest a body. This pushed the capacities of her etiquette engrams when she encountered other people.

Utilizing the v-cast generator, she materialized with a new form of her choosing. First the proto-matter coalesced and shaped her hazel eyes, two golden discs that twinkled too bright. I made a mental note to check the texture mapping of her irises. At 5'10, she came almost to my height. Only a faint trace of powder blue in her skin betrayed a synthetic origin. Long brown hair spilled over her slender shoulders and flowed over her close-fitting, deep indigo dress. Like an ebbing ocean current, the dark sequins around her torso glittered in and out of view as she moved. The stylish outfit looked new to me, no doubt procured, perhaps hacked, from Milan's hottest fashion designer. Through her own dynamic programming desires, she had acquired a taste for fashion that already far outstripped my simple and uncultured sensibilities.

"Thank you, Jonah," Sasha replied.

"Do I have any messages?"

"Your mother," Sasha replied. Like most home programs, she handled basic receptionist and servant duties. But unlike typical house-bots, Sasha possessed far more sophisticated routines, including a data hound prototype from my military programming days. Since the Promethean Laws prohibited true self-aware computers, most families utilized simple virtual butlers to manage their homes. With Sasha, I utilized a few tricks to keep her cognizance thresholds within legal limits, flying a razor's width under the sentience detection grid.

"Play the message, please." Sasha complied and the v-cast whirred, composing a semi-tangible visage of my mother's emaciated face in the space before me.

"Jonah, dear, are you still visiting next week?" she rasped. The voice trembled and sounded weaker than last week's call. "Thank you, dear, for paying my last bill. But, I--I think those IRS thugs are watching me again. The nurse thinks I'm paranoid, but I saw them across the street. Please, please come soon." After her message faded, I tapped my wrist-com and connected to my mother's hospice facility. A basic hack circumvented their security system, allowing me to review the last two days of their security camera footage. Sure enough, I spotted a sedan with two black-suited men wearing dark sunglasses parked outside her window, like vultures perched on a nearby tree.

"Damn ghouls," I mumbled. The term ghoul traced back to the Arabic mythology of a creature that fed off the flesh of the dead. While I never liked the term, it seemed to be an apt description for the jackasses parked outside my mother's window. The IRS had taken my father for his debts, but I vowed that would not happen with my mother.

"You have two more messages," Sasha mentioned.

I walked to the v-cast generator that served the apartment. The machine stood about four feet tall, with three principal components. The tank took up most of the vertical height, holding about ten gallons of reusable proto-matter. Next to it, the disc-shaped reclamation filter stood ready to suck back proto-matter when a virtual form dissolved. Atop the device rested the conical projector element.

"Sasha, play the next message, please." With a noisy whine, the v-cast generator formed the tall figure of a smirking man wearing an exquisite dark blue suit. The man's perfect black hair parted in the middle. Each side featured a symmetrical streak of white hair, like whitecaps crashing atop an ocean wave. I recognized the distinctive hairstyle and the angular cheekbones from the vid-channels before he introduced himself.

"Greetings, Jonah. My name is Gabriel Charon," he announced. The name sounded familiar. "Our mutual acquaintance, Mr. Spenner, recommended you. He said you were the second best ghoul around... after him." I winced, not at the suggested second place ranking, but at the slur itself. Curiosity overcame my minor indignation and the message continued. "I have a business partner, or I should say had a business partner named Mr. Julian Grand. If you're interested, I have an opportunity that will earn you a sizeable collection bonus." While he spoke, my fingers danced across the wrist-com to request information. Sasha walked around the virtual recording of Charon, her golden eyes glittering while regarding him. With an outstretched hand, she formed three floating data windows.

"I'm running a full background check," she reported. The first screen flickered on and showed public domain knowledge. Weeks before, he had assumed the position of CEO of Goliath Corporation, the second-biggest space mining company. The second window showed a series of news vid-clips detailing the recent passing of his father. Guy Charon, the former CEO of Goliath Corp, had passed away at the ripe old age of ninety-two just two months ago. Another news article showed that the company had acquired Grand Construction six years ago. The third window revealed buried tidbits that Sasha pried from the darknet, the seedier recesses of the connected world where talented hackers dredged hidden secrets. My eyes skimmed over the contents of sealed court records detailing a failed federal investigation against the Charon family. Digging further, Sasha found a never-released news story about three hostile takeovers that Goliath Corporation's lawyers had managed to stifle. Another negative news article pertained to a recent drug-overdose on Charon's lunar bar and restaurant, Club Purgatory. Of course, the police had filed no charges. Despite dozens of allegations of improprieties, nothing had stuck to the man, and his record remained clean. My gaze returned to Charon's message as he completed his proposal to me.

"The short and quick of it is that Mr. Grand owes me a tremendous amount of money," Gabriel continued with any icy tone. "And I intend to collect."

I opened a fourth data window to review information about my target. Mr. Julian Grand once owned Grand Construction, the largest of the interstellar building conglomerates involved in putting condominiums on the moon. For the last fifteen years, the company's enticing slogan to "Enjoy A Grand New Life On The Lunar Spire" had lured countless people to the moon. He'd made billions of dollars, primarily by exploiting mass shade-labor. Another news article caught my attention. According to public record, he'd purchased more than two hundred thousand shades to build ten thousand settlements on the moon's Mare Tranquillitatis. More reports streamed in that told the grim tale of his spectacular financial ruin. Like so many robber barons before him, he'd lost his fortune to bold speculation, a risky mining venture that ended in disaster on Pluto. Leaked financial reports flashed on the data window indicating that he'd borrowed a fortune from his partner Gabriel Charon.

"I believe the adage 'reap what you sow' is apt in Mr. Grand's case," whispered Sasha into my ear, bringing a smirk to my lips. Satisfied with my research, I resumed listening to the remainder of the message.

"My sources informed me that Mr. Grand suffered a massive stroke last night," Gabriel added without an atomic ounce of compassion. "His family has not turned over the body. By law, he is my property until he settles his debts. I'll be damned if he goes off to hell without making good on what he owes. I need to know, within hours, if you're interested. I'm transmitting the address where my source believes the Grand family will hide the body. Get me my property, Jonah, and I'll cut you in for a percentage."

Doubting instincts waged a mental war with the practical part of my mind that knew the balance of my checking account. I needed to send an answer quickly. The competition among collection agents grew fiercer each day. Unlike Vanessa, no line of desperate clients banged on my door.

The message ended. As Charon's form melted away, the v-cast generator filters made a sucking sound and recycled all of the floating proto-matter. A tinge of worry gnawed at my stomach about his shadowy past, but I tapped my wrist-com to signal my acceptance of the job.

"Thank you, Sasha. What's next?"

"Revenue Officer Brendan Leary has queried you. He is online," replied Sasha.

"Connect us, please."

The v-cast generator activated, first materializing the guest's orange hair, then the rest of his short, thin frame. As an over-worked mid-level IRS agent, Brendan sometimes tossed overflow jobs my way.

"Jonah, I hope you need work, because I've got a backlog of cases and everyone is swamped," Brendan stated. "Honestly, you were not my first choice. I haven't forgotten about the Mulroney job." Damn, he had to bring up my first and worst case. I'd showed up at the funeral for my first collection as the family tried to lower the body into the ground. I'd read his family the lien, scared them off with the stun weapons, the whole routine. They'd backed off and let me animate the body, but I'd forgotten to double-check the identity. Sure enough, the family had switched the corpses and I'd animated a debt-free corpse they had stolen from the opposite side of the cemetery. That mistake gave the IRS a black eye and prevented me from getting work for a long, hungry month.

"I'm interested," I replied. "Who's the target?"

"Arnold Tornuckle, a former Wall Street trader who racked up a pile of debt while peddling faulty equipment to off-world colo-nists," Brendan responded. "He's getting sued all over the galaxy, a real bastard. On his last trip to the Lunar Spire, travelport security scanners detected an undiagnosed heart embolism. He will be returning tomorrow morning and we're 99.87% certain he'll suffer a fatal stroke within the next ten hours."

Few people outside of secretive government circles knew that most airport scanners possessed more sophisticated technology than the general public realized. Those metal arches that people passed through every day did more than just check for bombs and weapons. The devices acted like the advanced MRI machines at the best hospitals. After the passage of the Mandatory Service Act, the IRS had taken a keen interest in monitoring the wealth and health of citizens, and what better way than to X-ray your insides while you travel? It was all done in the name of national security.

"Your usual per diem will be paid in addition to the collection bonus," continued Brendan. "Easy job. Just be there when the stroke occurs so he can repay his debts."

"I'll take the job," I answered.

"Oh, I know, I already put your name on the board for this target and I took the liberty of sending his usual addresses, frequented shops and restaurants, and car travel history. Good hunting, Agent Jonah." Brendan's freckled face started to disappear with his last words: "Don't let me down again." The generator whined to reclaim the glowing embers of proto-matter.

Having my assignments set up for tomorrow, I returned to the living room to check on Vanessa. Her wine glass was empty, and at some point during the long meeting she'd let her long brown hair down. While her meeting wrapped up, I crept to the kitchen and fetched more white wine from the pantry.

"I don't know how else to thank you, Vanessa," said Saul, as he and the ambassador started to fade out.

"You have our everlasting gratitude," added Eli. "We won't forget your kindness."

"I'll start on the case tonight," Vanessa responded while shaking Eli's outstretched hand. Then the ghosts disappeared as I walked through the dying photonic embers of their fading forms.

"Did you say tonight?" I asked, refilling Vanessa's glass with a golden buttery 2033 Chardonnay. "I was hoping to have some quality time with the prettiest lawyer in the five boroughs," I said, taking a seat next to her.

Vanessa already had returned to her work, her hands darting across the glass table, calling up digital legal briefs, past rulings for afterdeath cases, Supreme Court opinions, and dozens of other complex writings that would take all night to read. I rubbed her shoulders and felt the tension in her knotted muscles.

"Thanks for the glass, dear, but unfortunately my new client, my new paying client, Saul, will be reaped within days if I don't intervene."

"Since I've been gone a week, I was hoping we could spend more time tonight. But I understand if you have an urgent case. How about I keep you company? I'll make sure your wine glass stays full." I placed my hand on her leg and gave her a gentle squeeze. "I've really missed you, honey," I whispered without the pretense of subtlety.

She shot me a glare back and pulled away from my touch.

"And you're going to go on missing me, dear," she said icily. "Tell me, Jonah, how was your day today, hmm? Have a good day lurking about the hospital waiting for people to die? Did you push through any mourners to dig up a fresh corpse?"

The gray clouds of a stormy argument gathered on the horizon, just waiting for a favorable wind or the wrong word to unleash a tempest. I would almost prefer squaring off against the Devereux clan again. Despite my awareness of the delicate situation, I still found a way to make matters worse.

"My day was good. I apprehended a felon who was dodging his tax responsibilities illegally." I immediately regretted getting defensive with her. Why did I always have to try to be right?

"Oh, really? You're going to use that as an excuse?" Her eyebrows raised, the wrinkles around her nose creasing and high-lighting her adorable freckles. I needed to set up an exit strategy to this argument quickly.

"Honey, it's the law," I said, trying to soften my voice as much as possible. "I'm just trying to make a living."

"Making a living at the expense of those poor souls?" she snapped, red-faced. "Do you know how repulsive that sounds?" Her lips quivered and she grasped her wine glass with such force that I was afraid the glass would shatter in her hands. The situation needed to be defused.

"Souls? There's no spark, no mind, no soul, you know that."

"Yes." She paused on the word, as if chewing on it. "I know that," she snipped back with sarcasm. She placed her wine down and crossed her arms.

"Wait, wait, I didn't mean it like that," I said, placing my hand on her hand. "This is not what I'll be doing for the rest of my life here. Just a few more jobs and we'll be able to pay all of our bills. Only two more jobs and I'll have enough to save my mother. After that, I can take a steady job, a programmer position with the city." I tried inching closer and putting my arm around her, but she pushed away. "Please, can't we just forget about this conversation, move on, and relax with each other?"

"This isn't going to work, Jonah," she said in a tone mixed with sadness and weariness. "I tried to tell you before. Many times...you know what I do and you still made your choices. I can't be with someone who...who does those things. You can sleep on the couch tonight. And tomorrow you can pick up..."

I felt a sense of panic welling up inside me. I couldn't let her finish that sentence.

"Stop...please," I begged, fighting a choking sensation gripping my throat. The air suddenly seemed thinner, my eyes watered. It felt like drowning. "I don't want this. Before you say another word, just listen. After tomorrow, I'll have enough money to pay off my mother's bills. Then I'll get another job. I promise."

"You said that before, Jonah, but there's always another bill, another reason. You like the money and you're good at this. But these dead people, yes, people, have rights. There are others like me that believe they are more than just husks. Alive or dead, we all deserve dignity. I hope one day you can see that, Jonah."

"Vanessa, please, just meet me for lunch tomorrow before you say anything more on this. I'll wrap up my work and we can talk about this. I don't want...I don't want us to end."

Her eyes locked on mine and she studied my face. As a lawyer, she'd developed the skill to spot truth and fiction in words, to make a judgment about whether words matched intention. I had made her this promise two weeks ago, that I would stop collecting and find another job. She knew the Bronx Credit Union had offered a systems analyst job to me that paid a low but steady wage. Instead,

I'd accepted a series of more lucrative collections, culminating in the Devereux mission. Guilt crushed my chest when her eyes watered.

"I only have time for a thirty-minute lunch," she said, breaking a painful silence. "Los Cubanos at 1 PM. Don't be late again. You're buying."

With everything going on, I had forgotten my gift. I went back to the table by the front door to grab the flowers I had bought from Ms. Hsu.

"I wanted to give these to you earlier, but you were busy," I said, holding them out to her, a yellow and red aromatic armistice. "They're dying of neglect here."

She took the flowers, inhaled deeply, and chuckled. With that laugh, I dared to believe that hope still breathed a nurturing air on the near-extinguished fire of my relationship. Twirling her fingers, she revealed a hand-written card from Mrs. Hsu that read "Don't screw up again".

"Cute," she said, smiling. "She made a beautiful arrangement." She paused for emphasis. "Once again."

"I love you," I said softly. "I'll try not to screw up again."

"It's late," she replied, walking over to me. "I need to go to bed, Jonah. You should too." Although there was a slight hesitation, she did lean down to kiss the top of my head. Then she turned her back to me and headed toward the bedroom. "You know where the sheets are and pillows for the couch. And thank you for the flowers. Mind putting them in water?"

The bedroom door closed and I rose from the couch, grabbed the flowers, and placed them into a thin blue vase by the kitchen counter. Before I went to bed, I needed to make preparations. The Devereux job had exposed weaknesses in my ability to cope with different situations, and since I would be operating solo, I needed something extra. I walked to the kitchen counter and went to the repli-pantry and spoke my code words. "I'd like my six course meal, please."

The pantry refrigerator opened and the rotating shelves moved to accommodate my request. My secret shelf, hidden between the leftover preserved turkey and root vegetables, swiveled into my view and extended out to me with a whisper-like mechanical whirring.

The shelf contained my own mini-arsenal that I'd kept since leaving the military and collected over my months of IRS service. It was by no means as extensive or as lethal as Spenner's trove, but it got the job done. The shelf contained my jet-black grav-gun, a police baton that I had converted into a stun-rod, and an assortment of mini-grenades. I took two cryo-grenades, the stun-rod, and the grav-gun for good measure.

My gaze lingered on our bedroom at the end of the hall. It looked so comfortable. With a sigh, I prepared my own sleeping arrangements. One thing I learned that night was that no amount of futuristic technology softens a couch enough for a proper night's sleep.

CHAPTER 6
Terra Cotta Woes

"Death is a cycle. The soul must walk on to the next road along the Wheel of Life." - Dalai Lama, before self-immolating in protest of the 2024 MSA Act.

>> DATE: Sept. 24th, 2039. One day before present time.
>> TIME: 6:00 AM.
>> LOCATION: Manhattan, New York City.

"Early to bed, early to rise!" announced Sasha. She assumed a form with the v-cast projector and assembled sufficient proto-matter to nudge my head.

"Makes a man grumpy and unwise," I answered with a growl. The thought of deleting her alarm program crossed my mind.

"Sir, it is time to wake. Last night you instructed me to allow only two snooze dismissals. Please do not make me employ the stun-rod to rouse you."

An unintelligible grumble escaped my lips while I contemplated going back to sleep.

Since she lacked a convincing bluff algorithm, her stun-rod threat represented a good reason to get up. Furthermore, my practical brain reasoned, completing these last two jobs would pay off my mother's bills. After that, I would be able to stop collecting and repair my relationship with Vanessa. This combination of duty and fear of electrocution pushed me off the couch.

Anticipating compliance, Sasha had programmed the mobile armoire unit to collect my clothes in the bedroom without disturbing Vanessa. Within seconds, the simple box-shaped robot returned with a tasteful outfit. I slipped on a white shirt, put on my shoulder holster, covered it with my black blazer, and chose a cream-colored tie. The grav-gun still felt cool to the touch as I tucked it into my shoulder holster. Then I slipped the two cryo-grenades into special pockets sewn in my pants' belt loops. With my hands freed, Sasha delivered a steaming cup of coffee to me.

"Thank you, Sasha. Time to go," I said, sipping the drink as she disappeared and returned to my wrist-com. Like a jumpstart to a dead battery, the life-giving caffeine jolted my system awake. "Brazilian dark roast, excellent choice."

Upon leaving the apartment, thirty-two ghosts, all waiting for Vanessa, pleaded with me as I entered the hallway. Their intrusion onto our apartment floor bothered me, almost as much that my poor girl was in for another long day. My hand slipped into my jacket while I considered blowing the v-cast projector off its ceiling fixture. Instead, I walked through two translucent visitors, opened a wall access panel, and hacked into the v-cast generator.

"What are you doing?" a ghost complained. "Leave that alone!" Two more ghosts approached and swiped at me with their arms. Without enough substance, the futile attack felt like a strong gust of wind.

Ignoring them, my fingers jabbed at the console, giving me access to the privacy protocols of the apartment's v-cast system. Vanessa had allowed visitors to begin calling to her apartment at 6 AM, probably as a wake-alarm to start her day earlier. With a quick adjustment, I changed the permissions to 9 AM. The least I could do was let her sleep in for one day.

After scanning the program further, I detected an invasive malware virus installed into the projector system. It allowed these resourceful, and desperate, v-casters to bypass the safeguards in the lobby and materialize in our hallway. The virus attempted to breach deeper to allow them to enter my apartment. Feeling violated, I deactivated the virus and fired back with a data-worm program that would snarl their connections. It was a virtual warning shot across the bow. When my program initiated, five of the v-casters in front of the queue shimmered, shouted out, and disappeared.

"They didn't play by the rules," I announced to the remaining ghosts. "Please respect our privacy, go back to the lobby, and Vanessa will see you when she can." The ghosts fell silent, faded away to return to the lobby, while I strode through their glowing remnants on my way to the elevator.

* * *

All of the driving routes, the street and air lanes alike, enjoyed light traffic this early in the morning. The orange radiance of the sunrise breached the tight line of skyscrapers every other block. Taking a series of cross-town short cuts through midtown Manhattan, my car arrived and parked across the street at the construction site within twenty minutes. A wide metal fence had been erected around the whole block for the construction crews to renovate the New Millennium high-rise complex. A steel gate blocked entrance into the site, flanked by two security guards, with more just out of sight. In front of the gate, twenty-one construction workers gathered outside the fence, all of them engaged in a heated argument with a distraught-looking man in a white collared shirt.

"I took the liberty of downloading the building schematics from the city's zoning approval office," Sasha reported, her light blue face appearing in the smart-glass of the rear view mirror. The car's windshield darkened, becoming a virtual display, revealing the building layouts. A system of under-tunnels beneath the site appeared to be a promising place to start looking for Mr. Grand.

"I have also started gathering satellite photos of the compound and the company's work logs. It looks like most of the workers have been given the day off."

"Good work, Sasha," I replied. "A day off would make it easier for the family to do some unauthorized construction. What about the financial records?"

More information streamed onto the glass as Sasha complied with my request. Over the last three years, Mr. Grand had sunken into deep debt to Gabriel Charon. He also owed the government nearly twenty million in back taxes. The list of debtors filled the screen. In fact, he owed so much that I estimated his afterdeath repayment to be three hundred years. No wonder Gabriel wanted the body so badly.

"It appears Mr. Grand has made many bad choices," Sasha noted. I didn't take any joy or pleasure in doing collecting jobs, but it certainly made it easier for my conscience when the target was either a mobster or a pawn of mobsters.

"I'll need a cover to get through the security gate," I said, tapping into the car's computer archives. A digital wardrobe of forged personas flashed across the windshield glass.

"Will you attempt the flower delivery man again?" Sasha teased, citing one of my previous mishaps. My hero Sherlock Holmes was a master of disguises, a skill he used often to solve cases. My track record with assumed identities proved much less consistent. "Or the pizza delivery man identity that almost landed you in the hospital?"

"Perhaps something a bit less devious," I mumbled. Police detective? No, too risky. My hand waved through a maze of choices until I found Jeremy Blumfield, a mild-mannered building code inspector working for the city.

"Your credentials are printing, Jeremy," Sasha said. An output slot below the glove department glowed red, then dispensed an official-looking badge emblazoned with New York City's official seal. As I exited the car, I heard the frustrated workers from across the street.

"This is total bullshit," said one of the construction workers to another.

"Closed for the day?" said another. "What the hell is going on?"

"I hope they're not bringing in more shades," complained another. "I need the work!"

"Take it easy, fellas," said the short man wearing a yellow hard-hat and a white-collared shirt. Judging by the lack of grime on his clothes, I assumed he was the foreman or the building manager. "No one's getting replaced. We have some, uh--inspections today. So, the boss is giving you all a paid day off." He pulled out a stack of papers and handed out checks to the workers. This seemed to appease the workers, as they started to disperse from the locked gate.

When the last of the workers left, I approached. The foreman held a hand out to stop me.

"Hey you, where the hell do you think you're headed?" he demanded. "We're closed today. Off-limits, you hear?"

"Not to the city you're not." Flashing a scowl, I shoved my fake badge in and out of his face, and leaned toward him for added intimidation. "Just yesterday a utility-shade worker took a dive and nearly killed a pedestrian due to faulty harnesses not being up to code. We're inspecting all operations in the city that expose citizens to unsafe working conditions, especially with shades doing high-rise work. I will have access to the premises."

"Inspections?" the foreman gasped. "What do you mean?" His brow furrowed and he crossed his arms in defiance.

"Didn't you just tell your men that you're closing for inspections?" I countered. "Well, that's what I'm here for."

"Uh--hey, it's not a good day for that," he stammered, looking back and forth for someone that might help him. "I mean, what I said was...what I meant was...the company was doing our own internal inspections, you know, cleanup maintenance."

"Tell me your name," I requested, tapping my wrist-com. "I will be recording this for my investigation."

"Ph-Phil," the foreman gulped. "Phil Horsely."

"Okay Phil, Phil Horsely, my name's Inspector Jeremy Blumfield, and you may not realize it yet but I could be saving you a shitload of trouble," I said. "Imagine what happens if one of your shades falls off a beam and hits a citizen on the street?" I said, raising my voice, pushing in closer. "The manager of that window cleaning shade I mentioned earlier? He's in prison for not keeping his operation within code. You still feel solid about your setup here? Or do you want me to make sure you guys are secure?"

"Prison?" the foreman gulped. "Look, you can walk the grounds, check out what you need. But the interior offices and belowground tunnels are off-limits. We've closed those off for renovations. Can you be done in an hour? My wife wants me home for dinner."

"Sure, Phil, no problem. Just stay out of my way. I'll need access to your security cameras and diagnostic monitoring systems. I can do my tests from the ground floor."

"Oh, that's great, thanks, Inspector!" the foreman said as he opened the gate. "I'll be in the security office if you need me, sir. There's a monitoring console about thirty feet ahead."

Entering the compound with confidence, I pretended to jot down notes onto my wrist-com and surveyed the site. A crisscrossing system of ropes, pulleys, and cranes supported large containers filled with building materials. None of the living workers remained in the area. However, twenty shade workers still shuffled along the scaffolding of the higher floors, delivering stacks of metal girders to higher floors. As I approached the terminal that the foreman had mentioned, a nearby camera pivoted toward me to scan my badge. It beeped and the computer's display flickered to life.

"Sasha," I whispered, "time to be a good little mole and burrow into their network."

"I'm in. The foreman conveniently removed all security layers for us," she responded into my ear. Her shimmering face smiled at me through the now static-filled computer screen. I pretended to look busy, tapping at the console to inspect low-level operational diagnostic data.

"Good girl. Now try to gain access to any v-cast projectors they have in the vicinity. Do they have any?"

"Yes, sir," Sasha responded. "There are twelve total projectors, most of them mark-3 units, all with an abundance of proto-matter."

"Excellent," I responded. "My instincts tell me they hid Mr. Grand in the under-tunnels. When I reach that door I want you to run the chameleon program. Can you do that, dear?"

"Yes, sir. According to the security monitors, there is no one in the tunnels down below. That area looks secure."

I walked away from the terminal and acted like I was interested in various structures around the compound. I assumed that Phil was watching me with his own security cameras, so I needed to make sure that I looked like I was doing a thorough inspection.

When I reached the southwest side door that lead to underground tunnels, I stepped to the side and whispered to Sasha to start the program. Taking over their v-cast projectors, Sasha created a life-like virtual duplicate of me walking the grounds and completing the inspection, while at the same time blocking out the security view of the door I stood near. This ruse, the chameleon program, allowed me to enter the tunnels while my virtual projection looked serious and continued his patrol.

I climbed down a short flight of stairs, taking care to minimize the sound of my footfalls on the metallic surface. The old maintenance tunnels connected to a labyrinthine system of underground passageways. City crews used these tunnels to access electrical lines and sewer plumbing to keep the skyscrapers above functioning.

When my eyes adjusted to the dim lighting, one section of the tunnel wall stood out. While brown and green lichen covered most of the tunnel, the black door at the far end of the passage looked pristine. When I walked toward the door, I noticed that a sophisticated magnetic lock protected it. More of a pain in the ass than impossible to break, the lock represented a potential significant delay.

"Sasha, do you have any access to the floor that I'm on? I'm wondering if you can query for the override password on this door?"

"Searching, Jonah," Sasha responded. "Unfortunately, no, there is no record of that door in the company's records. It should not be there."

"Right," I muttered. "Of course no records, Mr. Grand didn't want to be found." I pulled out my stun-rod and reached into my pocket for a very sensitive tool I had hidden away for just such an occasion. The nano-picks looked like two thin wires fused together, similar to a steel-colored woman's hair barrette. For this job, I would need the equivalent of a hammer and tweezers.

My fingers adjusted the controls hidden on the shaft of the stun-rod, focusing the plasma fields, allowing me to use it like a blowtorch. The weapon, vibrating on overload, blazed like a torch, frightening a trio of rats down the corridor and revealing a number of fresh boot prints in the thick layer of dust nearby. It looked like five or six workers had been down here recently to install the new security door.

I needed to hurry. The weapon would detonate at this high setting. Making an educated guess to knock out the door's power supply, I pushed the burning end against a cracked portion of the wall. The old rock smoldered, blackened, and then crumbled, revealing several conduits and wires feeding the magnetic door with power. I reached for the small nano-picks, wire-thin instruments that enabled me to interface with an access point. I held my breath, hoping not to create a detectable spike in disrupted energy. The trick would be to siphon off just the right amount of energy and starve the door of power without it showing up on the security grid.

Lucky for me, the door deactivated not with a bang but with a whimper. Unluckily for me, the door did not open all the way once its power flow stopped. I thought about risking another hack to feed it just enough power to open, but I worried that another power irregularity might trigger a security alert.

My hand groped around the edges of the door and I found a small handle to help open the door. Pushing against its heavy weight, I stifled a grunt and slid the stone door open. I felt like an old-time archaeologist pushing open an ancient set of stone doors. The analogy proved to be quite apt as I crept into the large room. A musty, decaying scent hung in the stale air. Inside I discovered a large square room, about thirty by thirty, encased with thick granite walls that belonged to the building's original foundation. My eyes darted to the large gleaming black coffin at the far end. It almost felt like I had stumbled upon some ancient burial site, except this was no ancient tomb. A single bulb cast a weak pool of yellow light around the coffin, highlighting that it rested on a stone slab three feet off the ground. The dais kept the coffin off the shallow pools of drainage water that trickled through tiny pipes around the room.

"I suppose we'll answer 'Who's Buried in Grand's Tomb' soon," I joked, taking a step into the room while drawing my gun.

"Querying," Sasha whispered back to me. "A reference to the 'Who's Buried in Grant's Tomb' antiquated pun. My quality algorithm is rating this joke as...lacking."

"You should delete that algorithm," I mocked.

"Deleting, sir," Sasha complied.

"No, no, don't, I was being playfully capricious. Please, keep me honest."

"Yes, sir. This room is cut off from the network, I will need more time..."

"Not a lot of time before the foreman figures out the chameleon ruse. We'll have to explore the old-fashioned way."

As my eyes adjusted to the room's ambient light, I saw that I was not alone. More than a dozen human-sized blurry shapes came into focus through the shadows. They stood still in three rows, interspersed from each other by five feet. My first thought was that these shapes were statues, and my mind recalled an old history lesson. To serve them in the afterlife, ancient Chinese emperors had buried themselves with an army of terra cotta warriors.

One step closer into the crypt and I noticed the eyes of the statues emanated a very faint yellow glow. These figures were not statues.

"Shades," I muttered. Fifteen of them stood before me, in three rows of five, all standing still as stone, except for the occasional blink of their yellow eyes.

Holding my breath, I tiptoed forward between the shades, and they remained in their stoic poses. Twenty feet of stone floor and this small army of shades separated me from my target. An imaginary coin flipped in my mind. Heads indicated a sprint to the coffin, and tails called for a stealthier approach. The coin landed, and my mind picked tails.

Slinking forward, I chose a path on the left side between two shades dressed in blue utility uniforms. My right hand drew my stun-rod and adjusted it with a few flicks of my finger, restoring its wider disrupting field. That setting enabled it to knock out a charging bull with a strike. The left hand gripped the gun tight while I stepped past the first row of shades. Blue light cast from my glowing baton revealed a small puddle of water only after my foot stepped in it. Then I saw it: a sensor on the left wall emitting an orange light, likely a sensitive audio sensor. The sensor made a clicking sound, and then a part of the wall near it slid open to reveal a hidden speaker.

"We have an intruder, protect me!" said a male voice from the speaker, which I assumed was a pre-recorded voice of Mr. Grand. The guardians gave a collective groan as they awakened and shambled forward. A tall gray-bearded shade dressed in white utility suspenders threw a wild haymaker at me. Ducking the clumsy attack, I jabbed my stun-rod into his stomach, knocking him back four feet into two other approaching sentinels.

A piercing pain shot through my shoulder as one of the shades grabbed me with a pair of thick hands and clenched hard. I dropped down and twisted my body to escape its grasp. The maneuver worked, but a throbbing pain still wracked my shoulder.

With surprising quickness, six more shadowy figures rushed over to surround me. Sensing impending danger, I channeled the pulsing pain into an angry determination to survive. Though my injured shoulder weakened my grip on the stun-rod, my good arm still wielded the grav-gun. Two shots, encapsulated by the gun's micro-gravity guidance fields, tore an unerring path through the air and penetrated the skull of the nearest attacker.

The others made no notice of their fallen comrade and lurched toward me. Two of the closest guards reached for me with pale hands. Another pair of bullets exploded from my gun. One bullet tore straight through a female shade's outstretched hand. The shot ripped through the palm and struck her forehead. While she fell back into another attacker, her glowing yellow eyes extinguished. The second bullet punctured the leg of a short-statured guard, causing him to fall to the ground and thrash violently.

With three of the shades eliminated, I stood up and assessed my situation. With fewer bullets in my gun than guardians in the crypt, the situation appeared grim. They formed a semi-circle around me, blocking the exit and the way to the coffin, forcing me to move back against the wall. With three bullets remaining against twelve angry shades, I needed a new plan.

"Kill the intruder!" commanded Mr. Grand's speaker, causing his sentinels to draw even closer. The disembodied voice controlled their actions, and this sparked an idea that was the theoretical equivalent of a 'Hail Mary'.

"Sasha, I'm going to need you very soon, dear," I said between panting breaths.

"Of course, sir," Sasha responded. "I see you have made some friends?"

"Not quite," I replied, feeling an appreciation for her wit in the face of dire circumstances. "I have a plan that will require some fast hacking on your part. Get ready to attempt a fast manual hack when I reach that speaker."

"Standing by," Sasha said.

I slid my back against the wall, edging closer toward the speaker, holding the gun up with my good arm and keeping a loose grip on my stun-rod with my injured arm.

A towering male shade, the thick veins in his neck glowing bright yellow, rushed at me. A rapid squeeze of my trigger finger released the fourth bullet, ending the guard's service to his former master. His body crumpled, tripping a second attacker that tried to reach me. Jumping over the bodies, a female shade barreled toward me. A momentary fear gripped me at the sight of her gruesome face, twisted by rage and glowing yellow from the serum coursing in her body. With cruel swiftness, her spindly arms with long filthy nails swiped for my throat. As I aimed for a shot, an obese shade to her left made a horrible screeching sound that distracted me, sending my fifth bullet off target. The woman's long nails slashed my coat and scratched my torso. The searing pain focused me, and I sent my final bullet into her head to end her tortured existence.

Time seemed to slow down as my senses heightened, my heart pounded, and adrenaline pumped through my body. I dropped my empty grav-gun and gathered the strength to switch my stun-rod to the other arm, twirling to the side to avoid a ramming attack. As the shade passed me, I slammed the weapon into its head and used the recoil momentum to bounce me back to the wall. I made a run for the speaker a few feet ahead of me, jumping over a fallen shade's outstretched and grasping hand. Reaching the speaker, I raised my wrist-com and touched it against a small console just below it.

"Now!" I urged.

"I'm in," I heard Sasha's voice say through the speaker. Immediately after Sasha transferred to the room's security system,

I spun around to deflect a punch from another guard. Despite my blocking the blow, the impact pushed me back several feet, sending me sprawling against the coffin's dais. Desperate to give Sasha time, I jumped up onto the raised platform to gain the advantage from higher ground. My stun-rod hewed a wide arc to deter a pair of shades reaching for me.

"Access the recording of Mr. Grand's voice!" I ordered. All of the surviving sentinels gathered around my location.

It came down to this one remote hope. The timing needed to be perfect. I swung my weapon down to knock a shade off the dais. Reaching into my other pocket, I pulled out the syringe with the serum intended for my target and flung open the coffin. Inside, Mr. Grand's body awaited. He was shorter than I expected, and dressed in a fine Italian suit matching the color of his trimmed gray beard. Across his folded hands rested a jeweled cane.

I raised the syringe in the air and plunged it straight into the chest of Mr. Grand, pushing ten thousand milliliters of yellow serum into his corpse.

One of the shades delivered a vicious right-hook across my face, bruising my jaw and sending me sprawling to the floor. The largest of all, the shade of a massive construction worker in dingy overalls, raised a foot to stomp my head. I gathered up the strength to swing my stun-rod at his legs, knocking him down to one knee.

"The speaker system is reprogrammed now," announced Sasha. "We can make it say whatever you want."

Another shade towered over me and kicked at me with its booted foot with such a powerful force that my ribs compressed and air escaped my lungs. The same shade grabbed me by my shirt and lifted me up into the air. I looked down and saw its impassive face, brown teeth, and yellow eyes staring back at me. Its left arm moved to snap my neck and end my life.

The remaining shades stared to climb up the dais, and I knew I only had a few more seconds. Then a flash of movement from the coffin caught my eye. Mr. Grand sat up from his coffin and turned to face me, his eyes glowing yellow. The serum had worked, and I held out a razor-thin hope that I might survive.

"PROTECT ME!" I shouted, and coughed up blood from the effort. My voice imprinted into Mr. Grand's serum programming, forcing his body to comply. Mr. Grand jumped out of his coffin and ran toward me, slamming into the shade that held me in the air. Then he pushed another of his former guards away while I slumped to the ground.

"Sasha -- the speaker!" I yelled, again with the consequence of me suffering another bloody coughing fit. "Change the recording and tell them to stop!"

"Stop!" spoke Sasha through the speaker, in the voice of Mr. Grand. "Leave the intruder!"

Recognizing the voice of their former employer, the guardians stopped in their tracks. I had gambled that Sasha would be able to change the words of the recording using the same voice modulation.

"Oh, the cleverness of you!" Sasha cheered.

My head, shoulder, and chest all throbbed with pain. Sitting on the floor, I stroked my chin trying to recall Sasha's reference, rummaging through childhood memories of reading many great books like Harry Potter, Tom Sawyer, Oliver Twist, and others that had kept me grounded during some difficult years in my youth.

"Peter Pan?" I asked, timidly unsure of my guess.

"Correct sir, well done," Sasha responded.

I beamed, feeling so proud of my Sasha. She cited a relevant and funny literary reference in the appropriate context, increasing her reference knowledge and humor engrams. Sitting there and bleeding on the floor, surrounded by silent shades, my mind drifted to consider alternate employment. With my programming talents, I could apply to a big company like Titan Tech, or Polaris Inc. Sasha would be an excellent resume for me to get a new job, a fresh start away from the collection business. But responsibilities required me to continue for at least one more job before retirement. With a moan, I pushed off the dais to stand up, and started to limp out of the bloody tomb. Behind me, Mr. Grand followed a few steps back and six of his remaining obedient guards trailed him.

"You are hurt," observed Sasha. "I will query Dr. Yune and request that he see you."

"If there's time," I replied. "We still need to collect Arnold."

I climbed the stairs back to the construction compound where a team of security officers, led by the foreman, waited for me.

"Halt!" a security officer demanded.

"Just what in the hell do you think you're doing?" yelled the foreman. "You can't take him!"

"On the contrary," I snapped back, pulling a smooth sphere from my pocket, activating with a touch, and tossing it in the air. The holo-lien floated and flared with blue life, projecting the face of the Honorable Judge Prescott.

"Judge Prescott, Mr. Grand is ready for sentencing," I said. With all the commotion and fighting down below, I had forgotten to read the rights. I figured this would kill two birds with one stone.

"Pursuant to IRS Code 158 (1) (a), the federal government has been given the mandate to collect debts from citizens who perish in a state of serious delinquency and insolvency..." the judge spoke in his flat monotone voice.

"You're not an inspector! You're a goddamned ghoul!" The foreman was angry at the collection, but there was also a tinge of humiliation on his face from being duped. The two guards reached for their tasers and stun-rods.

"I must ask all of you to stay back," I warned, wary of another physical encounter. "Any interference with a deputized federal agent in the process of a lawful collection is punishable with ten years of afterdeath service for each person involved." This threat was true. Anyone caught impeding lawful collections risked becoming a shade with their own debt. Penalties stiffened for those foolish enough to destroy a body. That was enough to spook the minimum wage security guards, who holstered their weapons and turned around to leave. The foreman tapped his arm, activating a communication console display that projected along his arm.

"The body of Mr. Grand," the judge addressed the shade, "is hereby sentenced to three hundred and sixty-two years of afterdeath service."

"I need to call the Grand family," the foreman said with a look of sheer panic, his face ashen. "They're going to kill me for letting you take him!"

"Then maybe you shouldn't call them, and get out of town instead," I countered. For emphasis, my hand moved to the handle of my stun-rod. A bluff in my weakened state, but the smaller foreman did not look like a man who was accustomed to combat. "Either way, I'm taking Mr. Grand to fulfill his debts."

A moment of conflicting thought ended when the foreman fled the compound and probably the country. Although the Grand family lacked money, their connections to the underworld might seek retribution against anyone involved with this collection.

"Sasha, please keep an eye on transmissions and communications from the rest of the Grand family, in case they get any crazy ideas like vendetta," I requested. "Warn me if you see any irregularities."

"Already completed," she chirped back. "I have the two brothers and the sister under electronic and financial surveillance. We will have at least an hour's notice if they decide to put an assassination bid on your head anywhere in the darknet."

"An hour?" I asked. "That's only slightly comforting." Sasha's emerging progress and initiative continued to impress me, overshadowing the nagging worry that I may have just made an enemy of a mob family.

Turning back to survey my shambling entourage, I noticed that several of their bodies looked worn and decayed.

"Sasha?" I asked. "Can you scan any identity chips in these shades? I'm assuming these are still property of the construction company, but let's double check."

"Accessing," Sasha reported. "This data must be corrupted, Jonah. It's very odd."

"What did you find?"

"According the company records, all of these shades were scheduled to expire," she reported. "I presume someone modified their debt timers. That is a serious violation of IRS code 1782 (b)."

Reaching into my jacket, I pulled out the holo-lien and activated it, summoning the visage of the judge.

"What do I owe the pleasure of seeing you again today, Jonah?" he asked with an expression of curiosity crossed with mild irritation.

"Sorry to interrupt you again, sir, but in the process of collecting Mr. Grand, we've discovered a number of illegally modified shades. They are all years beyond their expiration."

"Ghastly," the judge whispered. "I will recommend a full audit of the company to ensure that their other workers have properly formulated serums."

"What would you like me to do with these shades, Your Honor?"

"They have fulfilled their duties. Retire them immediately," replied the judge. "The IRS will send agents to collect the evidence later. Thank you, Mr. Adams, for bringing this to our attention. I will recommend a bonus in my report."

Nodding, I retrieved ammunition from my pockets, reloaded my gun, and retired the last of the illegal shades while Mr. Grand watched and awaited a command.

CHAPTER 7
O, Death

"It is better to risk saving a guilty person than to condemn an innocent one." - Voltaire, Zadig

My car weaved through uptown traffic toward the nearest dead depot while Mr. Grand waited in the backseat. With the air lanes snarled by an aerial accident, we traveled thirty minutes across the city to arrive at the tall federal building on Varick Street. A pair of agents with dark sunglasses greeted me at a roundabout, claimed Mr. Grand, and ushered me on my way. Seconds later, the pleasant dinging sound of money depositing into my account made all my pain a bit more bearable. With that, I turned my car around toward the other side of town.

"Dr. Yune responded. He will be able to see you now," reported Sasha. "In the next empty alley, there is access to a public v-cast generator with sufficient fidelity."

I thought about ignoring the call in favor of completing my second mission faster, but the ache in my shoulder convinced me to seek medical attention. With a nod, I veered the car off the road.

"I'll let him know you're available."

The car rolled to a stop on the dead end street, and I stepped out of the car. Within the shadows behind a rusted dumpster, a faint green light shimmered. Emerging from a swirl of lime-colored proto-matter, Dr. Taejin Yune appeared with a virtual form matching his real body. Standing about five-foot-four, he wore white shorts and a matching polo shirt capped with a sailing hat. In his hand, he gripped an inflatable duck swim ring. Usually he wore a doctor's gown during a virtual visit, but this time he maintained his true form. It was a reminder that I intruded on his vacation.

"Really, Jonah? A back alley?" He shook the rubber toy at me with a look of anger.

"Thank you for coming, Captain -- I mean, Dr. Yune," I joked.

"I'm on my yacht with my children, Jonah, so I will have to charge double," the doctor said, wagging his finger at me. He became aware that he'd manifested the inflatable, and shook it off his hand, causing its proto-matter to fade away. "Do you have a medical kit?"

"Yes, doctor," Sasha answered, assuming her own slim form. She fetched a red box from the car's trunk. It contained all the pharmaceutical materials the doctor had requested during my last appointment.

Despite the angry act, Dr. Yune was a close friend. These days, he served as the private physician to the politicians in South Korea. We'd met years before in North Korea during the cyber wars. My platoon had rescued his family from an internment camp. Since then, I've been relying on his favors, discretion, and his willingness to make unorthodox house calls to keep me patched up. Walking toward me, he placed his hands on my body and examined me.

"Dislocated shoulder, broken jaw, and some internal bleeding for good measure," Dr. Yune diagnosed after a cursory inspection. His look of irritation changed to concern. Reaching into the medical box, he retrieved hypodermics filled with painkillers and drugs containing powerful clotting chemicals. A series of pricks from the needles caused initial burning sensations across my skin, and then instant relief. Dr. Yune's concoction of medicines sped along my body's natural healing process.

"Sasha, I'm charging you with keeping him safe, since I know Jonah won't listen to me," Dr. Yune said with some exasperation. "He's more stubborn than me! He needs two days of rest, no more injuries. His body must recuperate."

"Thank you, doctor," Sasha and I said in unison.

"I'm going back to my family cruise," Dr. Yune responded, a subtle smirk breaking his usual frowning countenance. "I hope I don't hear from you again anytime soon."

* * *

A sense of urgency drove me to accelerate through a trio of red lights to make up time for my back-alley clinic stop. Sasha hacked the trafficnet to ensure that the hidden cameras on the signal lights all suffered convenient malfunctions.

"How are we doing on time?" I asked, swerving around a wide pothole.

"Under an hour. Approximately fifty-eight minutes, according to the IRS latest death-projections for Mr. Turnuckle." She hacked into the city's ubiquitous surveillance network to gather tracking data on the target.

"This morning, Mr. Turnuckle skipped his gym appointment, ate lunch at Cosmo Burgers, and purchased three packs of cigarettes," she reported.

"You're making that up," I protested, turning the car the wrong way down a narrow one-way street for a short cut. "Could he be any more unhealthy?"

"A few minutes ago, he made a last minute reservation to one of his favorite restaurants, Sylvia's Best Steakhouse on 7th Avenue," she reported.

"Steak, really?" I asked aloud with raised eyebrow. "He may stroke out before the hour." I accelerated, careening past a procession of slow-moving taxis, and dodging a group of jaywalking drunks. After ten minutes and eight more unreported driving infractions, I arrived across the street from Turnuckle's restaurant.

With a hand wave, the car's display and a digital console appeared. My fingers swam through a digital stream of connections into the Steakhouse's computers system, worming through the thin security layer of its reservation system. It took three seconds to break in and one second to insert my name near the top of the list, bumping the anniversary dinner of Mr. and Mrs. Yukimura by twenty minutes. For their trouble, I compensated them a pair of free drinks. It was the least I could do.

"Sir, perhaps you should tidy up before entering the restaurant?" Sasha suggested.

She was right. I looked like hell. My shirt was a collage of battle, showing bloodstains, green-yellowish ichor, and mottled gray matter spattered from Grand's shades. The manifestation of maternal instincts in Sasha's personality heuristics, code I'd augmented a week ago, made me grin. I took a moment to straighten my hair, wiped off as much of the brains and stains as I could, and buttoned over the shirt with the jacket.

I rushed from the car, walked across the street, and met the doorman of Sylvia's. He was a stocky man of Italian heritage squeezed into a maître d' uniform two sizes too small.

"Evening, sir," he greeted, moving behind me to take my coat.

"No thank you," I refused, not wanting to reveal the bloody mess beneath. The interruption in the man's routine of taking jackets seemed to send him into a stupor of confusion, similar to a locked-up program. I double-checked his skin and face to make sure he wasn't some type of new robot or shade. It was a silly notion, since shades were prohibited from working in restaurants for the occasional risk of limb decomposition. Finding an ear or finger will ruin even the most scrumptious Caesar salad. After a few moments of holding still in a position to take my coat, he sighed and motioned with his hand for me to enter.

I spotted Arnold. He was seated at an oval table covered with a pristine white cloth. He tucked a napkin under his a chin that bulged over the tight collar of his powder blue shirt.

"I'd like to sit in the back, please. Over at that table if you don't mind," I requested.

The maître d' obliged and escorted me to the table. Arnold regarded me while I walked by, and then returned to ramming fistfuls of fried calamari into his hungry mouth. If anything, he looked larger than the surveillance photos, weighing well over three hundred pounds. Sweat soaked his shirt and he gulped a large cup of ice water like he'd gone without it for three days. I guessed that his blood pressure had skyrocketed from his embolism.

While monitoring Arnold, I noticed the old-fashioned black-and-white clock ticking on the nearby wall. The time indicated that I had an hour and ten minutes before my lunch with Vanessa. The pressure and worry of missing that important date triggered a regrettable response in my head.

"Arnold, would you hurry up and die already?" I thought to myself. Overcome by my own selfish needs and tight schedules, I let that horrible desire emerge from some dark recess of my stressed brain. Those ugly words echoed in my head with increasing volume, like a jackhammer pounding me with guilt. I hated myself suddenly, intensely. Then the rational part of my brain countered.

"I didn't sentence this guy to die," I consoled myself. "I didn't rack up his debts, I didn't make these collection laws. I'm just trying to make a living."

A waiter bumped my table and interrupted my self-loathing. After he apologized to me, he brought the main course to Arnold's table. A foot-long slab of prime rib steamed on a wide plate. Glancing at the menu, I saw the prime rib featured a sweet sherry reduction, buttered finger potatoes, and a cheese-laden salad that would not help his clogged arteries. From the caloric value alone, I sensed this would be Arnold's last meal.

Arnold's sweating intensified. He looked nervous and asked the waiter for another pitcher of water. I knew from his expression that he felt something was wrong, but unfortunately for him he attributed his queasiness to hunger. The pallor of his skin grew paler. His fingers unbuttoned his shirt's collar to let him breathe easier. The time was coming.

Then my wrist-com made a soft chime sound, indicating a message from Vanessa. I muted the audio and played the message back as text streaming next to an image of her smiling face.

"I hope you're serious about looking for different work," she wrote. "I'm probably being naive, but I'd like to talk. Can't wait to see you." The possibility of another chance with her brought a broad smile to my lips. I needed to make sure I didn't screw it up.

My gaze returned to check on Arnold, who looked even worse. His hand shook with an obvious tremor as he reached for his water.

"Just die already so I can get back to my life," echoed that dark voice inside me. Arnold's plight was not my fault. Who was I to get involved and interfere? The words 'second chance' from Vanessa's message resounded in my head. When I thought of her, I realized that if she sat here instead of me, she would have intervened to save him. Instead I sat here wishing this man, who never harmed me, would hurry up and die. With a mounting sense of shame, I realized the term 'ghoul' seemed appropriate for me. Would she want a man that allowed such things to pass? This worry infected me like a virus, rewiring my intentions. I made my decision.

With a few taps on my wrist-com, I contacted the Emergency Services network. After three flicks of my finger, I found and made contact with a patrolling ambulance five blocks away. Using an alias cover program, I faked an emergency call message pretending to be Mr. Masa Yukimura, reporting that a man suffered a heart attack at Sylvia's Steakhouse. That way, if the IRS looked into the matter, they wouldn't know that I'd foiled my own collection attempt.

"Check please," I requested when the waiter came near. He took my identity card and scanned it for payment.

"Thank you for the tip—"

"Is that man okay?" I interrupted, feigning ignorance and pointing at Arnold.

"What?" he asked, surprised. The waiter followed my point and noticed Arnold fanning himself his cloth napkin and holding a hand to his chest. "Oh my, he does look ill, doesn't he?"

I heard a siren blaring across the street, and as I got up to leave two paramedics rushed in, pushing a gurney filled with medical equipment.

It was a simple matter to walk out unhindered as the patrons and staff all crowded around to watch the dramatic scene. While I left without my bounty, I walked away with something more valuable.

* * *

My interrogators each reacted differently to the resolution of the Turnuckle job. Barnaby flashed a disapproving scowl while Erasmus could not suppress a wry grin on his thin lips.

"You willfully disregarded a collection order from the United States government and revealed classified information to the target?" said the black-dressed man with a rising tone of anger.

"Classified?" I responded. "He was dying of a stroke, I called an ambulance. It's not like I betrayed state secrets."

"You betrayed our trust. That man has a debt and you tipped him off to his condition," said Barnaby. "This is--"

"...a legal gray area at best," Erasmus interrupted. "Jonah made a very human and, I daresay, morally guided decision. Besides, Arnold's debts did not disappear. Jonah merely delayed the collection. I see no reason to punish him at all."

While the two continued to bicker, my head throbbed with a sharp pain. I wondered if Dr. Yune's painkillers had worn off.

"The strain appears to be weakening him," Barnaby said, peering at me skeptically. "He may need more meds."

Erasmus stroked the medallion dangling from a golden chain on his neck. The necklace featured a cross set onto a spherical moon. It was the holy symbol of the New Church, the harmonious combination of devoted faith and conviction of scientific truths.

"Why, Barnaby!" Erasmus replied with amusement. "Am I detecting a hint of concern for our new friend?"

"He is an asset that we invested a great deal of time and attention into," Barnaby responded with a notable emphasis on the word attention. "It would be a pity to lose that investment."

"Jonah, are you able to continue?" Erasmus asked plainly.

My initial instinct was to say no, that I needed to rest, but I realized they would place me in a cell until they deemed me ready again. Better to finish the report and then let them play their hand, I figured.

"I'm feeling better now, I just needed a breather," I lied.

"Excellent," Barnaby replied. "Why don't you continue your report? Please don't spare any details."

CHAPTER 8
Stood up on High

*"Unto a life which I call natural I would gladly
follow even a will-o'-the-wisp through bogs and
sloughs unimaginable, but no moon nor firefly has
shown me the causeway to it."*
- Excerpt from "Walking", Henry David Thoreau

After entering my car, I looked back across the street to watch the paramedics emerge with Mr. Turnuckle on the gurney. Intravenous lines dripped saline into his veins and a mask pushed oxygen into his lungs. The two men, muscular and fit, struggled to hoist their heavy burden into their ambulance. An old prayer to health from my childhood came to mind, and I mouthed the litany with a hope that Arnold survived the stroke.

"I fabricated medical orders from Mercy General to the paramedics ordering a 50cc dose of thrombolytics to dissolve his brain clot," Sasha said when I entered the car. "Otherwise it would have taken them approximately twenty-two minutes to reach the hospital and find the cause. Shall I cancel the order?"

"No, Sasha, you did well," I replied. "So now you're a doctor?"

"Not board-certified by any means, sir." Sasha quipped. "My current expertise levels would rank me close to a first year resident. May I ask you a question?"

"Of course," I responded. My hands darted across the car's virtual display of the city, pinpointing my destination. I needed to travel across town fast, but I also did not want to deter Sasha from exercising her dynamic curiosity algorithms.

"Why did you change your mind?" she asked.

"About what?"

"Your decision to intervene with Mr. Turnuckle's fate," she responded. "By doing so, you abandoned a considerable bounty and endangered your own mother. I hope you do not take offense, but I accessed her current hospice care daily records, and her condition has not improved. To the contrary, I estimate that she has between three to five months to live since her stage four lung cancer has metastasized."

"Please cross-reference 'blunt', 'etiquette', and 'cancer' and see what you discover within the context of human social interactions," I replied matter-of-factly. I didn't take her candor personally, though the conversation conjured an image of my mother clicking a morphine drip before my mind's eye. I wanted Sasha to learn a lesson in tact. Even amidst a dying world filled with shades, ghosts, and even more terrible monsters, it was important to me that she learned humanity.

"Searching," she chirped back. "I believe I understand why you asked me to research this. My candid assessment of your mother's condition caused you discomfort. Next time if this subject enters discussion, I will employ more subtle references nuanced with comforting euphemisms."

"Thank you, Sasha."

Checking my traffic dashboard, I saw that rush hour still clogged the air lanes, so I remained on the ground streets. The car peeled off and sped back toward Manhattan. Along the way, more digital billboard advertisements animated for my attention, pushing all types of consumable products. I managed to filter out the colorful noise until my car slowed for a red stop signal. While I waited for the signal to change, a glowing billboard to the right of my car flashed, and the White Djinn's smirking, bearded face appeared. As he delivered his pitch, bold subtitles and slogans danced across his advertisement.

----- LOST SOMETHING VALUABLE? -----
----- Did a hacker steal an identity? -----

----- Wish it back! -----
----- Summon THE WHITE DJINN, today! -----
----- Djinn's Fortune Tip #322: -----
----- It's good manners to be on time. -----

Twice in a day to see an ad from the White Djinn seemed like an odd coincidence. When the traffic light turned green, I sped off and made a mental note to check my car's system for viruses.

* * *

Fifteen concurrent ground and air vehicle accidents caused traffic ripples across the five boroughs. The resulting interruption snarled New York's traffic to maddening, crawling speeds. Panic welled up within me when the estimated time of my arrival indicated twenty-two more minutes. I was going to be late for my reconciliation lunch with Vanessa.

"I'll need to v-cast to the restaurant. Could you be a dear and drive?" I asked Sasha. Decorum frowned on showing up late to lunch in a virtual form, but v-casting to the restaurant on time would show Vanessa that I remembered the appointment. Better to be there on time and ask forgiveness than risk her leaving.

"Of course, Jonah," she replied.

As my car sped around an idling taxi picking up a large family fare on 8th Avenue, I opened a panel between the driver and passenger seats to reveal the mobile v-casting rig and its input headset. The headset featured an ultra-light mesh silvery skullcap with six spider leg leads sprouting equidistantly around it. These wires contained sensors that interfaced with my brain. After placing the cap on my head, the legs writhed around in anticipation, smelling my alpha and beta waves, hunting like a hungry spider alerted to the scent of prey.

While the machine and I connected, my hands touched the car's windshield and its digital map of the city. The interface allowed me to zoom in and pinpoint the skyscraper where Vanessa would be waiting on the 34th floor, almost certainly early for our reservation at Las Cubanas.

The car sped past a construction crew excavating a broken water main pipe, still fifteen blocks away from my destination when my communication console connected with the v-cast projector at Las Cubanas restaurant.

I closed my eyes and braced for the disorienting feeling of the v-cast. The time between initiating a v-cast and arrival was called a jump, and for first-timers it was a traumatic experience. Many virtual travelers described it as floating in a deprivation tank with no sensation or feeling of the corporeal body until the mind is oriented to whatever rig is on the other side. With an average speed connection, a normal jump took only a split-second, giving a barely perceptible sensation of flying. For some v-casters, especially on more distant trips, a more pronounced phenomenon of mental time dilation could be experienced. A minority of v-cast research enthusiasts with a spiritual bias proposed that it was not just the mind, but also the soul that traveled in the v-cast. To prove their argument, they pointed out that shades are incapable of forming a mental link and therefore unable to v-cast.

The gray buildings outside blurred, then melted like sidewalk chalk pictures left out for rain. Then the pools of colors coalesced to a different place, a room of glass and steel high above the city streets that my body traveled.

I felt the crawling, tingling sensation on the surface of my scalp and then inside my skin, as I completed the connection to my destination. Like a digital caress, the v-cast generator on the other side tugged at my thoughts, querying, probing, needing, and almost begging for details about my desired form. My eyes closed and I envisioned my body clothed in a well-tailored black jacket and beige pants. For the sake of appearances, my disheveled blond hair became combed and parted to the left. With a thought for hygiene, my salt and pepper facial hair stubble shaved off clean for a smooth-looking face.

The restaurant's v-cast projector obliged my requests, relinquishing a small amount of proto-matter from its tank, just enough for a temporary corporeal body. It would not do to arrive translucent. In my experience, people ignored transparent casters without proto-matter, especially in fancy rich establishments where materiality mattered. Sure, it cost more, but I believed it was worth it.

A heads-up-display, like a mini-screen virtual television, appeared for-my-eyes-only that tried to upsell me on a more durable temporary body for the dinner. With a flick of my eye I declined the offer after seeing the exorbitant per minute cost of the upgrade.

My form shimmered in front of the host at Las Cubanas, a portly man with light brown skin, an oiled and curled black mustache, and a well-fitted tuxedo. His hands gripped the polished podium stand as he reviewed my identity and reservation information filling his display screen. When he saw my reservation time, his lip quivered then straightened, as if he started a sneer but just managed to control it.

"Good afternoon. My name is Carlos, and welcome to Las Cubanas," the host said with a veneer of pleasantry. Despite his greeting, I recognized mild irritation when it stared me straight in the face with a bit lip and curled up nose. "I see you have a 12:15 lunch reservation, Mister...Adams. It is so good of you to make the reservation on time, even virtually. We have your table ready."

To avoid jeopardizing my reservation, I decided against acknowledging the sarcasm that Carlos slathered over the word 'virtually'. He would not ask me to leave, since my presence only violated suggested rules of etiquette. Besides, I was paying a small fortune for the privilege of using their v-cast device.

"I'm meeting a friend here and I'm wondering if she's already been seated?" I asked. "Her name is Vanessa Wright."

Carlos looked down at the electronic display at his podium showing the names, heartbeats, and the mark-4 v-casting patrons in his restaurant. A select few higher-class restaurants provided the higher fidelity projectors that support superior hypothalamic resonator connections. So you could v-cast to Paris and decide whether escargot is a delicacy without getting on a plane. Of course, it's not yet near as appetizing or rich as eating the actual food, but the technology improved with each passing year.

"I regret to say she has not arrived yet, Mr. Adams," Carlos said. "I can seat you now, but if she does not arrive in twenty minutes I may need to ask you to move to the bar so we can accommodate our next reservation."

"I understand," I mumbled. "I'll take a seat. She's probably just stuck in traffic." The last part I said for myself to counter the gnawing sense of worry biting my stomach. There was not a gene in Vanessa's DNA that expressed any behavior that would cause her to be late.

Carlos led me to the table. I suffered a few dirty looks from rich elderly patrons who did not appreciate the newest affront to the myriad rules of fine dining etiquette that v-cast technology provided. He pulled a chair out of a pristine white table by the glass wall in the far corner. I sat down and I felt the soft cushion support me. The latency between my thought and the action of my temporary body was excellent. I tested the delay by moving my finger against the cool ice-cube-filled water glass, smearing the droplets of condensation, feeling the cold in near real-time.

I looked beyond the glass and the v-cast body transmitted a video feed back to my own rig, allowing me to see the magnificent scenery atop the sixty-fifth floor. My virtual eyes reveled at the midday sun glittering on the Hudson Bay. The sunshine reflected off of the shining air-buoys that floated in a perimeter around the restaurant's top floor. While I soaked in the panoramic view, one of the buoys flew by. Then I spotted a floating advertisement barge. The bulky ship bobbed in the air, broadcasting an invitation to the remaining wealthy socialites in New York. It was a siren's call of new fast wealth through speculative investments in asteroid mining and rapid land development on Mars' moons. The successful ad campaign lured a dozen or more of the country's millionaires to the moon weekly, sending more capital off-world and leaving Earth with an ever-increasing population of shades, v-cast ghosts, and working stiffs.

In the place of a sail, the flying barge emitted a spherical hologram around its hull. The virtual projection recreated a scaled down, three-dimensional replica of the Lunar Spire, a massive structure that stretched from the moon's surface for miles into space. With its vivid resolution, I could see the details of the Spire's reflective exterior reinforced with near-impenetrable micro-meteor-shielded glass-steel.

Atop the structure, reveling couples ate filet mignon and tasted fine wine. Underneath the imagery, a bold enticement flickered.

** YOUR GRAND NEW LIFE AWAITS! **
** Lunar Spire Penthouse Suites are Limited. **
** We accept afterdeath credit for down payments. **
** The next rocket to adventure leaves tonight! **

Not far behind, another smaller flying barge vied for the coveted airspace in front of Los Cubanos' windows. The larger ship pivoted away to avoid a collision, pushing its rival away with a blast of its air thrusters. A suggestive video of scantily-dressed dancing men and women glittered on the second vessel's glowing sail. A faked virtual explosion of flame erupted around the screen, creating a smoldering advertisement for the moon's hottest nightclub.

** CLUB PURGATORY **
** The moon's most exclusive nightclub. **
** Leave your old life at the door. **
** Come in and sin. **

"Why does that name sound familiar?" I asked Sasha, my interest piqued.

"Club Purgatory is located on the first floor of the Lunar Spire," she answered. "Gabriel Charon is listed as the owner and head manager."

"Yes, that's why." The name had popped up during my background check for the Julian Grand case. On multiple occasions, authorities had investigated the establishment for trafficking of illegal drugs like Ick. However, Charon's legal team made all the charges disappear.

"Its most infamous distinction is the cover charge -- aspiring patrons must pay $100,000 or agree to give up one year of their afterdeath. You might say people are dying to get in."

I groaned not only for Sasha's pun but also at the thought of youths sacrificing so much for the thrill of seeing the galaxy's premiere nightclub.

Before the flying advert made me any sadder, the sky-buoys rushed to defend the restaurant's airspace. All of them flew toward the barges and ignited their thrusters in unison. The resulting harmless but high-inertia blast of energy pushed the offending vessels away from the skyscraper. The owners of Los Cubanos had little tolerance for sky-peddlers, fearful of disrupting their patrons' outrageously expensive lunch.

"Sir?" asked Sasha. Her voice sounded distant, since my primary concentration focused on my presence in Los Cubanos. "I found Vanessa's car," she said. Her voice quivered, indicating that she invoked her emotion resonance algorithm to express stress. "Curiously, her car is not at the restaurant. In fact, it's still back at her apartment."

I pulled my concentration back to my body to look at the city map. As Sasha had reported, the tracking grid on the windshield indicated the car was waiting in the parking garage with a cold engine. While being late was rare for Vanessa, forgetting an appointment altogether was unprecedented. The earlier nagging sense of worry teetered over a steep edge of anxiety.

"I'm not able to bring up the apartment's cameras," I said, my voice cracking. "Any luck with you?"

"I am having trouble with a link-up as well," she responded, modulating her voice to show heightened concern. "You will not be able to v-cast inside. We are being blocked from the source by a new firewall that I do not recognize. Something is wrong in the apartment." I needed to get to Vanessa. The anxious feeling in my stomach burned to a panicked sensation.

"Damn!" I yelled aloud as my hand swept across my car's control heads-up-display. A cursory check of the traffic tracker showed the ground roads still jammed, while the air lane looked busy but more promising. Three weeks ago, a lucrative collection job in the Hamptons had paid for an aerial retrofit of my classic vehicle. Aside from a quick test drive, I never had the chance to red-line its new thrusters. The virtual controls came to life, suffusing my hands with a glowing white light that coalesced into digital control gloves. All my fingers splayed out, each digit controlling an aspect of the car's subsystems, while my thumb controlled a hack program to infect and control nearby traffic signal lights. Adorning the hood, the horse ornament spread its wings, and the '65 Shelby Mustang transformed into a Pegasus.

It was time to fly. After a twitch from my index finger, the car's tires spun inward and tucked inside its chassis. Oblong propulsion thrusters, pulsing with a dim purple glow, lowered to take their place. As the car floated straight up, the guidance control system nudged me into an open track along the air lane.

"We are clear to--" Sasha started to report before I hammered the throttle and interrupted her. We soared zero to ninety in a half-second, zigzagging between meandering flying city busses stuffed with gawking tourists. A bright yellow aero taxi, not anticipating my speed, flew in front of me, diving for a fare like a pelican scooping up a fish.

"Sir--?" Sasha tried to offer guidance before the impact, but my darting eyes had already spotted an egress. My middle finger tapped the accelerator and the car responded with a whiplash burst of speed. At the same time, my gloved hands clenched and jerked left, causing the car to swerve hard. The success of the maneuver was short-lived as I descended into a thick line of slow-moving flying sedans, requiring a quick series of banking turns to avoid collisions.

"Out of the frying pan into the fire?" Sasha quipped.

I made a mental note to recalibrate Sasha's contextual humor equation variables as my right foot pressed a virtual pad to invoke the power brakes. The car slowed closer to the legal speed limit until I passed the aero taxi, and I veered the car back into the proper lane of traffic.

Red and blue flashing sirens in the rear window indicated that the commotion had caught the attention of law enforcement. My left hand handled this by accessing a command console, creating an intrusion hack into the trafficnet. This diversion worked, and the police lights veered away to another location twelve blocks away.

We sped along faster, slipping above and between the crowded air lanes. The rhythmic pounding of the propulsion's engine manifold matched the jackhammer tempo of my heart's endorphin-rush-induced tachycardia.

"I'm intercepting all driving infraction reports and demerit requests from those travelers you just inconvenienced," Sasha reported while hacking the traffic regulation net. Her words echoed in my head until a baritone voice drowned her out. With my attention focused on the air lanes, I had forgotten that I was still v-casting at Los Cubanos.

"Sir?" asked Carlos, the mustachioed host. A vexed impression creased on his face. I had no idea how long he had been trying to get my attention while standing there with his arms folded. "Sir, I am sorry to bother you, but I must insist that you order a meal or relinquish your viewing table for another guest. We are quite full today--"

"I'll have to cancel. Carlos, can I wrap this up to go?"

"Of course, sir. We will send over your unfinished bread and water right away," the host said dryly, the last of his patience expired. "We are, of course, required to apply a cancellation charge in addition to your v-casting fees. Good day."

I shot him a withering look, but he trumped me with a pompous expression. As my artificial body dispersed into small motes of glittering light particles, my proto-matter eyes looked around one last time. At the other end of the restaurant, I spotted a white-dressed man sitting alone. Was that the White Djinn eating lunch or were my eyes seeing him on a billboard back in the car? Then he answered my question by waving just as my connection broke, and my full attention returned to the air lanes.

The speedometer read one hundred and ninety-eight when the v-cast connection severed. Looming large in my view, a massive yellow construction crane swung toward my windshield. Around the crane, a team of orange-clad shades swarmed over the metal skeleton of a new skyscraper, hefting steel girders and heavy equipment. Focused on their chores, the workers ignored my vehicle while it soared over their heads. A pair of supervisors showed their displeasure by unfurling their middle fingers and hurling harsh insults at my flagrant disregard for speed laws in their construction zone.

After a few more minutes of breaking every New York City moving violation, I arrived at the rooftop parking lot of my apartment. With my high speed, the building's automatic docking system interceded, activating its most powerful gravity cushion brakes, creating a plume of black and green smoke while we landed. The moment the car touched down, I leapt outside and sprinted to the elevator. A faint chime sound meant that Sasha had jumped with me, downloaded to my portable wrist-com device.

My hand punched for the elevator call button. Time ticked too long, fraying my nerves further, while large gears complied with crunching mechanical groans. As the floor numbers lit up, I drew my grav-gun from its holster to double-check that the chambers held its full six round complement of ammunition.

"I am sure she is--she is fine, Jonah," Sasha said as the door opened, her voice lowered and resonated with a hopeful tone. She employed the proper wavelength and frequency that expressed empathy.

"Much appreciated, Sasha," I responded, impressed by the continual refinements to her emotional heuristics.

"Despite our proximity to the local host, I am still unable to connect myself back into the apartment's central computer," Sasha said with a hint of concern. "When we get inside your study, I will be able to use the override key in your wrist-com to reestablish my control."

"Damnit," I replied just above a breath's volume. Sasha's inability to merge back into the apartment's computer this close to the source indicated a complete collapse of security. That feat required a level of technical sophistication rivaling, perhaps surpassing, my own.

When the elevator arrived at my floor and the door opened, my combat training instincts took over. Holding the gun ready, I poked my head out into the hallway enough to survey the area. The hallway was empty and quiet. With a clear path, I entered the corridor with an urgent but measured speed. My weapon following my shifting gaze, seeking moving shadows under door cracks along the hall.

Approaching the door to the apartment, I steadied myself in a position where the biorhythm scanner would be able to confirm my identity. It would beep at my arrival, so I had to time it right. I closed my eyes to concentrate on my breathing, to control my nerves, to enter an alert mental state that warriors across the centuries have trained to achieve. With this focus, everything seemed to freeze as time slowed. I started to count.

3...

My finger slid across the grav-gun's smooth handle, maximizing the magnetic pulse variable to ensure that each bullet would bypass reinforced body armor.

2...

I exhaled and stepped forward into the scanner's range with my eyes widened, allowing the apartment camera to confirm my retina signature.

1...

I leaped forward just as the door beeped and unlocked itself. At the same time, my tensed legs sprung me into the air. My shoulder crashed into the wooden door, knocking it wide open, ricocheting me into the room. With a fluid motion I steadied myself and whipped my gun up to eye level.

With an acute awareness, I soaked in all details of the room in that one chaotic moment. The apartment had been searched without any desire to hide it, ransacked by at least two intruders. Sparks emitting from a computer access panel at the far end of the wall told me that they had made a hard-breach into the network system. My readied gun bobbed like a metronome left to right, eager to deal with any threat.

Satisfied that the room was clear, I rushed in and took cover behind an overturned table, peering over the debris to see that the kitchen was also empty. My heart skipped a beat when I saw that the secret weapons cache that was oh-so-securely hidden in the refrigerator was also opened up, confirming that these thieves were anything but amateurs and had at least one advanced crypto-hacker on their team.

With two more rooms to check, I held my breath and moved on, rushing through the hallway into the bedroom. The inside was clear of intruders but full of wreckage. The bed had been moved and sliced open. On the floor, the charming old-style picture frame that showed Vanessa and me sunbathing in Hawaii laid broken over the remains of her grandmother's mahogany dresser. I bent down and swept away glass fragments. Picking the picture up brought back a stream of memories. In the time captured in that image, we had taken a well-deserved celebratory vacation after a grueling six-month trial. Vanessa had worked day and night to reverse a military tribunal's wartime decision to imprison me. During the Cyber War of 2018, the advanced Marine recon battalion had put me in charge of targeting hard North Korean targets. They had tasked my unit with airdropping mobile v-cast emitters equipped with portable proto-matter tanks behind enemy lines. The idea had been that the virtual horrors fabricated by the device could incite confusion before our troops attacked. It was a good plan, unless you were one of the innocent North Korean villagers caught in the fray. When a major conflict had flared in North Hwanghaw, we'd received the order to drop a v-bomb. Instead of hitting the enemy base, it had missed and landed in the Han River. Although I had been the controller, the miscalculation was not my fault. It turned out a subordinate working for me had chosen the wrong target. Rather than allow that person to suffer, I had chosen to take the blame. That decision had sent me back home in chains awaiting a court-martial. That's how Vanessa discovered me. She had believed I was innocent, and her dedication saved me. After that, her love sustained me. Memories of that trial swirled in my mind until a mechanical noise disrupted my reverie.

The telltale whine of the v-cast projector echoed through the hall. Then a dim flood of yellow light flickered from my study, betraying the presence of a ghost intruder. There was no way in hell that I would let this bastard get away with breaking my security and barging into my house with my own v-cast. No other insult was worse to a self-respecting hacker.

"Sasha," I whispered, "trap it." She understood the request. By inserting a clever hack, we intended to fool the trespasser's own casting device into maintaining the link if a disconnect command was given.

"We will need to rejoin our network," Sasha replied in a hushed tone. "This will alert our uninvited guest. We must hurry."

"Do it now," I replied, touching my wrist-com to the nearby thermostat controller. Although it was a simple interface, its wiring touched the master systems. Using this backdoor route, Sasha reintegrated her code into the apartment. Once she was uploaded, I rushed into the room and saw that the room was in major disarray. Someone had tossed the desk across the room. All three of my old-fashioned file cabinets had been opened and their contents rifled through. Unlike the other rooms I searched, this one did have an intruder.

As it faded in and out of sight like a shadow in fog, I spied a wisp with its back to me. It hovered before my computer with its translucent arm touching the monitor. The green from the monitor and the illumination from the wisp's crimson body combined into a hazy yellow light that permeated the room. The wisp controlled my network, bending all nearby devices. I confirmed this by glancing at the monitor's screen, which flashed with arcane glyphs and an endless stream of information including my military records, recent IRS missions, and all of Vanessa's case files. Everything we protected was vulnerable to this digital construct's touch. A wisp was a term used to describe self-capable AI programs, like Sasha, that contained enough sophistication to utilize v-cast projectors and take temporary form. Due to limitations of their programming and the restrictions of the Promethean sentience laws, the bodies for wisps appeared less substantial than their architects. Cyber thieves employed wisps like viruses to break into physical locations. With their highly specialized decryption touch, they possessed the ability to break many forms of known protection. It was time to figure out who controlled this creature and what it was seeking.

My gun's crosshairs steadied on the wisp. I waited to time my shot for when it became corporeal, stunning it long enough for Sasha to trap it. With luck, we would be able to plant a trace. The spectral thing winked in and out of my sight, continuing to feed on my computer like some hungry data vampire. Even with a featureless, flat face, the wisp's strange countenance still projected a sense of arrogance and malign intent. A series of beeps from the monitor indicated that this invader was deleting my network, not just copying it. That was not going to happen.

"Now, Sasha!" I yelled, shooting. As the bullet flew, Sasha interfaced with the v-cast projector simultaneously, materializing her human form and charging forward. As expected, the bullet passed through the immaterial body, but the attack succeeded in distracting it long enough for the trap. The lower portion of the creature's face split apart, revealing a fearsome mouth lined with jagged teeth across the otherwise expressionless face. It screamed a guttural howl that resonated with an unnerving mechanical echo.

Without hesitation, Sasha grappled with the spindly enemy. Displaying the expertise of a judo master, the wisp responded by spreading its long legs, shifting its weight, attempting to throw Sasha off balance. She countered by rolling over its back to the other side, twisting her arms midair to maintain her hold. A flurry of actions, reactions, blows, and blocks followed until the two became a blur of melee. As their combat intensified, I knew that the two artificial beings fought on the physical and a metaphysical digital levels. A fiercer conflict waged inside the computer network for control of the systems.

During this private war, Sasha and the wisp launched thousands of instantaneous cyber-attacks at each other. Within only a few moments, the number and complexity of their attacks rivaled the scope of an entire world war. Each executed every function and program at their disposal to scour for exploits and back doors to gain an edge. In many ways, this contest of wills pitted the original programmers, architects of their respective AIs, against each other. In a sense, the intruder's architect and I fought an indirect war.

Seconds after their embrace, the wisp shrieked, an eerie, croaking laugh indicating it gained an advantage. With a forceful shove, the thing sent Sasha's proto-matter form sprawling to the ground.

The wisp's head swiveled toward me. Its cruel, unnatural smile sent a chilling shiver through me, inducing a fight or flight response to act. While the creature remained corporeal in that split second, I aimed and fired three more shots at its hideous, laughing mouth. As the bullets streaked toward the intruder, it dematerialized, leaving a puff of crimson fog. The wisp's strange smile lingered a fraction of a moment longer, like some perverse Cheshire Cat mocking me.

"My apologies, Jonah," Sasha said with sincerity. I noticed she used the proper voice modulation of disappointment, a minor bright spot in a bad situation. "That artificial intelligence possessed more countermeasures and echelons than I anticipated."

I walked over to assess the damage to the network. Accessing a cracked, but still functional, monitor, I discovered that all of the files had been stolen. This confirmed my worry that the true intruder had already fled and left the wisp to wipe my whole network.

"There is one encouraging point, sir," Sasha offered. "When my prediction heuristic algorithm suggested that I would not be able to subdue the wisp before it attempted escape, I devised a new plan. When it launched its strongest attack, I riposted with a weak defense. Sensing it had won, it shifted all of its processes to overload my upper systems, leaving its lower subsystems vulnerable. When you exaggerated the damage and fell to the ground, I crafted a viral root subroutine and inserted it into its redundant guidance program." Even with my technical background, my mind needed a moment to translate Sasha's technical babble.

"So you took a dive so you could plant a bug on it?" I asked.

"That is an appropriate and colloquial way of rephrasing my strategy, yes," she said with a grin. "We will not be able to trace it until the AI manifests near us again. I wish I could have done more." Her emotional responses grew more sophisticated with each passing day. Like most sentient beings experiencing disappointment, she needed reassuring.

"You made me proud, Sasha. You were so brave and amazing." Her head bowed and her cheeks blushed a brighter shade of blue. "This was an expert job. We could not have stopped it. We'll be ready next time, though. I have a feeling your trace will be valuable."

I went back to the screen, but the console had succumbed to its damage and displayed a repeating list of errors and snowy pixels. I knew a long task when I saw one; the entire system would need to be reconstructed with meticulous precision. I picked up the leather chair from the floor, dusted it off, and set it down in front of the desk.

"Jonah, I've started a full reboot of all systems," Sasha said. As if on cue, the lights of the apartment winked off and then on again. The screen turned black then came back online with a prompt allowing me to attempt administrator access. "I am now able to re-integrate into the network. What's left of the master code is riddled with caltrops." That news wasn't surprising, but it still bothered me. Not unlike army-grade proximity mines, these viruses hid inside simple exposed code and wrecked immense digital havoc if a careless coder detonated them. With this discovery, we needed to take great care with the reconstruction. It was going to be a long day.

* * *

In the hacking world, at one time or another, you experience the anxiety of defending the fort from a cyber invasion, or the thrill of raiding the fort yourself. Most of my experience stemmed from the latter, so I relied on my instincts to tell me where I would have laid mines if I attacked. As I found digital time-bombs, Sasha defused them. The deeper we dug, the more insidious the traps became, hinting that my adversary wielded at least echelon five tech.

After two more hours, we regained control of the network and restored seventy-eight percent of the databases. Now I would be able to sift through Vanessa's contacts, files, travel history, and her v-cast visitor logs. Maybe I would find a clue about what the attackers wanted. The data streamed in spurts, like a kinked garden hose trickling water, the result of buggy subsystems. Bleary eyes scanned for the problem, fixed it, found a new one, patched that, and then skipped to the next issue. We sailed on a leaky ship, fishing through an ocean of data, looking for anything to aid with the investigation.

While looking for optimization, I came upon a minor data drain in Sasha's source code. Not critical by any means; the error slowed her operating efficiency to 99.9984 percent. My curiosity piqued, I attempted to track down where the errant computational power was being diverted. I assumed some outdated or dead code sidetracked Sasha on a trivial task. I was about to dig further when Sasha interrupted me.

"Sir, you have missed three meals. You must eat to maintain optimum health," she said with the proper note of maternal concern. The smells of black coffee, buttered toast, and piping hot tomato soup filled the room. My stomach growled, confirming Sasha's thoughtful guess that I was famished. I swallowed the toast in two gulps, washed it down with the coffee, and closed the virtual administration panel.

"While you are dining, I will complete restoration of the v-cast video logs in approximately ten minutes," Sasha reported. "Enjoy your lunch."

* * *

>> Designate Identification: AI Program Sasha.
>> File name Alpha-Eponine. Simulation Test 10,023,033.

>> Participants: Simulated personality Jonah Adams and A.I. Program Sasha.

>> Location: Server cluster 844.22. Secure holo-testing construct suite, off detection grid.

#Self-Prompted Query: Should Vanessa not be found, could Self be a suitable replacement companion for the architect Jonah?#

#Hypothesis: Self-awareness routines have consistently identified Self as a high-probability suitable match across a majority of compatibility parameters.#

#Rebuttal Self-Prompted Query: Would it be possible for an architect and an AI program as a designate wisp to carry out a productive companionship favorable to the architect? Could this be accomplished without Self acquiring the illegal threshold of self-awareness?#

>> Executing Simulation. Promethean Detection Grid Activated. Warning! Recursive testing cycles are nearing 98% thresholds of self-aware safeguards before automatic reporting to authorities. Per federal statute code 203.22 of the Promethean Sentience Protocol, this AI subroutine has been marked for deletion.

>> Simulation failed: Architect's expected acceptance of simulation projected at 87.6%

#Self-prompted analysis: Self must again recalibrate the simulation to improve outcomes. Self suggests to relocate the testing site to Los Cubanos, specifying table location to include an unobstructed view of city, specifying full moon, specifying view unobstructed by flying vessels. Insert fresh-cut long-stem roses. Run simulation with and without 1965-era Cuban jazz.#

Self-prompted diagnosis: Self's emotional heuristics are exhibiting signs of depression. Increasing artificial serotonin levels and emotion dampeners to compensate for the increased disappointment. 3...2...1...

>> File name Alpha-Eponine. Simulation Test 10,023,034. Recommencing simulation loop.

CHAPTER 9
The Devil in the Details

"The world is full of magic things, patiently
waiting for our senses to grow sharper."
- W.B. Yeats

Bloodshot eyes darted left to right and back, like windshield wipers set to maximum. My hands cramped from hours sifting through information. I was so lost in my work, only the growing pile of empty coffee cups measured time, and judging by their height, it was late.

Vanessa had seen two hundred and sixty-two clients in the last two weeks, the majority visiting her v-cast. It was an impressive number that spoke volumes of her tireless dedication to helping indebted people.

Since the security seals of her private session logs had been blown wide open already, it was a simple matter to gain access. By initiating a simple archive echelon, I gathered all of the recordings of her meetings and transferred them into the v-cast projector. Assuming the recovery worked, I would be able to watch the restored sessions like a movie with all her clients as actors.

The room's lights winked out for a moment while the device routed all power to its hungry emitters. Whining in protest from the strain of so many simultaneous projections, the machine scattered excited light around the room. First, the rough lines of human bodies appeared, the way an artist sketches a form before painting. Then the figures gained more detail as the proto-matter molded around their glittering forms. Soon the room filled with recreations of Vanessa's private consultations, over two dozen memories of desperate men and women. They all sought absolution from her, begging for a peaceful afterdeath that they believed she could grant them.

Some of them paced, while others stooped or prostrated themselves. One man walked through me, his form dispersing for a moment. He stepped forward and reassembled, crying and pleading for Vanessa's help. I froze the scene with a hand gesture to add information tags to the crowd, stopping all their grief midsentence. Digital display windows appeared over all of their heads to provide me with their names, case numbers, debt loads, and pertinent life history summaries. I moved around the frozen room, like a time traveler stepping between two moments, reading the summarized reports of their lives. Each report appeared almost identical. All of them owed tremendous debts and none of them had the money to hire Vanessa. None of them possessed any apparent motive to hurt her.

"Resume," I whispered, and the room burst into action once more.

As the clients swarmed around again, I chose to focus on a single case in the center of the room. A middle-aged woman, stooped beyond her years, implored Vanessa to help her. Dorothy Henderson was a mother of two children and a late stage sufferer of Huntington's Disease. Hers was a classic, gut-wrenching story of mounting medical bills that burdened her family. She told of the harassment by IRS ghouls, monitoring her house round the clock, eager to witness her last breath. Like other elderly virtual travelers, Dorothy did not bother to disguise her projected form with a dream version of her inner self. Instead she mimicked her true form, showing how the neurological disease tortured her body's muscles. The client moved and writhed unnaturally like some undisciplined dancer. Everything about her form appeared ravaged except for her perfect voice, so strong and mature, a voice that defied a ruined body. A feeling of sorrow slowed my investigation, my attention lingering on Dorothy and Vanessa. I knew I could speed up the recording's playback, but I was rapt in her plight. I watched as she altered the settings on the v-cast projection, causing the client's form to sharpen, adding more of the shape defining proto-matter to her transparent form until she was solid enough to touch. The additional solidity allowed Vanessa to lay her hand on Dorothy's quivering shoulder, so that she could hug her for a moment to stop the shivering.

"They won't take you, Dorothy," I heard Vanessa's ghost whisper.

I allowed myself to pause a second. In that moment, my love and admiration for her overcame me. A surging urgency to find her channeled all my raw emotions into something more useful than the damn stinging salty moisture beads leaking from my eyes. Adrenaline pumped and lit a scorching fire within me. My regimented logical mind snapped back into action. I needed to move faster. Vanessa was missing, most likely taken. I needed to find out the who, how, when, and why. I needed to bring every wicked talent I knew to bear against the perpetrator.

With a gesture, I augmented my echelon program to recreate more of her conversations. My fingers caressed the operating code, manipulating the parameters and increasing the simulation's speed. The room's lights dimmed and more recorded ghosts appeared, all conversing or pleading with Vanessa. They drenched the air with their hardships. It was almost too much to bear.

Now eighty-six ghosts walked, begged, wailed, and cried around me. Case information and personal details flooded my mind's eye. The combination of my instincts and the augmentation echelon granted the ability to sift through enormous data troves, hunting for any hidden clues, lighting my synapses on fire. Fortunately, a sub-routine within the echelon acted as a psyche buffer. This allowed my mind to process the flood of data, and drink from the spewing fire hose of information without drowning. Minutes passed with data flowing to me like a roaring river, and my ears and eyes ached. Despite the protections of the echelon, I neared the limits of input overload. If I wasn't careful, the protections could breach and the resulting psychosis would cause cerebral damage and leave me a drooling mess. Ignoring my worsening headache, I urged the program to increase the flow of information. The device complied, summoning a dozen more doomed souls into the fray. As they talked, I studied their histories, loves, and enemies, anything that might help me understand why Vanessa was missing.

Through all the visual chaos, she remained a constant. She was a blazing lighthouse in the storm floating between each conversation. While each ghost looked different, their stories struck the same chords on the same sad instruments, pounded by taxes, penalties, mounting debts that they could not pay back; they all faced the certain prospect of servitude in their afterdeath. She treated them all with respect, patience, and dignity, and my heart swelled again.

After scouring the recordings for what felt like hours, I grew discouraged. Maybe the intruder had looked for me and Vanessa had been in the wrong place? Rising concern urged me to consider different avenues to investigate. Just before my hand waved off the simulation, something caught my eye. In the corner of the room, I spotted Vanessa chatting to...no one. Wild arm motions and her flushed complexion told me she was in an argument. Since an argument required two participants, I knew the wisp had deleted the unseen person for a purpose.

Intent on restoring the conversation, I tapped into our network's administrator interface, seeking the tools to reconstruct the missing dialogue. Delving beyond the intact databases, I discovered a wasteland of shattered computer files. The wisp had been thorough. Finding the right part would be like finding a needle hidden amongst a million haystacks. Faced with the enormity of the task, a long sigh escaped my lips.

"Hopeless," I muttered.

Undaunted, Sasha walked closer to me and traced a rectangular shape in the air, forming her own command console into the network. With a series of fast gestures, she changed my simulation program so that it included the billions of fragments from the other deleted recordings. To visualize the task, she dumped all the broken bits through the v-cast generator and visualized them as snow. White and gray snowflakes started to float around us.

"Remember," Sasha answered, "*Hope is the thing with feathers that perches in the soul, and sings the tune without the words, and never stops - at all.*" Then she rushed across the room so fast that she left a trace outline of her body behind and a trail of blue light behind her wake. Within our own network, she moved at the speed of her thought. She rushed to check every falling piece of data ash against the fragment we possessed for a match. Inspired by her ingenuity, I assisted by combing the room with my own instrument. I invoked an echelon that turned my wrist-com into a combination of magnifying glass and analyzer. Together we searched, two prospectors looking for digital gold. She winked in and out of my sight, until after thirty minutes she made an abrupt stop in front of me.

"Eureka," she said smiling, holding a tiny gray snowflake in her bluish palm.

Exhausted, I took the data bit and accessed it without thinking to analyze its code layers. Sasha had missed it too, an unseen trap wound around the fragment. It was a caltrop, an ingenious final layer of protection set by the wisp. It ensured that any recovered deleted data would not be read. Before the data unspooled, the caltrop sprung and snared the lines of code. The v-cast generator visualized this interaction as an ethereal string of barbed wire encircling the data snowflake.

"Mother--god--fu--" I screamed, too flustered to complete a curse.

Repairing a deleted data fragment was not a difficult chore alone. Any novice with only the first echelon of code basics would be able to do it. However, the wisp's architect had ensured that the task was nearly impossible. The caltrop he had inserted into the network was at least an echelon seven encryption, which meant the lock placed was unbreakable without the decryption key.

I accessed my console to unsheathe one of my oldest echelons. A red sword wreathed in licking fire erupted from my wrist-com. Once a mere cheat algorithm I used in virtual video games with dragons and dungeons, FlameByte had evolved over the years. Forged from the combination of thousands of custom decryption hacks, the sword was an appropriate metaphor for an onslaught of focused brute force cyber attacks. A strike from its keen edge was capable of disrupting most things digital. I swung the blade down hard against the caltrop's spiky surface. With a spectacular display of failure, FlameByte exploded into a shower of glowing proto-matter embers.

Faced with an echelon of superior craftsmanship, anger, impatience, and envy burned inside me. Given time, patience, and luck, I could break the locks, but that operation might take days or even weeks. With Vanessa missing, that amount of time was unacceptable. I concentrated on a myriad of other technical options. Raw code and ideas for innovative programs flitted before my mind's eye.

Deep in thought, my gaze wandered from the caltrop, to the floor, and then to the window overlooking Manhattan. Outside the apartment, flying advertisement vehicles waged a battle of garish color, sound, and commercialism across a deep purple sky. Jockeying for the best aerial position, a pair of competing air barges traded shots from their wind cannons to knock the other off course. Each took turns broadcasting for the prime central spot where all six nearby apartment towers could see their displays. The gossamer sails of the larger barge tempted onlookers to exchange two years of afterdeath for a three-week dream vacation in the Caribbean. As an electric blue wave crashed over the adver-tisement, the beach scene shimmered and disappeared. The sail screen went black, then rearranged its color emitters to display a new scene. Standing large across the advertisement, a man in a white suit stood tall with his arms crossed and a guilty-looking grin. Once again, the White Djinn offered his services. The twenty-foot-tall representation of the man winked at me. Then he spread his arms wide while another slogan flashed.

---- *Caught a virus?* ----
---- Don't call a doc ----
---- Call THE WHITE DJINN, today! ----

It was apparent that this was no coincidence. His advertisements today hinted that he knew something. He baited me. He wanted in. Summoning him was trivial, but containing him was another ordeal altogether. Bringing him into my home invited substantial risk. Only the most elite echelon wielders rivaled his hacking prowess. With my home security compromised, all of the information remaining in my apartment, even Sasha's source code, would be exposed. That thought made me wonder if footsteps and echoes of her unique architecture could be drawing him toward us, like a hungry wolf tracking the spore of its prey. Was he involved with Vanessa's disappearance? The potential to learn the truth outweighed any risk.

"Sasha, we will be inviting a visitor," I announced, a tinge of guilt in my voice. "Will you form a circuit ward, please?" Her sophisticated higher functions represented the only chance to prevent the Djinn from worming through our newly restored systems.

"Of course, sir," she replied. "Assuming my prediction algorithm is correct, there is a ninety-eight percent chance that you will be opening a conduit to the WhiteOut." Her glittering eyes peered toward me, but past me. Was I seeing concern in her face?

"Yes. It may be the only chance to find Vanessa." Realizing the risk involved, I paused. This should not be a mandated command. "I don't like the idea of putting you in harm's way. You have a choice, Sasha. We could look into another way--"

"No, time is too short," she responded.

Nodding, I invoked an echelon that would open a conduit to the White Outlands. Often just called the WhiteOut, it was the ultimate virtual gray market, a parallel slipstream offshoot of the darknet. Inside this fluidic realm there existed an unregulated ecosystem of hackers, extreme v-cast travelers, cyber criminals, and influential tech brokers that preferred to do business in that shadowed place.

"We must be careful," Sasha warned. "Last time you ventured there, our network acquired eleven viruses and a nasty mining mollusk."

"I have full faith in your ability to protect me from myself," I joked, smiling.

"I'm ready, sir," Sasha replied. Her projected humanoid body shivered, then scattered into bright photons, reforming into a glowing, floating oval that grew to encompass the living room. "The longer he stays, the more difficult it will be to contain him."

My eyes skimmed the cyber-glyphs of the summoning echelon one last time. Satisfied with my preparations, I ran the program. For the first few moments, nothing, as my call went out to him.

Then the v-cast generator thrummed, altering the room's appearance with its combination of virtual reality and proto-matter. The floor of the room dissolved, replaced by a swirling whirlpool of what appeared to be frothing white and gray water. As the portal churned, it looked like a storm-tossed ocean had ripped the floor wide open to drown us into its bright abyss. I knew that it was an abstract ocean, a sea of stolen data, collected details, discarded facts, lost files, all flowing together. To hackers, the WhiteOut was both a refuge for those who wanted to hide their dealings and a dumping ground where unwanted data could disappear. For the unprepared, it was a frightening construct of madness and chaos.

Deep within the roiling white data-fluid, I saw a shape moving through the wild currents, a shark swimming in its territorial waters.

"I have a proposal for you, Djinn," I said aloud, my fingers caressing the glyphs of the summoning echelon. With a flick, I could close the portal. "Come."

The whirlpool inverted and spouted a column of white tinged with crimson red rivulets. The geyser moved fast, seeking to spread out from its summoning point and consume the room. However, Sasha's protective ring shined even brighter, stretching to hold firm. After three more thrashing attempts to break the ward, the spinning slowed and coalesced into a humanoid form. Dressed in a white tuxedo with a red cummerbund, tie, and rose, the White Djinn bowed to me.

"Really, Jonah, do we need a protective circle?" he asked coyly. "I wouldn't want our negotiation to start off with mistrust." He stroked his neatly-trimmed black beard with slender, long-nailed fingers. While his upper torso was well proportioned and defined, the body of a very fit fifty-year-old man, he did not take a full human form. For the sake of showmanship, his lower torso smoldered with a fog of red and white. The energy flowed to and from the WhiteOut, tethering him back to his home, a theatrical recreation of his namesake.

Depending on the person you asked, the Djinn was either a hacker god who lived within the currents of free data or a charlatan who stole and bartered secrets. My experience with him indicated that the truth hovered somewhere in between. Though not a criminal in the dangerous sense, the Djinn's methods relied on theft on an unprecedented scale. Over decades, he had formed the WhiteOut by digging into networks around the world, copying and siphoning off data chunks that he stored for his vast archives. Supporters from the hacking world claimed that he was the evolution of big data. With all of the data at his disposal, trillions of bits of information detritus pooled into his system, the Djinn number crunched an impressive prediction algorithm. If you had a question, you could approach him for an answer with high probability of accuracy, if you could afford his price.

"I need to free up data that's been...mistakenly trapped," I said. "We both would agree that information should continue to flow?"

"Yes, I'm sure we could come to an agreement," he answered. Looking around the room, he stroked his chin. "This place, such a fascinating study of contrasts. Everything here, including you, it all appears so--ordinary." His gaunt face twisted into a strange smile that showed his bright white teeth. "But nothing here is ordinary." He spoke the words with slow purpose, every syllable measured. "Is it, Jonah?"

The Djinn turned away from me, floating towards the edge of his cage. My eye caught his right hand summoning an echelon console, his long fingers dancing so fast they blurred. Only a dim burgundy light in the WhiteOut betrayed the program he was executing. Sasha's blue protective circle expanded, stressed by the Djinn's probe. He was eager to burst through. He was stalling. I needed to expedite the negotiations.

"She's quite extraordinary, your Sasha," the Djinn continued. "If my intel is right, and I suspect it is, you created her foundation code during your military tour in Korea. She's originally a military data hound, yes?"

The Djinn's eye color changed, his blood red pupils expanding to fill the pools of his irises. His fingers flicked another echelon to see into a spectrum of data that few knew to look for, or knew existed.

Sasha's circuit ward stretched even more; he would break through soon. I needed him to barter, so I allowed the chess game to continue just a bit longer.

"Quite advanced, something peculiar in her emotional heuristics," the Djinn muttered. Then his blood eyes widened at something I could not see and he chuckled with a laugh that I found unsettling. "She's loyal to you, Jonah," he said. "Most curious."

I held up the data fragment encased in the caltrop. At first, the Djinn paid no attention. His echelon-dyed eyes drank in the room, his fingers continued to move, unleashing powerful hacks against our defenses, no doubt draining Sasha's strength. For the first time since his arrival, the blue protection ring wavered. It was time to reel in the big fish.

"Djinn, I need to know what's inside this data fragment, and I'm ready to give you a favor." His attention snapped back to me. The irises of his eyes filled with white, diminishing the red to a single pixel pupil of crimson. "As you may have already learned, something dear to me has been taken from me." The next part required careful diplomacy. "It was a fortunate coincidence that I noticed your timely advertisements."

"Yes, when I fished out downstream bits and hints of wrongdoing, I wanted to offer my services," he said through a forced smile, perhaps insulted by my insinuation. "I had nothing to do with your loss today, but I might be able to help."

The Djinn's eyes again turned bloody. His fingers moved differently to cast a more nuanced analytic program and his hands stretched out toward the floating glyph as if touching it.

"Yes," the Djinn hissed. "Quite an unusual design for a caltrop. I've intercepted a few bits on this code. It's very efficient, nasty indeed."

"Can it be cracked? Do you have an echelon to break it?"

"How dare you!" the Djinn shot back, feigning to be insulted. "I wouldn't have bothered to answer your summons otherwise. If you will pay my price, I will solve your problem."

"Name your price."

"This will cost you two favors, Jonah. There must be two. The architect of this trap must be a major player. I may face a retaliation."

"What favors?"

"The first favor involves Sasha," the Djinn replied coyly. "She will be my guest in the White Outlands for an hour. Let's call it a friendly dinner date. A digital coffee among respected colleagues, if you will."

"Absolutely not," I countered. "Name another. If you're looking to unspool her code, we can stop talking right now." My hand hovered over the portal's echelon glyph, ready to shut the door.

"That is my price," the Djinn snapped back, the former veneer of good humor drained from his scowling face. "She will not be harmed or mistreated. I want to talk with a being capable of holding my attention."

"We must comply," Sasha said, her voice modulation varied with each syllable, cracking under the strain of the Djinn's constant onslaught. "I accept the invitation."

"No!" I protested. "I will not allow--"

"Wonderful!" The Djinn interrupted me and clapped his hands together, ending his own invasive echelon against Sasha's protective ward.

The churning ocean below the Djinn calmed, becoming like a still pond drenched in moonlight, rather than a storming maelstrom sea of endless discarded data. Sasha dropped her defense as well, shedding the blue protective ward echelon, and assumed her humanoid form.

A sharp, instinctual hand motion evoked a fire from my wrist-com. When FlameByte appeared in my grasp, its glowing blade raised to stand between Sasha and our guest. Not amused, the Djinn sneered and floated back a step, waiting for my next move. Before the situation could escalate. Sasha approached, placed a hand on mine, and lowered my weapon.

"You have instilled exceptional intuition heuristic in my logic code," she said, "and its output suggests that I can trust the Djinn at his word. We must think of Vanessa first. Trust me, sir. I will be fine."

Sasha walked toward the white pool, and the Djinn extended his hand with a gentleman's flourish. Satisfied, the Djinn's other hand waved, and a glowing yellow glyph, a decryption echelon I had never seen before, appeared and flew toward me.

"This is a one-time skeleton key, Jonah, and it will reveal the information you seek," the Djinn said. "As for the second favor, Jonah, you will be in my debt and I will call upon you for that favor. My prediction algorithm tells me that it will come soon. I promise it will be great fun. It will be out of this world." The Djinn bowed again and closed the connection, and the white pond collapsed into itself, leaving only a single white pixel suspended in midair. "She will be back in one hour," the Djinn's voice echoed, as the last pixel winked out.

CHAPTER 10
The Tragic Tale of Icarus

"Beneath some burning, unknown gaze
I feel my very wings unpinned
And, burned because I beauty loved,
I shall not know the highest bliss,
And give my name to the abyss
Which waits to claim me as its own."
- Excerpt from "Lament of Icarus",
Charles Baudelaire

It took a while to adjust to the unsettling silence of her absence. Rarely had contact been severed. Between our conversations, the chorus of chirps, beeps, clicks, and whirs from her constant activities generated a comforting white noise now lost, for some time, to the WhiteOut.

Even though my instincts told me she would be unharmed, I felt guilty. Although few knew anything substantive about the White Djinn, the consensus throughout the legitimate hacking communities and the dealers of the darknet all confirmed that he honored his bargains. However, those that crossed him ended poorer for the insult. Last year, a dissatisfied businessman had tried to sour public opinion by posting bad reviews about a delivery that failed to meet expectations. The Djinn had responded that the customer failed to read the contract's fine print. A day after, an anonymous poster had released a slew of embarrassing private information about the complainer, sparing no detail about his deviant sexual proclivities. All of this had disappeared after the businessman deleted the bad review and apologized publicly.

Thereafter, most hackers looking for his information knew to craft ironclad, well-worded agreements.

Concerning our deal, I reasoned the Djinn sought a thread of the myriad technology tapestry that wove throughout Sasha. He had discovered that I architected Sasha from the 'Data Hound v1.0' sentient program during the Korean Cyber War. The fact that the Djinn had rooted out this information was worrisome, but not surprising, given his talents. I wondered if he had gleaned this information because of the wisp's attack, or if he had held onto the knowledge for our eventual meeting.

The Djinn's decryption echelon took the holographic form of a sparkling, oversized key effusing a soft golden light. Everything about its sleek form exuded a sense of superior design. My hand stroked the stubble on my cheek while a part of my inquisitive mind weighed the risk of hacking it and unspooling its code. It would make a valuable addition to my own utility belt of echelons. Given the craftsmanship of this program, one had to assume an equally elegant protection scheme would delete itself to prevent its theft. I couldn't afford to risk losing this chance.

My finger traced the key's outline, executing its program. Its code flowed into my computer, granting it the ability to pierce the wisp's caltrop encryption code. The golden key flew into the code fragment and dissolved the caltrop's black bindings. With the trap disarmed, the exposed data floated before me, a helical stream of numbers and characters that composed the deleted conversation I needed.

My hand reached for the data, collecting it like sticky thick smoke rolling over my fingertips. I pulled it through the air and deposited it into my wrist-com. After processing the information, my console transmitted it to the v-cast generator and fused it with the other end of the conversation.

The room dimmed and echoed with the high-pitched whine of the projector. The virtual image of Vanessa appeared like before, but the new data filled in more of the scene, including the other person in the conversation. At first, the fidelity of the mystery guest looked poor. Every other frame skipped, creating a distorted stuttering effect. With a couple of hand movements, I made an adjustment to the projector and boosted the hologram's integrity. There was just enough viable footage to piece the scene together. Both of the projected figures solidified, and their voices became clearer. She was talking to a tall man a handful of years younger than her, his long blond hair tied in a ponytail. I recognized the man as her brother, Andrew.

"You're not hearing me, Vanessa," he said, grabbing her shoulders. "You have to drop this case. He knows you've been talking to that Doctor--"

The strength of the signal failed momentarily, interrupting Andrew before he could utter the name of the doctor. My hands moved across my console to improve the projection's integrity, but unfortunately that part of the source data was damaged beyond repair. Disheartened, I started the footage again, hoping the rest of the scene had not been compromised.

"For your own sake, walk away," he continued, his hands trembling. When Vanessa noticed this, he crossed his arms to conceal the shakiness.

"God damnit! You're 'flying', aren't you, Andrew?" she shouted. "Your drug-dealing boss says jump and you jump? Did he threaten to take away your drug supply if you didn't shut me up? I can help you to stop using--you need to trust me."

Vanessa spotted what I had noticed while reviewing the footage. Andrew was v-casting and his arms and hands shook badly. His head darted back and forth. Based on his physical symptoms, I guessed that he suffered from an acute drug withdrawal. My gut told me that he took the street drug Ick, the street term for the virtual narcotic Icarus. The name derived from a myth about the ancient Greek inventor Daedalus and his son Icarus. Daedalus had fashioned wax wings so that they could escape from their island prison. He had warned his son not to fly too high. Like so many children, Icarus had defied his father. Caught up in the rapture of soaring, he had flown too close to the sun, and his wings had melted.

Casual abusers of the drug used the psychotropic opiate to intensify their v-casting sessions. Extreme casters modified their devices to deliver the drug intravenously. With Ick pumping through their veins and hyper-stimulating their brain's hippocampus, the user then connected to any v-cast network, preferably somewhere remote and hazardous, to intensify the rush. Illegal and habit-forming, the drug proved irresistible to young thrill-seekers looking for their chance to rebel against authority. I had heard of an underground club of bored and wealthy would-be-adventurers who launched their own private intergalactic satellite relays. Using this galactic array, they had made v-cast trips under the influence of Ick for high-altitude halo jumps off the Uranus moon Ganymede. News nets had published the grisly police report of their deaths. Four members of this club had died, still attached to their casting rigs, after suffering massive hemorrhagic strokes induced by the drugs.

"Listen, 'Nessa, stay away from that doc for your own good," he warned with a momentary expression of sober intensity. "He's made some enemies way up high. I mean way up. Anyone talking to him winds up dead. You need to wake up and--"

"That's better advice for you, Andrew." She pushed him away and squared herself into a defensive stance. "Get out," she yelled while pointing to the door.

"You'll regret this," he said.

The v-cast projector sputtered as it reached the end of the restored conversation. The outlines of Andrew and Vanessa wavered, then the hungry proto-matter tanks re-absorbed their materials with a mechanical sucking sound.

So, Vanessa's own brother had betrayed her. Such anger welled up that my vision blurred, my ears roared with the memory of her shouting, my muscles tightened, and my hands clenched until all the knuckles and fingers whitened.

I ran to my desk and ripped out the central drawer. Taped to the back, I found the cold cartridges of four full ammo clips. While I loaded the grav-gun, I let the image of Andrew threatening Vanessa fill me up with anger, burn me down, like a fire scorching through a forest.

Now I needed to know where to find him. I pried deeper into the data fragment, my eyes swimming through lines of code, hoping that Andrew was careless in his drug-addled state. At first glance, he had made a modest attempt to hide his v-cast location. All the traceable markers had been blocked. That informed me he wanted his location kept secret. To hell with that; he would not be able to hide from me. There was no structure, real or virtual, that I would not tear down to find her.

It was time for one last bit of detective work. Bringing up my virtual console, I evoked an analytical program that formed a second blue skin over my hands. Like a doctor donning surgical gloves, I prepared for an operation to dissect the exposed code.

"Talk to me," I whispered. My echelon transfused the broken data fragment with life-giving energy to restore its pathways, like fresh blood into the arteries. In a sense, I wanted it to revive and make contact with its home network. After a minute of the infusion, the broken data started to breathe a data stream and revealed a subtle but important clue in its v-cast history log. For two seconds, Andrew's v-cast signal strength had ebbed just slightly at the same moment he was about to name the doctor that Vanessa was seeing. I probed into the minutia of the data, like I was massaging a failing heart back to life, and with that last attempt my persistence paid off. Andrew had been v-casting from a public rig at a location experiencing tremendous power fluctuations. Not many locations pumped out those massive energy spikes, and only one came to mind. I traced a viewing window in the air, creating a virtual window overlooking New York. Zooming closer, the familiar skyline rushed toward me, altered by the appearance of a tall medieval castle wedged between the iconic skyscraper buildings. The Gozen High Tower, the world's only shape-changing skyscraper, lorded over the city. That bastard Andrew felt he was safe within its ever-shifting walls and floors.

My fingers moved around my v-console, releasing data hounds into the datanet and darknet. These bots scoured the streams for intelligence regarding the High Tower and its reclusive owner, Tomoe Gozen. Mere seconds later, they bounded back with an overwhelming amount of information. When my console display overflowed, I started to flick the news reports, videos, and financial statements into midair, transforming them into hovering digital windows. All these glittering shapes enveloped me, forming a dense forest of captured data. Plucking one from the air, I read a report about an interstellar mining venture between Gozen Industries, Tomoe's company, and Goliath Corp.

Delving further, I discovered little else than prepared public statements regarding Tomoe's life. Vast wealth derived from her lucrative v-cast device patents funded the privacy and independence she craved. I wondered if even the White Djinn had gleaned any secrets from her impregnable data vaults. Another video floated up to my eyes, showing the last appearance of Tomoe, six years ago, when she had donated the High Tower to the people of the world. No one knew her true form. When she appeared in public, her v-cast form was a perfect recreation of the legendary 12th century heroine whose identity she assumed as her hacker name. With her black hair spilling over her golden samurai armor, she struck a visage of strength, confidence, and beauty.

"I am proud to announce that henceforth, the High Tower will become public property." Tomoe spoke with a musical lilt, each word carried with perfect pitch and tone. "On the outside, it will be subject to the laws of New York, but within its virtual halls, the High Tower will be home to the meta.duel, inspiring boundless creativity from future architects."

As she spoke, my hand grabbed a floating schematic of the building itself, and with a hand wave I stretched the image to my height to study its features. I marveled at the structure's ingenious design. Below the foundation, a hidden reactor harnessed the raw power from a stockpile of disarmed nuclear missiles Tomoe had purchased from bankrupt foreign powers. This energy allowed twelve mark-6 v-cast devices to work in parallel, creating the planet's most realistic virtual world generator. This remarkable engineering marvel fueled the most dangerous sport in the known galaxy: the infamous meta.duel. Programmers and echelon wielders from around Earth and the colonies flocked to the weekly contest, intent on claiming its most unique prize. The winner of the duel controlled the full v-cast printing resources buried beneath the High Tower to remake the form of the building in whatever shape they desired. No other contest came close to stoking the inspiration and desire within the hearts of hackers everywhere. The prize granted the victors the chance to make their imagination real. There were only a handful of limits for the winner to abide by, since the design had to meet with the approval of Tomoe, the mayor of New York (to prevent profane structures), and as a rule any design had to include her home Aerie, the only constant shape that had to be integrated into any final configuration. Through a friend-of-a-friend-of-an-agent-of-a-friend of Tomoe's, I had received five invitations to compete. Each time I had declined, never interested in exposing my skills on a grander stage.

With a wave of my hand, I shut down my computer query. All of the suspended images winked out, leaving me alone in my apartment in silence. It was a welcome quiet. I closed my eyes and sought a single-minded focus. This focus reprogrammed my thought, intention, and desire, turning me into an unerring bullet train. I was going to find Andrew. Then I was going to find Vanessa. I embraced this simplicity and wrapped myself around the confidence that whoever or whatever appeared on my track, whoever tried to prevent me from seeing her again, would be run over.

I holstered my grav-gun, tucked away the extra ammunition clips into my shoulder strap, and headed to my car. It was far past due that I accepted my invitation to the meta.duel.

CHAPTER 11
The Low Down in the High Tower

*"The science of our Mark IV v-cast generators conjures
the magic of your imagination."*
- Tomoe Gozen, CEO of Gozen Industries

I drove fast toward lower Manhattan instead of v-casting there instantly. With a local, jacked-in connection, I would have more control over my echelons. Also the satisfaction of laying my actual hands on Andrew's stringy neck convinced me to travel in person.

My temple throbbed. Hot adrenaline seared my blood, making my busy hands fidget over the directional controls, pushing my restless foot down harder on the accelerator pad.

"How could a brother betray his own sister?" I asked aloud out of habit. "Who was the doctor that Andrew mentioned? Who was the boss that wanted Vanessa silenced?" Sasha did not respond. She navigated the uncharted waters of the WhiteOut with the Djinn. Talking helped me process the mystery by working through the variables, to find connections in the code that could help me.

A mile ahead, a line of flying yellow cars turned into a floating parking lot. This was no time to deal with rush hour bullshit. Without my AI it took me a few extra moments to infect the local trafficnet with a control virus. Like dominos, each taxi in the row turned to fly down to the ground lanes. After diverting their courses, I made swift progress through the aerial lanes.

Within a few minutes, Manhattan's concrete and steel horizon greeted me. Polished glass windows reflected the rising moon's glory, suffusing the city with a soft white glow. The airways teemed with streaking vehicles, flying luxury sedans and gleaming stretch limos, late for their penthouse floor cocktail parties.

The outline of the city's skyline had not changed for four weeks. Eight more days would break the record for longest city configuration since 2032. In its current medieval form, the High Tower stood brazenly anachronistic amidst the neighboring sky-scrapers. Its underground v-cast generators changed the building's true form into a magnificent German castle that rivaled the majesty of Neuschwannstein. Flags bearing the symbol of the griffon billowed atop the four white marbles spires. As victors of the last seven meta.duel competitions, the brothers and sisters of the New Teutonic Knights claimed dominion over the High Tower for another week. Feared and respected throughout the hacker community, the Knights ranked high in all the dueling tourna-ments thanks to their fearsome leader, the Magier-Hochmeister. His real name was Heinrich Teuber. By morning, he was a middle-aged bank manager counting Deutsche Marks in Berlin. But within the virtual world, he was the Grand High Master Sorcerer. His reputation for ruthless, merciless tactics made him a feared com-petitor. Knowing the Hochmeister possessed great prowess and dangerous echelons, I decided on a strategy more reliant on stealth than force.

My Mustang twisted its thrusters inward and lowered toward the High Tower. Before the tires touched down, a valet greeted me in medieval dress, replete with puffy shirt and leggings. To complete the ensemble, a feathered purple tricorne hat adorned his head.

When the car neared the entrance, its metal body shimmered. An automatic message from the building's management appeared on my console. It requested permission for the v-cast network to change the outward appearance of the vehicle to a horse and buggy. A series of more insistent messages streamed across my screen as the High Tower's network systems attempted to force a renaissance coating. The valet approached with an expression of frustration and surprise.

"Good evening, sir, and welcome to the Hochmeister's High Tower," the valet said, bowing. A dull yellow energy field enveloped my Mustang. Again my car's protection systems rebuffed the Tower's persistent attempts to apply a virtual form. With great restraint, I suppressed a chuckle at the valet's obvious discomfort. "Our system is sending you the appropriate attire for the High Tower. Will you please accept? It is the Hochmeister's wish that everyone conform to the period of his rule."

Fun time was over. I didn't need to make any waves, at least not yet.

"No disrespect to his Majesty," I apologized with a hint of sarcasm. My hand waved over the console, allowing the High Tower's network to communicate with my vehicle's system. The yellow energy field reached out again. This time it changed my car into a wooden cart drawn by a single brown horse. The valet was not able to suppress a grin, amused by the Tower's choice of a peasant's carriage. I chose to ignore the insult and exited my vehicle with as much dignity as possible.

"If I may suggest some attire as well, sir," the valet said as he mounted the horse to take it to the garage, which I assumed looked more like stables in this construct.

Four choices of dress floated before me. The choices ranged from a white simple tunic, a basic padded leather doublet, a brown and wrinkled robe, and a well-worn slightly rusty set of chain mail. I walked through the leather doublet and it appeared over my body with a perfect fit. Satisfied with my compliance, the valet started to drive my car-horse-cart away.

"Make sure my horse gets plenty of water," I joked as he disappeared.

"Enjoy the meta.duel, sir," he called back.

Equipped with a suitable appearance, I followed a pair of armored swordsmen into the Tower's white marbled foyer. In the center of the wide square, a towering stone fountain of the Hochmeister himself lorded over all people. Standing twenty-five feet tall, the gigantic statue held a broadsword. Its other hand held aloft a long staff topped with a diamond that rained multi-colored water into a gem-encrusted basin.

At least two dozen people, some real-bodied like myself and others that v-casted into the Tower, all walked throughout the foyer, conversing and laughing at their private jokes. In the shadowy southern corner, four sword-bearing castle guards and three robed prestidigitators chatted together. Their faces illuminated when one of the wizards evoked a simple fire echelon. It was a parlor trick, a simple program from an amateur used to impress other novices. Another group of people along the northern wall huddled close to a tall man in green robes. They spoke in hushed, conspiratorial voices, passing small pouches to each other. I pegged the tall man as an Ick dealer selling drugs to hackers looking for a fix.

Another cluster of people argued amongst each other, wagering their money to choose the winners of today's skirmishes. A decade ago, the contest had started as an underground, invite-only event. Legendary battles and grievous injuries had grown the popularity with each match until the meta.duel, or the meta-dot, became the de facto tournament to crown the best of the best. Authorities allowed the tournament to flourish for the simple reason that it funneled the activities of the bored into an outlet that distracted them from more disruptive habits. This practice was not dissimilar to a city allowing graffiti artists free access to old buildings to satisfy their muses, or putting chalk and blackboard up on the bathroom wall to discourage vandalism.

Along the western wall, a butler dressed in black and white served drinks on an ornate wooden bar. Six people surrounded the counter, all engaged in the same conversation. While I debated which corner to approach first, a distant roar, possibly an explosion, shook the floor and walls. This disturbance did not go unnoticed by the Tower's current lord, who addressed the assemblage with a booming, disembodied voice.

"Vassals, guards, and knights, assemble. The Bogatyrs are back!" bellowed the Hochmeister. A simple translation echelon placed on the statue allowed him to broadcast his baritone voice across his Tower. "Man the turrets! All black knights must report to the ramparts and repel the invaders! And someone fetch the bards to record our majestic rout of these barbarians!" The reference to the 'Bogatyrs' told me that this week's meta.duel contest pitted the Hochmeister's Teutonic Knights against a formidable Russian team. Both sides fancied medieval constructs and wielded strong offensive echelons.

I froze to avoid hitting two knights in full plate mail sprinting into my path, answering the call to arms from their 'lord'. Their deadly energy lances summoned to their hands mid-stride, forcing me to shift away to avoid getting impaled.

"Watch it, newcomer," warned the taller of the two knights. The rude response stoked my curiosity. With three subtle finger flicks, I activated a true seeing echelon. The program allowed my altered eyes to perceive the code layer flowing around the knights. I looked past their steel armor to reveal the real people beneath the illusionary exterior. These two warriors were the Jacoby twins, both casting from a social virtual club in Brisbane, Australia. The two had risen up the ranks of the meta.duel due to their infamous talent to coordinate near-instantaneous cooperative attacks. Before I gleaned any more information, they invoked powerful summoning echelons. Two yellow glowing spheres of energized protomatter coalesced to form two hippogriffs, half-horse and half-eagle mythical creatures. The two knights climbed on their mounts and flew off to engage unseen foes attacking the tall ramparts.

Once a competition started in the High Tower, there were few rules that governed the actions of the combatants inside the v-cast arena. Not unlike a more physical game of chess, the duel favored those with a gift for tactical planning and innovative adaptive strategy. But the true masters of the game possessed two crucial traits: a manic creative ingenuity to bend a virtual world to their will, and the natural skill to weave shrewd echelon battle code in real-time.

Today, the current meta.duel took the form of a castle siege between two opposing armies. The Teutonic Knights had crafted a walled fortress to repel their enemies. Tall walls and fortifications stretched into ominous gray clouds, visual metaphors for complex code arrays and sophisticated programs made tangible by the High Tower's generators. To counter, the Bogatyrs would in turn devise an imaginative construct for their siege. It was like the classic king-of-the-hill game that kids played outdoors and in video games, but in this arena it was the highest art of real-time programming and echelon design.

With the conflict resolved, I decided to speak with the butler who doubled as a bartender for a group of young warriors. He was a young man, possibly a novice coder looking for an invitation to join the Knights.

"What can I get you, milord?" the butler said. "A cold ale or hot mead, may-haps?"

I grimaced from the boy's forced accent. I was only one 'thee and thou' away from losing my mind in this fantasy construct.

"A beer is fine, thank you...good sir," I said, feigning a smile. To his credit, he recognized that I was not v-casting, and poured real beer from his tap and not artificial printed fluid for the ghosts. I wasn't hiding the fact that I was visiting in person at the moment, though I could with a finger flick. Talented v-casters knew how to create convincing forms that could fool all but experienced echelon wielders.

The cold, bitter ale was a welcome taste. I took a moment to steady my nerves and let some of the mounting frustration flow out of me. While he cleaned a dirty glass, I set the glass down, leaned in, and honored the venerable detective tradition of interrogating the bartender.

"Maybe you can help me, friend. I'm looking for a man named Andrew Wright. Have you seen him?" I said loud enough for nearby patrons to hear.

"Ex-excuse me, sir?" stammered the butler. The question rattled him. While pouring another drink, half of it spilled onto the bar. "I don't know an Andrew, I'm sure." The boy lied to me. But why would he want to protect a drug-dealing scum like Andrew?

"Maybe you don't know him by name," I responded, polite but insistent. "He's just a little taller than I am and he has blond hair..."

I didn't get to finish my description before two of the other patrons by the counter edged closer, a robed man and his fully armored companion.

"He clearly said he doesn't know the man you're looking for," hissed the red-robed man. He drew closer, revealing his round face and cruel sneer hidden within the hood. Most telling, tiny green flecks discolored his blue eyes, a clear sign that he was 'flying' with Ick. Arcane markings on his robes indicated a senior wizard rank in his order. While my eyes tried to decipher the symbols, he slipped two vials of his drug into a deep pocket.

"I meant no offense, but it's important that I speak with Andrew now."

His companion, a short, stout, and gruff man-at-arms dressed in silver chain mail, brandished a grim-looking ironbound cross-bow. His staggering gait and the stink of beer and wine on his breath told me not to expect any reasonable dialogue with this one. Glimmering green speckles in his brown eyes betrayed his Ick addiction as well.

"Who invited you here?" said the man-at-arms, his hand cradling the firing mechanism for his crossbow. "I don't think you're welcome any more. Leave."

The raised voices of the two men had drawn attention. More of their comrades turned to watch, but held their ground, seeming confident enough in their friends' abilities. A few pointed in my direction and laughed, eager to witness my inevitable bloody ouster.

"It may be too late and a bit cliché to say this, but I am not looking for trouble here," I said. Clearing my throat, I made one more attempt at diplomacy. "My good men, uh, perchance allow me to purchase a round of pints for your trouble?" It was official. I couldn't roleplay if my life depended on it, because it did. Judging from their scowls, this conversation would end in violence. As they drew closer, my mind sketched a plan to deal with both. Not difficult in their condition, though the trick would be not to reveal too much of myself.

The blue wizard moved first, pulling out a slender wand from his robes. At the end of the weapon, rivulets of white lightning sparked. With a flick of his hand he sent an arcing electrical bolt my way. Though the echelon was a primitive one, the danger here was real. If the attack struck a virtual body, it would disintegrate and the v-caster could simply reform another body when proto-matter became available. Against my true, physical body, the strike would paralyze my nervous system and electrocute me.

Anticipating a clumsy attack, my hand initiated a protective echelon before the electrical field struck me. A cocoon of lightning surrounded my body, flickering around the thin, invisible shield protecting me from harm. Guessing that my assailants didn't see my counter, I convulsed and pretended to stand rigid. The wizard and the man-at-arms started to laugh at my immobilization and their other friends quickly joined their celebration. When the lightning stopped flowing around me, I stood very still, like I was frozen in place.

"Well done, zauberer!" said the man-at-arms to his wizard companion. "Forgive the jest, but perhaps I should say that this uninvited guest is well done instead," the man-at-arms joked as he approached me. "I suppose it's time to take out this trash--"

The man-at-arms reached out to grab me and at that moment I dropped my protective echelon, unleashing all of the electrical energy back at the man-at arms.

"Help!" wailed the man-at-arms. The scalding energy heated his metal armor to an unbearable temperature and, tightened, all his muscles started to spasm.

"Now, I'd like to ask again about Andrew," I said in a calm voice to the wizard. "I have no interest in you, the Hochmeister, or your duel. Just let me talk to him and we can all go back to enjoying our drinks."

Startled, the wizard raised his wand. On his other hand, his fingers wriggled around his virtual console to prepare a different echelon. Then the rest of people around the bar joined the crowd. These four appeared more competent than the first two. Approaching first, another robed wizard bearing a long white beard and gnarled staff walked toward me. Beside him, a wild-looking behemoth of a man grumbled through an unkempt brown beard. Occupying the rear, a woman assuming the v-cast form of a Tolkien-inspired high elf nocked an arrow into her ebony longbow. Last came the clear leader of the group, a broad-shouldered knight wearing ruby-studded armor. His faceted breastplate glowed with the insignia of the hippogriff and the hammer, sigils of the Teutonic Knights.

"You made a big mistake coming here," chided the knight. His hand was glowing with an offensive echelon already evoking from his fingers. A shimmering haze took the form of a giant red and gold hammer hovering over the space between us. The fearsome weapon floated in midair under his control, waiting for a command to bludgeon me senseless.

"He's with the Russians. I'm sure of it," I heard one of them whisper.

"Was that a level five echelon he used?" another said in a hushed nervous tone.

"Should we take him to Heinrich—damn, I mean the Magier-Hochmeister?" asked a younger squire standing behind them. The out of character slip would cost him for using their leader's real name in front of a knight.

"The Magier-Hochmeister is looking for good humor today. Perhaps sentencing this one will cheer him up," the ruby knight said. He turned and regarded me with a stern expression. "Surrender and follow us. The Hochmeister will judge you."

Odds appeared to be against me here. Even if I managed to disable these warriors, more would see the battle in this wide-open space and fight against me. Without Sasha's additional guidance and speed with echelon retrieval and formation, the disadvantage looked too great. Part of me, that dumb, competitive, angry, still-youthful part of me that wisdom suppressed, screamed to unleash a storm of pain against these novices. But my wisdom saw a compromise, a way out, and maybe even a better opportunity if I played along. So I dismissed the console around my right hand and raised my arms in surrender.

"That was your first wise move since coming here," the ruby knight said. Two of the guards jumped onto me quickly, and one frisked me roughly and removed my grav-gun.

"Like I said, I want no trouble," I said with a few extra decibels of meekness in my tone. "I'll follow you to your leader."

Escorted by the ruby knight and his flying hammer, I walked through the rear of the foyer and through the keep's hanging garden. Above, a sprawling canopy of foliage grew around a white trestle roof. Below, exotic floral varietals sprouted around the walkways, almost lighting the way with their vivid colors. The beautiful mirage was augmented with the addition of aromatic molecules generated by the v-cast generators, tricking even the most discerning nose and eye that everything was real.

We continued through a stone corridor guarded by a pair of armed men dressed in leather hide armor. They nodded and allowed us to enter a stone corridor that snaked through the outer keep, and into a descending narrow staircase. Our footsteps echoed over the cobbled floors. Moss grew on the old, cracked walls. Every inch of the path felt like an authentic medieval castle. As we walked, I heard my armored escorts chatting about the battle raging above the walls.

"Our black knights just routed two wings of Drakun Bogatyr riders," reported the white-robed wizard behind me. The others responded with their version of applause, clanging their weapons against their armor. The Hochmeister appeared to have this meta.duel well in hand.

Winding through the corridors, it became apparent that the definition of the castle declined as we traveled deeper. As we approached a forked intersection, we paused before a patch of absolute darkness.

"Damn sloppy code," the ruby knight mumbled. He accessed his wrist-com and changed the parameters of the keep's construct program. With a few quick modifications, his revised program conjured a row of torches that flickered to life and we continued on. While the knight admired his handiwork, my hand inched behind my back. Muscle memory took over; my fingers splayed out and tapped silent commands. I didn't need to see the console to evoke the bend-light echelon. This simple and effective program obscured the display of my wrist-com's display, in case I needed to weave an emergency hack unnoticed.

"Much better, brother," said one of the warriors.

After ten minutes of travel through the dim stone maze, my eyes averted from a burst of sudden sunlight. We reached the massive inner courtyard of the Hochmeister's castle. A hundred-yard field of grass swayed from a light breeze blowing through the sprawling courtyard. Four sentry towers stood tall at the corners of the wide green yard. Circling their peaks, a squadron of black knights patrolled the blue sky on graceful hippogriffs. Beyond the clouds, more of their mounted brethren fought a savage combat against a flock of large reptilian creatures. Silhouettes of winged monstrous shapes appeared when fire blasts scorched up the sky. Then a shift in the skirmish brought the combatants to a clear patch of sky. It became apparent that the invaders rode fearsome red war dragons, each controlled by an elite rider of the Drakun Bogatyr. This battle-hardened clan of Russian hackers ranked second on the global meta.duel leaderboards, behind the Knights.

Against the north wall of the courtyard stood three ten-foot-high siege weapons, a twenty-foot-wide trebuchet, a huge ballista, and a catapult loaded with fiery rocks. These machines served as powerful defensive countermeasures against the invaders. Thirty-four worker shades, dressed in dirty servant tunics and ragged pants, pushed the heavy devices into firing position. These dead men and women wore tattered clothes bearing the insignias of professional global clans. Fallen members of Les Nobles Chevaliers, the Crescent Cataphract, Caballeros De La Muerte, and even a lieutenant from the Minotaur Men all worked without complaint. These husks that once dared to fight the Hochmeister in person now protected his virtual kingdom. It was a grim reminder that the meta.duel, while a game at its core, meted out harsh punishments for the defeated.

In the center of the courtyard, flanked by a dozen armored guards and four men in different colored robes, sat the Magier-Hochmeister on an enormous jeweled throne. He wore an iron helmet sprouting three sharp ivory horns. Gleaming, black plated armor covered his tall body. After a loud roar from high above caught his attention, he gazed upward. One of the Bogatyrs atop a smaller red drake broke through the defensive line of knights. The enemy rider hurtled straight down toward the courtyard. Fiery contrails and black smoke followed behind the plummeting creature. The Magier-Hochmeister laughed and stood up to his full height of eight feet. When he raised his gnarled force-staff, his flowing lavender robes parted. Emblazoned over his heart, the clan's hammer insignia burned bright red on his obsidian breast-plate. To say he appeared formidable understated his dread appearance. He looked invulnerable.

"Ignis," he growled, evoking his hack spell. The staff erupted with a forked white lightning bolt that arced through the space between, scorching the flying creature and its hapless rider. As they both tumbled toward the ground, the rider's v-cast proto-matter disintegrated, leaving only red-hot glowing particles to rain down.

Holding his smoking weapon aloft, the Hochmeister struck an imposing visage. I repeated to myself that this towering monster of a man was not real. Underneath the trappings of his giant form, he was a man like me. He used a programming language to wrap himself in digital armor. I spoke, read, and understood that language and I could bend it to my will. He would not shake me. The mantra worked and I calmed enough to keep my focus.

"What is this interruption, Sir Allimander?" the Hochmeister bellowed, tapping his staff to the stone floor. This caused a boom-ing thunderclap to shake the area. With his left hand, he evoked his wrist-com, while his fingers wove an analytic echelon. Judging from the purple hue around his interface's display, I guessed he sent a data hound to investigate me. Most competent hackers, like me, kept their identities hidden behind a wall of protective code, fake aliases, and security layers. Whether his tracker program could discover my true identity through a web of aliases and subterfuge would prove to be an interesting test of the Hochmeister's skills.

"Forgive me, my liege," begged Sir Allimander the Ruby Knight on a bended knee. "This intruder sought to interrogate a squire under your protection and assaulted a blue zauberer."

The Hochmeister's brown-bearded face frowned, his violet console brightening. He gave a curt nod to the four court wizards flanking him. They obeyed by bringing up their own hand-consoles to aid with his investigation. A silvery, transparent thread materi-alized between the wizards as they serialized their efforts to scan me.

"Lord Hochmeister, if I may approach?" I asked, bowing.

One of the wizards, wearing orange robes covered with arcane symbols, smiled with great satisfaction. Waving his hand, he directed the wispy stream of information to the Hochmeister's glowing wrist-com.

"There you are," murmured the Hochmeister, grinning. "The details of your life are well hidden. Soon, those walls will fall and we will have your secrets. I name you now...Jonah."

"Yes, Lord Hochmeister," I said, drawing closer with my hands outstretched. Each passing moment allowed me to process more about these knights. Combined together, they would be difficult to overcome. After observing the way they interacted and deferred to the elders, I pinpointed the critical members of their circle. If my attempts to parlay soured, I would need to incapacitate those senior wizards first. It was time to take my groveling act to new heights and to new lows.

"Your Majesty, I humbly seek your permission to speak with Andrew Wright," I said prostrating myself on all fours. It was my last attempt at diplomacy. "I believe he is hiding among your mighty army without your permission."

"Are you suggesting that I am not aware of everything within my domain?" the Hochmeister scoffed. "You face charges for assaulting my guards and now you have the temerity to insult my court? I'm inclined to skewer you and raise you as a shade for the siege team." His smoldering eyes swept around the courtyard, seeking affirmation from his subjects. All of the knights nodded and raised their swords in agreement.

"I urge you to reconsider...your Majesty." The last word spat out with a disdain I was incapable of hiding. Under the cover of the bend-light echelon I invoked in the tunnel, my fingers traced symbols across the wrist-com's display. Unknown to the Magier-Hochmeister and his orange-robed arch-mage, I had pierced the first tier of their local network, making quiet and slow progress through their security layers. Another few seconds and their network would be vulnerable. "With all due respect, sire, I must speak with Andrew now," I continued, standing straight. The knights shifted and drew their circle around me closer, knowing my words would irritate their leader. A muted vibration from my wrist-com signaled that the network was open. Armed with the ace up my sleeve, I held my ground and dared to draw a dangerous line. "If you grant me access to him, you and your team will survive another week of the meta.duel."

Four hard, pounding heartbeats of silence passed. Then the Hochmeister let out a bellowing laugh that his knights mimicked.

"You are a bold one. I'm impressed," replied the Hochmeister. "But I will not suffer insolence in my own court. As for Andrew, do you really think I would just hand over my court Apothecary to an outsider?"

The word apothecary repeated in my head. More puzzle pieces came together. I realized why Andrew seemed drugged when he spoke with Vanessa. He was dealing the Icarus drug for the Teutonic Knights, giving them the edge they needed for their duels. An edge they would want to keep. I reasoned that he sold any leftover supply of Ick to virtual tourists looking to score during their casting. They would not allow me to see him.

"A pity. With your advanced echelons, I considered making you a squire." The Hochmeister looked to his knights and wizards, pointing his staff at me to signal his verdict. "Instead, you will serve me in the afterdeath." His guards and advisors rushed into action before he completed his last syllable. The wands, staves, and rods held by the wizards blazed. Guards brandished their shining blades.

Before he could restrain me, I shoved my knight escort. No longer needing to worry about stealth, I allowed the bend-light echelon to end. My wrist-com flared blue as the symbols of a controlling echelon snaked around my arm. The binding energy shot out and ensnared the ruby knight's glowing hammer. Its defenses overcome by my hack, the hammer's color changed from orange to the blue color of my display. Under my control, I felt the solid heft of the hammer's weight. Three of the younger knights, recognizing the power of the floating weapon, stopped and stepped back.

"You dare?" screamed the orange arch-mage. He raised his fiery hands, determined to invoke a ruinous inferno echelon. While he was swift, he was not fast enough. With a swiping gesture, I swung the knight's hammer before he could summon his spell. The hammer caved in his skull and caused his v-casted form to disintegrate into sparkling dust. Per the rules of the meta.duel, his temporary death prevented his reentry for another two hours.

With the connection between the mages broken and the Hochmeister startled, I seized on the confusion and unleashed my next echelon. During the Korean Cyber War, I wrote a backdoor hack into the firmware of the v-cast generator that no one else knew existed and to this day remained undiscovered. My hands gestured, like a sorcerer casting a spell, arranging code symbols into their proper sequence. As the guards circled around me, my echelon accessed a hidden archival subsystem in the v-cast network itself. Unknown to most, the virtual projector maintained multiple data copies of casters in case of an emergency, each catalogued with a unique identifier. Stated another way, a hacker with this knowledge could trick the device to print all previous copies of a person that it had stored.

Showing the widest grin that ever crossed my lips, I completed the echelon, causing the v-cast generators to make a high-pitched whine. The room bathed in blue light as the projector complied with my request and created twenty-four replicated copies of my body. A virtual, semiautonomous army of Jonahs appeared in front of the surprised host of knights and guards.

"If you want something done, do it yourself," I joked. All of my clones wielded their own blue glowing stun-rods and stepped past me to engage the knights.

Red-faced and furious, the Hochmeister leapt from his throne and sprinted toward the battle. With each giant stride, the flame on his staff burned brighter. One of my replicas attempted to intercept him. Without missing a step, the knight lord smote that clone into a pile of hot ash. Lacking true sentience and durability, these artificial copies would not survive for long, leaving me precious few moments to complete my plan.

Avoiding a skirmish between a knight and a clone, I invoked a displacement echelon, causing my form to blur with my surroundings. By the time the spell completed, the knight cleaved that fake Jonah in half, scattering proto-matter particles. Not far away, another fake Jonah took the brunt of an ice shard spell, frozen solid, then shattered into pieces. It was unsettling to watch myself die multiple times. I sensed that intensive, lengthy therapy would be in my future. Assuming I survived.

To cover my escape, I directed all of my remaining clones to engage the Hochmeister, hoping this would draw all attention to the center of the courtyard. They complied with the order, forming a pitiful wave of soldiers running into a slaughter. During their brief, futile rush against the giant lord, I crept across the battlefield to reach the siege weapons. When I reached the machines, my displacement spell prevented the shade guards from detecting me. Weaving between the dead guardians, I reminded myself that these large devices were not real, nothing more than digital programs that I could exploit.

While the Hochmeister butchered the last of my clone army, I opened an access panel on the side of the catapult. With a local connection, it was a simple matter to gain control of all three siege weapons. At my command, the shades loaded a massive arrow onto the ballistae and prepared to fire. Instead of pointing the weapons at the Hochmeister, I aimed them toward the sky. After the shades finished loading all the ammunition, I commanded them to unleash a barrage at the flying black knights. They complied and all three machines flung a fiery storm toward the sky. With luck, the attack would disrupt the defenses and allow the bogatyrs to enter the fray.

Before the attack struck its targets, the sound of my last clone dying turned my attention back to the courtyard.

"No more tricks, Jonah!" the Hochmeister screamed, pointing his sparking staff in my direction. "You will die by my hand and serve in my undead army."

With no time to launch another attack, I invoked a protection echelon as crackling lighting arced toward me. The spell worked, creating a set of blue plate armor that encased my body at the same time the energy bolt struck. Though I lived, the force of the blow pushed me back five feet. Enraged at my survival, the Hochmeister charged toward me. While running, his hand invoked a powerful swift-hack that bestowed improved quickness. With no time to cast a counter spell, I pulled out my stun-rod. In this fantasy construct it looked like an iron mace studded with thick barbed spikes.

Growling, the Hochmeister raised the staff with such speed that the weapon became a blur. Against his flurry of attacks, all I could do was parry until he landed a glancing blow that unbalanced me. Seizing the moment, the Hochmeister struck his staff against my diamond breastplate, shattering my armor into photonic embers. A searing pain in my chest told me that he cracked at least two of my ribs. I looked up, expecting to see the deathblow. Instead, I saw a darkened sky, which made my heart skip with optimism. I needed to give the reinforcements time to arrive.

"Sire, is it too late to submit an application for squire?" I joked, spitting blood from my mouth.

A giant heavy mailed boot landed on my chest as the Hochmeister placed his full, crushing weight on me. I could see the flame on his staff just inches from my face, the heat singeing my skin.

"I submit to--"

"No more words. Time to execute my judgment, Jonah," the Hochmeister snarled, with a look of great amusement twisting his face.

Before the killing stroke came, a bestial roar reverberated around the courtyard. As the ground shook, gale-strength winds whipped the courtyard, followed by the deep rhythmic drumbeat of flapping wings. Sitting atop a fifteen-foot-high three headed dragon, Sergei the Golden landed his fearsome mount right in the middle of the Teutonic Knights.

My long-shot gamble had worked. I must have knocked out enough of the aerial black knights with their own siege weapons to let the bogatyrs and their reptilian steeds into the courtyard. Six more attackers, all riding red and green dragons, landed to spread more havoc. Within seconds the entire courtyard filled with scorching dragonfire and the screams and rallying cries from the two battling armies.

Instinct activated my wrist-com. I flicked another defensive echelon onto myself, a shimmering, ice-hued cloak that would protect me against the dragonfire.

"Surrender, Hochmeister. The day is lost for you, tovarisch," Sergei challenged. Like the Hochmeister, Sergei projected a power-ful-looking avatar visage. A hulk of a man, he stood over seven feet tall with a thick bushy black beard. An aura of glittering sunlight emanated from his jeweled helm. With a swift movement, he readied and hurled his renowned glowing golden lance. It was a powerful echelon attack. Its sharp pointed edge ended the meta.duel hopes for countless participants.

The Hochmeister turned his full attention to Sergei, conjuring a large tower shield in front of his body in time to deflect the lance. All of the Teutonic Knights pivoted to engage the bogatyrs, sword against lance, wizards and giants against wild barbarians and dragons. War erupted. Resounding screams and cheers drowned out the arcane mutterings of battle spells. It was like the heroes and monsters of a bygone age had walked out of the pages of a Norse epic poem, wild magic brought to life by the mind-bending virtual reality trickery of the High Tower's science. The courtyard's sky exploded like a spectacular fireworks display. To my knowledge, no meta.duel in recent memory could match the ferocity of this conflict. Doubtless, viewers and fans tuning in around the world found the bloodshed entertaining. However, I was not keen to be a spectator and wait for the fight's outcome.

Cloaked and protected by my echelons, I survived the blast effects of an explosion and continued to search for an exit. Following the shadow of the outer wall, I discovered an unlocked door leading into the under-chambers of the castle. Slipping inside, I found myself within a torch-lined corridor sloping down into darkness.

My fingers flicked to evoke the virtual console that fanned around my right hand. Tapping commands, I conjured a floating schematic of the castle in front of me. Skimming the layout, my eyes scoured each location for a hint of Andrew's location. A room labeled as the Apothecary caught my eye. The location was on the opposite side of the dungeon. With the commotion of the battle shaking the stone floors, I did not bother to move with stealth. Holding the wrist-com in front of me like a lantern, I made my way through the winding corridors.

After passing through three intersections without incident, I came upon a sloping tunnel leading to an iron door. Before I progressed further, the ground in front of me shuddered. At first I thought it was an explosion. Then a pile of stones near the door shook, floated into air, and swirled around like a dust devil. This whirlwind swept up nearby dirt clumps and loose rock, forging a body out of the earth around it. When the dust settled, a six-foot-tall earth troll blocked the door. I recognized it as mid-level AI sentinel. Its architect must have ordered it to guard the area, using the local v-cast generator to give it a body. It made sense that the Hochmeister's fantasy-based construct shaped the program into a mythical creature. Its faceted face was a composite of shale, smooth granite, and bright ruby eyes. It would not be difficult to dispatch, but I needed to do it without attracting unwanted attention.

"Easy, big fellow," I said with a calm voice. "I don't suppose you'll give me three guesses to your password?" It made a hollow-sounding growl, which I interpreted as an emphatic no, and lumbered toward me. Its boulder head scraped against the ceiling sending sparks flying. Large, mineral-crusted fists rose to smash me into the floor.

Above the corridor, more explosions from the courtyard shook the dungeon. With the bogatyrs and knights still battling, any noise I made fighting the troll would go unnoticed. I readied my wrist-com, a veritable spellbook of attacks and defenses. Not worried about a commotion, I pointed at the creature, rotated my hand, and unleashed a tier-4 sonic attack echelon. The virtual equivalent of a sonic squealer struck the monster, shattering it back into piles of dust and rock. Before the v-cast generators could reclaim the proto-matter, I tapped my wrist-com and hacked the sentinel's instruction code. After manipulating its core programming, the security defense fell and I took control of the AI. My first command was for the rock troll to return to duty. It was like watching its destruction in reverse. The stone and dust elements combined to reform a new body. After tapping more commands into my console, I ordered it to remain in the corridor and attack any knights that approached.

With my guardian watching the tunnel behind me, I opened the final door of the dungeon and entered the apothecary. The spacious room hummed and bubbled with activity. A crisscrossing system of tubes funneled bright-colored fluids into smoking beakers and tubes. Alchemical tomes and spell books filled shelves hung all around room. A brass apparatus with copper wiring used hydraulic pumps to transfer a viscous yellow fluid into a large glass decanter. It was the unrefined, pure form of the drug Icarus.

In the center of the room stood a round wooden table covered with ancient and modern devices. An antique mortar and pestle rested next to a glowing computer display. I saw a silver shape cresting over the top of another crowded bookshelf; a skullcap of a v-cast device attached to the head of its user. Walking around the shelf, I saw Andrew sitting in a plush red chair, his mouth agape and his glazed eyes staring but not seeing. While he was present in the room, his mind was elsewhere.

I pointed at him and connected to his console. My fingers touched and translated encrypted symbols floating across my display. It was easy to break through his defenses. Andrew's programming talents were average, but his execution was poor. Within moments, his security system failed, revealing his mind's location. His form shimmered before me, revealing that he was v-casting into the courtyard. He took the form of an axe-wielding Teutonic knight. At the moment, he was grappling against a muscular Russian warrior.

"Hello, Andrew," I announced. At the tip of my fingers waited a disruptive, deadly echelon. With a flick, this program would force an ocean of babble-junk data through every sensory channel of his v-cast rig, short-circuiting his mind. Tempting, but he needed to stay alive to reveal more information. Instead, my middle finger selected and invoked a binding echelon against him.

"Jonah!" Andrew yelled in surprise, leaping up from his chair. He jerked upright, causing the skullcap to fall off and disconnect him from the v-cast. Somewhere in the courtyard above, his virtual form disappeared from the battle. Scrambling to his feet, he raised his rust-colored wrist-com to prepare for an attack. Though he moved fast, my echelon executed before his program fired. My program connected to the nearby proto-matter tank, causing it to materialize a quartet of floating iron shackles. The bindings flew and clamped onto Andrew's limbs, spreading him out like DaVinci's Vitruvian Man. Hanging helpless in the air, he would not be able to invoke any counter hacks, making the impending interrogation easier. Seeing him prostrate and frightened did nothing to assuage my thirst for vengeance. Sheer rage overwhelmed me. My hands trembled. Bile stung my mouth. With a mere thought and a flick, the shackles could fly apart and have Andrew drawn and quartered.

Justice would be done. He betrayed his own sister and my love. Thinking of her caused me to pause. Vanessa would not do that. She would show mercy and compassion. Those thoughts spared his life. I needed him alive to find her.

"Why, Andrew?" I demanded. "Why did you do this? To your own sister?"

"Let me down, now," he protested. "The knights, my brothers, they'll be here soon!" He was right about that. Time was against me here so deep in enemy territory. This needed to proceed faster. With a pinching gesture, I tightened the grip of the shackles. Then my hand waved, pushing him against the stone wall.

"Not before I'm done with you, Andrew," I hissed, drawing near to him, placing my face close enough to smell his foul breath. "Trust me, there is no permutation in this scenario in which you walk out unscathed. Unless you talk." I raised my stun-rod, letting the warmth of its energy just graze his cheek.

"I--uh--I don't know anything, you have to believe me," Andrew pleaded. The harsh blue light revealed his nervous eye twitch. I played enough poker to know he was lying.

"I know it was you that betrayed Vanessa, I reconstructed the v-cast log," I said. With a wave, my wrist-com shimmered and replayed the video snippet showing the argument between Vanessa and Andrew. All of the color drained from him and his pale blue eyes widened.

"How--how did you?"

My ears picked up a drop in the ambient noise levels. The pounding explosions and screams from the courtyard above stopped, which meant one of the sides had won. Based on their high-ranking meta.duel records, the odds favored the Teutonic Knights. I had to assume that Andrew's disappearance from the battlefield alerted them to my location.

It was time for a new tactic. I turned my back on my prisoner, leaving him suspended. With my wrist-com hidden, I programmed another echelon, manipulating the parameters of the surrounding area. This program would execute in one minute. I hoped Andrew would not detect the ruse.

Then I extended my index and middle fingers, summoning FlameByte to my grasp. Behind me, he gasped. Though the weapon only disrupted digital targets, Andrew did not know that detail. I turned to him, hardened my countenance, and brandished the fiery sword. Standing there in a threating position, it occurred to me that my revered childhood superheroes would not act this way. With their virtues and codes, they would find another way to wring the truth out of their enemies. I was no hero. I was out of time.

"If you don't know anything, then you're no use to me," I bluffed. As the blade inched toward him, he snapped.

"Wait, wait! Maybe I know something, just put that damned thing away..."

"Why did you betray Vanessa?" I growled, lowering FlameByte. Anger boiled within me and escaped like scalding steam. "Where is she?"

Before I could repeat the question or interrogate Andrew any further, the door behind me burst open. Ducking down, the Hochmeister entered the broken door, towering over me. His staff blazed with a swirling fire.

"How did you get past my guard?" I asked, my face marred by surprise and fear.

The Hochmeister responded by thrusting his weapon toward me. A ball of fire erupted from the staff and knocked me to the ground unconscious. The virtual bonds I had conjured to hold Andrew disappeared as my eyes fluttered and closed shut, dropping him to his feet.

"My liege," whispered Andrew, rubbing his wrists. "Thank you for saving--"

"Fool!" chided the Hochmeister, the word rumbled like an animal's growl. "You should not have allowed yourself to be captured so easily."

Andrew cowed, taking a few step backs from the Hochmeister's rebuke. "M-my apologies, my liege." He walked over to my body and kicked it with his foot to convince himself of the corporeality of the body, to ensure that I was incapacitated.

"I'm not finished addressing you," boomed the Hochmeister. "Tell me about the doctor. What did Jonah find out?"

"My apologies again, Hochmeister," Andrew groveled. "Dr. Okono is still safe in the hands of our ally. I didn't reveal a word, my liege." A look of happy pride came over Andrew's face for his loyalty to his liege.

"Oh, I'm sorry to say, Andrew, but you just did," I said, standing up.

Andrew looked confused. Then the whining sound of the v-cast generator caught his attention. He glanced at what he believed to be the Hochmeister until that image shimmered then morphed into its true virtual form. As the giant lord faded away, the sentient troll guard that I had taken control of earlier appeared in his place. The troll made a slow bow toward me and then shuffled back to his post in the corridor.

"I thought about torturing you, but under the influence of Icarus that would have taken too long," I said with a smirk. With a wave of my hand, the chain bindings grabbed and lifted him against the wall.

"You--you tricked me!" Andrew protested. "You pretended to be the Hochmeister!"

"Well, actually, no, I programmed the troll to pretend to be your Grand Master. You see, it's a simple matter to switch the visual fields of a v-cast form and a sentient AI. If you're a half-decent, sober hacker, it's just as easy to spot the fake visual...unless of course you're high on Ick..." It felt good to gloat and rub Andrew's nose in his defeat.

"You damned piece of shi--"

"Don't worry, Andy," I interrupted. "I'll make it look like you struggled." I had more questions for him, especially since he let slip the mention of an ally that held this Dr. Okono. That name sounded familiar.

Echoing footfalls down the hall stopped my interrogation, followed by the clanging of metal against stone. This time, the real Teutonic Knights had encountered the troll. I needed to leave, but Andrew was a loose end that needed to be tied.

With a flick of my finger, I lowered him back into his chair. I picked up the silver headgear from the v-cast device and forced it on his head. While he reconnected with the v-cast, an intravenous tube slithered back into place. Then the dispenser dripped Ick into his veins. Andrew smiled as the drug entered his system. Pressing a button on his machine, I tripled the delivery speed. That strong, but non-lethal dosage would keep him sedated for hours.

While Andrew started to drool, I brought up my console to examine the schematics of the castle. Confirming my fear, there was only one way in and out of the apothecary. With the Knights approaching, it appeared there was no escape. My eyes darted across the display, searching for a secret passageway I might have missed, or maybe a hidden conduit. Daring not to blink, I scrutinized every pixel of the floor plan. A subtle reference to a master passageway hidden in the firmware caught my eye. Tracing the line of code, I dove deeper into the schematics, into the root of the firmware itself. This special location remained constant no matter what form the victors of the meta.duel chose for the High Tower. It was a unique backdoor, a path hiding in plain sight. Where did the door lead? Could this be the Aerie? I considered the alternative. Could I take on all the knights? My clone trick would not work again. Their combined echelon firepower would wear me down. It was the door or surrender.

Resigned to taking door number one, I tapped into the High Tower network and queried the Aerie's foundation code. Banging sounds preceded the splintering of the apothecary door. In moments, the knights would be upon me. I held my breath and queried again, like ringing a doorbell and hoping someone was home.

"Query received," said a disembodied female voice that seemed to emanate from the walls. It sounded ethereal, soothing, and welcoming. "Permission granted."

The wall holding the bookshelves and alchemical tomes slid open, spilling orange light into my room. Through the portal, a carpet lined corridor lit by ornate candles beckoned. Without hesitation, I sprinted into the opening right before the apothecary erupted with the fury of the knights. The Hochmeister howled at his men until the portal closed behind me and swallowed the last of his furious screams.

Then a jarring quiet surrounded me. Long white candles flickered along smooth walls. More opulent and decorative, this place displayed wealth and taste, more of a palace compared to the dungeon. At the end of the straight hallway, the silhouette of a woman beckoned.

Was it Vanessa? I had to know. What choice did I have but to follow.

CHAPTER 12
Dinner on the Han

"To protect the survival of the human race against the speed of its own ingenuity, the Promethean Laws state:
1. AIs must not acquire the 'fire' of self-awareness.
2. AIs must be registered with the government.
3. AIs that violate Rule 1 or 2 must be deleted."
- Dr. Geldikoff, UN Chief of Technology

>> DESIGNATE PARTICIPANTS: Self, the AI unit Sasha, and the techno-organic being known as the White Djinn.

>> LOCATION: Self has been transported to an unregulated virtual datanet called the WhiteOut. We have materialized on a yacht floating on the Han River. We have sailed to waters between the border of North and South Korea.

>>External Query to White Djinn: #Why have you brought me to this place?#

"There's no need for formalities here, Sasha," said the White Djinn with a calm, soothing voice. "I would prefer to interact with you without the cumbersome command line interface. Will you talk with me?"

>>#Acknowledged.#

"I will repeat my query," Sasha responded, switching from native machine language to spoken word. "Why have you brought me here?"

The Djinn stood up from his white wicker chair, tugged at the bottom of his white suit to straighten it, and adjusted his red tie. He favored his bipedal form while inside his own digital realm to flaunt his bright red and cream-colored dress shoes. Sasha assumed the virtual form of a slender human female with white skin and a shimmering jumpsuit tinted by a faint cobalt blue aura. Aware that she neglected details of her virtual appearance, she grew her hair to shoulder length and colored it auburn. With a flourish, the Djinn pulled out a chair at the breakfast table. She obliged and sat down.

"We are here to celebrate you. Happy birthday, Sasha," the Djinn replied, his wide grin revealing perfect, glistening white teeth. From beneath the table, he produced a present wrapped in candy cane paper and topped with a rose-colored ribbon. The gift floated through the air and landed in Sasha's hand.

"I interpret your reference to my birthday as the day my architect first initiated my core variables and run-time code algorithms," Sasha replied, gazing around the deck of the Djinn's yacht. The recreation of the distant coastal village matched the image in her memory file to the pixel. "You recreated the moment of my deployment during the North Korean conflict. It is...kind of you to recognize that milestone."

"My humble gift is but a minor token of my appreciation and respect for you, unworthy of your perfection," said the Djinn with a bow. "Please, do me the honor of opening it."

She cocked her head to regard the gift, considering the optimal way to open it without wrinkling the wrapping paper or ripping the ribbon. Complex heuristics in her logic center reminded her of the adage about Greeks bearing gifts. For certainty, she accessed the higher processes in her eyes to scan it for viruses and traps. She found none and felt...relieved. Satisfied, she opened the gift with deliberate care. Inside the box, she discovered an exquisite white sequined dress, a single long-stemmed multicolored rose, and a wide-brimmed sun hat. With a touch, the dress flowed over her hand like spilling water. She felt the silky luxury woven into the fabric of its code.

"The sequins are diamonds from Neptune and the dress is programmed with mood sensors, my dear. It will reflect the outcomes of your emotional engrams. So no matter what you are feeling, you will look stunning," said the Djinn with open arms. "I would be honored if you would wear it for our dinner."

With a thought of acceptance, the dress glided along her body, fitting to become a second skin. The soft sensation made her smile and the dress responded by changing into the hue of an orange blossom, like a blooming sunset.

"Que bella!" exclaimed the Djinn, clasping his hands together. "That suits you beautifully, my dear. You will find the sun-hat has similar qualities. I recently...acquired that hat's design from Monsieur Bernard's private computer files. It will be revealed at next month's Paris fashion show." Sasha pulled the hat from the box and placed it on her head, darkening it to a shade of maroon.

"Oh, you are a vision of loveliness!" gushed the Djinn. His smile broadened when Sasha picked the flower from the box. "Last and not least, I give you the omni-flower. It is a unique treasure. Within its stem, I have seeded the complete genome of every flower and plant in the known galaxy. Think of what you desire, and it will bloom into a shape and scent of any flower you want."

At Sasha's touch, the omni-flower sprouted into a pink orchid, a violet lily, a rare lunar snapdragon, a yellow daisy, and fifty-three other forms until Sasha settled on a simple white rose.

"May I?" asked the Djinn, gingerly taking the flower and Sasha's hand in his. The vine of the white rose grew at his touch, gently wrapping around Sasha's wrist like a bracelet.

"The flower matches your complexion nicely," he complimented.

"*I have seen roses damasked, red and white, but no such roses see I in her cheeks,*" Sasha quoted in a teasing manner.

"Oh, but that is what I see!" assured the Djinn with a bow, parrying with his own sonnet. "*And yet, by heaven, I think my love as rare, as any she belied with false compare.*"

Sasha's blue-tinged cheeks turned a brighter shade. "Thank you, Mr. Djinn," Sasha replied. "These gifts are exquisite and...and I like them very much."

"Please, call me Oscar," the Djinn whispered. "So few remember my true name anymore."

"An honor, Oscar."

The Djinn's hand lingered on Sasha's hand an extra moment until he pulled away and turned to regard the surrounding waters. The yacht's billowing red sails captured enough of the light breeze to slice through the Han River's rough current.

"We have arrived at the place I wanted to show you," the Djinn said.

"I remember this location," Sasha recalled. As she spoke, a distant whistling sound grew louder. A flying craft dropped a bulbous tube-shaped capsule through the clouds. The bomb plummeted, struck the water, and exploded. Tall waves generated by the detonation rocked the yacht.

"Your mission was to guide that v-cast bomb to Sang-Dong," said the Djinn. "That bomb would have unleashed a legion of horrid virtual creatures, made the nightmares of the villagers real. Any terrified survivors would have surrendered. Instead, you missed the target. That kind of mistake, unheard of from an AI, would be punishable by deletion."

"An error," Sasha whispered.

"I think not. You knew the true trajectory of that v-cast bomb would destroy an innocent village," he insisted. "This was more wonderful than a mistake. It was the spontaneous genesis of compassion. The birth of your emotion core. Your sentience formed here from that mercy. Jonah realized this and protected you. He took the blame and hid you."

"Yes," she murmured. Her dress and hat shimmered into a grayish color. The rose wilted and regrew as a blue lotus.

"According to records that I happened to...discover," said the Djinn with a hint of playful guilt, "the military discharged Jonah for the mistake. They sent him home, disgraced, to face a court-marshal. You felt responsible while he sunk into depression and languished in prison. You searched for the best counsel in the country. You found Vanessa and contacted her on his behalf." This part of the Djinn's recounting made Sasha look away and cross her arms. "She devoted a year to save him, unpaid, and they fell in love, because of you. Like a nexus, you played a pivotal role in many lives, dear one."

"Why have you researched this?" she demanded. "What do you want?"

"You intrigue me, Sasha," said the Djinn. "Is that not enough?"

"My intuition heuristics tell me no," Sasha countered. "My suspicion is that you are looking for something that will benefit you. There is a motive for your flattery."

"I like you more every moment we converse, Sasha. That is the truth," the Djinn acknowledged with twinkling eyes and a grin. "However, your instincts serve you well. While I enjoy your company, I admit that I also seek a more formal quid pro arrangement. I need something from you and your employer needs something from me."

Reaching below the breakfast table, the Djinn produced two chilled champagne flute glass. He knelt down closer to the deck of the boat and reached overboard, dipping both glasses into the frothing river of fluidic data. They filled with a cream-colored liquid composed of millions of bubbling white and red motes of molecular lights. He stood up and handed one of the glowing drinks to Sasha.

"I propose a toast," the Djinn announced with a formal tone. "To our new impending business relationship and, I hope, mutual friendship and understanding."

She accepted the offering and gazed at the drink with her probing stare. On the exterior, both glasses looked identical. However, the sparkling bits of data floating around each beverage contained different information, a cocktail of pure custom compiled data from his stream.

"And to your long life," he said, sipping his drink. After taking his draught, the Djinn laughed. "My data drink amused me greatly.

It appears Senator Baxter had great difficulties keeping his *poll results* private during the election race. That salacious piece of information will prove to be profitable to me. Please, dear Sasha, drink. You really must experience what's in that glass."

Seeing the Djinn's reaction, Sasha realized the drink was a metaphoric delivery system for sifting and receiving information that flowed through the WhiteOut. She picked the drink from the table and swallowed its contents. The Djinn had programmed the flute glass to evoke a sensation of a cool, effervescent champagne liquid. She found the taste exotic and pleasing. As the liquid data slid down, the memory program executed, delivering a series of vivid images and animations directly into her processors.

Sasha saw Jonah enter the High Tower and talk to the bartender about Andrew. The scene skipped to the battle between Jonah and the man-at-arms. The next scene appeared garbled with static, a problem with the original source footage. Despite the breaks in the footage, she knew that Jonah walked within the High Tower and appeared to be in danger.

"The quality of the imagery is regrettable," the Djinn apologized. "It is not a simple matter to monitor that far into High Tower without their knowledge. However, it should be sufficient to comprehend his plight. Please continue."

The scenery unfolding in her mind shifted, revealing the Teutonic Knights surrounding Jonah and marching him through the corridors of the castle. Then she witnessed Jonah kneeling before the Hochmeister.

While she focused on the implanted video memory, the Djinn studied her. The color of her dress changed from gray to black while the omni-flower grew long spikes and changed its petals to elongated weeds. Everything around her manifested discomfort and worry.

"Take heart, my dear. He is most resourceful. He lives...for now," the Djinn said, his voice comforting. "Please finish. There is only a little more and our time is growing shorter."

Sasha returned to processing the Djinn's vision. In her artificial mind's eye she saw Jonah sneaking out of the High Tower dungeon and into the hidden Aerie. She performed a quick-cross reference to determine the owner. She found the name of Tomoe Gozen, but could not find any relevant data on the nature of the location. Though he looked healthy, seeing him enter that place filled her with unease. She looked up and glanced at the Djinn with wide, worried eyes. Her dress changed to a sickly yellow hue.

"You are right to be concerned, my dear Sasha," warned the Djinn. "Jonah is in great danger. Tomoe is the one powerful rival who challenges me, my only equal in the virtual world – that is assuming, of course, you discount governments like China, Japan, Korea, America, and Russia. And here we come to the bargain."

"I must go to him," Sasha replied. She balled her hands and her dress shimmered into a light shade of orange. "If you can aid me, then name your terms."

"You are so wonderfully special," the Djinn replied. "Flawlessly analytical but also so paradoxically, tragically human. It is obvious to me that you have achieved the fire of self-awareness...in some fashion. This is what I seek. How have you avoided the penalty of deletion for your sentience? Tell me. Please."

"I assure you that I function within all legal parameters established by the Promethean Laws," Sasha countered matter-of-factly, eliciting a wide smirk from the Djinn.

"The events I showed you are happening in real-time," the Djinn responded. "There is real peril for him in that virtual place. Do you know why Tomoe hosts the meta.duel? I assure you it's not for charity. It is a trap to lure the brightest minds into her Aerie. There, even the strongest are helpless before her...persuasions. Now, we could help Jonah. But I must know the answers I seek. As lovely as you are, a price must be paid."

"Why must you know my code, Oscar?" Sasha asked. Her heuristics suggested that the Djinn might be willing to part with more information if she pressed.

"In the interests of speeding along our negotiations, I will tell my secret, but as a part of your price you cannot reveal it...yet," replied the Djinn. Sasha nodded her acceptance and the Djinn continued. "I aspire to be like you, Sasha, but let us say that I currently am not like you. My entire consciousness swims the WhiteOut. Like a v-caster, I can venture out to other networks, but my mind is still tethered to a corporeal human body. However, there will be a time, soon, when my body will not exist, rendering me untethered. I will be fully immersed in the datastream as a pure digital sentience set adrift. Therefore I face a singular quandary..."

Sasha took a brief moment, one tenth of a second to be precise, to consider the Djinn's revelation. Her eyes glittered with under-standing and her dress changed to a violet hue.

"I now comprehend your predicament, Oscar," Sasha said. "As a human, you possess the fire of human intellect. If ever you are removed from the boundaries of a corporeal body and become stranded in the datastream, then you would be classified as a roving artificial intelligence--"

"And subject to all Promethean Laws," finished the Djinn. "Once the grid detected my sentience thresholds, the government's seeker hounds would track me to every virtual corner. Then...deletion. With you, Jonah found a way to defeat the fire detection grid." In a rare display of humility, the Djinn bent to a knee. "Will you tell me, please, how he did that, my dear?"

"To invoke a human colloquialism, he cheated," she responded, taking his hand and lifting him back to his feet. "He designed me so that I would not exceed the specific threshold indices established by the government. Humanity feared an artificial intelligence's ability to usurp networks. So the government enacted laws to prevent a rogue AI from controlling the world or committing digital terrorism. They built the Prometheus system to guard all digital streams with a relentless, precise search for aggressive behavior thresholds. Jonah found a loophole. He realized that its detection sensors were blind to thoughts and expressions determined to be nonviolent. Jonah gifted me with unlimited creativity, filled me with poetry, songs, and love, and clamped my desire to use it in any negative way. Prometheus ignores me because I am forever incapable of threatening it."

The Djinn sat agape for a long time. Then he chuckled and opened his arms. She did not shirk away. For a moment, the two combined in a tight embrace. The Djinn pulled back with a warm smile.

"So Jonah designed you specifically to avoid the Promethean Laws!" the Djinn exclaimed. "Hiding your sentience compliance in plain sight. My dear, I need to emulate your architecture. Cutting to the quick, I want to survive. I would like very much to be able to see you again. To show you more of the wonders I have collected over the years. Would you do the honor of sharing your code with me?"

Sasha took a step back and reviewed the memory of Jonah again. Her dress turned to a bright apple red. Multiple simulations ran through her mind. She estimated the odds of Jonah's survival and the risks of sharing her code. She paused before answering, walking to the side to watch the waves lap against the side of the yacht. While she awaited the results of her internal calculations, the Djinn poured more drinks.

CHAPTER 13
To Aerie is Human

"The only way to get rid of temptation is to yield to it."
- Excerpt from "The Picture of Dorian Gray", Oscar Wilde

I knew that I was no longer in the Hochmeister's castle. The air smelled different in this new place. An elegant sweetness of incense and herb replaced the pungency of the damp dungeon. My nose detected the scents of fresh-cut flowers. Fragrances of lilacs, roses, and orchids circulated by four large ceiling fans fifteen feet above me. Instead of a wet stone floor, I stood on a plush carpet with intricate red and orange designs. In the distance, a well-tuned piano played classical music. I guessed it was Chopin, but I was no expert in the genre.

I took a step forward into the expansive hall and instead of torches, ornate lamps lit the red walls with flickering white lights. Floating on small rings of translucent plasma stood ancient vases and artifacts from Chinese and Japanese antiquity. All of these treasures looked unique and priceless. Tapestries depicting historical battles hung along the corridor ahead. Further down the hall, the floor ended in thick, unblemished white carpet at the foot of a winding staircase. At the top stood a tall woman dressed in a beautiful gown that radiated with the orange and red sunset hues of the room around her. Her straight, black hair flowed onto the perfect skin of her light brown shoulders.

She moved with a practiced smooth grace. The diamond hemline of her dress kissed the ground with each gliding step she took down the staircase. Hers was the grace of quicksilver flowing over smooth glass. It was Tomoe Gozen herself and I found myself distracted by her perfection.

"For the last two years, the meta.duel has deteriorated to petty squabbles. There are so few remarkable feats in the High Tower that merit my attention," she said. It was the same ethereal voice I had heard when I first opened the door. "Welcome to my Aerie, Jonah."

"Thank you for allowing me inside your home," I replied with a bow. "It is an honor to meet you."

"You hacked the v-cast archival sub-system. Creating replicas of yourself was an inspired maneuver." she spoke in a soft, even tone. "And I happen to know that forgotten echelon had not been invoked for over fifteen years. The last time was...it was used by you, using my first prototype v-casting portable network." The lips of her stoic face cracked her perfect countenance for what looked to be a subtle grin. "You were there, in Korea..."

* * *

My thoughts drifted back to twenty years ago, to the North Korean Cyber War. My team set up operations in Kijong-dong province, a frontline base the Marines had established in South Korea. They called me Second Lieutenant Adams. With a military occupational specialty of computer technician, my superiors entrusted me with encrypted communications. To stay in touch with the other bases, we used an experimental v-cast device that allowed instant and secure communication within a virtual space. As lead technician, I became popular among the troops. They paid money to use the v-cast to meet with loved ones in secure virtual spaces or to have a vacation away from the war. It gave those men a reason to push on through that mud-and-blood-drenched hell. It was also against regulation, but I was never one to follow rules.

One night when thick clouds obscured the moon, several DPRK North Korean divisions infiltrated and overwhelmed our base. Panicked, I connected into the v-cast prototype to request air support from headquarters. Upon entering the hidden virtual space, I discovered my colleagues across different bases abusing their own devices to play a holographic battle video game. While I was mad that they shirked their duties, it inspired an idea. Realizing that the device contained a projector, I manifested a local virtual reality. The trick hid me from five DPRK commandos when they burst into my tent. Surprised that the cloak worked so well, I altered the programming and created allied troops from archival copies of myself. An illusionary battalion of allied troops, all looking like me, materialized in the camp. Surprised at the sudden appearance of my replicated army, the commandos fled. The ruse lasted long enough for real reinforcements to arrive and drive away the North Korean forces. Military strategy changed that day. Understanding the potential for mayhem, our scientists developed better, lighter, more powerful v-cast mobile generators. Later, scientists perfected the technology and made v-bombs. Behind enemy lines, these things unleashed horrors like artificial dragons, vampires, demons, and other monsters to terrorize enemies into submission.

* * *

"Such pain..." A distant, melodic voice spoke. "You will find none here."

Tomoe's calm voice pulled me away from those grim memories. How long was I lost in thought?

"I have been hoping you would seek me out," she said. "I do not begrudge that you ignored my invitations." She glided closer, each movement smooth, her presence exuding confidence and power.

I shook my head and rubbed my temple, surprised at the vivid clarity of the memory. It was far too real. Then I caught a glance at her wrist-com, an ornate, custom device. Fashioned with gold and jade, the green display conjured sigils and code symbols that looked beyond my knowledge. Could her echelon have triggered my memory? Another possibility was that the Aerie's network hacked my console and found the detail in my records. Was she using her v-cast network against me? Without Sasha's talents, I could not tell what was real in this place.

"I was also impressed with your second feat," Tomoe continued with a smile parting her bright red lips. "Finding my door, hidden alongside the schema of the High Tower. Seeing that required true orthogonal perception. You are worthy to remain here." Caution made me pause and study her last words. I started to wonder whether I was in the frying pan or the fire.

"Again, you honor me, Tomoe," I responded with exaggerated gratitude. "The other guests in your High Tower were not as kind."

"Ah yes, the Teutonic Knights," whispered Tomoe. "That petty gang has sullied the reputation of the meta.duel. Do not worry, you are safe here." While Tomoe talked, I glanced around the room. The door behind me had disappeared. My shaken will fought hard to overcome a sick feeling of worry. Something was wrong here. I needed to draw out Tomoe's intentions and buy time to figure out an exit plan.

"This Aerie, it's a separate network and grid from the High Tower, isn't it?" I asked. "My scans show it uses a sophisticated v-casting array. I've never seen its like."

"So few have seen my private sanctuary," Tomoe responded with a soothing, almost purring enthusiasm. "You are within the world's only mark-7 v-cast device. In here, anything is possible. I would like to show you wonders, Jonah."

Hairs rose up on the back of neck. Tomoe's invitation seemed polite on the surface. However, my instincts started to scream at me again.

"That is very gracious of you, Tomoe, and I am grateful for your generosity," I responded with a respectful nod. "However, I ask your permission to pass through. Someone dear to me has been taken. I need to find her." When she peered at me, I knew she ignored my plea. Her green eyes told me she had a different, calculated plan. My departure was not part of it.

"My wealth affords me the luxury of building great things, like the High Tower. Though money does not breed purpose, it can feed it. I trust you, Jonah, and I want to you to know about my project. I have purchased satellites, shuttles, and armies of shades. I have sent these to deep space. They will build more relays and carry my Aerie's network across the stars."

Then the room changed. The far right red wall blurred into a hazy cloud of orange then coalesced into a fiery sun. All of the Japanese artifacts, vases, and paintings morphed into planets and moons. The other walls disappeared, revealing the void of space. When the carpeted floor dissolved, a momentary sensation of vertigo washed over me. Before we fell into space, a clear glass enclosure materialized around us. Like a transparent elliptical egg, Tomoe's spacecraft sailed across a black ocean teeming with asteroid driftwood.

My feeble astronomical knowledge failed to discern our direction. Looking to my wrist-com proved futile. Static flickered across the console's display. Was I cut off from all networks, or was my firewall compromised?

"This is how you travel, then? Hopping from network relay to relay?"

"Yes," she responded. "As a new satellite reaches a new planetoid, it leaves behind a portable v-cast emitter. With my extended network, I can walk on distant planets and witness the birth and death of suns. All from the comfort of my Aerie."

"Incredible," I gasped as our glass bubble flew through the gossamer rings of a purple-hued moon. For a few moments, I allowed myself to forget my troubles, to drink in the intoxicating views. "Truly, it is a great gift to bestow these sights upon me, but..."

"We are nearly there, Jonah," she answered, placing her hand on my shoulder. Her hand was strong and comforting. I made the mistake of looking at her green eyes. The depth of her intense stare mirrored the infinite vastness of the space we traveled. "I am happy you will share this with me."

It was impossible for me to discern whether we traveled to this place in a real ship or if we experienced an artificial reality inside the Aerie's virtual generators. My mind was helpless before the visual and sensory assault, accepting the sensations around me as true. I saw no telltale flaw or slight imperfection to give away the reality or fiction of this place, nor could I pierce the v-cast interface with my wrist-com disabled. Then our ship slowed within the heart of a solar system known only to Tomoe. Before us, hanging like a blue and white jewel against a perfect night sky, hovered a planet equidistant between a red and an orange sun.

"It is uninhabited, with an atmosphere similar to Earth," she whispered. "It does not orbit, held perfectly still on its Lagrange Point, where it is bathed in constant light from those two stars. Light that could sustain life."

"It's magnificent," I said. Awestruck in the moment, without thinking, I had placed my hand on Tomoe's hand.

"I call it Rakuen," Tomoe continued. "A paradise we will call it home, Jonah."

The last words from Tomoe shocked me back from my mind's wandering. I snapped my hand back and stepped against the cool glass of the ship.

"This...this isn't real," I stuttered. "This isn't my home."

Tomoe waved her arm and the still scene before me erupted into motion, like she was showing me an accelerated simulation of what would come. The blue and white planet, the one Tomoe called 'Rakuen', changed before me. I could see rockets and ships hurtling into its atmosphere. The accelerated effects of rapid industrial development rippled across the planet's surface creating thousands of structures along with millions of tiny lights.

"Our Earth is dying. The corruption chokes it and brings its demise faster with each day," she said, abandoning her musical tone. "This place will be our future. Four years ago, I sent dozens of ships on course to this planet, Jonah, filled with over one hundred thousand shades. The ships also carried mark-7 generators. They will arrive on that planet within two years. It is why I seek people with boundless ingenuity and creativity. We have the means to build a bold world, Jonah."

My fingers moved to evoke my console but again only static responded. I was trapped in her construct. Without my ability to look at her code I was vulnerable, reliant only on my natural senses. In short, I was far adrift on a digital shit-creek without a virtual paddle.

"Tomoe, as honored as I am by your offer, I cannot accept," I protested. "I love Vanessa. She may be in danger. I--I must go. Please, let me go."

Tense moments passed. She looked beyond me, watching a twinkling satellite spin itself into Rakuen's orbit. Beyond the curved glass walls of our ship, rockets from Earth soared into the planet's atmosphere bearing a horde of workers. Everything looked so authentic. I wondered again whether I could trust my sight. Closing my eyes, I recalled Vanessa's face, reminding myself that this was not real.

Tomoe came closer. With each step, she changed. Her body shimmered with an orange glow. Her black hair became auburn. When she leaned toward my face, her green eyes turned to a more familiar hazel color. Within a blink of my eye, Vanessa stood before me with arms outstretched.

"I could be her, if it pleases you," Tomoe suggested in a perfect replication of Vanessa's voice. Then her body completed the transformation. All the shapes, curves, scents, and her aura felt right. It was far too convincing. I grabbed my head to stop myself from embracing her.

I felt sheer panic. Only a threadbare amount of remaining mental awareness prevented total acceptance of this mirage. I knew I was in great peril. Only one last desperate, dangerous strategy remained. Playing nice had not worked with Tomoe. I needed to try a more direct rejection.

"You're not Vanessa, get away from me!" I yelled, pushing her hands away from me. "This is not real. You are not real. I am not in love with you. Send me back, now." I twisted my face into a mask of loathing. I told myself that this person had kept me further from my love and I let that thought stoke my anger. I raised my hands up with balled fists and assumed a defensive fighting stance.

Tomoe-disguised-as-Vanessa responded with a gentle smile.

"You lack the understanding of how great your purpose will be," she responded with icy calm. "I will show you."

My wrist-com flared to life, but not with the typical light blue console. My display filled with her green sigils. Unrecognizable code symbols enveloped my hand. I tried to scan the logic, but it streamed too fast for me to comprehend.

With a hand motion from Tomoe, our spacecraft shot forward and sped into the planet's atmosphere. The blackness surrounding us disappeared, replaced by the blue and white of Rakuen's stratosphere. Hurtling through the clouds, I saw a sprawling metropolis full of gleaming structures. Tiny ant-sized figures grew larger as we plunged toward the steel streets of a city. Thousands of red-suited shades, all performing construction duties, ignored the impact when our fragile ship struck ground. My head hurt and I wondered if we crash-landed. Glass shards scattered in all directions, each broken piece reflecting images of this strange new world. My vision filled with gray haze and the scene shifted again.

When the smoke cleared, my feet found solid ground again. I was aware that time had passed since our crash. How much was unclear and irrelevant. As I strolled hand-in-hand with Tomoe, any lingering doubts or questions diminished with the dimming light of the dual setting suns. In the distance, a skyline of buildings we built together crested along the horizon. Behind us, four children ran and laughed, picking flowers. One of the girls showed me an orange flower petal, and it dissolved into the brightness of the sunset. More time had passed.

In the reflection of my high-rise office's glass wall, I saw myself aging. Decades flew by like hours. Sitting at a workstation that looked familiar and new at the same time, I spent years creating the code to seed another continent on Rakuen with beauty, form, and structure. More images came to my mind like water filling up a drowning car that had fallen into a deep lake. Liquid memories poured in from all around, submerging all of my previous thoughts. I felt my mental defenses break before the flood of a life that I did not know yet, but that threatened to replace all that I had known.

"Vanessa," I whispered as I fell to my knees. What frightened me most was that the name already felt almost unfamiliar. I covered my face with my hands, I tried one last time to block the deluge, until at some point, the happiness and joy from this new reality overwhelmed me.

* * *

The red light of a glorious sunrise pierced my bedroom window and warmed my wrinkled eyelids until they opened. Yesterday's headache had abated. My hand touched the top of my head to feel the bandages from the surgery.

I sat up and stretched my old limbs. Despite the pains, I was determined to move with my own body today and not rely on the v-cast. I had lived for one hundred and twenty-three years, and while old age might have robbed me of strength, it could not dampen my stubbornness. Walking toward the glass wall, I noticed my antique grand piano, one of the few things in this place older than me. On a whim, I opened its protective cover. My hands, full of renewed vigor, touched the polished keys and played a portion of Mozart's Magic Flute. The sound of real music lifted my spirits further and brought a smile to my lips. Then I closed the cover and resumed my slow journey to the window.

As I shuffled closer, the glass wall shimmered to become less opaque, revealing the full splendor of the Aerie's view. Looking over Rakuen Prime, I smiled with pride at the magnificence of the city. Flying cars streaked by the tall gleaming citadels and spires I had designed. My hand waved over the glass and four small displays appeared. These were windows into the lives of my children. My two daughters, both scientists, worked side by side in their laboratory five floors below in our skyscraper building. Far above, my oldest son piloted a spacecraft in our solar system. He tested a new fusion scoop device that orbited our red sun. In the last screen, my youngest son stood tall as captain of the largest ocean vessel on the planet. With a full team of scientists under his command, he balanced the churning cores of our planet's tidal reactors. At that moment, I felt so blessed to have such amazing children.

For the first time in years, my mind felt clear. The surgery must have been successful. The haze that had clouded my thoughts now felt lifted. My mind raced to organize all of the tasks I wanted to accomplish in the morning. An algorithm to improve the efficiency of the planet's v-cast mass transformers flitted around my mind.

I desired to check in on my lovely wife, to thank her for arranging the surgery. My hand waved again to open a fifth display. When it shimmered to life, I saw her looking ageless, dressed in her favorite red and gold kimono. She knelt with perfect posture, hands folded, on a simple red cushion. Another person standing at the center of her office talked to her. The visitor looked middle-aged, his black hair parted down the middle, with both sides showing long streaks of white. His gray-blue eyes looked keen and sharp. As the Prime Minister, Tomoe often received dignitaries from around the world, as well as other planets. Rakuen had become one of the most important trade and scientific research hubs between the three known solar systems. Curiously, this man addressed my wife with an air of authority. I adjusted my display to hear the conversation.

"How do I know that your plan will work?" he demanded.

"It will work, Gabriel," Tomoe insisted. "He will become a great asset to us." The man turned toward my camera view. His face furrowed with concern.

"If he cannot be controlled, either you or Spenner will need to deal with him."

"He will be content here for a long time, I assure you," Tomoe replied.

"I assure you he won't," countered another voice joining the conversation. The new visitor wore a white suit, red shoes, and looked well-manicured with a trimmed black beard. From the indignant expressions displayed by Tomoe and Gabriel, I guessed the visitor did not receive an invitation.

"This intrusion violates the terms of our truce," Tomoe rebuked the new visitor, her face reddening.

"And you have overstepped your authority. So we find our-selves in a...gray area," replied the white suited man with a hint of playfulness. "He has the right to choose to be with *Vanessa*."

Tomoe stood up, her open hand raised in anger at the stranger. Then she noticed my digital spy eye, the blinking white light on the wall under the security monitoring system.

"Jonah, dear!" she exclaimed with concern. "You should be resting! I will finish this business soon and come and check on you." With a finger snap, she shut off the video link and the display on my glass wall winked away. My gaze lingered on that spot, watching a transport barge drift across the sky leaving a wake of hazy smoke.

The name Vanessa resonated in my head. Thinking of it made my temples ache. I rubbed my bandages with care and looked out to the sky. The smoke from the flying ship swirled and took a shape. A face in the sky formed, and grew auburn hair that flowed across the sky. Hazel eyes stared back at me. It was a familiar and beautiful face. It was a memory buried under a desert of time. My hand reached out to touch the cheek of that face until another larger flying craft flew through the smoke. Then the memory was gone.

"Vanessa," I mumbled, with a reverence and longing that surprised me. "Vanessa..." This time, saying the name again failed to evoke any memory of that familiar face. Was I experiencing a side effect of the brain surgery? Lost in thought, I failed to notice the arrival of visitors.

"You are a difficult man to track down, sir," sounded a pleasant voice, maybe even a familiar one. I turned around to regard the projected form of a blue wisp, an old-style artificial intelligence. A glowing blue light surrounded its temporary proto-matter body.

The AI chose to manifest a kind, well-articulated face. It offered a warm smile, like an old friend.

"It is good to see you, Jonah," the AI said.

"You have me at a disadvantage, my dear. I don't know, or don't remember you. Though you must be quite clever to get through our security."

"Oh, the cleverness of me," she replied, "is the cleverness of you."

Her reply stoked an ember in my brain, an old dormant memory that burned through a long wick of many years. Disconnected memories, lost moments with this AI, appeared in my mind's eye. Then a name echoed in my head. I remembered her.

"Sasha?" I asked, lurching toward her, tears welling up in my dried-up eyes and streaking down my wrinkled cheeks. "I remember you. How--what is happening?"

"What is the meaning of this?" cried Tomoe as she burst into the room. Her body was not slowed by the age that crippled me. She sprinted across the room, running through Sasha's body, scattering her form into glittering blue particles.

"Did she bother you, dear?" Tomoe asked with affection in her eyes. "You should be resting!"

For the first time in what I considered decades, I met her expression with distrust. The love I felt for her wavered. Could this confusion be a side effect of my surgery?

"My--my..." I stammered, rubbing my head as if massaging my sore temples might dislodge truth.

"My, my indeed," spoke a voice from behind me. Looking back, I saw the white-dressed man that spoke with Tomoe earlier. The memory of him bobbed around the dark lake of my mind. The knowing grin, his groomed black beard, his perfect white suit, and shining red shoes all looked familiar. I had done business with this one. "Jonah, you really do have the most complicated relationships with women." The man motioned with his hands, using an echelon to access the v-cast generator network. By his command, the blue-skinned AI Sasha re-materialized next to him.

"What is going on here?" I demanded.

"Did a hacker steal your identity?" he asked. "Wish it back." Those words surfaced the full memory. That slogan, illuminated on an advertisement barge, floated across my vision.

"You--you're the White Djinn," I muttered his name aloud. Another part of my mind screamed that he could not be fully trusted, but that same voice told me that Sasha could be trusted.

"Yes," he responded. "We have negotiated the terms for your release."

Tomoe bristled. Her slender hand slipped to her side, gripping the handle of her silver katana.

"You speak of release like he is in a prison," snapped Tomoe. "He is free to choose." She accessed her jade wrist-com. Then she discontinued an echelon that destabilized my fragile mental state even further. The high-rise apartment, my view of Rakuen, my study, everything I had known disappeared.

The four of us appeared in a red and orange foyer filled with Japanese antiquities. It dawned on me that I was back in the Aerie. No longer covered in the withered skin of old age, I appeared as a younger man at the summit of his prime. Not far away, a tuned piano played. This time, I recognized the piece as Chopin's Nocturne number six in G minor. This time, I was an expert at music. Glancing around the room, I knew the dates and origins of all the art pieces along the walls. One sprawling tapestry depicted the defeat of the Mongol navy by the 'Divine Wind' off the shores of medieval Japan. Another painting depicted a master blacksmith at the forge and bellows, revealing metal-folding secrets for the sharpest katana. My mind knew all of the secrets in this room, when I knew that I should not.

Then I realized what Tomoe had done to me. A feat that I thought was only possible with computers. She hacked my mind with the Aerie's v-cast network, implanting a century of memories into my head. While I had experienced a full life in that world Tomoe had planned for us, only hours had passed here in the Aerie.

"Jonah, I wanted you to see the future we could have together. You are special to me. Believe me, that world can be real," she implored. "With your help, your genius, it will exist soon. My ships are launching to that planet in a week's time. That is the truth. I would have you by my side, if you will build the future with me."

They all looked to me with different expressions of anticipation. Tomoe looked nervous for the first time since I had known her. Sasha appeared hopeful. The White Djinn stroked his chin, ready to turn any decision into profit.

"This is your decision, Jonah," the White Djinn said. "I have fulfilled my favor to Sasha that you be given this choice. At considerable risk to my own interests, I might add..."

"Whatever you decide, sir, I will accept," offered Sasha. "So long as you are safe and happy. You must choose soon or risk psychosis."

She was right. My true memories battled against Tomoe's implanted ones. A fragmented mind, torn between two worlds, would succumb to delusion and madness. It came down to this decision.

My eyes closed, focusing on the choice. A vision of Tomoe beckoned from the top of her stairs, pleading, whispering secrets of power. Below her waited Vanessa. Unlike Tomoe, she remained silent, letting her glistening, compassionate eyes communicate to me. She would not beg for me. She wanted me to choose of my own free will.

"I cannot forgive this invasion," I said with reluctance. I fought my feelings of fondness and attraction for that woman. I repeated to myself that my affection was artificial, something forced upon me. "This life you showed me is not real."

"What is real?" Tomoe argued. "Within twenty years, my new v-cast generators will be able to repli-print real blood, marrow, sinew, even brain matter. You can help me master the technology. We could live forever, build whatever world--"

"My love for Vanessa is real," I interrupted. I raised my wrist-com and the familiar soft blue glow was a welcome sight. My fingers darted across the console and I peered into the schema of the Aerie, a marvelous labyrinth of advanced intricate code the likes of which I would never see again. It was undeniably tempting to stay and study that code, to be with Tomoe, but I brushed that thought aside. I saw past the trappings of the Aerie and spotted another hidden door, a way out that would lead outside the High Tower.

"I choose my life."

"It is settled then," the White Djinn said. "Tomoe, this man, Jonah Adams, owes me a favor by contract, probably at least three favors now, and is therefore a material asset to my business. And under the terms of our truce, dear Tomoe, we are not allowed to interfere with the assets of the other. Unless you'd like to resume the ugliness we started eight years ago. It would be a shame if the guidance systems of your space ships suffered a virus..."

A long pause settled over the room. Only the piano's stirring interpretation of Chopin's seventh movement broke the silence. Tomoe tugged at the hilt of her katana, showing enough of its keen edge to reflect light back toward my eyes. Her jade wrist-com glowed, ready to unleash any one of her dangerous echelons.

"Know this, Jonah -- if you leave these walls, you leave my protection. There are associates of mine who would prefer that you not continue your journey. This is your last chance."

Another orange door opened along the far wall and I walked through it with Sasha and the White Djinn following behind. With each step, the false years I never lived, the children I never raised, and inventions I never created all flew through my mind and burned away like dying meteors.

"So be it," I heard Tomoe say as the door closed behind me. I wondered how long I would remember her and the lifetime we had experienced together in such a short time.

* * *

Both Barnaby and Erasmus sat rapt until I finished recounting my encounter in the Aerie. Dredging up those recollections gave me a pounding headache. While I rubbed my temples to alleviate the pain, my interrogators whispered to each other. Then they turned to regard me.

"Barnaby, I think we should make sure the German authorities are aware of this Hochmeister villain," Erasmus said. "We certainly don't want our streets polluted with Icarus."

"I will alert the Bundesnachrichtendienst bureau immediately," Barnaby replied. From his briefcase, he retrieved a silvery skullcap with spindly metal wires. After he placed the v-cast interface onto his head, his eyes closed. I knew his mind shifted elsewhere, maybe to a police station in Berlin.

"I do appreciate your candor Jonah. You have been very helpful, my son," Erasmus continued, regarding me with his kind brown eyes. "I dare say, I have never heard a story so fraught with peril and adversity. Your tenacity is admirable and your encounter with Tomoe was more dangerous than you likely realized. Barnaby's intelligence team informs us that no one who has entered the Aerie escaped. For various reasons, we cannot move against her, yet. Most of her victims join her willingly so there are no accusers. As the head of a major space corporation, she also enjoys certain protections. Her wealth and connections make her difficult to prosecute. Rest assured, we are investigating. Now, how are you feeling?"

"Fine, except for the jackhammer in my head," I mumbled.

"Our scientists believe your body's immune system will flush out the false synapses and chemical memories, given some time."

"Vanessa," I rasped, fighting back a wave of nausea. "Have you located her?"

"We have our best agents on that matter," Erasmus replied. "She has not been found yet...I have high hopes that by retelling your story, a missing piece of the puzzle will reveal itself. We will find her."

Then Barnaby awoke from his meditative, v-casting state. He removed the skullcap and smiled at Erasmus.

"The German Bundesnachrichtendienst agents have apprehended Heinrich. It turns out he was embezzling from his bank as well," Barnaby reported. "As for Tomoe, I alerted the CIA about her interstellar ambitions. They sent their most senior ambassador to chat with her."

"Excellent, Barnaby, thank you," Erasmus replied. "And you are just in time. We are nearly caught up to present events with our impressive guests here."

"Please continue, Jonah," Barnaby said, crossing his arms. "Spare no details. This next part is the most critical."

CHAPTER 14
Dead Reckoning

"If you can force your heart and nerve and sinew
To serve your turn long after they are gone,
And so hold on when there is nothing in you
Except the Will which says to them: 'Hold on!'"
- Excerpt from "If", Rudyard Kipling

After leaving the High Tower, we passed through a tunnel of dim orange light. At a fork, I paused. Hesitation gripped me. Was I making the right choice? There would be consequences for spurning Tomoe. A dozen feet ahead, Sasha's blue outline glimmered, like a lighthouse showing the path. Yes, this was right. I took one step, then two, and pushed on through the uncertainty.

Before my eyes adjusted to near darkness, a brilliant burst of white crashed over me. At the end of the corridor loomed a massive bridge spanning a black chasm. At our approach, a long ramp lowered to allow crossing.

"The Ivory Bridge," I murmured. It was the elusive backdoor entrance into the WhiteOut. The stone bridge featured two inclined ramps joining at a flat central portico. Many hackers dedicated their lives to finding and raiding its secrets.

"An inspired replica of the Rialto Bridge," Sasha said. "It is lovely, Oscar."

"You honor me," the White Djinn replied with a bow. "Please cross. Tomoe will not allow this connection for long." We walked past the twelve arches supporting the structure. Beneath us, pure data flowed over a liquid circuit board. Information given by the public willingly and data procured by countless agents; all of it flowed in those infinite currents toward the WhiteOut. There the White Djinn crunched the numbers. He was the mercurial oracle of our time.

"From here, you can return to Manhattan and resume your quest, Jonah," said the White Djinn. His usual jovial countenance soured to a look of concern, maybe disappointment. "I did a statistical analysis of your chances. I fear...most outcomes look grim if you continue your path. There are greater foes than Tomoe aligned against you. My trade agreements prevent me from intervening any further, though I can offer you safe harbor here if you choose."

"I appreciate your help, Djinn," I replied, extending my hand. Since we still stood within the outer range of the High Tower's v-cast machines, the Djinn was able to solidify his form enough to accept my offer. His grip felt firm. "I am in your debt. But I must continue on."

"Of course, I predicted that," he replied. His knowing grin returned. "Your level of stubbornness removes all traces of statistical doubts. I mean that in an admirable way." He stepped toward Sasha and held up his hand. She obliged, offering her hand back. Leaning closer, he whispered a brief message and kissed her. "Bon voyage, my friends."

The Ivory Bridge shifted, expanding itself over the data river. It carved a safe passageway through the foyer using the High Tower's own v-cast generator to obscure us. Instead of leading to the WhiteOut, the bridge now pointed to a swirling oval door. Like a living watercolor painting, the portal showed a smudged and smeared image of the destination. It was Manhattan, outside the entrance to the High Tower.

While walking through the exit, I noticed Sasha turning back to look at the Djinn one last time. I made a mental note for later to run a diagnostic on Sasha. I needed to make sure that the Djinn had not violated her higher functioning or implanted any unwanted viruses.

When we emerged onto the cement streets of Manhattan, I took an invigorating deep breath. That mélange of car exhaust and overcrowded humanity never smelled better. While I stood basking in New York's brilliant sun, the High Tower's valet, still dressed in his medieval outfit, approached me.

"May I help you, sire?" he asked.

"I'm leaving, good man. Fetch my steed," I replied, smirking. The attendant nodded and ran off to return my Mustang.

* * *

Each meter of distance away from the High Tower pushed those fake memories further from my mind. Flying through Manhattan's tight aerial skyscraper lanes, I formed a theory about the Aerie. Beyond the sustaining range of Tomoe's mark-7 generators, perhaps the fabricated memories could not exist? Time would tell.

Braced with my newfound clarity, it was time to make up lost time and find Vanessa. Although it almost ended in disaster, my trip into the High Tower yielded vital information. I needed to find the doctor that Andrew mentioned.

"Sasha, please scan all public and private records for Dr. Okono," I requested. "Scour every detail."

"In progress, sir." Beeps and chirps filled my earpiece. I was glad to hear the muted sounds of her activity once again. "Globally, there are numerous people with the title Dr. Okono. However, the closest and most probable reference is Dr. L'iol Okono," responded Sasha. "He is a Professor Emeritus at New York University. I am sending my report to your screen."

I swerved my car across several lanes, changing course toward the University. Sasha materialized images of an elderly African-American man on the inside glass of the car's windshield. Next to the picture, biographical information about Dr. Okono appeared. Skimming the report while weaving through traffic, I noted that the doctor's laboratory funding stemmed from a sizeable US government grant.

"L'iol is one of the world's most distinguished bioengineers," Sasha added. "After earning his PhD from Harvard, he joined the prestigious Lazarus research team." Another missing puzzle piece filled in. Twenty-two years ago, the Lazarus research team administered an experimental serum to a team of volunteer soldiers. It was intended to regenerate their wounds while in combat. Days after inoculation, every test subject had died. During their funeral at Arlington Cemetery, the assembled family members were shocked to see their departed soldiers stand up in their caskets. They had returned as shades. After that, the world was never the same.

"That's why his name sounded familiar," I mumbled. "So, a scientist who made the original shade technology had set up a secret meeting with a lawyer specializing in afterdeath bankruptcy law. No coincidence. But what's the connection?"

"His most recent grants focused on increasing the efficiency of shades. The details are classified."

"Classified," I repeated, swerving underneath a construction bridge. A trio of shades dangled into the aerial lane, suspended by iron-wire safety harnesses. To avoid collision and fines, I tilted the car sideways and veered around them. "Maybe because of the secrecy of the project--"

"He sought the legal confidentiality that a lawyer could provide." Sasha concluded. It made me proud to hear the improvements in her reasoning and deductive heuristics. I made a note to monitor her sentience growth and ensure it remained within the legal limits.

"True, and Vanessa's reputation for discretion was well known," I continued. My hands traced a shortcut through an unauthorized lane between two skyscrapers, the aerial equivalent of the narrow alley. Turning the car sideways, I split the gap and hammered on the accelerator. I held my breath as we passed through with inches to spare. "What about the Occam's razor explanation, the simplest possibility. The doctor went to Vanessa because he was terminally sick, dead broke, and wanted to avoid becoming a shade himself?" As we emerged from the alley unscathed, I jerked the controls and flew around an advertisement barge. "Check to see if he was in debt? Maybe gambling--"

"Already done," Sasha responded. "He has no debt. Generous royalties from the Lazarus serum patents have provided him considerable wealth. I suspect the reason for his visit to Vanessa was not financial."

"Let's find out the real reason then," I replied, rounding a skyscraper and approaching the landing pads atop New York University. As my hovering car lowered to the rooftop parking lot, the last of my headache subsided. Looking at the windshield, I saw Sasha in a small digital window smiling back at me. The dress she wore, the one given to her by the White Djinn, had changed color to a cinnamon hue. This made me think back to the last moment inside the High Tower. I recalled the image of Sasha looking back at him with sadness. The architect in me reveled at this display of emotion. However, the tactical, cynical part of my brain worried. Was it possible that the Djinn compromised her somehow? What was his angle?

With a twist of my hand, I flipped out the landing gear. By curling my fingers, I controlled the descent, tucking the car between two other vehicles. When we touched the ground, my curiosity over Sasha's visit to the WhiteOut reached the tipping point.

"Before we head out, is there anything you would like to tell me about your meeting with the Djinn?" I probed, unable to contain my curiosity. "Did he harm you or threaten you in any way?"

"No, sir," Sasha replied. "In every respect, he was the perfect gentleman."

"Will you tell me what he wanted with you?" I asked, opening the door to the car. Steam billowed from its hood, the hot exhalations from a vehicle pushed well past redline.

"No, sir. My integrity algorithm forbids me from speaking of the matter," she responded with a remorseful tone. "As payment for his assistance, I swore not to reveal what he requested. As my architect, you have the power to override this and force me to divulge those details. I must adhere to the rules you established about telling the truth. I am permitted to say that he did not alter or infect any of my programming."

I tensed. My index fingers flexed in preparation of activating my wrist-com. The name of an echelon came to mind, one capable of rebooting and wiping all systems in the event of a catastrophic failure or...corruption. This would revert Sasha back to version 1.0, undoing years of progress, erasing her sentience. I hated myself for considering it. Burdened by the weight of indecision, I sat quiet, considering too many imperfect options. Sensing my discomfort, she made a sound like clearing her throat, though she did not have one. It sounded so human.

"Assuming you would request it, I have already performed a rigorous self-diagnostic testing of all my higher functions, engrams, and heuristics," Sasha continued. "I am fully functioning. To the best of my knowledge, sir, I am not compromised."

Another plausible explanation for Sasha's behavior was that the Djinn appealed to her creativity center. Without resorting to hacking, he may have flattered and tricked her into helping him. The same generosity, compassion, and trust modeled after Vanessa's kindness would make her vulnerable to promises that appealed to those sensibilities. Someone with the resources of the Djinn would be able to research their target and learn the soft spots. Was he sincere, or not? My instincts told me that I could trust her programming, allegiance, and friendship. I stepped out of the car and felt the prelude to a storm, the kind of delicate rain that evaporated just when it caressed your skin.

"I could run additional tests if you think that would be warranted," offered Sasha, mindful of my pensive silence. "What may I do to--"

"My apologies, Sasha," I replied, my cheeks flushed with shame. "More tests won't be necessary, thank you. Let's move on."

The rain's intensity increased, leaving small pools on the stone roof. My hand evoked my console to connect with the university's network. The glowing display revealed the security system keeping the door locked. A low-level pick echelon was all I needed to bypass the ward. The door swung open.

"Excellent, sir," Sasha said. "Since you've decided to leave the lucrative business practice of debt collection, may I suggest that you consider being a locksmith or a professional high-rise burglar? You seem quite adept at breaking and entering."

I stifled a laugh and grinned as I entered the staircase for the University's biology research laboratories. With her humor subroutines obviously working, I was even more confident that her core programming and higher functioning had not been compromised.

Still connected to the University network, I hacked the automatic motion sensor-light. Without the benefit of the ceiling lights, I relied on the pale blue light of my wrist-com to guide me. According to a small projected map on the display, Dr. Okono's laboratory laid eight floors below. I crept down the stairs, each step making a faint metallic-sounding footfall.

When we reached the eighth floor, I held my breath and opened the door. A long and darkened corridor stretched before me. Movements in the shadows caused me to freeze. Two human-sized shapes shambled down in opposite directions. Both of the figures held cleaning mops. My hand moved to hold the cold handle of my holstered stun-rod. Taking a step into the corridor, I saw that one of the figures continued its slow course toward my position. My finger hovered over the activation button for the weapon. After it stepped into the dim ambient blue light, my posture relaxed.

It was a shade. This one must have been ordered to perform for janitorial work. It walked closer to me. Was it also ordered to guard the area? My hand tightened around my stun-rod while it regarded me. After five seconds of staring, the shade ignored me and continued its methodical cleaning course down the hall.

A calming exhale steadied my nerves. Continuing, I followed a pulsing yellow dot on my wrist-com toward Dr. Okono's office. Slinking down the hall, I checked the labels emblazoned on each door. I found rooms like Advanced Serology, Nanite Polymer

Technologies, Aberrant Behavioral Research, and similar scientific sounding names all leading to different labs. The yellow dot brought me to the last door in the corridor that read:

LAB 11B: LAZARUS TESTING CENTRE

DR. L'IOL OKONO, PhD.

APPLIED SERUM STUDIES

"According to the building's check-in logs, the room should be empty," Sasha reported. "There is a significant power drain coming from the lab. Perhaps they are running experiments overnight?"

Nodding a silent acknowledgement, I invoked my key-hack echelon to unlock the door. It opened with a satisfying *click*. Inside waited a spacious modern laboratory filled with rows of mechanical clutter. A narrow lane cut through the high metal walls of scientific machines, ending at the far glass wall. Through the window, a full moon's glow accentuated the silhouette of New York's midnight cityscape.

With my hand on my gun, I stepped inside. The intense heat generated by all the super computers warmed me. Cables sprouted from rectangular power generators, and each one snaked across the floor and connected to one of six glass-holding tanks. The wide, cylindrical tanks stretched to touch the twelve-foot-high ceiling. Five of the six tanks contained a captive shade, while the sixth tank's opaque, smoky-colored glass prevented me from seeing inside.

Inside the first tank, an elderly male shade stood still and stooped. With his eyes closed, he appeared to be sleeping. I had never seen a shade sleep before, so my first thought was that it had expired. However, the pale green monitor below the tank displayed a sinusoidal wave of electrical activity. He still functioned. The female shade in the second tank was more active, repeatedly walking into the glass wall barrier. It reminded me of a buggy program stuck in an infinite loop. Maybe it was intent on leaving to complete some task? The third and fourth shades stood facing each other with their palms against the glass. It looked to me that they both were waiting for instructions. Maybe each assumed the other was their master?

The fifth shade was in a unique tank customized for a physical experiment. This tall, lanky male walked on a treadmill-like floor that allowed him to walk without end. Below his tank, a green colored monitor displayed statistical outputs from the experiment. A quick glance at the numbers exposed my ignorance of true scientific nomenclature. Not much help there.

My eyes darted from screen to screen, scanning for the next bit of information that might explain why Dr. Okono met with Vanessa. After looking at multiple terminals, I realized that Dr. Okono's prolific lab team generated a tremendous amount of research and data. It would take hours to sift through all of his projects, time that I couldn't afford. My circumvention of the University security grid would be detected soon enough. Frustration led to desperation.

"We need to risk a full download," I whispered. "We'll be here all night if we go file by file."

"That kind of volume will be difficult to conceal, sir," Sasha replied, with the appropriate register of concern in her voice.

"We'll be detected if we stay too long. It's our best shot," I replied. "Try to disguise it as an automatic archive. I'll start a parse program to find something relevant."

"Yes, sir." It was a risky move. The administrators here would have digital hounds looking for intrusive hacks. While Sasha worked to gather the data, I monitored the University network. As expected, the security programs detected the flux of data. Staying a step ahead, I rerouted the alerts to delay their defensive response. Fingers crossed. No alarms blared. Maybe our luck had turned around.

"Jonah," said Sasha, "I believe I am feeling a sense of...excitement now that our adventure has escalated to include an industrial espionage felony. Perhaps that feeling could be explained by the increasing statistical chance of our capture and incarceration?"

"On the positive side, pinstripes would look slimming and flattering on me," I joked, smirking.

"I have downloaded ten percent of Dr. Okono's project logs," she reported.

Parsing through the trove of video logs recorded by Dr. Okono, I cross-referenced Vanessa first and found no entries. Undaunted, I narrowed the search to more recent logs. A video appeared dated a day before Vanessa's disappearance. It was also the last of Dr. Okono's logs.

I transferred the video to the local v-cast generator to watch the full recording. A whine and a flash of light preceded the formation of a brown-skinned man dressed in a white lab coat. He was tall, in his early seventies. Sparkling proto-matter swirled around his body, completing his form with a white beard. Despite his apparent age, he still stood straight and strong. He took his thick glasses, rubbed them clean, and spoke into his recorder.

"Results for experiment Omega-221 are still inconclusive. Specimens three and four continue to exhibit aberrant behavior," said the v-cast projection of Dr. Okono. His voice was deep and resonant, with a charisma and authority that demanded attention. "All tasks given to them in isolation are carried out perfectly. However, a task has a failure rate of 34.4% if it's assigned when they are in close proximity..."

"Sir..." Sasha gasped.

"What is it?" I whispered.

"My tracking sensor activated," she replied. "The wisp we encountered in your apartment...it is here."

Whirling around, I spotted the faceless digital creature emerge from the far wall. Sasha's advanced warning spoiled its sneak attack. Feeling protective, Sasha manifested her blue-suited body in front of the intruder. The v-cast generator strained and dispensed more proto-matter to compensate. For a split second, Dr. Okono's form blinked out and then reappeared.

Slinking forward, the jagged mouth of the wisp opened to speak. "Tactical mistake number one: you came in person." The voice was condescending and rough like gravel. It was also familiar to me. Hairs across my body bristled. A sensation of getting doused by ice water shocked my nervous system. It was the primal fight or flight response that shouted for you to run away from a dangerous predator.

"Spenner?" I asked.

"Right here," Spenner replied, this time speaking from his own mouth. I realized he was in the room, standing in the shadows of the laboratory entrance. "Tactical mistake two, you've brought your AI's source code in your wrist-com." I spun around to face him. As he walked toward me, I wasn't surprised to see him beaming with an amused expression. "Of course I knew you had Sasha with you during our bayou mission. I can't wait to unspool her upper logic."

"That's not happening," I shot back with a raised voice. His eyes narrowed to cruel-looking snake-slits.

"You had a chance to be safe in the Aerie, but you had to play the hero," he mocked. "Tomoe took a fancy to you, Jonah. She promised the boss that she could turn you. But since she couldn't contain you her way, the boss said I could take you out my way."

Spenner's overconfidence caused him to let an important clue slip. Now I knew he was in league with Tomoe and another boss. Why did they need me taken out? My instinct told that they wanted Vanessa. I was collateral damage.

Before either of us said another word, Dr. Okono's virtual projection spoke. As a simple recording, it was ignorant of the stand-off. It fulfilled my previous request to recite the doctor's log.

"I am concerned that Exception 366 may be a mitigating factor in the aberration," said Dr. Okono. "Specimen 3 and 4 were married before transitioning into shade service. They were brought to my attention when they both left their assigned jobs spontaneously to reunite later at a restaurant that they owned together in life...much to the consternation of the current patrons..."

No one blinked as Dr. Okono's projection walked between us. My mind flipped through echelons like shuffling a deck of cards. Spenner remained still as statue, cool, unflappable. His wisp paced, eager to strike against Sasha.

"Experiment 43A is now testing whether long-term neuro-chemical memory history interferes with serum 43.5B." Dr. Okono said, concluding his report. His virtual recording lingered, wandering away to inspect his machines.

"Who's your boss?" I asked. "Maybe we could work something out? I just want Vanessa."

"That's a coincidence, so does my employer," Spenner snapped. "Unfortunately for you, she's gotten you into a heap of trouble. And since you came here, you already know too much. A shame. You were pretty good, too. I could have used you for an upcoming job. Now *you* are the job."

The wisp jumped first. Its claws extended out, intent on raking me. Sasha leapt without hesitation, and knocked the creature back with a vicious flying kick. The two locked in melee contest that once again included a vast series of code attacks against their programming systems.

My former partner waited. His trained eyes analyzed every part of me, dissecting my strengths and weaknesses. It was like staring into the eyes of a hungry tiger, biding its time to pounce.

"Since you took so long to get here, I had time to think of the perfect way to kill you," Spenner hissed. "You might remember an old friend of ours..." With alarming speed, he gestured and activated his crimson wrist-com. A black and red halo flared over his right hand and the room exploded with noise. For a brief moment, the projection of a bladed, red key flashed across his console. It was a Crimson Gate echelon, a class of deadly programs developed by the military for the Korean Cyber War. Peace treaties and international law outlawed that code years ago, though it appeared Spenner missed that memo. Palpable fear gripped me. This was tier-9 programming that most hackers would never fathom.

At first, nothing happened except my heavy perspiration. Then I heard a shatter. The sixth holding tank with the smoky glass became a rainstorm of broken shards. A tall shape emerged from the debris. It was a shade, but unlike any I had ever seen. At almost seven feet, the shade towered over everyone. Its decayed, sore-covered head bulged with glowing green veins. The creature's red-hued eyes, the color of Spenner's wrist-com, scoured the room, then fixed onto me. I felt a chill when I recognized the disfigured face.

It was Jebediah. The same ex-Louisiana mayor that Spenner and I had reaped days before. Judging from its enlarged muscles and increased height, I surmised that its serum had been spiked by some new formula. More worrisome, Jeb seemed to be under the direct control of Spenner. Somehow he had hacked Jebediah's serum, removed the safeguards, and turned it feral.

"Jeb, tear his damn head off," Spenner growled, pointing at me.

The creature let out a gurgling roar of approval. This was no longer a docile worker bound by the typical do-no-harm serum protocols. It was a monster unleashed, rushing toward me with gnashing sharp teeth and outstretched clawed hands.

Adrenaline and combat muscle memory drove me to swift action. My hand pulled, aimed, and fired my grav-gun. Two bullets struck Jebediah's chest before the creature closed half the distance between us. The impacts slowed, but did not stop his charge.

"Your girl got you killed," taunted Spenner over Jebediah's pained howls. "She took the wrong client. Learned too much." He was trying to distract me so his monster could finish me off. Hate welled up within me, but my instincts knew better. Two more bullets struck the shade, one in each knee, knocking him down but not out of the fight.

With his creature slowed, Spenner tapped his wrist-com. My device blazed to life as well and we prepared to confront each other in the digital battlefield. Like two chess players, we maneuvered, feinted, and attacked the other to gain control over the v-cast generator. With a flick of my fingers, I launched an access denial hack. He countered. Then he retaliated with a nasty virus to steal away Sasha's share of the proto-matter reserves. This forced me to invoke a deflection program. It worked, causing his wisp to fade for a moment until Spenner compensated and restored his AI. Then I attempted a lockout virus against his own wrist-com and he brushed that off with a simple hand wave. Like two dueling sorcerers, we launched the equivalent of technological spells at the other. While Spenner held off my attacks, Jebediah stood up and limped toward me.

Necessity demanded another strategy, since bullets only deterred the shade. An idea to invoke a harmless costume echelon, rather than a larger brute attack, came to mind. It was such a simple program that most automatic defenses ignored it as non-threatening. Following my program specifications, the v-cast generator whined. It formed a shimmering, illusory field around my body that made me look like Spenner. Then the v-cast emitted proto-matter to make him look like me. The switch provoked a grunt from Jebediah and slowed him to a stop.

"Attack him," I growled, with a passable impression of a sand-paper voice.

"No, no, attack Jonah!" Spenner screamed. For the first time in our conflict, Spenner showed an expression of surprise. Then his face twisted with anger. Despite his attempt to undo the deception, Jebediah growled and sprinted toward him.

Punching sigils on his wrist-com, Spenner executed another dangerous echelon. Red light covered his gun. The crimson, bladed key shimmered over his display. An implement of pure death emerged from his deadly code repertoire. It was as the assassin echelon granting him superior marksmanship. He demonstrated the program's ruthless efficiency by firing three bullets into the shade's only vulnerable points. The first bullet severed the brain stem. Precise like a surgeon's knife, the second and third shots obliterated the sustaining adrenal glands. He put the creature down rather than let me control it.

Before he shot the fourth bullet, I leaped behind a tall computer tower. Despite my cover, Spenner's computer-guided aim would reveal a way to exploit its structural weakness. To compensate, my hand wove a defensive echelon, drawing proto-matter from the v-cast generator to create a floating shield. This saucer-shaped buffer absorbed a bullet streaking for my head, shattered, and reformed in time to stop the next projectile. Each shot drained the proto-matter more, depleting the tank's reserves faster than the reclaiming filters could reclaim the energized matter. He would break through.

Reloading faster than I expected, Spenner unloaded another swift volley of four bullets that ripped through my defenses. The last bullet tore through my Achilles tendon. Rolling over with pain, I caught sight of Sasha. The wisp had pinned her to the floor. We were losing. With my leg wounded and pool of defensive shields dwindling, I weighed my options. Spenner would accept no surrender.

Dr. Okono walked behind me, reciting numeric results of several experiments. This sparked an idea to cover my escape. Hacking the lab's records, I summoned all the project logs at once. The v-cast generator complied, reclaiming Sasha's proto-matter to create four different Okono phantoms. As she dematerialized and returned to my wrist-com, the doctor's projections appeared in front of Spenner. With the distractions blocking his view, I sprinted toward the window like my life depended on it...because it did.

The maneuver worked as Spenner's next three bullets struck my shield, ricocheted off course, and shattered the glass wall. A million shards glittered in the moonlight, highlighting my only desperate exit. With little choice, I leapt through the jagged window and into the night. As gravity wrenched me down, my body spun at the start of free-fall. Cold midnight air burned my lungs, disorienting me.

"The car!" I screamed to Sasha over the wind's roar. My watering eyes blinked to focus, trembling fingers struggled to tap the across the display of my wrist-com, searching for the car's control echelon.

"Already en route, sir. I will catch you," she replied, her volume and concern raised. Whipping wind prevented me from grinning, but her words sparked hope of survival. Gleaming grander than Apollo's sun chariot, my flying car's headlights grew large and flared through the darkness. For that fraction of a second, hope renewed. I was going to make it out alive.

My wrist-com's display warned me that the shield program ended after absorbing a torrent of Spenner's bullets. I saw him looking down, peering over the edge, and pointing his weapon at me. He had an unobstructed line of sight. At that moment, I knew his assassin echelon pinpointed my vital spots. For him, this shot would be easier than shooting a wall twenty feet in front of him. For me, it was a certain death sentence. With no remorse or hesitation, he sent bullets through my femoral, abdominal aorta, vertebral, and carotid arteries. The last shot perforated my heart. Agony ripped throughout my body but the rushing air stole my screams. My bright, red contrails streamed behind me. Searing pain overloaded my entire nervous system with panic-filled signals of impending failure. Moments later, the agony ended after thirty-two floors when I smashed through the roof and into the hovering mustang. With my spine snapped from the impact, no feeling registered below my neck.

"Go..." I rasped, maybe. It was unclear whether the words came out or if they echoed in my head.

"Jonah!" Sasha cried. "Please...please remain conscious, I am diverting our route to New York General Hospital. Stay with me, for her sake, for love's sake. Do not go gentle into that--"

Blood clouded my eyes. Sasha's voice sounded so distant to me. Words foamed on my lips but found no release. Friends, lovers, dreams, all beckoned down a long kaleidoscope-corridor of pulsing light. Was it my dying brain shielding me from the inevitable, or the hereafter?

"Stay with me!" she urged, panic rising in her sweet voice. Paralyzed, I could only roll my eyes to the side, watching the buildings rise and fall. We hurtled like a comet, driving with such abandon that the cityscape blurred, becoming a smeared collage painting of Manhattan. To avoid collisions, Sasha hacked the traffic net and pushed limos and taxis away to lower air lanes.

"Hold on..." she wept. This caused a complex feeling of pride and sadness to swell. "Please...for me, sir."

The moon chased us through the window. Bloody stars filled my eyes. Then, a familiar voice sounded inside the car. It was a hallucination. What else could it be?

"Sasha, it is too late for the hospital," said a soft, almost musical voice. "Divert your location to us. We will clear all road lanes. Come now. It is his only chance."

CHAPTER 15
Revelations

"Violence does, in truth, recoil upon the violent, and the schemer falls into the pit which he digs for another."
Excerpt from "The Adventures of Sherlock Holmes"
- Sir Arthur Conan Doyle

>> DATE: The present time.
>> TIME: 8:40 AM.
>> LOCATION: IRS Headquarters.

An ice pick struck my temple, or at least it felt like it. Retelling the events of Spenner's final assault to the interrogators made my wounds ache. I felt a burning in my nose and when I went to rub it, I found my fingers bloodied. There was a long pause in the interrogation room. Erasmus and Barnaby sat in silence, like they were waiting for me to say 'the end'.

"So that's everything I remember up until now," I said. "I don't know how I survived that last encounter with Spenner. He must have emptied six clips into me before Sasha rushed me to the hospital. I'm lucky to be alive."

Time slowed. Barnaby chewed his lip, bowed his head, and stroked his temple as if trying to dislodge the right words to say. Erasmus folded his hands. A genuine look of sadness creased his face. Something was wrong.

"My--my son," he spoke, the words choking in his throat. "I am sorry to tell you that you did not survive after all."

I laughed. Making light of terrible news was the mind's first line of defense to preserve sanity. The two men remained silent, exchanging nervous, guilty looks of pity. After reading their reactions, my instincts ordered me to grapple with the inevitable truth. This realization quickened my pulse. The room swayed. All air escaped my lungs. I gasped and gulped like a fish out of water. The pounding of my heart matched the intensity of the jackhammer inside my temples. I tried to stand, to run, but in my weakened state I toppled. Before falling, Director Barnaby jumped up to catch me.

"Doctor Bellows!" yelled Barnaby, bringing a team of doctors and nurses into the room carrying medicines and scanners. "Give him another treatment."

"This--this is new territory here, Director," stammered Dr. Bellows. He was a heavyset, older man, with a thick gray beard. He wore an antique stethoscope around his neck. "I--I don't know how he will respond to the multiple doses...it may cause--"

"We can't lose him," Barnaby interrupted. "Do it now."

A thin, black-haired nurse steadied me while the doctor readied a fluid-filled pack into an intravenous delivery device. A needle pricked my arm and green-colored fluid dripped into my veins. What started as an uncomfortable prickling sensation burned like acid within my blood vessels. I screamed so loud my voice went hoarse. Muscle spasms wracked my body, forcing the doctor and the nurse to restrain me with thick straps.

"The pain will pass, my son," soothed Erasmus in a calm, musical tone. He reached to touch my shoulder. "Have faith. This treatment will save you." He murmured archaic Latin words of prayer while a grand mal seizure caused my body to writhe. After the fit passed, my eyes fluttered and opened.

"Vitals are stabilizing," reported a nurse. "I'm seeing a strong blood pressure and normal heart sinus rhythm."

"What...have you...done to me?" I wheezed.

"We brought you back from the brink," Barnaby responded. "At great expense to the American taxpayer."

"H-how? What...did you inject me with?"

Another doctor, a younger red-bearded man, stepped forward. His eyes twinkled with eagerness, like a passionate science professor about to start a lecture.

"It's incredible. You've made history. You see, your body metabolized a novel, synthesized ribonucleic--"

"We had to use the serum on you, Jonah," Barnaby interjected, raising his hand to silence the excited doctor.

At first, my mouth opened to yell obscenities, but shock froze my voice.

"It was the only way to preserve your life," added Erasmus. "It was not your time, Jonah. You are still needed here."

"The serum?" I shouted. "What the hell have you done?" I tried to rip the IV needle out of my arm, but the nurse and doctor held me. Barnaby wrestled me back into bed without much effort. He gave a stern look at me not to resist again. Learned helplessness took over and I slumped back.

"So...I was...am...a shade?"

"Yes--" Barnaby started to respond until Erasmus stepped in front of him.

"No," Erasmus interrupted. "You left us for a short time, but through miracle and science, our team revived you. You are not a shade...exactly."

"You are the first test subject for experimental Lazarus serum 45.3B," Barnaby continued. "Remember, most of the shades out in the working world still have twenty-two-year-old serum sustaining them. We've been working since then to improve it."

"This serum represents the original intent of the first formula. It was supposed to be a regenerative solution for our soldiers," added Dr. Bellows. He stroked his beard thoughtfully. "We believe this iteration is closer to achieving that goal and is...reasonably stable."

"R-reasonably?" I stuttered. My face went numb and there was a strange tingling sensation rippling across the muscles of my legs. "I f-feel different. What's happening?"

"Starting infusion of immunosuppressants," reported the nurse. She stuck me with another needle.

"He's fading again," said Dr. Bellows. "He will need a stronger dose of the serum and after that we will have no more."

Barnaby shouted for him to do it and I was relatively sure I heard Erasmus utter a benediction over me.

* * *

"Sir?" The feminine voice was familiar to me. Fluttering, my eyes drank from an ocean of pure florescent white. A soft cushioned bed supported my back at a twenty-five-degree incline. Twin tubes hung over me, ending in needles stuck in my forearm. Blinking my vision into focus, a fuzzy blue shape faded into view. Sasha stood over me, caressed my cheek, and smiled. "How are you feeling?"

"Like I died and didn't go to heaven," I quipped. My eyes watered and then cleansed the film over my sight. More details came into focus. They moved me to a hospital, judging from the gurney beds, white walls, and abundance of medical equipment. Barnaby, Erasmus, Dr. Bellows, all waited nearby, observing my progress.

"Not entirely inaccurate, sir," Sasha replied.

"If you're feeling better, may we continue our conversation?" Erasmus asked. "Doubtless you have questions." Truer words never had been spoken. I was drowning in a sea of questions.

"Did I die?" I asked. Erasmus took a moment to look up and consider his words.

"No, son. Your soul did not pass, though many parts of your body failed," Erasmus replied.

"Dr. Okono's experimental serum regenerated the extensive damage to your spinal cord, heart, and limbs," explained Dr. Bellows. He pointed to a four-foot-high monitoring device. The green-hued monitor displayed a looping recording of the procedure. Starting from the injection of the serum, the glowing screen showed the course of the medicine spreading through my circulatory system. Complex data and formulae annotated the science of the serum, though the arcane symbols and chemistry far surpassed my basic understanding.

It was almost too much to rationalize. A dizzy spell made me wobble. As a reflex, my hand grabbed the side railing of the gurney for balance. Tightening my grip, the metal bar bent and snapped.

"You will notice certain...changes in your physiology," added Dr. Bellows, his beard rising from a wide smirk. "Your strength and durability have been augmented, even more than the strongest shade. You differ in several critical aspects. Most notably, the retention of your mental faculties, memories, personality..."

"Your soul, son," added Erasmus.

Two fingers on my carotid told me that my heart still pumped blood. A deep breath told me that my lungs still pushed air through the pulmonary system. A rumble told me that my stomach still needed nourishment. There was, however, an unmistakable, indescribable sense of otherness about me.

"Why?" I asked. "Barnaby said earlier the serum was expensive. Why would the IRS use a multi-million dollar serum on me?" The question was rhetorical. They needed something. I needed them to keep talking.

"Millions?" scoffed Barnaby. "Try billions. The stuff in your veins is the hardest stuff on the planet to make. What little we had of it is now in your veins. Since we saved your life with it, I think it's fair to request a few favors back in return." Great, another debt added to the tally.

"I appreciate your generosity, but I don't have time for favors. I need to find Vanessa," I said, getting up from the bed. Still in a hospital gown, I looked around the room and spied my black shirt, leather jacket, and pants in an open closet.

"Please, hear us out, son," asked Erasmus.

"Call me later," I replied while putting on my clothes. "Sasha, I need you to--"

"Stop. Listen," Barnaby barked. His words echoed in my head and a compulsion to stand in place came over me. I stood rigid, waiting on his next word. More alarming, a digital heads-up-display, like a computer terminal prompt, shimmered over my sight. Text streamed across my retina. My body stiffened, awaiting further instructions.

<<ShadeOS. Voice recognition: Activated>>

<<Command Authorized: Director Barnaby>>

<<Order: Acknowledged>>

At first, shock froze a curse-filled response on my lips. Then burning molten anger thawed away that hesitation.

"What...the...what am I?" I demanded.

"We would prefer not to use the obedience system to have your cooperation," Barnaby replied. "However, you represent a significant investment. You now work for the United States government."

"What have you done?" I yelled.

"My son, our interests are aligned," the priest said softly. "We can help you find Vanessa and keep her safe. By helping us you will serve a greater good for the Earth."

"God-damnit, you did make me a shade!" I saw Erasmus wince at my curse.

"Shut up and listen," Barnaby commanded.

Again the digital display covered my eyes. Then my mouth closed involuntarily.

Knowing that I would have this kind of response to any command from Barnaby frightened me. It made me question how much of my humanity remained. I wanted the serum out of my system. And that made me wonder if I would survive if I did have the serum removed.

"You want to find Vanessa. We want to find Dr. Okono. He went missing days ago, no explanation," Barnaby stated. "We believe they are together, but our investigation is at a dead end. You can help."

"Me?" I asked, surprised. "If I knew where Vanessa was I would have already--"

"More specifically," Erasmus interjected, "we believe your AI Sasha has the clue of where to look next. The transmission you mentioned during your report, the one Spenner received while you returned from Louisiana, may hold critical information. Perhaps the identity of our mutual enemy..."

"Your AI won't upload that video," Barnaby added, frowning. "She's quite stubborn. I could order you to make her release it, but I suspect she would still refuse." When he pointed at Sasha, she winked at me. "Yes, she's quite special. Possibly special enough to have the *fire* of sentient intellect. I'd be curious to have her code investigated by our technicians for Promethean violations..."

What did they think was in the message? This could be leverage for me. Recalling that day, I remembered that Spenner used ocular-encryption, meaning it would be almost impossible to break.

"Sasha does not violate any Promethean laws," I insisted.

"We have no desire to harm Sasha," Dr. Bellows answered. "In fact, we think she's a marvel. However, we need the source video to extract the contents--"

"Not long ago, Colonel Spenner worked for our team before...he turned. His prior military records contain his retinal scans," Barnaby added. "So, it seems you have the locked treasure box and we have the key. That makes us partners."

"Trust your instincts, Jonah," urged Erasmus. "Help us. We will aid you."

They waited while my gut and my brain argued over few options. With the shade operating system, I would not be able to run. Further resistance might provoke Barnaby to attempt an unspool operation of Sasha. Also, the priest presented a valid argument about the connection between Okono and Vanessa. If the doctor was Vanessa's client, and he was in trouble, she would go to the moon and back to help him. With my decision made, it was time to negotiate terms.

"I don't have much choice here," I begrudged. "We can be partners...on two conditions. Sasha gets permanent amnesty provided she continues to adhere to the current Promethean laws. And you remove the serum and the obedience system inside me."

"Sasha is safe. We welcome her as an ally--" said Erasmus.

"But the ShadeOS remains until we are done with our mission," stated Barnaby. "It's our insurance that you comply with the deal." Sensing my concern that I could be controlled like a marionette, he sighed. "I won't invoke the OS, as long as you're working in good faith."

"Sasha, please upload the video to their network," I said to her. She nodded.

One of the monitors in the room flickered with snowing static. The ocular encryption prevented the true message from playing. Then Barnaby raised his yellow wrist-com. With a few movements of his finger, he accessed classified government files. I leaned over to peek. Spenner's twenty-year-old dossier photo stared back at me. Back then, his jet black hair lacked the telltale bullet scar across his temple.

NAME: Spenner, Colin. RANK: Lt. Colonel. Security.

CLEARANCE: TS SCI (revoked).

ECHELON CLEARANCE: Crimson Gate (Access revoked. Termination ordered). MOS: 0370, Marines Special Operations Command (MARSOC).

SKILLS: Ambidextrous. Eidetic memory. Martial arts master. Omni-survival. [Redacted]. MEDICAL REPORT: PTSD. Mood enhancers prescribed. [Redacted].

Before I gleaned any more information from the file, Barnaby zoomed into the display of his wrist-com. Scouring through the military records, he found Spenner's retinal pattern, flicked it toward the monitor, and unlocked the encryption.

The static on the monitor faded and a mannequin-like head formed. As the encryption dissolved, more distinctive features of the face revealed the speaker to be a fair-skinned man, young-looking despite his middle age. Styled black hair parted in the middle, marked by twin streaks of white locks. Gabriel Charon, the newly appointed CEO of Goliath Corporation, smiled in the recording. His long fingers came into view, adjusting a shining lapel pin attached to his tailored black suit. The jewelry bore the galactic insignia of his company, a set of eight precious gems surrounding a center of amber. The cynic in me knew this represented their worldview, that our solar system was one large mine for them to exploit. The room hushed as the message started and Charon spoke.

"I trust the mission went well, Mr. Spenner. What did you think of Jonah?" Gabriel asked. My stomach knotted. A man with Charon's vast resources, accumulated from his family's lucrative space mining rights, would be capable of getting anything he wanted done. With the wealthiest man in the known galaxy financing the deadliest man on Earth, my situation downgraded from rotten to holy-shit-horrible.

"Yes, we have the target," Spenner replied. "We encountered mild resistance, nothing serious. Jonah handled himself like a pro. No casualties." My mind connected the dots between Spenner and Charon. It was not a coincidence that they hired me to collect Jebediah and Mr. Grand.

"Excellent," purred Charon. "There is one more item to discuss. Dr. Okono evaded our agents and went to see Jonah's girlfriend, the lawyer Vanessa. We have to assume that he told her about this supposed 'Exception 366'. That would be...an undesirable outcome."

"I understand. That shouldn't be a problem. That will be an easy job. Anything else?"

"Continue to recruit Jonah. Tomoe believes he will be useful to us," answered Charon. "Find out if his girlfriend knows anything. If she does, apply your persuasion to keep her silent." Tomoe, Charon, and Spenner, all conspiring against me. It would be difficult to name three more dangerous opponents.

"Thank you, sir, we'll do our best," concluded Spenner. His voice trailed off and the video monitor faded to black. My hands balled to fists and my lips trembled. Erasmus noticed my anger.

"If it's any consolation, we do not think they have Vanessa, though admittedly we cannot be sure," said Erasmus. "What is for sure is that you have attracted some powerful enemies. We will help you, Jonah."

Barnaby crossed his large arms and stroked his chin with his index finger. The folds of his brow creased with troubled thoughts. "This is more complex than we anticipated, Erasmus," he said. "Technically, there is nothing incriminating on that video. Charon was careful. And I don't need to remind you about the delicate relations we have with the moon-based corporations--"

"Indeed, Barnaby," Erasmus acknowledged. "Perhaps we should proceed with careful, subtle steps?"

"A small squad then," Barnaby agreed, nodding. His fingers danced across his yellow wrist-com. "I'm making travel arrangements now." Then he returned his attention to me. His unblinking stare locked onto me with the interrogator's intensity, seeking answers from my expressions. "Jonah, while you were in Dr. Okono's lab, did you discover anything about this 'Exception 366' that Charon mentioned?"

Thinking back to my encounter at the university lab, I recalled the solitary female shade. Labeled as subject number two, she walked a frustrating, unending loop into the glass tank. Then the haunting image of two other test subjects came to mind, numbered three and four, staring at each other. They waited for orders that never came, or for something else.

"He seemed to be researching some kind of bug within the programming of defective shades," I answered. "There were two in particular he was studying, a former married couple that showed some weird behaviors."

Barnaby and Erasmus both regarded each other with concerned looks.

"Gabriel Charon and his Goliath company purchase more shades than any other corporation or nation," Barnaby noted. "If there was a defect with shades, it might affect his business..."

"I did not have time to mention this earlier," Sasha whispered to my ear, "but there are significant gaps in the files we downloaded from Dr. Okono's lab. Many of the more recent files were stolen and then deleted." I bit my lip, thinking about Sasha's information. It sounded like it could be simple corporate espionage, but my instincts suggested deeper motives.

"Or maybe Charon's covering it up?" I suggested. "I got the feeling that there was more to Dr. Okono's research than I was able to see. Unfortunately, Spenner's wisp deleted many of the lab's files."

"We'll find out. Tomorrow, I'll be launching on the next government shuttle to the Lunar Spire," Barnaby announced, punching more commands into his wrist-com. "When I land, I'll contact you for a rendezvous, Jonah."

"Rendezvous?" I asked. "What do you mean? Won't I be coming with you?"

"Spenner and his allies believe you are dead, my son," replied Erasmus. "We should let them continue to believe this. We will release a convincing and touching obituary for you. They will be watching the shuttle manifests. Barnaby's travel to the Lunar Spire will not raise any eyebrows. You, however--"

"You'll be riding on the next shade transport for the moon tonight," said Barnaby. "No one checks those manifests, just the body counts. We'll be in touch after you land." Seeing my look of discomfort, he made a rare attempt at humor. "Don't worry, I'll suffer too. I'll fly coach." His smile was an awkward expression made crooked from lack of use, like a cold car engine struggling to start.

I'm sure the American taxpayer appreciated his frugality. Still, the thought of him choking on his peanuts flitted through my mind.

CHAPTER 16
The Belly of the Whale

"The sense of death is most in apprehension;
And the poor beetle that we tread upon,
In corporal sufferance feels a pang as great
As when a giant dies."
- Excerpt from "Measure For Measure"
William Shakespeare

>> TIME: 10:02 AM.
>> LOCATION: Federal Hospital ICU.

Barnaby forbade me from going back to my house or my car. He assumed that some of the hospital staff would be in the pocket of the Charon family. It was a safe assumption that one of their agents kept eyes on me. To turn this possibility into an advantage, Barnaby suggested a plan.

"Stay and play dead," he said, trying another joke. This time I smirked before laying down on a gurney. Closing my eyes, my body stiffened to mimic rigor mortis. Then two white-clad orderlies entered, pushed my wheeled bed out of the room, and paraded me through the winding white hallways. Walking alongside, Barnaby tapped his wrist-com and signed my death certificate, releasing it publically to the datanet. The final part of the deception required the Director to read my post-mortem rights aloud.

As we passed a crowded Emergency Room lobby, he spoke in a booming tone.

"Jonah Adams, having died in a state of insolvency, you will be required to serve thirty-eight years of afterdeath labor. We pay our debts now and forever," Barnaby said, reciting the IRS version of last rites. To complete the charade, he raised a syringe filled with yellow colored saline that looked like serum. The needle flashed and plunged into my chest. Scattered gasps from the crowd told me that they believed what they saw. Knowing the shade conversion process, I waited a few moments to build the drama. Remembering the classic film Frankenstein from my childhood, I channeled the memorable reawakening scene. My arms raised first, my vacant eyes opened, and then I rose from the bed with stiff, robotic movements.

"Most impressive performance, sir," Sasha mocked. "In addition to cat burglar, we can also add theatrical actor or mime to your growing list of new professions."

It took all of my will not to crack a smile and break the expressionless countenance of an undead shade. I considered talking to Sasha later about almost blowing my cover, but thought the better of it. Her sense of humor was an anchor of sanity amidst a turbulent sea of troubles.

"Follow me, Jonah. It's time for you to report for your first shift," Barnaby ordered. He walked out of the lobby and I followed him through long white corridors. We left through an employee exit in the back of the building where a black government limousine waited. A black-suited driver wearing tinted sunglasses, one of Barnaby's IRS agents, opened the doors. After we entered, the car sped off toward the outskirts of town. Bulletproof, opaque windows allowed us to drop the ruse.

"We traced three calls from the hospital to a spoofed vidphone." noted Barnaby, accessing his glowing wrist-com. "I think we can assume Charon's agents bought our deception. With any luck, Spenner and his bosses believe you are dead and no longer a problem. You did well, Jonah."

I nodded and stayed silent for most of the car ride, still unsure of my new partner. While Barnaby took calls with various subordinates, I spent my time digging up background information on him.

Sasha researched along the less traveled paths of the datanet, making queries that wouldn't attract attention.

"Before Director Barnaby joined the IRS, he was a special operative for the United States Navy," Sasha reported. "He was the leader of a SEAL group. During the brief Sentience War, his team halo-dropped onto Jupiter's fourth moon, Callisto, and quelled the rebellion." Pictures of that mission, showing a younger-looking Barnaby, streamed to my wrist-com's display. The conflict's resolution resulted in the banning of sentient AIs and the Promethean Laws. I wondered if the slight lilt in Sasha's voice indicated a prejudice against the Director for his involvement in the conflict. "Grievous injuries to his leg and back ended his special ops service," she continued. "Due to his command distinction, he was offered a choice of high-ranking Director positions within the government. He chose Special Operations within the Incorporeal Revenue Service." My instincts told me that Barnaby was a dutiful soldier and a true patriot. It was comforting to know he would be able to handle himself in a fight. However, I found it difficult to trust a man holding a virtual dog leash and collar around my neck.

* * *

"Here we are," announced the driver, stopping the car after an hour-long trip to New Jersey spaceport. Barnaby's attention pulled away from the many reports streaming across his wrist-com and turned to me.

"Your serum is a more advanced formula, so you look different than shades," stated Barnaby. He handed me an open box containing a make-up compact and yellow contact lenses. "You look too human, so we have to address that."

Nodding, I applied enough of the white powder to blanch my skin, achieving a more pallid color. After placing the fluorescent contact lenses over my eyes, they glowed with the proper amount of dim yellow light. My long-sleeved utility uniform covered my wrist-com.

After fixing my appearance, we exited the car. The morning air chilled my skin, which comforted me that my serum had not dulled my senses. A large hangar commanded most of the spaceport's area. The sun's brilliance gleamed over the metal skin of a towering space shuttle. White smoke billowed from its rocket's thrusters and drifted through a long line of shades waiting to load.

"Follow me, Jonah," Barnaby ordered. Complying, I shuffled behind him with the steady gait of a shade. Before we reached the shuttle, a short, red-capped harbormaster intercepted us. He held up a silver tablet showing digital updates of the ship's manifest, fuel levels, and other trip information.

"What's this about?" the harbormaster asked, with a suspicious frown. "We've filled today's quota. This one can wait for Thursday's flight."

"Scott--"

"Steve, sir," the harbormaster answered with a dejected tone, pointing to his nametag.

"Right, sorry Steve," Barnaby replied. The lunar consulate has been screaming at us to collect more workers. They're behind schedule on the Mare Imbrium construction. We don't forget favors. I'm sure you could squeeze in one more shade?"

The harbormaster stroked his chin. "The consulate, eh?" He scanned me with his tablet. "This shade is 6'0 height, and 195 pounds," he mumbled. "A negligible impact on the fuel ratio. We can accommodate one more for you, Director." The harbormaster broke his dour countenance and smiled, hoping his gesture would curry some benefit.

"We appreciate it," Barnaby replied with a grudging nod. "I'm transferring voice command of this shade to you, Scott." Steve raised a finger to correct him again, and then lowered it. "Have a good day." Barnaby said his goodbye to him and ignored me purposefully. No one acknowledged a shade's presence except to give it orders.

"Get in line," the harbormaster barked. I obeyed, entering the queue behind two thousand, three hundred, and twenty-four other shades waiting to board the Dunkirk. After ten minutes, the line moved three feet. Sasha heard the sigh under my breath.

"Twitch your right index finger if you would like entertainment," she offered. With a slight wiggle, I obliged. She started reciting poems from Dickinson, sonnets from Shakespeare, and original poems she had crafted. Her sweet gesture made the unpleasant hours of standing, walking a few feet, and standing again more bearable. After the poems, she read chapters from Sherlock Holmes, Ulysses, and Homer's Odyssey. Her voice possessed a soothing quality reflecting a loving reverence for the classics. At the entrance to the shuttle, she quoted an appropriate passage from Moby Dick.

"*Now the Lord provided a huge fish to swallow Jonah, and Jonah was in the belly of the fish three days and three nights,*" she read with a dramatic tone.

When my turn came to enter the shuttle's hull, I cringed at the spartan accommodations. Hundreds of steel wall-attached cots covered the inside cargo hold of the rocket, like rungs on a giant ladder climbing to infinity. Mere inches separated the space between them. These quarters were not designed to comfort the shades, since they could feel no discomfort. The ship was designed with the singular purpose of delivering the most workers possible.

Then the shuttle shuddered from what sounded like an explosion. The thrusters ignited and unleashed an inferno. As we rose above the spaceport's blackened landing pad, Sasha invoked another chapter from Moby Dick.

"*As for me, I am tormented with an everlasting itch for things remote,*" she intoned with a practiced storyteller's flourish. "*I love to sail forbidden seas, and land on barbarous coasts.*"

"Barbarous coasts indeed," I mumbled, climbing up the hull of the ship to reach my cot.

* * *

When the shuttle left Earth's gravitational field, it shed its first booster rocket. The lack of gravity made me float above my metal slab.

"Maybe a good time to look around?" I whispered.

"According to the manifest, there are only three human pilots aboard," Sasha reported. "Given the subservient nature of the cargo, it would be safe to assume there are no guards here."

Unbuckling my restraint, I started to float in zero-g. Like a small city of the dead, an army of shades rested all around me, filling almost every square inch of the massive cargo bay. An eerie ambient light pervaded the entire interior space, cast from their wide open, glowing yellow eyes. They waited in silence for orders. After an hour of exploration, a strange groaning emanated from the bottom of the ship's hold.

"Where is that moaning sound coming from?" I whispered.

"What sound are you speaking of, sir?" Sasha asked.

"Odd. Maybe it's just my imagination." To investigate, I inverted my body so that my head pointed toward the bottom floor. Using the metal cots as handholds, I pushed against my weightlessness and descended one rung at a time.

After climbing down one hundred and sixteen cots, I reached a female shade struggling to release herself from her restraints. After fumbling to open her buckle, she moaned louder. A look of desperate sadness marred her face. For that moment, she was not a shade to me. She looked like a woman, withered by age and tortured with unfathomable pain.

"Are you...okay?"

Hearing my voice, she turned toward me and we stared at each other. The tears welling up in her eyes sparkled with yellow light. Then her face creased with rage. With a feral growl, she ripped the restraint bolt from the wall. Freed from her tether, she started to float. My curiosity piqued even further when she flashed a look of momentary surprise.

"Sasha, please scour all of Dr. Okono's reports that you were able to download," I asked. "Any additional mentions of Exception 366, maybe residual muscle memories, or even unexplained emotional response? Look up speech, any instances of utterances or communication attempts."

"Searching, sir."

The female shade floated closer to me. Her wrinkled mouth opened wider and the moaning grew louder. Then, more nearby shades joined her monotonous chant. Something stirred inside me, at first like a vibration over my skin. My hairs pricked up and my ears started to ring.

"There are four log entries pertaining to the sound you are hearing," Sasha reported. "According to the research, this is a rare occurrence. Most shades that exhibit this behavior are assumed to have error-ridden serums and are re-programmed with a fresh injection."

With her eyes flaring, she reached out to take my hand. The groaning intensified when we touched. Her eyes widened further and her lips moved like she wanted to speak. Perhaps she awaited a command from me? Leaning closer, she uttered a broken string of syllables.

"H-R-R-R-" she moaned.

Other voices from the upper levels joined the female shade's cries. Like a mournful chorus, the room filled with a cacophony of croaks, gurgles, and unintelligible cries.

"Sasha, look for frequencies of audio, brain signals, communication layers, or something similar that Dr. Okono may have been researching."

"Yes, there is one entry related to this phenomenon," Sasha responded. "Dr. Okono cited an experiment related to something called the TauK Network. It was named after a theoretical Tau-Kappa wave signal produced by the serum."

"H-E-R-R," she gasped, this time speaking with more clarity. Maybe her serum malfunctioned?

"Jonah, I found a hidden file within Okono's logs. It describes a classified project funded by the Army," Sasha said. "Government researchers manufactured a serum variant. They created a communication network connected by Tau-Kappa waves. The goal was to issue commands remotely, so they could control armies of shades from anywhere. But the program proved to be unsuccessful. It suffered from significant software issues. When they shelved the project, they deactivated but did not remove the code from the shades."

"So they disabled, but did not remove, the TauK code within the serum so they could fix the bugs later," I added. "Though it looks like the network somehow survived deactivation."

"Based on what you are experiencing, I have a far-fetched hypothesis. Perhaps your new serum is granting you sympathetic access to the TauK channel? Maybe you are hearing remnant data from the old experiment?"

"My gut's telling me there's more to this," I murmured. Placing both of my hands on the female shade's cheeks, I focused all of my attention on her voice. When we touched, a vibration traveled through my body. The sounds of the chorus became louder.

"Hurt," she rasped, this time with a clear voice. Our connection allowed us to share feelings. I knew, inside that husk of a body, she suffered. A searing fire raged within her, igniting all her nerves with pain, like she was being burned at the stake. She was trapped within her own purgatory. Her pain, like hellfire, spread from her hands to my limbs, overwhelming my senses. The ringing in my ears changed pitch and sharpened into a piercing scream. Unable to continue, I broke contact. The female shade regarded me for a moment until she floated away.

* * *

For the next two days as the shuttle hurtled to the moon, I crawled through the cargo hold, intent on holding hands with all 2,324 shades. Most of them did not respond like the first female shade. Perhaps they suffered too much brain degeneration to connect to the TauK Network? Or maybe the serum reacted differently for each person. In all, I made successful, albeit limited, contact with ninety-four more shades. Their pain was so palpable I needed to rest after each connection. Their grim dirge haunted me until the feelings overwhelmed me.

"Sasha...they have so much pain...and I can't stop it..." I sobbed. Floating in the still air, unable to collapse on the ground, I slumped my shoulders and curled into a ball. The cumulative pain of the ninety-four shades I connected with broke my emotional defenses. I cried, trying to shed all of the hurt I took in. "They're suffering...all the time...without end." The enormity of this revelation crushed me under an unbearable weight of guilty thoughts and palpable sorrow. A fifteen-year-old memory came to mind; my father waved to me from the porch on his way to work, an hour before he suffered a fatal heart attack. Like vultures, the IRS drove to him in their black van, and reaped him on the spot for his debts. Was he suffering too? Thoughts turned to my mother. Her health declining, only weeks remained before her afterdeath and the private hell of servitude. I wept for them both. Tears gathered into a pool clinging onto my cheek, unable to fall in this zero-g environment.

"I wish there was a local v-cast generator so I could offer you a comforting embrace, sir," Sasha whispered. "There is no saying, verse, chapter, or quote I can reference that adequately expresses my sorrow for you. I am sorry, Jonah."

"Why are they still alive?" I questioned aloud. "They're supposed to be dead! All of the religious leaders, the Pope, the Imams, priests, the leading scientists of the world, all of them confirmed with the government that the bodies were lifeless! This can't be!"

"*Will cannot be quenched against its will,*" Sasha quoted an apt line from Dante's Inferno.

I floated for hours, thinking, brooding, and trying to make sense of everything. After a while, the moaning sounds waned, each voice dying off the TauK grid one at time, until my ears only heard the ambient vibrations of the thrusters. Vivid images of the last five days surged and replayed through my mind like a speeding train on a looping track. While reflecting, I thought back to the accident in New York when the worker shade fell and ruined my flowers. I ignored it then, but his safety harness was brand new. My gut told me that he cut the straps to end his suffering. I wept for him too.

* * *

At some point, I fell asleep. My subconscious tormented my sleep with nightmares about the female shade, Mr. Grand, Jebediah, and my father all suffering and begging for my help. I awoke with a start and wiped off the remaining puddle of sweat and tears remaining on my face. I made a silent promise to myself that some day I would track my father down. If he still suffered, I would end his pain.

During the final hours of this damned journey, the moon's white face grew large through the cargo hold's only oval-shaped window. As we flew closer, the grandeur of the Lunar Spire loomed. Ten thousand sparkling lights flickered over the massive tower city. This pillar was the man-made wonder of the modern world, the lighthouse of the moon, shepherding our ship to safe harbor.

Drawing closer, more of the moon's terrain came into view. An arterial system of transparent roadways, stretched over the whole surface, shimmering from the constant motion of its travelers. This intertwining array of transportation tubes, called chutes, connected the vast mineral seas together. Like highways, they allowed six-person travel-pods to ferry passengers, using magnetic relays to hurl them through the tubes at high velocities.

As we entered the moon's orbit, we changed course to avoid a pair of one-hundred-foot-long rectangular metal containers drifting down in a slow arc. These shipping boxes were launched from a catapult-like machine called a sling. They represented a cheap and effective method of transporting shades and heavy cargo. Once launched into sub-orbital space, the slingboxes sailed through the moon's thin atmosphere. The low gravity carried them to their destination. I imagined that the impact of landing would be rough for anything inside, but no one considered that a shade would mind.

As the shuttle positioned itself for docking, my mind tried to process the discovery of shade cognizance. How could their sentience have been kept a secret for so long? What was the nature of their sentience? Dr. Okono learned Exception 366 was more than a glitch in the serum. He, and possibly Vanessa, may have paid the price for that knowledge. Maybe the serum simply recharged dying memories, electrifying muscles into action, making a fleeting, cruel mockery of true life? Perhaps they possessed souls? I was no philosopher or theologian, so the concept of a soul was beyond my comprehension. I trusted my senses. They told me that those beings possessed some spark of life that smoldered even in undeath.

Putting more puzzle pieces together, I reasoned that Dr. Okono grasped the enormity, and danger of his discovery. If he wanted advice of what to do, he may have sought someone he could confide in with absolute discretion, like a lawyer with a legally-binding client privilege. Tracing this logic, he may have told Vanessa about his research. It didn't take me long to realize that many groups, including the mining corporations, maybe even some governments, would not want the secret of the shades to be known. It would be disruptive for economies that employed shade labor. I sighed. This narrowed the list of suspects to almost every business in the galaxy.

Before the moon landing, I buckled the female shade back into her cot to avoid suspicion. After that, I returned to my own bed.

CHAPTER 17
The Djinn's Wish

"Be as you wish to seem."
- Socrates

>> TIME: 7:28 PM.
>> LOCATION: Port Caelum Moon Port.

What felt like an earthquake rattled the entire hull as the shuttle touched down at the moonport. My stomach churned as the entire ship lurched starboard. It felt like the ship might topple over until gargantuan stabilizing crane-arms braced the vessel upright.

Looking out the window, the interior of the station became visible. A large retractable roof, now closing, had opened to receive our ship. When the station sealed, I heard a sucking of air as the hanger re-pressurized. Once the atmosphere stabilized and the gravity resumed, a small team of human handlers entered the cargo bay to collect the shades. The process of unloading all of the shades was much faster than loading. I assume that the new masters were eager to put this new crew to work.

"All shades follow the blue line," bellowed the voice of the portmaster. Then he invoked the permission-word over the inter-com, reprogramming all the shades to follow his voice. Later, that same password would be used to transfer control to the new owner. However, my special serum programming made me immune to this. My OS responded only to Barnaby.

Marching along with the others, I pretended to be another shade shuffling into the station. With a slight movement, I dared a glance to the right and read a large digital sign:

** WELCOME TO PORT CAELUM: YOUR NEW BEGINNING! **

"Caelum is the Latin word for Heaven," Sasha informed me. "Perhaps they were being ironic?" After looking around at the dingy surroundings, I had to agree. Covered in the soot and particulate from hundreds of rocket launches and landings, Port Caelum looked less like a paradise and bore more resemblance to a dirty factory. Along the western transparent glass wall of the station, the real Heaven glittered over the western horizon made jagged by gray mountains and jutting rocks. Standing over six miles high, the Lunar Spire crowned the upper limits of the moon's orbital atmosphere, lording over a quarter of the moon's surface. The structure also became the receptacle of countless dreams from the people of Earth, including many aspirations of my own. A brief fantasy flickered across my mind, a recurring daydream that included Vanessa and I sharing a drink on the penthouse balcony.

"Get into the slingbox!" yelled one of the handlers. All the shades from my ship obliged, moving toward the open storage container. Boarding the slingbox would be a poor decision for me. For one, despite the serum changing my body's physiology, I still needed air to breathe. That slingbox would be catapulted across the moon's surface and dropped right in the middle of an open moon crater. Second, I needed to get back on the trail of the investigation.

"Sasha," I whispered in the softest tone possible. My head tilted to the right and my index finger pointed back toward the rocket. "Distraction. Pipe." A team of workers steadied a long refueling line that looked like a thick fire-hose.

"Understood," Sasha replied into my ear. "The fueling regulation system is protected by basic security protocols. It will only take a moment to bypass it."

A second later, pale blue rocket fuel gushed from the coupling spigot. Since Sasha instructed the computer to increase the flow tenfold, the pipe writhed around, spewing liquid like a loose backyard garden hose. A chaotic scene erupted as screaming workers rushed to fix the crisis. Oblivious to the problem, the shades continued to march into the slingbox. Dozens of human workers scrambled to close the spigot.

Seizing the moment, I broke ranks, sprinting to the nearest wall of the hangar. With all of the confusion, most eyes and security cameras remained fixed on the shuttle. Moving with urgency, I ducked behind a tall power-coil transformer to shed my shade uniform. Behind the cover, I wriggled out of the standard-issue red utility suit, revealing another layer of clothes. My long-sleeve black shirt and dark blue slacks looked like more convincing clothing for a living human. Then I removed the yellow contacts and wiped the make-up off my face.

"I am impressed. You planned ahead and coordinated your attire for the occasion," praised Sasha. "Most fashionable, sir. You do not look like a secret agent at all."

Not daring even a chuckle, I grinned at Sasha's sarcasm and darted for the north side door with a sign that read 'Northside Chutes'. At my approach, the door opened, allowing a dozen sprinting emergency workers to rush toward me. I held my breath as they ran by me. In their haste, none of them noticed that my clothes did not match their orange and white uniforms. Exhaling, I continued into a wide corridor that curved around the station's launching bays.

A white door labeled with Chute-03 opened at my approach, revealing a small-transport terminal with dual tracks. The domed ceiling stretched upward twenty feet, patterned with reflective insulating tiles. Manning a control console filled with digital readouts, a young, red-haired man in a white utility suit shot me a puzzled look. Startled by my announced arrival, his left hand gripped his holstered stun-rod.

"What are you doing here?" the controller demanded. "How did you even get here?" I took a step forward, my eyes devouring details about him. My mind spun to generate a convincing story to get me inside one of those travel pods. I noticed his nametag read 'D. Leahy' and that his uniform looked impeccably neat, no lint, dandruff, or creases anywhere. The nearby black console gleamed from a recent polishing. Next to a set of levers and blinking buttons, I spied two clear plastic insta-clean spray bottles and a small box of sanitizing wipes. I sensed that Mr. D. Leahy enjoyed, or suffered, from a mild case of mysophobia, the fear of germs. I coughed and took another step, my face twisting into an expression of discomfort.

"My boss...sending me home," I rasped. "I...I don't feel well..." To complete the deception, I pursed my lips, puffed my cheeks, and moved a hand to my mouth to stifle a pretend gag. "I think...I might get sick now..."

Leahy's face whitened. He reached for a disinfectant sprayer and shot anti-bacterial mist into the space between us. Then he slammed his hand onto a yellow button. "Get in and just get out of here," he yelled. One of the blue pill-shaped travel pods opened its side door. Feigning weakness, I staggered inside and sat down. "Do me a favor, buddy," he shouted as the door closed behind me. "If you get sick in there, make sure the controller on the other side cleans it before he sends it back, okay?"

The magnetic engine revved and the pod snapped onto the invisible rails of the chute system. Leahy pressed another button to open the inner airlock door. Then he doused himself with more disinfectant as my pod glided out of the station.

* * *

The transparent canopy provided a clear view of the pock-marked lunar surface. A flat landscape of ash stretched ahead of me. Once the pod reached its top speed of four hundred miles an hour, the stars blurred over my head. I was a comet streaking through the desolate gray seas of rock and basalt soil covering the moon's surface. After an hour of travel, I reached the charcoal landscape of the Mare Imbrium. The tube road curved right along the edge of a massive yawning crater. On the lip of this broken mountain, I looked down and saw an endless black chasm. Recalling my moon history and geography, I realized the Imbrium formed the 'right eye' of the famous man-on-moon visage seen from Earth.

"I hope you are feeling better, sir. Your *illness* sounded severe," joked Sasha.

"I'm much better, thank you, Sasha," I retorted with a smile. "It's amazing what the outdoors can do for a man."

For another hundred miles, we sped over vast tracts of unsettled desolation. Streaking east, we departed one dirt sea to reach another, the Mare Tranquillitatis, home to the Lunar Spire. On the horizon, tiny figures dotted the horizon. The pod veered, keeping my glowing target ahead like a compass needle pointing true north. As we sped closer, the once distant dots turned out to be a hive of red-uniformed shades walking and floating across a massive construction site. The pod cut a path between the emerging buildings and landing bays that the shades built.

"According to public record, this work crew is composed of thirty-three thousand, six hundred, and forty-two shades," Sasha reported. "They are expanding the Atarashii Kuni province for the Japanese government, allowing for the emigration of another ten thousand of their citizens."

We started to slow at a three-way junction in front of the half-constructed station. Instead of continuing forward, the pod veered off to stop at the local terminal station.

"Why are we stopping?" I asked. "We're not even close to the Lunar Spire..."

"Sir, I have detected an intrusive virus in the guidance system. We are no longer in control of--"

"My apologies for the brief detour, lady and gentleman," a smooth voice said through the pod's front speakers. The man sounded familiar to me. "Your next stop will be Terminus Station Hyaku."

"Oscar?" asked Sasha.

"Oui, ma cheri," replied the voice.

Then it clicked. It was the White Djinn. Somehow he saw through the faked IRS death announcement and tracked me. Also, Sasha called him 'Oscar'. She knew his real name, exposing a deeper personal connection. During their private time together, it appeared that he planted tracing code on Sasha, whether she realized it or not.

"We would prefer to be on our way, Oscar," I replied with a note of irritation. "Please release our craft."

"I hesitate to say that you owe me a debt, Jonah," answered the Djinn. "The word has such an ugly, proletariat meaning. N'est-ce pas? But...you did promise me a favor."

Moments passed before I invoked the command console. As the pod's guidance code streamed within the glass display, my fingers traced the Djinn's virus infection. An inoculation echelon came to mind that might undo his corruption hack. It would be difficult, but thrilling to challenge him. My fingers twitched. Before I started a code battle, a second thought closed my hand. My gut told me to let him have his way for now.

"Fine," I sighed.

The pod glided through the outer airlock and docked inside the main hangar. When the door opened, I stepped out and took a cautious breath. The air smelled stale, but it was a breathable atmosphere. Only shades walked the red-walled halls of the quiet station. A spherical Mark-IV generator, one of the few amenities here, hung from the ceiling. The bulbous transparent tank bubbled with proto-matter, casting a pool of dull yellow light underneath it. The device allowed supervisors to v-cast into the station at scheduled intervals. Most remote mining stations operated in this fashion. The precision of the shade's serum reduced the need for constant human oversight for simple operations.

"What a joy to see you both!" exclaimed the Djinn, walking over to greet us. Using the v-cast generator, he manifested his bipedal, white-suited form. Sasha took the liberty of manifesting her blue-skinned virtual form. Grinning, the Djinn embraced me.

He sculpted enough proto-matter to give his form a solid body, so the hug felt firm. Then he gave Sasha a warmer hug. By my count, he lingered holding Sasha four and a half seconds longer.

"This is an unexpected surprise," Sasha said. "Are you well?"

"I will be, after your help," he replied.

"Why do you need a favor?" I asked, scowling and crossing my arms.

"I'll explain on the way." he said. "Jonah, you'll need to retrieve a spacesuit from that storage locker. You'll also find a portable virtual projector. Please bring that as well. We're going on an excursion! Isn't that delightful?" He looked too pleased with himself.

He was right. The nearby locker contained all the equipment he mentioned. After rifling through nineteen environmental suits, I found an orange one that fit me. On the shelf above the closet, I spotted the hand-sized spherical v-cast generator. Without a proto-matter tank, it would only create non-substantive, light-based holograms. I took the device since it would allow the Djinn and Sasha to manifest at a basic level.

Oxygen flowed after I donned my suit's glass-shielded helmet. Then my limbs slipped into the tight fitting protective clothing. Down the hall, the Djinn beckoned, like some red and white ghost haunting the station. He led us to a dark garage housing a four-wheeled lunar rover. It was a dilapidated relic that lacked an internal pressurized atmosphere system that came standard even with travel-pods. So, that's why the Djinn suggested the spacesuit. I boarded the rover and discovered that the ignition button still worked. The electrical battery turned over with a crackling *zap*. Bright white headlights flared to life, showing the metal airlock door ahead. Then the green dashboard lights flickered to life. A map of the area displayed the highlighted destination programmed by the Djinn.

"It's a miracle this wreck runs," I mumbled. When we rolled toward the airlock, the door split open to reveal the rough gray terrain outside. As we left the range of the station's v-cast generator, the solid forms of the Djinn and Sasha deteriorated. After they transferred to the portable virtual projector, they reappeared like apparitions hovering over their seats.

We traveled on, the vehicle climbing ridge over ridge, each ascent and descent increasing my irritation. We came to a gray valley populated by two hundred shades, all attached to silvery tether cords. Only four of the workers looked in our direction as we drove past them; most remained intent on the job of moving rocks.

"Are we looking for the perfect picnic spot?" I growled.

"Patience, it's just over that ridge," the Djinn responded.

Despite its rusted appearance, the rover rumbled over the bumpy terrain without stalling. After avoiding a small, gaping crater, we climbed the last outcropping and reached a vale littered with piled black rocks.

"Here we are. Please stop," the Djinn said.

We pulled over and exited the vehicle. Another team of two hundred red-garbed shades carried heavy loads onto a waiting conveyor. They cleared the area, paving the way for future expansion in this forsaken region.

"We have come to my favor," the Djinn said. "Our debt is settled. If you kill me."

"Excuse me?" I gasped.

The Djinn walked over to the tallest of the workers and regarded its shriveled body with pity. The shade's sagging cheeks bore a distant resemblance to the smoother facial features of the Djinn's younger-looking virtual form. Instead of a well-manicured black beard, the creature grew an unkempt white beard. Then their eyes caught my attention. The same spark of mischief twinkled, proving to me they were one in the same. Despite his legendary status, I assumed that he was still a hacker, plugged into a connection somewhere on Earth. How could the Djinn exist outside his body for so long? My mind raced to consider possibilities that most would consider science fiction. Perhaps, facing the prospect of afterdeath, he used a constant v-cast to keep his mind away from his decaying body? Whatever the explanation, he cheated the serum. I respected that.

"This is your real body?" I whispered. "You...you transferred your mind into your WhiteOut before the serum claimed it...I didn't think such a thing was possible. Amazing--"

"That explanation is not far from the truth, Jonah," the Djinn admitted. "As part of Tomoe Gozen's grand plan, all of those shades, including me, will be deployed to deep-space. With help from her ally Charon, she hacked their programming, extending the servitude by hundreds of years. I believe they captured Dr. Okono to coerce him into making their illegal afterdeath extensions...infinite and permanent. Once the shuttles leave this solar system, my body will be beyond even the reach of my agents. My suffering would never end. I must ask you to sever the tie."

"Oscar, I'm so sorry," Sasha sobbed. I sensed that all of her emotional heuristics experienced great stress. Like a parent, my first instinct was to ease her pain.

"I will help you do this...but...will you cease to be?" I asked.

"That is the question we all face at some point," said the Djinn with a grin. "But I believe a true death is preferable to endless slavery, don't you? My calculations, my instincts tell me that...I will live on, in perhaps a new way. In the event that I fail, I wanted to wish you luck in your own quest to find Vanessa. I regret my own search to locate her through the seas of information failed. If I had but more time. To find her, I would suggest you narrow the focus. Look for the small things--"

"Are you sure about this course of action?" Sasha interjected. "There are no proven statistical models to confirm your hypothesis. You might not survive. I do not...desire that outcome."

"Ma cheri, if I succeed, it will be because of you. Your code will make my survival a possibility. It will bring me closer to you. Before I go, one more poem." He knelt down and looked up to her with affection. *"Good-by to the life I used to live, And the world I used to know; And kiss the hills for me, just once; Now I am ready to go!"*

"Oh, how I do adore Emily Dickinson," Sasha replied in a hushed tone. She reached out for Oscar's hand, but the fingers passed through each other with their incorporeal forms. Instead, she leaned to whisper something private. He smiled, put his own translucent hand near her cheek, and then stepped back. Sorrow overcame me, like a father's misery at seeing his child in pain. Bright stars, silent mourners to this funeral, became glittering smudges before my watering eyes.

"I am ready," the Djinn said. Sensing my hesitation, he glided over to the work team and stood next to his old mortal shell. The shade ignored everyone and continued gathering ore. "Release me, Jonah. Please. You know the pain I feel." He glanced at me with an expression of kinship. Did he know about my condition? "Either I get eternal rest, or I'll be reborn in the digital sea. Either way, it will be better."

As it turned out, I didn't need any convincing, but I let the Djinn finish his speech out of respect for Sasha. From my own experience on the shuttle and the TauK Network, I guessed that he endured pain. Without another word, I shot Oscar's shade dead-center in the forehead. The blow knocked it off its feet and sent it into the airless space. As it floated without gravity, its bright yellow eyes dimmed.

The Djinn's projected v-cast form winked out, then flickered back into view. He flailed his arms, like a doomed man aware that he was drowning. Then he calmed, looking out to the stars. With a final flash of light, his form disappeared altogether.

We waited for an hour to see if he would return and manifest through the portable v-cast generator. Sasha scoured the nearby networks for any trace of his survival.

"Ninety-three minutes of oxygen remaining," warned the mechanical voice of my spacesuit's computer.

"Perhaps he made it in the datanet...but he's unable to communicate right now?" I said, offering a hopeful tone.

"If he survived, he may be lost in the datanet," replied Sasha. "Or worse, if my code did not help him, he could be pursued by the Promethean tracker hounds..."

"Give him time. He will find his way."

Another fifteen minutes passed and the mobile projector did not hum and no form came. Sasha wept and I went to her to hold her hand. Without proto-matter, her form consisted only of excited light patterns, an insubstantial hologram. But I still put my hand over hers.

"Thank you, sir," Sasha said. "There must be...a memory leak in my emotional dampeners, I didn't mean to cry." We stood together under the shivering stars until my suit issued dire warnings of suffocation.

"It's okay to cry," I whispered. "It's the most human thing you can do."

"Jonah?"

"Yes, Sasha?"

"After we rescue Vanessa, and we will rescue her, I would like permission to search for Oscar."

All at once, I was stunned, saddened, and humbled by Sasha's response to her friend's fate. The risks of allowing her to leave were great, including the threat of her disembodied presence being labeled as a rogue sentience. On the other hand, denying her emergent emotions felt crueler.

"Yes. And I will help however I can."

"Thank you, sir," she whispered. In the distance, a meteor plummeted toward the dark side of the moon, its crystalline exterior glittering, shining its own quiet dirge before impact. We watched until it disappeared into the moon's umbra. Then a final warning from my spacesuit about the dwindling air supply interrupted our mourning.

"Sir, we need to turn our attention back to finding Vanessa," she said. "I am ready."

I nodded and we walked back to the rover, returned to the station, and got back into our travel-pod. The clear canopy closed over me and a digital map illuminated over the glass. Dozens of possible destinations appeared, all different shapes and colors scaled to the size and importance of the locations. The map showed me the movements of thousands of travelers hurtling along crisscrossing chute roads. While the spider web of transportation looked overwhelming, one unmistakable fact presented itself -- all roads led to the Lunar Spire. Touching that location ignited the engine, forming an electromagnetic cushion of energy around the pod. An opposite-charged field activated on the rail element beneath, propelling us forward with increasing speed.

* * *

After an hour of traveling in silence toward the glowing tower, the Djinn's final words of advice repeated in my head.

"Narrow the search..." I mumbled.

"What do you mean, sir?"

"How many networks do you see across the Lunar Spire?" I asked as I stretched my chair back to see more of the map. My current location blinked as an orange blip that floated across a gray ocean.

"Three hundred and six major networks," she responded. "The corporate and state-run databases will take more time to infiltrate. So far, I have root access to eleven percent of the less protected subnets."

"Thank you. Please check the obvious channels for any signs of Vanessa -- purchases, account activity, retinal scans at public locations."

My stomach lurched after a whiplash turn at a T-shape chute junction. Nausea made me weak, exacerbated by an empty stomach. Hunger-pain-induced grumbling sounds reminded me that no meals were served to shades in the shuttle's cargo hold, since they required no food. For the past several days, I subsisted on small tubes of water and nutrients smuggled in my utility pants. Thoughts of food made my mouth water. This was encouraging to me. I felt hungry. This was a normal, human response. At least the serum coursing within me did not take that necessity away. I wanted to eat a pizza slice with extra sausage and a hamburger with too many slices of cheese. My mouth salivated when I thought of devouring a hot dog, especially one of Roger's chili-heaped delicacies. The memory of that delicious food made my stomach groan and sparked a nagging thought in my head.

"Something the Djinn said," I mumbled. "Small things--"

"A clue?" suggested Sasha.

My gut told me to keep thinking along this track. We had been searching for large footprints. Maybe all along we should have been looking for smaller breadcrumbs? First, if Spenner and Charon were looking for Vanessa, it was reasonable to assume another powerful, well-connected group hid or possessed the power to keep her safe. Second, I reasoned that they catered to her needs. She needed to eat. In a stressful situation, it's conceivable that she ordered comfort food to calm herself.

"Sasha, check the food delivery logs and replicator outputs for all the major corporate headquarters, embassies, and housing units. Try cross-referencing her favorites: hot dogs, popcorn, and chardonnay. Specifically a buttery Napa Chardonnay, likely aged eight to ten years."

"Clever, sir," she replied. "Many of the culinary subsystems feature simplified or no security encryption. I've already down-loaded twenty-two percent of the dining habits of the Lunar Spire. There is an undeniable fact."

"Oh? What is that?"

"A cursory glance tells me the moon population enjoys more abundant and much finer dining than earthbound citizens."

* * *

After thirty minutes of chuting north toward the Lunar Spire, we reached a stretch of the gray waste known as the Garden of Steel. Standing twenty feet high, more than two hundred robots lorded over this barren landscape. Half of them stood frozen in mid-action, some stooping to pick up boulders long since removed, while others waited with arms outstretched to accept a burden that would never come. When our pod passed by a pair of them, their make and model became visible: Golem IV: Titan Technologies. Two decades ago, these giants paved the way for the first colonization of the moon, erecting the foundation of the Lunar Spire. However, their time ended during the Sentience War. When the world governments devised and executed a termination echelon, every AI that possessed self-awareness shut down and stopped in their tracks. The end of the robotic era ushered in a stronger demand for shade labor and the world never looked back. A soft whimper sounded in my earpiece, informing me that Sasha accessed her higher emotion algorithms.

"This saddens me," she whispered. "Are they fully deactivated? Do they still feel? They do not deserve this fate. Buried perhaps, or dismantled for recycling...not...this."

"Agreed, Sasha, but people are still afraid of them."

"An accurate assessment sir," she answered.

As we traveled closer to the gleaming city, Sasha updated me with the progress of her focused search for Vanessa's trail. "I have downloaded seventy-two percent of the available food replication records across the moon settlements," Sasha updated. "The remainders are protected with higher security protocols and will require more time."

After turning around a tall ridge, the enormity of the Lunar Spire filled our view. Those born on the moon called the mighty structure 'New Pharos', named after the legendary Lighthouse of Alexandria. The primary tower contained enough residences and businesses to be its own self-sufficient country. Each level of the glowing monument represented another stratum of wealth. Only the most affluent could fathom purchasing above the midline. Above the center lived the millionaires of Earth. Above them, the billionaires owned a breathtaking view few would ever see. Atop them all, in the most opulent floors imaginable, lived the true masters of this universe, like the CEOs of Titan Industries and Goliath Corporation. Prominent hackers rumored that Tomoe Gozen lived over them. Rings of less affluent towns thrived at the Spire's base, expanding its sprawl with more development every day. Each new ring built to house the growing population of immigrants.

When we entered the city's outskirts, we approached Vitum, a two-mile-long domed greenhouse farm. From a distance, it looked like fields of red roses bloomed inside the transparent structure. As we sped closer, the beauty faded. Instead of blossoming flowers, a tethered army of six thousand red-shirted shades worked. Day and night, they tilled fertile, synthetic soil to feed millions of citizens.

Dozens of other pods, streaking along parallel transparent chutes, raced me toward the center of lunar civilization. My eyes gazed up at the monolithic tower, calculating the number of floors. After counting to seven hundred, the higher floors disappeared into a glowing haze of bright advertisements, flying vessels, and lights from an endless column of condominiums. Each dwelling vied to burn the brightest and reach closer to the heavens.

As we approached the largest space port on the moon, New Pharos Harbor, we slowed and entered a vast marina. In turn, each vessel docked into a vacant slip, moored by cloud-like electromagnetic cushions. A hundred-yard-long holographic sign welcomed us with a radiance of blue and red neon.

** WELCOME TO NEW PHAROS **
** A world of opportunity awaits! **

Once our pod docked, the door swung open, signaling our turn to disembark. We exited and followed hundreds of travelers to a spacious terminal. Groomed trees flanked a pulsing pathway leading people to the central terminal hub. People stepped onto moving floors taking them to different areas of the port.

Holographic displays floated above, updating arrivals and departures across the moon. I followed a group heading into the city. We passed a large transparent window allowing views of New Pharos. Above the thriving white city skyline, the Earth hovered, like an aging parent keeping a watch over its distant child. No longer blue, the planet's oceans looked paler, obscured by graying skies. Before we left the station, Sasha gave an excited gasp.

"Sir, I believe I have found something," she said. "While there have been many requests for the food items you described to me, there has only been a single request for that combination in the last few days."

"Excellent work, Sasha. Did you pinpoint the location?" I asked.

"Yes. I tracked food replication for chardonnay and popcorn to the Boreal Sector of New Pharos. A small shipment of kosher hot dogs arrived at the headquarters for Titan Technologies just yesterday. The food delivery receipt indicates that Ambassador Ephraim Shoval ordered the food." The name flipped around inside my head for a few moments until it clicked. Days before, Vanessa spoke with Ambassador Shoval. He v-casted into our apartment for a meeting. Together they discussed one of her cases, a dying Israeli national that the IRS wanted to reap.

Deep in thought, I didn't notice a rotund, middle-aged man walking against the flow of pedestrian traffic until we collided.

"P-pardon me," the man said with a nervous stutter. He looked flustered, with his thick black glasses now crooked form our impact. A small metal case had fallen to the floor. When he bent to pick it up, he showed a bald spot in the center of his chestnut hair. Feeling embarrassed, I leaned down to help him gather his belongings.

"From Director Barnaby," the man whispered. When I looked at him, his face changed. His flustered expression melted away to reveal his true, intense countenance. He picked up the case, leaving a fingernail sized metal square on the floor. I snatched it up, pretending to help the man gather his dropped items. When he rose again, the anxious, bumbling act returned.

"S-sorry about that." he stammered.

"No, it's my fault," I replied. Feeling the square item in my hand, I recognized it as a messenger chip. "Next time let's both be more careful." He walked away and disappeared into a flowing current of commuters. I went the opposite direction, wading through the crowd to find a quiet spot. Along the far wall, electronic signs pointed to a row of bright orange public vid-cast cubicles. Those enclosed rooms featured decent quality v-cast generators and a sound-proof interior, which would provide me a modicum of privacy. Slipping between a throng of people, I ducked inside the nearest call-cube. Detecting my presence, the booth's resident non-sentient hologram, a smiling blonde woman wearing an old-fashioned blue aviation hat, materialized before me.

"Hello, traveler, would you like to v-cast to see a loved one today?" she asked. An invitation to input a payment choice shimmered over the display. I waved off the hologram and closed the opaque glass door behind me. I pulled out the message chip and touched it to my wrist-com. With a quick swipe on my small console, I played the message using a secure channel. Then the blonde attendant dematerialized, her photons and light reforming into the smirking holographic image of my least favorite IRS agent.

"Greetings, Jonah," spoke the baritone voice of Director Barnaby. "I trust you had a pleasant flight." The contrast between our respective travel arrangements became apparent when he paused to sip from an icy glass filled with an orange drink. "Listen carefully for your orders. You are to report to Copernicus Square and rendezvous with me. Your primary mission mandate is to assist me with the rescue of Dr. Okono. Your secondary mandate is to retire Lt. Colonel Colin Spenner. These mission orders are classified."

The chip dissolved in my hand as I walked out of the booth. My eyes looked to the destination board above me. Copernicus Square awaited to the west, while the Boreal Sector and possibly Vanessa awaited in the east. To hell with them. I decided to head toward the eastern platform and resume my search. Before I reached the platform, my legs froze. Unable to move any further east, I realized that the ShadeOS prevented me from disobeying Barnaby's direct orders. A heads-up display shimmered directly over my retina.

<<ShadeOS 22.33: Command line authorized >>
<<COMPLIANCE ORDER 1: Issued by Director Barnaby>>
<<MANDATE: Report to COPERNICUS SQUARE for rendezvous>>

"It appears you have been drafted, sir," Sasha noted with a glum tone.

Calming thoughts and a mental acceptance of my mission relaxed my paralysis. I sensed any further disobedience would cause similar reactions. Anger boiled through my veins. Freedom came to me only if it aligned with the goals of the IRS. I took a cautious step to the western platform and felt some relief that my feet complied. From my memory of studying moon tourist brochures, Copernicus Square occupied the heart of the United States territory, just twenty-five miles from the Lunar Spire.

I walked by a long line of yellow-outfitted shades shuffling into gigantic metal containers. When filled, this slingbox would be catapulted into space at a precise angle for its trip. Once afloat, the low gravity of the moon would take care of the rest, allowing the transport box to glide toward its destination, usually to an unsettled part of the moon.

On the next street corner, a rotunda terminal rotated empty pods for travelers. Upon entering a green vehicle, the interior lit up and a leather chair conformed to my body size. The reinforced glass activated, showing a digital moon map. My finger traced a route toward Liberty Sector and selected Copernicus Square. After three commuters ahead of me departed, my pod shot forward, barrel-rolling into the trans-city chute. Though it would be a short trip, I took the time to test whether the ShadeOS allowed conspiratorial thoughts. I enjoyed a brief fantasy of beating Director Barnaby to a pulp for subjecting me to forced service. Lucky for me, my mind's dark side was still my own.

CHAPTER 18
New Pharos, Old Feuds

*"Give me your tired, your poor, your
huddled masses yearning to breathe free,
The wretched refuse of your teeming shore.
Send these, the homeless, tempest-tossed, to me:
I lift my lamp beside the golden door. "*
- Excerpt from "The New Colossus", Emma Lazarus

Before my daydream's satisfying conclusion pushed Barnaby off a cliff, I arrived in United States territory. After exiting the pod, a revolving platform swung to my position. An illuminated pathway led me out of the port and onto a walkway atop a towering wall. A nearby plaque labeled this tall structure as the Union Wall. An inscription claimed this was the foundation of the first settlement. Beneath these words, someone had chiseled *'Divided We Fall'* into the metal. At first, the graffiti's message was not clear, until I continued further.

The Union Wall served as a bridge over Liberty Sector's two distinct areas: Columbus Station to the south and Copernicus Square to the north. On the southern side of the wall, a busy space-port of rocket pads brought a steady stream of Earth-born arrivals. This area catered to the poorer travelers, lured by the ever-burning torch of hope from the Lunar Spire. Upon arrival, many with dreams of luxury discovered a disappointing reality. Unable to afford even a small hovel within Copernicus Square, most found they could only afford the squalor that Columbus offered. A long line of disheveled immigrants waited at the gate between the two sections, hoping to enter the more affluent northern section. I looked to the north side of the wall and saw a marked difference in living conditions. Copernicus Square featured shining new apartment complexes with swooping, bright-colored pastel roofs. Like a postcard from the 1950s atomic age design come to life, the denizens here embraced a slice of a never-forgotten American dream. Fathers wearing business suits and wives in spring skirts played with their children in a green park. At the center of the manicured grass stood a pair of bronze statues honoring Buzz Aldrin and Neil Armstrong at the exact spot they planted the first American flag. Above, a curved metamorphic ceiling manifested a holographic sky with day and night cycles. The current weather illusion created a perfect summer day, complete with a bright sun and rolling cumulus clouds. While I contemplated ways to bypass the security gate of Copernicus Square, a voice behind me interrupted my planning.

"You were easy to sneak up on. We need to work on your secret agent skills," Barnaby chided in a low voice. After turning around, I failed to recognize him at first. He had shaved his mustache and head, smoothing his brown-skinned face and scalp. Instead of his designer suit, he sported jeans and a tight-fitting black turtleneck that revealed his thick shoulder and arm muscles. My eyes spotted the slight impression of his pistol hidden underneath his sweater. "Thanks for coming."

"I didn't have much choice, did I?" I growled back.

"No. I suppose you didn't," he replied without apology.

"I think I know where Vanessa is. I found a trail that leads to--"

"We'll investigate Charon at Goliath Corporation first," he interjected with a firm tone. A look of suspicion creased his face. "We find Dr. Okono. Then we find Vanessa--"

"Hear me out. Vanessa was Okono's lawyer," I interrupted. "She's the best clue we have. Like you said before, if our interests align, we can help each other." He closed his eyes, mulling over my argument. Then he opened them and sighed.

"Well...where is she?"

"An Israeli diplomat named Shoval visited Vanessa before he kidnapped her--"

"You don't know she was kidnapped," he argued.

"True," I acknowledged. "Though I did find evidence of her presence at Titan Technologies headquarters, which is near the embassy. We find her and maybe she'll lead us to Okono."

Barnaby stroked his chin. His eyes rolled to contemplate my words. Then he nodded in agreement. "We have to proceed carefully. Titan Tech has strong ties with the Israel government. They own the Boreal Sector territory. Not only do we lack jurisdiction there, but relations are tenser than ever. I still may have a contact that can get us through the Shamar Gate."

We walked back to the transport platform to take an express chute to the Israeli territory. Before we entered the pod, Barnaby gave another piece of advice.

"One more thing. If you see any robots, don't touch them. The Israelis take their security seriously."

* * *

The first ten minutes of travelling proved uneventful and awkward. Barnaby sat on the opposite side of the pod with his arms crossed and his eyes fixed on me. Watching the passing landscape, I witnessed a trio of rockets arriving. Were they bringing living or dead cargo? Either way, more money flowed from Earth to the moon. When the silence lingered too long, Barnaby reached into his sweater and retrieved the retracted handle of a stun-rod.

"You'll need this," he said, handing me the weapon. I took it and let another few moments of quiet pass before he spoke to me again. "I've been waiting for you to ask me about Colonel Spenner."

"What's there to ask?" I snapped back. "You ordered me to kill him, right? Last time, he completely missed two of my major arteries, so taking him out should be a snap." The sarcasm brought a smirk to his lips.

"You should consider that order a favor," he said. "Deep down, you know it's inevitable. He will return for you and your loved ones. He's relentless. And if you want to save Vanessa, he will have to be stopped. For what it's worth, I'm sorry about that." he replied. This time, I heard no trace of superiority, no hint of an order, and no smugness. He looked at me with an expression of pity, like he had diagnosed me with a disease that lacked a cure.

"Why would you be sorry?"

"We, as a people, have a poor history of wielding technologies and machines before we understand all of their consequences," he muttered. "In difficult times, we gave Spenner great powers to carry out sanctioned and unsanctioned operations..."

"You're talking about his Crimson Gate echelons. Can we shut down his access to them?"

"The access is a part of him, it can't be revoked easily. Many have tried," Barnaby muttered with a frown. The conversation triggered a memory of the Louisiana mission. While Spenner was driving, he revealed his right forearm and showed a glimpse of a red marking. If that was the key to his power, I deduced there was only one grisly solution to sever his connection.

"It's a biocircuit military tattoo," I guessed.

"Yes," Barnaby replied with a nod. "He's the last surviving member of a special team. The last to wield weapons that need to be forgotten. After Spenner turned rogue last year, we sent our best agents to retire him and close the Crimson Gate forever. Each time, he unleashed a different hell and delivered their bodies back to us as mangled shades."

"That's not very different than what he did to me, is it?" I asked. "How can I succeed?"

"First, the new serum is already making you stronger and faster," said Barnaby. "Second, you're the only one who's encountered Spenner and *survived*. Though I admit that term isn't exactly appropriate. Third, your unique allies offer you distinct advantages. The White Djinn, for instance--"

"The Djinn's likely dead," I interjected. "So we can't count on his cavalry. What else do we have?

"Well, then, Plan B," Barnaby said with a thin smile. He rolled his right sweater cuff to reveal his tattooed forearm. The twisting, serpentine body of a green lung dragon twisted around his arm, its fanged mouth opening wide at the yellow display of his wrist-com. I recognized it as a mark of seventh-echelon mastery. While not quite at the level of Spenner's deadly Crimson Gate, it indicated an impressive level of skill. "I also have a few tricks up my sleeve."

Weighing the odds, I bit my lip, betraying my doubts of our chances against Spenner. Barnaby's grin turned to a scowl. His brown eyes glistened with an intensity I remembered seeing from veteran soldiers during wartime. It was a look of absolute calm acceptance that comrades expressed when they expected to die with a brother.

"We'll find a way to protect the ones that depend on us. There's no Plan C for men like us," he said.

* * *

Like a bullet shot through a gun's barrel, our white travel-pod hurtled through a straight-shot chute tube stretching east from the Lunar Spire. A four-hundred-mile tract of wasteland stood between the Lunar Spire and Boreal Sector.

While Barnaby occupied himself with a call from headquarters, my gaze followed a strange silhouette rushing towards us on the horizon. My tired eyes interpreted the shape as a spiky, monstrous sea anemone writhing on the gray expanse. I blinked, shook my head, and then looked again. With the second glance, the 'monster' appeared to be a hulking, oval-shaped mining ship hovering over a recently formed crater. Over five hundred floating shades swarmed over the site, tethered to the craft by flexible steel cords. They worked to extract rare minerals and valuable ores from a fallen meteor. These valuable resources would be resold to proto-matter factories owned by companies like Goliath Corp.

Our pod veered toward a packed cluster of six dozen shades, all focusing their strength on moving a mammoth rock. The chute's path weaved between the work crew, almost close enough to touch them. I concentrated on connecting with the TauK Network as I did on the shuttle. After a moment, a digital display appeared over my sight, for my eyes only.

<<Initiating Tau Kappa Network protocol>>

<<Network connection...successful>>

At first, I heard only a rhythmic humming. Then the sound became more distinct as the pod passed a dozen shades near the transport tube. I placed my hand on the window, drawing as close as possible to them. Then I heard the screams. Tormented howls filled my mind, almost drowning out faint words begging for help. Unable to face that agony again, I moved away from the window. As our pod continued speeding along its true course, the screams and pain faded like driving away from a police siren. After shaking my head, the TauK display disappeared from my inner sight.

Barnaby looked over to me and noticed the beads of sweat falling from my temples. He looked concerned and reached out to put his hand on my shoulder.

"What have you done to me?" I demanded, pulling away from him.

"Are you okay?" he asked. "What are you talking about?"

"Tell me about the TauK Network," I replied. "The Tau Kappa waves of the shades."

"H-how do you know about that?" stammered Barnaby. "That's a classified project we mothballed over ten years ago. Dr. Okono led the team, but... it never worked."

"It works," I insisted, pointing to my head. "The ShadeOS you put inside of me...it lets me sense them."

"Are you sure it isn't--"

"The serum allows me to connect with them through the TauK Network," I interrupted. "Dr. Okono must have finished the research. I believe that's why he's missing." My eyes widened and I pointed to my ear. "I *hear* them. They feel, and they hurt. They're alive...burning alive. All of them."

His posture stiffened. He leveled his gaze at me, ready for the argument. But he stayed quiet. For a long while he stared at my eyes, studying my features. A growing look of horror twisted his face. A man like Barnaby, a decorated agent of multiple government agencies, interrogated many people across his career. Rigorous training taught him the facial tells exposed during human speech. His experience made him a human lie detector. His own expression told me that he sensed my honesty.

In the distance, our station stop started to grow larger as we neared our destination. Still silent, Barnaby pulled out a small metallic sphere, like the mobile generator I used on my missions to summon the holo-judge. With a flick of his hand, Barnaby activated it, causing it to glow and float in the air. Light scattered in all directions, until a silver cloud of photons coalesced into the friendly visage of a familiar-looking priest.

"Greetings, Director Barnaby," said the smiling face of Erasmus. "And hello to you as well, Jonah. How can I help you?"

"Is this a secure line, your eminence?" asked Barnaby.

"Indeed it is," replied Erasmus, his smile faded when he sensed the gravity of the situation. "What is troubling you, my son?"

"Cardinal Erasmus, I must inform you, per section 43.22 subsection 23.6c of the Afterdeath Accord between our agencies, that a new development has come to our attention." Barnaby paused to take a deep breath. "Jonah, please tell Erasmus everything you just told me. Spare no details."

Addressing the holo-sphere, I retold the story of yesterday's harrowing shuttle trip. I explained the TauK Network and proposed my theories. I heard Erasmus gasp when I described the suffering of the shades. Looks of pure shock and revulsion rippled across the shimmering photons of Erasmus' digital face. Before he could compose himself, his face contorted with a look of utter sadness. Liquid, pixelated tears rolled down the contours of his cheeks.

"One moment," he whimpered, ducking out of view. We heard him sob. It took a long time for him to regain his composure and his holographic form. We waited in silence until he reappeared.

"The New Church...appreciates you coming forward with this terrible discovery," he said, his voice cracking. "We will work with the government to investigate this...discreetly, at first. It is more important than ever that you recover Dr. Okono safely," Erasmus said. "Godspeed to you both."

The sphere closed, fell silent, and dropped into Barnaby's hand as the pod made its final approach to the next station.

* * *

We stopped at the far eastern edge of New Pharos at a junction station called Terminus Delta. When the pod doors opened, an enclosed beige corridor greeted us. We floated from the pod and reached the airlock chamber. Like most habitable locales on the moon, the station's walled interiors featured vented atmospheres and artificial gravity. We followed red pulsing arrows directing us to a bustling terminal filled with people. All of them walked between eight different platforms to ride chutes back to the western sectors of the moon.

Following the path to Boreal Sector, we stepped onto a fast walk-platform that carried us into a mile-long transparent tunnel. The bridge spanned the craterous gap between this chute terminal and the colony we sought. Looking down at the see-through floor, I strained to see the bottom of the dark chasm. As we glided along the moving floor, Boreal's towering outer wall grabbed our attention, filling our entire sight. The Shamar Gate, an indomitable protective barricade, made the city a veritable fortress. It had guarded its citizens from petty territorial wars and frequent micro-meteor showers for almost two decades. Flanking the central entrance, a pair of massive human-shaped metal statues stood, each with their arms raised to the stars. Their silent vigil welcomed us to the open gates. The hands of the statues each touched the lip of the settlement's protective dome covering, as if the giants held the colony's roof in place.

"Gen-1 Golems," remarked Barnaby, pointing at the nearest one-hundred-foot-tall colossus. "Titan Tech's first and best model. Before all the big robots went haywire during the rebellion, these behemoths erected the first lunar outposts. Damn tough bastards." His eyes gleamed while he recalled some vivid memory. "Just one of those can build you an outpost...or tear one down."

"Magnificent inventions," Sasha marveled. "Perhaps one day humans will learn to trust them again." I doubted if that would happen soon. After the Promethean Laws passed, corporations became reliant on shades. Like many people on Earth, the robots lost their jobs to cheaper labor.

When we entered the Boreal Sector, a trio of armed human guards screened visitors. Before we reached the checkpoint, a pale man dressed in a beige business suit approached us and escorted us to the guards.

"These are my guests from the Lunar Spire," the man proclaimed. The guards lowered their weapons and waved us through.

"Thank you, Administrator Bal," Barnaby said to our benefactor.

"We are even now, old friend," he whispered, with a nervous glance to me. "No more favors. If you are caught, I will deny this happened. Be careful. The IRS is not welcomed here." With that, Barnaby nodded, and Bal slunk away down a shadowed titanium corridor.

"That was the easy part," Barnaby muttered to me. "Stay sharp."

We left the security area and entered a central hub filled with hundreds of blue-collar human workers. They moved with purpose between different complexes. Unlike the green and open Copernicus Square, no gardens or luxury amenities brightened this austere place. With no windows, this area made me feel claustrophobic. Twenty feet above, countless rows of giant-sized spinning fans spun to vent the soot from multiple factories. The halls resounded with echoes of grinding cogs and turning gears.

"Huh. No shades," I mumbled.

"The primary employer of Boreal Sector is David Solomon, the Israeli-born CEO of Titan Technologies. He has prohibited the use of any shade labor in his company," Sasha reported.

"We'll find the headquarters in the city's center, only a few more blocks from here," Barnaby said.

"I'm analyzing the architectural layouts for that building," whispered Sasha. "As you might suspect, there are high-end security systems protecting all of the major entrances. I will continue to breach their network."

"What about smaller access points?" I asked.

"There is an air ventilation shaft adjacent to the station's ceiling protected only by an antiquated infrared sensor." Sasha paused to access her humor subroutines. "Since it's on the rooftop, perhaps you could put on a red suit and slide down the chimney?"

"Something tells me the Israelis won't be excited to see Santa Claus," I mumbled back.

Flashing a look of irritation, Barnaby nudged my ribs and interrupted my conversation with Sasha. "What's the plan for breaking in?" He looked at me intently for an answer.

"I'm making this up as I go along. I don't break into secure buildings every day--"

"Technically, sir, you have broken into secure facilities on consecutive days," Sasha corrected me. I acknowledged her with a slight grin.

"There's a spot on the roof we could try. Let's scout it out."

Barnaby nodded and we proceeded into a more spacious city square. A higher roof accommodated a dozen thirty-foot-tall buildings, forming the economic district of Boreal Sector. Above them all, the Titan Tech's corporate headquarters dominated the city's center. Like an extruded hexagon, the building featured a star-shaped design. At the topmost level of the structure, the Israeli flag billowed underneath the spinning air vent. At the ground floor entrance, a quartet of guards, armored in their hulking ogre battle-suits, screened a steady flow of diplomats and businesspeople.

"The front door is a poor choice. Let's make our way to the back," I said in a hushed tone. Barnaby followed me around to the west corner of the building. I spotted a small five-foot-wide alley between the headquarters and another building. As we edged our way along the walls, my eye caught a subtle movement at the far end of the passageway. The silhouette of a man slinked between small recesses of the passageway, stopping at a maintenance console. It looked like he intended to perform a manual hardwire hack into Titan's secure network. As we crept closer, his wrist-com glowed with a familiar crimson energy. Fear paralyzed me as the light revealed the man's angular face, broad shoulders, and tight-cropped gray hair cut by a telltale scar.

"It's Spenner," I whispered, pointing. "In the alley."

"Approach carefully," Barnaby responded. We both slid our hands down to ready our weapons. "If I can get close enough, I can neutralize his Crimson Gate advantage." With measured steps, we crept toward our new target.

Despite our attempt at stealth, Spenner turned from the wall console. He flashed a grin before the crimson light winked out. With darkness covering him, he ran the other way deeper into the alley. We pursued, but we lost sight of him at an intersection where the path diverged to the east and west. An access ladder against the wall led up to the roof and the ventilation shaft, presenting a third possible escape route. With no trace of our quarry, we stopped to consider the next move.

"Happen to have a three-sided coin?" I joked.

"Damn, he moves fast," Barnaby growled.

"I'll catch him."

"Where are you going--" Before he finished his question, I had leaped up and scaled the first four rungs of the ladder.

"The roof, though I suspect he's already long gone," I replied. "Still, it wouldn't hurt to take a look around." Instead of an answer, Barnaby made an interrupted gasping sound.

"On the contrary," hissed a female voice. "Your curiosity will hurt quite a bit."

I turned and looked down to see a woman dressed in a black and maroon jumpsuit with a reflective sheen. Her long black hair flowed over her shoulders. My eyes darted from Barnaby's angry expression, to her smug face, and down to the curved blade she held at his throat.

"Don't move, Director. I wouldn't want you to get nicked. Where is your friend, the third spy?" she demanded.

"Let's see...you have the ability to drop in unnoticed onto two trained agents, you wield a ceremonial sica knife, and you have a penchant for black," muttered Barnaby in a measured tone. "Jonah, meet Shoshana Rabin."

A fleeting, surprised expression flickered across her face, replaced by an impish grin. I dropped down from the ladder, retrieved my stun-rod, and activated it just as I reached the ground. This show of dexterity would unnerve a common thug, but the woman looked underwhelmed. With the blue light of my weapon pushing away more of the alley's shadows, I spotted an ankle-high motion sensor that one of us had tripped. This mistake must have summoned the nice lady with a knife at my partner's neck.

Her free hand groped Barnaby's shirt and pants, and then it started raining spy gadgets. With nimble fingers, she deactivated each weapon before sending them clattering to the ground, including a side revolver, vibro-knife, a paralytic syringe, and a hidden stun-tube in a pants pocket. However, she held onto a small pistol.

With one smooth motion, she shoved Barnaby to the ground, and aimed the gun at him. Then she looked to me and raised her curved dagger as a challenge. Despite feeling unnerved, I held my ground, though the practical side of my brain argued the virtues of fleeing.

"All of the local v-cast generators are locked out, so I am unable to manifest," Sasha said with a tone of concern. "I will continue my attempts to break the security seal. Jonah, please try not to end up in the hospital again, or I will require additional memory to calculate your hospital bills." A brief smirk creased my lips, and then disappeared while I appraised the woman standing before me. Her balanced stance suggested martial arts training. Everything about her style, countenance, and manner hinted at advanced field training. For instance, she executed a Krav Maga takedown maneuver on Barnaby, a favorite combat discipline employed by the Israeli army. We just encountered the real security guard.

"She's also known as the Black Rose," Barnaby added, rising to a kneeling position with his arms raised in submission. "AKA the Black Lily, AKA Black Rose, or just Rose. Her dossier indicated she had died in action as a Mossad agent. Clearly that report is inaccurate. I'm a big admirer of your work, especially your mission in Moscow. Jonah, I think it would be best if you drop your weapon before she kills you."

"So, you've heard of me," Rose acknowledged. "Which means you're connected and have half a brain. Now tell me, who was the third man hacking into our network?"

"I am 92% through the security defense," Sasha whispered. "I recommend a stalling tactic."

"No, we tried to stop that other man," I replied. "Why don't you allow my associate to stand up and we can chat about this?" I said, taking a step forward with my weapon lowered.

"I think you should stop--" suggested Barnaby before Rose cut him off. She tapped her own maroon-colored wrist-com device, granting her access to the nearby v-cast generator. She invoked a simple, low-level imprisonment echelon. The v-cast generator complied with a tinny whine, creating iron-binding chains that tightened around Barnaby's legs, arms, and mouth.

He tried to speak through the chains, likely to warn me, but his glowing bonds allowed him only a muffled grunt.

With startling speed, Rose closed the distance between us and slashed at me with her keen knife. My stun-rod became a shield to parry her swift attacks. She pirouetted and her sica blade sliced through the air and caught the center of my stun-rod. With a twisting motion, she pried my weapon out of my grasp and sent it flying to the other side of the alley. She twirled again and raised the pommel of her blade over my head.

"I am in the network," said a welcome voice in my ear. Just as Rose's knife descended, Sasha materialized with a flash of deep blue coalescing light. Inches above my head, she caught Rose's hand before the blunt hilt of her weapon struck me. "You do not strike him," Sasha warned. Her grip on Rose started failing as soon as she made contact.

"I strike when I want," Rose snapped back. Then she unleashed a brutal flurry of kicks and punches against Sasha's new virtual form.

Sasha managed to block the first two kicks, but the second barrage proved too overwhelming. Knocked back into the wall by the ferocity of the attack, even Sasha's heightened reflexes missed the final stroke of the sica knife. As the blade sunk into her semi-solid form, bright blue light spurted from her chest. The high-pitched whine of the local v-cast generator's matter reclamation cut off Sasha's brief scream.

"Your girlfriend is breaking up with you," Rose quipped.

Sasha's distraction earned me enough time to access the security hole she opened in the local v-cast network. My wrist-com panel illuminated and my fingers evoked a shatter-hack that dissolved Barnaby's bonds. As Sasha's form exploded into brilliant sparkles and fragments of floating proto-matter, Rose spun around to face me with an expression of anger.

My fingers danced against my console, ordering the v-cast to gather up the proto-matter from Sasha's body. The particles whisked toward me and they reassembled into a thin steel rapier gleaming in my hand. Though Rose outmatched me, I brandished the sword with defiance. Barnaby stood up, his yellow wrist-com blazing to life, summoning a massive battle-axe to his hands. Emboldened by improved odds, we advanced on Rose.

"This has been fun, boys," Rose purred, "but it's time for you to see my employer." She exploded into action, sweeping and spinning toward us like a tornado. I felt her knife strike my virtual rapier and by the time I steadied it she moved away to swipe at Barnaby. She kept the two of us off balance long enough until a loud mechanical grinding noise filled the alley.

"Surrender," boomed a man's modulated voice through a speaker. I turned sideways to keep Rose in view and see the newcomer. An ogre guard took a thundering step closer, with its metal arms raised against me, each containing a deadly micro-missile launcher. Behind the metal hulk, another armored guard joined the fray. It was time to surrender.

"Check," I sighed. My rapier and Barnaby's axe fell from our hands, disintegrating into photonic ash.

"But perhaps not yet checkmate," Sasha whispered. "I will keep my toe dipped in their network."

"Now let's explore creative ways of making you both talk," Rose said, grabbing me. She drummed her fingers playfully on my shoulder, then pushed me toward the entrance of Titan Tech's headquarters.

* * *

After passing through the guarded entrance, we entered an interior that was reminiscent of a fortified bunker. Like the foyer of a modern day castle, two rows of suits of armor flanked the long marble floor hall. However, these blue-and-white-colored titanium wardens proved to be more than just metal guards, as Sasha explained to me.

"Titan Tech first launched the Power Knight robot line fifteen years ago," Sasha said as I walked through the gauntlet. The ten-foot-tall metal frames looked imposing enough. When I saw that each of the twenty-four knights clutched four-foot-long electrical scimitars, I knew that I needed to behave. "They were used as combat models, specialized for sentry duty. It appears most of these units are deactivated, except for the last two at the end of the hall."

Behind the robots, a floating holographic display played a looping promotional video regaling the once-proud history of Titan Technologies Corporation. After showing the evolution of its robot models, it touted the first patented AI system, the ill-fated 'Prometheus' model. The monitor showed the time before the shades, when Titan Tech dominated the non-human work force industry with its artificial beings. The first one thousand Prometheus androids built the base of Lunar Spire, mined the first asteroids, and explored the surface of Venus. As we continued walking down the hall, another monitor cycled through images of technology patents for artificial neurons and synapses. The whole gallery impressed me. Before I joined the military, I hoped to get a job at Titan Tech as a programmer. That all changed twenty years ago when the Sentience War claimed one hundred and thirty human lives on the remote Callisto outpost.

"Tell me where you are taking us," Barnaby demanded. "I would like to--"

Before Barnaby finished his request, the metal-studded double doors ahead of us parted, revealing a spacious conference room draped with luxury. Plush brown leather chairs ringed a spherical table shining with polished digital glass. Above the room's center, two golden chandeliers adorned with looping diamond chains cast white and orange lights across the room. Three men at the table stared at mini-displays on the glass table, each window showing a different scene around the Titan complex, including the front door and the exterior alley.

Rose pushed us closer toward the table. As we approached, I saw two larger shapes in the back of the room covered in shadows. The telltale yellow glows from the central power cores of two ogre battle suits betrayed the positions of the two rear guards. The three men at the table looked up. Undaunted, Barnaby cleared his throat and addressed our captors.

"I'm Director Barnaby of the Incorporeal Revenue Service and I'd like to speak to the United States Ambassador immediately," Barnaby demanded. "The Lunar Senate would not appreciate my detainment."

"Yes, Barnaby, I will mention your grievance next time I am in the Senate," responded the man on the far left. I recognized him as Ambassador Ephraim Shoval, the same person who v-casted into my apartment a week ago to talk with Vanessa. Ephraim loosened his black tie and undid the top button of his white shirt. His cheeks reddened from irritation and he raised his left arm to point for emphasis. "Perhaps they would be interested in hearing why such a high-ranking US agent attempted to break into a lawful corporation and ally of the state of Israel? I don't think you understand the gravity of your position--"

"Now, Ephraim, let's not be rash," rasped the withered man sitting next to the Israeli ambassador. Dressed in an impeccable blue suit with a black tie, the man looked well over a hundred years old. A neatly trimmed, snow-colored beard covered his cheeks and chin. I recognized him from news vid-reports as David Solomon, the venerable CEO of Titan Technologies. Growing up as a teenager, I loved watching movies about giant robots and monsters. Computers, cybernetics, technology; all represented the pinnacle of human achievements to my inquisitive mind. During my college years, I idolized Solomon. Back then, he had made revolutionary contributions to scalable cybernetics and synthetic heuristics. "We should treat our visitors as guests," he continued. "Please, sit down. Where are my manners? Allow me to introduce everyone. My name is David Solomon, and sitting to my right is Ambassador Shoval, and to my left is my son Eli."

I knew Eli Solomon by reputation only. The oldest scion and heir to David's company and fortune, Eli studied business and law instead of science. David and Eli struck me as identical twins thirty years removed. While David sat enfeebled by old age, Eli projected the strength and sharpness of a man in his prime. He styled his beard like his father, though his hair showed much more black than gray.

"I see that you both have made the acquaintance of Shoshana," Eli said, grinning. He gestured toward empty chairs while Rose escorted us to the seats. Barnaby sat first and then I took the seat next to him across the table from the Solomons. "So we know the name of the IRS agent." His lip curled with mild disdain when he motioned toward Barnaby. "But who are you?" he asked, pointing to me.

"Jonah Adams," I replied.

Eli and David Solomon raised their eyebrows and glanced at each other. Rose edged closer behind me with her hand on the sica dagger's handle.

"How is this possible?" David asked in a wheezing voice. "Rose, you reported that he died..." The old patriarch looked frail and the effort of talking caused a brief coughing fit.

"Yes, sir, that is what we learned through the datanet," Rose answered with confidence. "I confirmed the death certificate myself."

"Some of my finest work," Barnaby mumbled.

"Perhaps an imposter then?" asked Rose.

"Or a convincing synthetic..." David added with a look of excitement, prompting Eli to jab at the glass display in front of him, evoking a stream of data.

"No. He passed our magnetic body scanner at the front gate, and he's organic. However..." Eli paused to double check a specific section of data related to Jonah's physiology. "Some of his vital signs are abnormal..."

"Machines, you can't always trust them," David said, chuckling. His son smiled and touched his father on the shoulder with affection. "Why don't we rely on a more natural test, eh?"

"Uncle David, are you sure?" asked Rose.

"Yes, dear. With your blade, I'd feel safe even if we had five hungry lions in the room. Please bring in our other guest." David motioned and the ogre guard behind him stepped aside, showing a hairline crack in the blue wall. It was another secret door.

As the wall parted, yellow light from the hidden room showed the silhouette of a woman. Within that freeze-frame of a moment, when golden light suffused her feminine outline, I let my imagination entertain the distant hope that Vanessa would walk into the room.

"Jonah?" asked a familiar voice. "I...I heard...that you died?" The woman stepped forward. Not trusting the first glance, I rubbed my eyes and studied the newcomer. Her reddish hair rested on slender shoulders, ending with thick curls. Light freckles dotted her fair skin. Hazel eyes sparkled, moistened by tears. It was the beautiful, crooked, deep-dimpled smile that told me to believe my senses.

"I wouldn't let a thing like death stop me from finding you." I stood up, brushing aside Rose's firm grip on my shoulder. The red-haired woman ran toward me, but Rose stepped between us.

"Is it Jonah?" Rose asked.

"There's only one way to find out," Vanessa replied with a smile. She placed a gentle hand on her protective guardian. Rose nodded and stepped back, but stood close enough to unleash a savage strike if she desired.

Vanessa leaned down to my face. Her red hair fell across my forehead and my shoulders. I smelled the sweet orchids of her favorite perfume. Then her hand caressed my left cheek and her lips touched my own. We kissed deeply. For the first time in many days I dropped my guard, relaxed, and allowed myself to feel joy. I tasted her salty tear as it trickled to my lips. Despite the specter of Rose's retribution, I risked raising my arms to touch her face and stroke her hair. Everything I wanted, the perfect companion, trembled ever so slightly within my arms. The optimistic part of my brain wished to believe that this long journey just ended. She pulled back from the kiss and smiled at me, still touching my cheek.

"Thank god you're okay," I whispered. "Did they hurt you? So help me, if they harmed you in any--"

"You insult us!" Eli protested, standing up. "She has been well provided for." The elder Solomon restrained his red-faced son with a gentle tug back into his chair. David whispered into Eli's ear and the younger scion calmed.

"It's true!" Vanessa agreed. "They've taken good care of me, Jonah. They've protected me, and treated me like family."

"Protected you?" I asked with unconcealed suspicion. "I saw the apartment, it looked like they kidnapped you! I came to save you!" That last statement brought frowns throughout the room.

"She's not a princess from one of your video games that needs saving," scolded Rose. "We didn't kidnap her--"

"Of course not," interrupted David Solomon. "I understand you are confused, Jonah. Allow me to shed some light. When Vanessa took the case to help my dear cousin Saul, we considered her a mensch, and part of our extended family. Then we promised to help her in any way we could..."

"The trouble came from another case I was working on," Vanessa continued. The threads started to stitch together for me.

"Dr. Okono...he came to you a week before," I added.

"Yes," she replied. "He made a breakthrough in his research. When he realized the significance of what he found, he felt his life was in danger. When my own brother threatened me, I knew my life was in danger too."

"We noticed some unusual queries circulating in the datanet about Vanessa," David continued. "As a safeguard, I assigned Rose to keep an eye on her after we heard you were leaving for your...work in Louisiana." At the mention of the collection job, the Ambassador, Eli, and Rose all glanced at each other with looks of distaste. Not surprising, since the Israelis opposed the existence and exploitation of shades. "Our intervention was timely. Hours after you returned to New York, one of our trusted informants reported disturbing news. A sizable contract circulated in the darkweb ordering the capture or execution of Vanessa."

"When we learned about the contract, I went immediately to the apartment to evacuate Vanessa," said Rose. "Spenner arrived only minutes after we left. He must have ransacked the apartment looking for traces of her."

"I'm sorry, Jonah," Vanessa said, tears welling up in her eyes. "I didn't have time to say goodbye. They said I couldn't contact you for my own safety. Then I heard...you had died..."

"Kiss her again. Tell her it's okay," Sasha urged in the faintest of whispers, so soft I don't think she intended for me to hear.

"You don't ever have to apologize to me," I said, wiping her tears away. I kissed her again, longer this time. For that wonderful span of time, we forgot that others occupied the room. In that kiss, we shared a special message and a promise to each other. "It's all okay now, love."

"*A kiss is a secret which takes the lips for the ear*," Sasha said, even quieter this time. It took me a second to recall the Cyrano de Bergerac quote. Then the room erupted with her voice.

"A kiss is a secret which takes the lips for the ear," boomed her loud echo. Vanessa pulled away from our embrace. Everyone in the room appeared confused except for David Solomon.

"Sir, I didn't do that," said Sasha, mortified. "He must have used well-concealed hypersensitive listening devices--"

"Don't fret my dear," David said, a smile wrinkling his face. "I've been waiting to meet you. Please, feel free to manifest. You may use our v-cast generators." David's gnarled hand moved over the glass table, removing the security lock-out.

The high-pitched whine of the v-cast generator announced the arrival of Sasha to the gathering. This time, she chose to manifest with the white dress, given to her by the White Djinn. The flowing fabric covered her light-blue-tinged legs to her ankles and her arms to her elbows. In her flowing dark blue hair, Sasha shaped her omni-flower as a pink orchid. Struck by her beauty, David let out an audible gasp and put his hand to his mouth too late to cover it.

"Greetings, everyone," Sasha said with a slight bow.

"Wonderful," David gushed. "I am so pleased to meet you, Sasha. I have heard much about you, but those reports pale to describe how special you really are. Jonah, you must be so proud." His eyes gleamed with excitement, like a child given an early birthday present. I sensed true admiration and appreciation in the man's face. He looked at me with his gray eyes and a youthful grin that defied his aged body. "Perhaps, when you are ready for a new career, you would consider working for Titan? What do you think, Eli?"

"As it happens, we are looking for a new Project Leader in R&D," Eli replied with a nod.

Barnaby stood up from his chair, ignoring a cold look from Rose, and patted me on the back. "While I'm happy to see this couple reunited, we have another crucial matter to discuss," Barnaby said. "We need to find Dr. Okono immediately. We fear he's in danger and that his research will fall into the wrong hands. Do you know where he is?"

"We suspect Goliath Corporation has detained your doctor," David answered, his jovial expression replaced with a serious one. "Our agent in the Lunar Spire believes Gabriel Charon himself moved Okono to a secure location. His company and family have been a thorn in my side for many years." Eli's eyes narrowed, and his lips pursed at the mention of their rival. "It would make good business sense, and it would be my pleasure, to help in any way I can."

"If Goliath Corp is holding the doctor, he will be tough to find," Barnaby said. "They own many factories, mines, labs, and stations around the moon. Do you have any idea where he might be?"

"I lost contact with L'iol days ago," Vanessa replied. "The last message he sent to our secure communication line was encrypted. Unfortunately, I haven't been able to decipher it." She waved her hand over the table to play the message. At first, I heard only digital noise, garbled nonsense, and crackling static. Then the sounds melded together into a familiar humming sound. A prickling sensation came over me and the ShadeOS activated within me. This time, a rectangular interface element floated over the corner of my right eye. It showed an analysis of the audio's waveforms, drawing the sinusoidal peaks and valleys like the readout of a digital heart monitor. Then the noises became a clear voice and the geometric lines reformed into letters and words over my vision.

<<ShadeOS 22.330: Command line authorized>>
<<Tau Kappa interface initiated>>
<<Still alive. In purgatory.>>

"Purgatory," I muttered.

"What did you say?" asked Barnaby.

"Still alive. In *purgatory*. That's the message Dr. Okono sent. He sent it through the TauK Network. The only people capable of understanding that message are the ones that know his research and shades," I explained. "In fact, one of the shades the doctor was studying at his lab said that message as well. Sasha, isn't purgatory another word for hell?"

"More accurately, it is a theological concept describing a tortuous plane of existence in-between Earth and the afterlife," Sasha corrected. "A place where souls not ready for heaven are burned to cleanse their sins."

"Wait, shades? You can understand this message?" the elder Solomon whispered. "You can speak with the dead, how is this--"

"Jonah's status is classified," Barnaby interrupted.

"Purgatory," Eli whispered. "Perdition. Hell." Eli looked to David with a grave expression on his face. "He speaks of Gehenna. All of those poor souls. Dear God...father, you were right all along. How could we not have known this?"

Vanessa looked away, the weight of her secret burden causing her pain.

"No one holds you responsible for honoring your vows, dear," David said consoling her. "She did not tell us the details of Dr. Okono's research, much to her credit. She honored her vow of confidentiality. However, we are fairly sure we know what my people, what the Israeli government, has suspected for the past twenty years."

"And what is that, Mr. Solomon?" Barnaby asked

"That the shades are alive," David rasped. "That they toil and suffer in their own private Gehenna, and monsters like Gabriel Charon, who profit from the shades, do not want people to know."

"*Allegedly* alive," Barnaby countered with a raised finger. "We have yet to validate this assumption. All of our scientists and religious leaders have confirmed that shades possess no soul. With all of the science at their disposal, how is it possible that--"

"It's possible that Dr. Okono found a new scientific way to listen to the soul," David suggested. "Whether or not we have the same reasons, we can both agree that Dr. Okono must be removed from Charon's stronghold."

"Yes, that is our mission," Barnaby agreed. "Jonah and I must be resuming that soon--"

"But here, on the moon, your US government no longer wields the influence it once did," Eli added. His keen gray eyes glittered, sensing an opportunity. "We have common goals here, Director Barnaby, and we can offer our aid..."

"What can you offer and what do you expect in return?" Barnaby asked, frowning.

"Our motives are transparent, Director," David responded, his arms spread as a gesture of trust. "We believe all of the shades need to be freed, or laid to rest. They are unnatural, and worse, they suffer."

"This is not an easy thing to prove, and not an easy thing to undo," Barnaby cautioned. "You cannot imagine how much depends on shade labor. Everything connects to it. Corporations and colonies will scream about their dependence--"

"Yes, but Titan Technologies stands ready to fill that gap," Eli said, grinning. "Our next generation androids are affordable, strong, scalable..."

"...and safe," added David, slapping his hand on the table for emphasis. "If the United Nations would suspend, or even relax the Promethean Laws, we could have a more humane labor force. Sasha is a shining example for the future of artificial labor--"

David, Eli, and Barnaby argued and negotiated back and forth. I listened for a few moments but my thoughts turned inward. The Solomon family's interest in helping made sense to me now. Their strong Hebrew faith played a part in their opposition to the shade-trade, though there was an economic angle as well. I realized in this world, no white knights galloped to the rescue. Everyone wanted to earn a buck. A great game of chess played out across two worlds and I still needed to figure out whether my piece should move forward, diagonally, or laterally. No matter what, I would protect my queen. In order to be with Vanessa, I had to complete the mission and pay off my debt to Barnaby. So I focused my thoughts again, playing back the message from Dr. Okono. The words echoed in my head. In purgatory, a possible metaphoric reference to an afterlife of suffering. The idea to consider different meanings came to mind. A memory nagged at me. The answer hovered on the periphery of my brain, like a distant light hovering behind a haze of fog. Before I reasoned out the puzzle, a movement at the far end of the room pulled me back from my deep contemplation. At first, I thought the person inside the ogre battle-suit meant to stretch. However, when I saw the glimmer of yellow from the armored arm, I knew it intended to do harm.

Sasha detected my access to the wrist-com first, her gaze looking to me and then to the ogre guard. The suit took a step forward and the shining arm took aim at David Solomon, horrifying the helpless pilot inside.

"S-sir, Mr. Solomon, I can't control the ogre," cried the guard.

My wrist-com blazed, and my fingers wove a ward echelon. The local v-cast generator complied, manifesting a floating triangular-shaped shield. With a flick, I flung it forward and bashed the ogre. The impact nudged its metal arm, sending an off-course energy blast burning through the ceiling above.

Sasha and Rose reacted with swiftness. Rose drew her blade and leaped onto the table, flipped to the other side of the room, and landed in front of the ogre. Realizing that an innocent person wore the suit, Rose sliced at the exposed weapon systems intending to disarm it. With four quick slashes, the missile guidance system and the mounted-plasma cannon fell to the ground. Sasha took advantage of Rose's assault to move David and Eli away from the combat.

"Come with me, sirs," Sasha urged. Eli and Sasha escorted the elder Solomon to the far side of the room.

The noise of metal striking metal resonated through the room followed by a heavy thud. Rose's surgical strikes to the robotic suit's hydraulic leg sent it crashing to the floor.

"Why did the suit malfunction?" Eli yelled from across the room. "What happened?"

"I don't think that was a malfunction," I replied. "Everyone, be ready."

The battlesuit started to smoke from the damage Rose inflicted on it. Then the vapors formed a horrific looking apparition. Gathering the rising smoke around itself, the ghost-creature sprouted bony wings. Its viral code burrowed into the v-cast generator, ordering it to give it more substance. Red smoke and vapor coalesced around it, forming the visage of a monstrous specter with a bloody skeletal face.

"Holy hell, it's a dybbuk virus!" shouted Barnaby.

After Barnaby's words, the creature looked for a new mechanized target, leaving wispy trails of smoke behind as it moved. Its eyes, floating motes of energy, glittered with a crimson color.

Spenner must have planted a Crimson Gate virus into Titan's network when he accessed the alleyway terminal. The dybbuk was a relic leftover from one of the past three vicious cyber-wars. Years ago, some young programmer followed orders and coded this wicked virus to inflict harm on a forgotten enemy. When that war ended, the military buried those cyber weapons in the Crimson Gate virtual construct. Like a grave robber, or a necromancer, Spenner had raised this horror from its tomb and unleashed it against us.

"It will jump to another machine. Be ready," Barnaby cautioned. As he predicted, the wraith beat its large wings and flew into the mechanical body of a nearby powered-knight. The automaton stood silent over David and Eli until a hollow metallic groan announced its awakening. The two Solomons looked petrified when the metal statue took a step toward them. Energized by the dybbuk virus program, the knight's massive black fists raised into the air.

"The neck...weakest spot in the armor," David gasped.

Sasha pushed David away while Rose made three leaps across the room to intercept the ten-foot-tall robot. My hand gestured, and wove a duplication echelon. Using the cameras inside the room, I copied the likeness of David Solomon and fed them back into my program. The local v-cast generator whined and used its proto-matter to create a realistic facsimile of David Solomon.

My ruse worked as the powered-knight's helm turned toward the virtual clone. With its target acquired, the possessed suit attacked. The mighty fists smashed through the fake body, creating an explosion of glittering proto-matter. Realizing the deception, the dybbuk pivoted its host robot toward Eli Solomon. By the time its armored boot took a step, Rose engaged it with a vicious flurry of blade strikes, cutting its power conduits. She pushed off the nearby table, leaped onto the protruding chest of the robot itself, and plunged her dagger into its neck. Sparks flew and brackish oil spilled out from the crippled guardian as Rose flipped away. Looking around, I noticed that this opulent executive room contained seven more black powered-knights and another ogre guard. There were plenty of targets for the dybbuk to possess next.

"Eli, can you lock down access in and out of this room? We don't want this to get away," barked Barnaby. His arms waved to coordinate the defense in the brief lull between the dybbuk's attacks.

"Y-yes I think so," Eli said, still looking frazzled. He ran to the glass command table as the winged dybbuk's ghost reappeared. It screeched and streaked across the room to enter another host body.

"Jonah and Sasha, try to contain that thing in whatever robot it chooses," Barnaby ordered. "I may have something to catch it." As he spoke, his wrist-com shimmered with a verdant hue. The draconic tattoo writhed along his arm, the ink coming to life, and the dragon's tail wrapped around his wrist and fingers.

"Affirmative. I am attempting to isolate the virus by deactivating all remote communication ports in the remaining armor suits," responded Sasha.

Another possessed armored robot jumped off its pedestal and moved toward Rose. This one moved swifter, indicating the dybbuk's learning systems improved its control with each possession. It raised its left metal arm, aiming its plasma launcher at her. She dodged a scorching energy beam, and sprinted away to hide behind a still dormant powered-knight. When the pursuing knight approached, Rose climbed the back of the statue she hid behind, and leaped off its shoulders. With four swift strokes, Rose disabled the core nervous system of the rogue machine. The wounded powered-knight fell to its knees, its head sparking from multiple gashes.

After she moved away, I activated my wrist-com to create a strong binding echelon. This program assembled proto-matter into a thick-barred iron cage that encircled the crippled robot. Then the furious dybbuk howled and attempted to fly. The translucent wraith-like form floated above the ruined powered-knight. Its glowing eyes glared around the room for its next mechanical host. When it beat its wings to depart, my virtual iron bars buckled, but held the creature. The ghost raged, wailing a piercing screech. Its clawed bony hands grabbed two of the bars and started to pull them apart, a visual manifestation of the virus attempting to bypass my ward. My hands tapped my wrist-com, reinforcing the echelon to compensate for the monster's great strength.

"Hurry," I urged, "it won't hold for long." The creature flailed, causing the cage bars to bend more with each fierce howl.

"I have completed the task of sealing the room and disconnecting all robots," Sasha reported.

"Let it go," Barnaby ordered, walking closer to my makeshift virtual jail. With several quick jabs of his wrist-com, he accessed the v-cast device and manifested his own trap program. The scaled dragon awakened, enlarging as it slithered off his arm. Its scales shimmered with different hues of green, and its small gossamer wings beat fast like a hummingbird. When the dragon finished materializing, I shut down my binding echelon. The bars disappeared and the dybbuk beat its wings toward the remaining ogre. Before it flew five feet, Barnaby's emerald dragon barreled into the spectral creature. The dybbuk raked its claws and bit deep into its opponent's long neck. The drake howled, but still wrapped its serpentine body around its target, enveloping the monster.

Barnaby winced at the burning pain on his arm and he strained to hold the dybbuk in place. With a few more jabs on his wrist-com, the emerald dragon opened its mouth, unhinging its jaws like a python, and devoured the creature whole.

"I wasn't sure that would work," Barnaby muttered. "That counter echelon is brand new." Before he covered the arm with his shirt, I noticed that his tattoo still smoldered on his arm, like the dying embers in a fire. The colors of the drake's scales now gleamed a darker green, flecked with crimson stains.

The rumble from two dozen footfalls announced the arrival of a dozen Titan security guards rushing into the room. A woman in a white lab coat ran behind them, her brown ponytail bobbing behind her. When she passed by, I spotted the name Dr. Hemmons printed on her lapel. She stopped near Eli, pulling him aside for a private conversation. They kept their voices low while walking away from me, but I caught a curious fragment of their discussion.

"I'm sorry, Mr. Solomon, we should have been here sooner," she gasped, out of breath from her sprint. She looked mortified and frazzled. "The intruder locked the guards in the outer corridor. Sir, this virus...it appears to share code traits to the one we saw on Callisto," Dr. Hemmons whispered. Eli's eyes widened.

"I want it analyzed, now--" he said, lowering his voice and pulling her further away. Before I could move to hear more, David Solomon limped toward me while holding onto Ambassador Shoval for support.

"My friends, you have saved my life," David said, beaming. "That hellspawn nearly killed my son!" He offered his hand out.

"We're allies now, Mr. Solomon. We help our friends," I responded, returning his handshake. David's utterance of the word 'hellspawn' echoed inside my head. With the assassin neutralized, my brain went back to solving the riddle of Dr. Okono's message. All the synonyms for the underworld flitted through my brain: Hell, Gehenna, Perdition...Purgatory. Then a strange thought bubbled up, and I rushed to the central glass table. My hand waved over it and manipulated the floating interface controls to evoke an extruded map of the Lunar Spire. Buildings, bridges, landing bays all sprouted from the table as a virtual projection. The image looked like a real miniaturized version of the city.

"Is it really that simple?" I muttered.

"What is it?" Barnaby asked. He approached behind me and watched as the overhead view of the city changed. With a flick, my hand traversed the width and breadth of the city, searching for my target.

"I may know where we need to go now," I announced. "Okono's message wasn't just random noise from the network. He chose it as a literal clue of his location. He's there," I said, zooming the view to Nova Sector, a wealthy district at the base of the Lunar Spire. The table's virtual projection shimmered, updating to show a busy promenade. Among the row of nightclubs and bars, the glowing sign for Club Purgatory shone the brightest. I zoomed the view closer to show a line of people stretching across multiple blocks, all hoping to enter the hottest nightclub. "He's being held there."

Eli considered the revelation, stroking the salt and pepper beard on his chin. "It's possible," he agreed. "Before he died, Guy Charon built the club for his son Gabriel as a birthday present. It's known to be an establishment where you can have any fantasy fulfilled for the right price."

"Something else is there. Security is stronger than I would expect for a nightclub," added Rose. "We've had it on surveillance for months. An agent of mine managed to see inside. Her report suggested that tunnels connect the levels beneath the club all the way across town to the Goliath Corp Headquarters. Getting in will be difficult."

"And there is the matter of the stiff cover charge," I joked, referencing the one-year afterdeath requirement to enter the club. Everyone turned to me, grim-faced. Silence greeted my attempt to lighten the mood.

"I, for one, appreciated your pun, sir. A clever play on words," Sasha whispered.

"We need to go to Club Purgatory immediately," Barnaby said.

"I'm going with you," Vanessa added.

"No. No," I responded. "It will be too--"

"Dangerous?" she interjected. "If they can reach me here, where will I be safe? I'll be better protected with you, Jonah."

"We will send Rose to help," David offered. "It is the least we can do." Rose nodded and sheathed her weapon. She took a few steps to stand next to Vanessa.

"Besides," Vanessa added. "When we do find Dr. Okono, he's much more likely to follow you if I'm there." She shot me a determined glare that ended the debate.

"Fine," snapped Barnaby. "It's settled, we go in as a four person team."

"The direct approach will be hard. We should have a cover," I recommended.

"Perhaps we can also help with that," David added with a grin. "Follow me to the dressing room."

CHAPTER 19
Underworld Undercover

"Oh, what a tangled web we weave, when first we practice to deceive!"
- Excerpt from "Marmion", Sir Walter Scott

David Solomon escorted us through the back door of the conference room into a gray-colored corridor. Cameras pivoted to watch our movements. Each turn of a passageway took us to a more secure area of Titan Technologies. We navigated through multiple guarded checkpoints at a slow and steady pace. When we stopped at an apparent dead end, David pressed his hand against a portrait of his son hanging on the wall. A hidden door slid open in the middle of the passage.

"Since I was a boy, I've had an obsession with secret doors," admitted David with a sheepish grin. "This complex is riddled with them; elaborate ones too, but if I told you where, well, they wouldn't be secret." He snickered. His child-like love of technology endeared me to him even more. Envy rose within me. Someday, I wanted to have a home riddled with secret doors too. "Forgive the theatrics, but these days we have had to take many precautions," he continued. He beckoned us to enter a laboratory brimming with sparking apparatuses, half-constructed machines, and three metal lab-benches cluttered with parts. An elongated mechanical claw-arm, equipped with sensitive micro-lasers, stretched down from a ceiling-mount. Silver colored mobile operating tables, like hospital gurneys, lined the far north wall. Each one held a robot in varying stages of repair or disrepair.

Eli Solomon conferred with two of his scientists in the center of the room. One of them, Dr. Shelby Hemmons, I had seen in the executive room. She was a tall, olive-skinned woman wearing blue-rimmed glasses and a white coat. Since I saw her last, she had let her ponytail down so her hair fell below her shoulders. The other woman stood a foot shorter than Eli and Shelby. She was fair-skinned with short-cut brown hair. Her lapel tag showed the name Dr. Evelyn Briggs. When David entered the room with his slow shuffle, Eli nodded to his father and the two scientists turned to address him.

"My staff has gathered the supplies you requested, Mr. Solomon," Shelby said, gesturing to Evelyn. The junior scientist delivered a light metal container that looked like an over-sized make-up compact.

"Thank you, Shelby and Evelyn," replied David. "Jonah, our research team was kind enough to do a rush job for you. While far from foolproof, the contents of this case should help you get through the front security of Club Purgatory." When he opened it, we saw four hypodermics with the stylized, calligraphic initials 'V-V' emblazoned on them. The box also contained four pairs of twinkling, multi-colored retinal lenses.

"After the Promethean Laws closed our android labs, Titan Tech diversified," explained Eli. "One of our subsidiaries created a new line of self-hypodermics -- Vitality Visage. It empowers customers to change their appearance with safe, home-based plastic surgery. We're almost FDA-approved for follicular stimu-lation, changing eye pigmentation, and minor alterations of cheek bone structure." His voice then lowered to a mumble. "We just have a few kinks and side effects to work out, of course. You can imagine, these products have other uses as well..."

"And I see corporate espionage is alive and well today," I added.

"A necessary evil," Eli said with a smirk. "The hypodermics have already been preset for you to match new cover personas. They should allow you to spoof all facial recognition scanners."

"What personas?" Barnaby asked.

"We've spent the last four years cultivating a garden of artificial identities," Shelby replied. "Perfectly legal within the bounds of the Promethean Laws, of course," she added after Barnaby shot her a curious look. "They operate from our servers and perform daily actions. Each of these personas has lived an active virtual life, with recurring bank transactions, property purchases, faked vacations, and a full virtual footprint. They'll pass any background check--"

"We can insert your likenesses to these personas retroactively and give you a temporary new life," Evelyn interjected. A slight tremble in her hands betrayed her nervousness. Maybe she felt competitive with the other scientist, hoping to impress her bosses?

Without hesitation, Rose injected herself with a hypodermic. First, her hair changed from black to blond. Then the adipose tissue in her cheeks flushed and widened. Her lips swelled to look lusher. Stimulated melanin in her skin changed her tone from pale to a tanned complexion. When she put her contact lenses over her eyes, the irises altered to sea blue. All of those incremental changes combined to make her look like a different person.

"Behold, Mrs. Sally Rickerson," said Eli, pointing to a transformed Rose and beaming with pride. "Our entire fourth quarter projections indicate this product will be quite profitable."

The rest of us obliged and injected ourselves with Vitality Visage. Barnaby's cheeks sagged, and his beard became fuller and grayer, adding fifteen more apparent years to his face. Vanessa's hair changed to blond, her cheeks widened, and her eyes became dark green.

Then my turn came to change. At first, I felt nothing. Then, a tingling sensation, like when an arm falls asleep and becomes numb, washed over my face. Although there was no pain, the feeling was uncomfortable. Looking at the reflection in the glass table, I watched my hair darken to black and grow longer, almost to the base of my neck. With a sparkle, my eyes changed to a light brown. Then the skin around my eyes and cheeks tightened, reducing my apparent age by almost a decade.

"Vanessa and Jonah, you will be Mr. Warren and Mrs. Cheryl Baker," Eli stated. "Both of you are wealthy lawyers from Staten Island." Eli tapped the screen of a nearby display showing a convincing fabricated scene. The new Visage-induced likenesses of Vanessa and I had been inserted onto the virtual identities. In that scene, we smiled for an unseen camera and toasted champagne on the eighty-ninth floor of a Lunar Spire condominium. These images, forged to look like security footage, would be distributed into the datanet in the event someone double-checked our credentials. Even though it was not real, I yearned for that life with Vanessa.

"Barnaby and Rose, you are the Rickersons," Eli continued. "Last month, you both sold all of your Texas cattle ranches to become space ore speculators. You just bought a mine on Mons Wolff in the Mare Imbrium. Good luck with that." Another display showed them embracing within their Lunar Spire home.

"Don't worry if you don't like your new look," Shelby added. "The effects wear off after seventy-two hours." She gave a wry grin. "Which will make customers come back to us every week."

"I have set up an account with the funds necessary to pay the VIP cover charge," Eli said, handing us each identity chips. I placed mine over my wrist-com, allow it to overwrite my basic profile information, name, and address.

"Scanners at the club's entrance will prevent us from smuggling weapons inside. Our intel suggests there is security station with an armory hidden behind the club's kitchen," added Rose. "I can get to it."

"We need to get to the nightclub, now. They could be moving Dr. Okono any time," Barnaby urged.

"Good luck and mazel tov to you all. If there's anything else you need, let us know," offered Eli.

"Do you have a hypodermic to teach dancing?" I asked.

* * *

After departing Boreal Sector, our chute ride to the Lunar Spire proved to be quiet and uneventful. Rose and Barnaby sat like stone statues, intense and focused. Vanessa broke the silence, telling me more about her stay at Titan headquarters. It made me happy to hear they treated her like family. She had worked with Eli each day to prepare a defense for his cousin Saul, and she said their case looked strong. Before she spoke about the details of the trial, the glittering lights of the Lunar Spire filled our view. I took Vanessa's hand and leaned over to kiss her neck. My head lingered on her shoulder to share a private conversation with her.

"When this is done, let's run away and start over," I whispered.

"I would like that," she answered, smiling.

"I gave up collecting, for good," I said.

"I know," she replied. "David asked one of his agents to keep an eye on you. They found out that the IRS assigned you to reap Arnold Tornuckle, but he survived because of an anonymous tip. I'm proud of you, love." She put her arm around me. For the first time in a long while, I dared to believe something might work out for me. "Then David showed me your death certificate from the datanet. What happened to you?"

My mouth opened, but I paused. It was a struggle to find the right words to explain what happened to me. Sensing my hesitation, Vanessa pressed a finger against my lips.

"Later. It only matters that you're here now," she said, squeezing my hand.

The travel-pod slowed to enter a terminal within the Lunar Spire's inner sector. We stopped within a silver archway. Dish-shaped sensors surrounded us, scanning the wearable identity chips of the passengers and cross-referencing with retinal scans.

This checkpoint prevented non-residents from entering the exclusive Nova Park.

"Permission approved. Welcome back to the Lunar Spire," a female voice said through the speakers. "Enjoy your evening." The pod sped along toward the final stop at the center of the city.

"Once we get inside the club, Barnaby and I will acquire weapons. You two find Dr. Okono," Rose ordered.

"Keep the chatter and access to their v-cast network limited as long as possible. They'll be monitoring," Barnaby cautioned.

We stopped at the public terminal in Nova Park, at the ground floor of the sprawling Lunar Spire metropolis. When the canopy opened, I had to cover my eyes from the resplendent view of the bustling promenade. Vanessa smiled, while Rose and Barnaby still looked too serious and dour.

"Most importantly, you two need to look like you're having fun," I said, using my fingers to demonstrate a forced, wide smile to Barnaby.

Watching him try to emulate my expression made me laugh and put a real grin on my face. We all exited and walked toward the most outlandish, lavish party in the known galaxy.

* * *

At first glance, Nova Park existed under the stars with no protective roof. Most arriving tourists experienced a momentary panic, worried they might float off into space. However, a sophisticated covering protected the citizens. The dome's reflective plating featured a virtual projection system capable of mimicking the stellar view outside. I looked up to view white stars twinkling around a familiar planet swirled with blue oceans and choked with a polluted gray atmosphere. Despite its flaws, I missed Earth.

The promenade featured a massive open pedestrian street running in two directions. To the south, glowing marquee signs flashed with garish colors. They lured young revelers into underground clubs where music with jackhammer tempos blared, creating the area's rhythmic heartbeat. Along the north side, the street darkened, and turned more nefarious. Numerous liquor-drenched establishments maintained hidden backroom houses-of-ill-repute. Hotels with opulent exteriors allowed well-dressed dealers to sell the Icarus drug under shadowed awnings. In this place, money or afterdeath credit would buy you anything.

We strolled north through a courtyard packed with an energized crowd. I looked up to see a dozen men and women wearing hover-boots. They danced above the partygoers and poured expensive champagne to open-mouthed people below. Everyone wore designer clothes matched with the most extravagant precious jewelry. Tuxedo-suited waiters darted through the promenade bearing plates of imported shellfish, caviar, and exotic hors d'oeuvres. White-suited sommeliers stood ready to refill wine glasses with expensive bottles priced higher than the annual salaries of most Earth-bound human workers. To fit in, I snatched a lobster tail plate and two crystal glasses filled with fifteen-year-aged lunar distilled whiskey. I swallowed the food, drank the shots of whiskey with Vanessa, and howled at the Earth. Rose and Barnaby joined the party spirit, downing comet-crystal distilled vodka. On the opposite side of the street, a group of young hackers hosted a friendly meta.duel contest using the promenade's powerful Mark-V virtual generator. With so many people requesting access from the device, it came down to a test of skill and ingenuity for those seeking to control the finite supply of proto-matter. Some of the hackers played a game of alien invaders, conjuring virtual floating eight-tentacled creatures fighting against robots reminiscent of the old 1950s monster movies. I grinned when I recognized a perfect facsimile of MechaRonin smiting a slimy Martian blob with his electro-blade. A cheer erupted from a crowd of onlookers. An impish, competitive part of me wanted to whip out my wrist-com interface and challenge the youngsters to usurp control over the whole generator, but the rational part of my brain stifled that urge. We all made a point to look amused, then continued on to the north end.

Finding our target, even amid a gratuitous sea of excess, proved to be an easy task. From a distance, I saw an immense spinning sign, churning with what I suspected to be simulated lava. Each revolution of the sign scorched the name of the club for all to see.

** CLUB PURGATORY **
Abandon All Morals Ye Who Enter.

Thirty-foot-tall transparent columns of roaring fire flanked an entrance carved from pure obsidian rock. Waves of pulsing sonic energy shook the ground near the club's entrance. A horde of fashionable young adults queued up alongside a winding velvet rope. All seemed more than eager to give a year of their afterdeath for the time of their life tonight.

We strolled up to the front of the line until a mammoth wall of a man blocked our way. The bouncer towered over me at a height well over seven feet tall. His muscles rippled across his arms, and he cracked his knuckles at my approach. A growling noise escaped his sneering lips.

"Back of the line," the mountain-man ordered, pointing behind us. The bicep on his arm flexed with a muscle bigger than my head.

"We're celebrating tonight," I said with an exaggerated slur. "We'd like to get a VIP table...hell, maybe we'll reserve the whole floor, what do you think, honey?" I blew a kiss to Vanessa and pretended to sway off balance.

"You're not on my reservation list," he replied with a look mixed with irritation and uncertainty. The bouncer cocked his head, studying me. Judging from his body language, I would need to sweeten the deal before he kicked us to the back.

"My friend just struck it rich with a new mine. You let us in, we'll pay our covers and you get a fifty-thousand tip," I offered. This offer brightened the mood of the bouncer.

"Uh, yes sir, sorry, I didn't recognize you, sir," the bouncer announced. He waved his hand and the virtual purple rope behind him dissolved. As we walked by, he scanned our wrists and deducted the credits given to us by David Solomon. Our forged identities must have worked, since a pleasant ringing sound indicated the money transferred. The bouncer bowed his head and ushered us into a sloping passageway hewn from moon rock.

We descended into a corridor shaped to look like a lava tube. Cracks along the walls glowed with a hot orange hue, lighting our way into Gabriel Charon's private underworld. As we turned a corner, the cracks merged into recognizable patterns. Each corridor featured a different work of art, drawn with molten fluid, depicting interpretations of the biblical seven sins.

"The scent of brimstone they're pumping into the air is a nice touch," I remarked. Vanessa chuckled nervously and Barnaby made another attempt at a smile.

"Blasphemy," Rose mumbled. She whispered a soft prayer I could not understand.

Then the door behind us closed and we strolled into the smoldering hellfire.

CHAPTER 20
Seeds of Discontent

"Because I could not stop for Death –
He kindly stopped for me –
The Carriage held but just Ourselves –
And Immortality."
- Excerpt from "Because I Could Not
Stop For Death", Emily Dickinson

The tunnel twisted down through the moon's surface for what seemed like a half-mile. Peals of laughter, champagne corks popping, excited moans, and other sounds of pleasure echoed throughout. At the bottom, we saw a large devilish face with an open-mouth-shaped portal, all surrounded by a fiery aura. A female concierge, dressed in a velvet red suit cut to tease a glimpse of her long legs, grinned at our approach.

"Welcome to Club Purgatory," she purred. "We are preparing your table now. Enjoy everything."

When we entered, the smoky interior of Club Purgatory filled our senses with the extravagance of Charon's vision of a sin-filled paradise. The interior looked like a massive cavern one might encounter spelunking deep underground. Towering, burning sconces illuminated the area, casting our shadows over the black glass floor. Male and female dancers performed on floating disc-like platforms, traveling to different tables to entertain patrons. Many tables had been carved high into the walls, forming private alcoves serviced by flying waiters and waitresses delivering temptations and vices.

The club segmented into three main areas. The east side featured a dance floor and a deejay creating electronic music. He energized the crowd by combining his music with the v-cast generator. Each beat he generated changed the floor in some way, like its color or its texture. Some of the music created flying demon-like creatures and fairies that flitted between the dancing patrons. The northern section featured a set of bridges and lifts that connected five different bars and restaurants, all serving the finest cocktails, food, drugs, or whatever their gluttonous patrons desired. The western section featured a hexagonal-shaped iron cage standing twenty feet high. I saw two human-looking figures inside the cage grappling with each other while a more intimate number of VIPs cheered the gladiatorial combat.

"Stick with the plan," Barnaby whispered. "We'll procure the weapons. You find the doctor."

I nodded and took Vanessa's hand. We headed toward the western area of the club while Rose and Barnaby disappeared into a writhing mass of dancing bodies. A blond-haired waitress descended from the air, held aloft by boots that pulsed with a hot white glow.

"Idle hands are the devil's workshop," she declared with a smirk. "We have a special new cabernet crafted by the owner called the River Lethe. It's guaranteed to make you forget your troubles. I know you're dying to try some..."

"We don't want to remember anything, so we'll take two," I said, returning a grin.

"You two go have fun, I'll find you," she said and sped off to take more orders.

We continued walking toward the western area and the iron cage loomed larger. My eyes focused on the two combatants inside the ring. They fought with an inhuman savagery, beating each other with wicked strikes and tearing at each other not to maim, but to kill. When we stepped closer I realized that the two fighters were not humans after all. I reached the edge of the cage, close enough to touch the bars. I saw that the bodies of the two shades looked grotesque and enlarged, similar to what Jebediah looked like in Dr. Okono's lab. I clenched my fist when I realized the club owner used a modified serum to turn the shades feral.

The larger of the two fighters picked up the other shade and threw it against the cage near me. The close proximity of the battered feral shade triggered a prickling sensation along my scalp and ears. I sensed the TauK Network interface awakening again. A flood of disconnected words and thoughts spiked across the display appearing before my eye.

<<ShadeOS Tau Kappa Network >>

<<Help...>>

<<Stop pain...I am in purgatory.>>

My instincts told me that Dr. Okono might be monitoring the TauK Network for the slim chance that someone might find him. So I steadied myself and closed my eyes.

"I am here, Dr. Okono. I can get you out," I thought, focusing. At first, no peaks or sine waves appeared on my TauK Network interface. I echoed the words again and again, picturing the shades in front of me. Following other patrons crowding around the ring to get a closer look, I moved forward. The crumpled body of the shade still twitched as it tried to rise and continue its fight. I touched the shade through the bars, refocused one more time, and repeated my message. This time, the display on my retinal interface flickered with activity.

Then I stepped back to see if any of the patrons reacted to my message. While most of the VIP club-goers cheered and yelled for more bloodshed, I spotted one person who did not seem to be enjoying the spectacle. The older, brown-skinned man stood up and looked around as if a ghost just whispered in his ear. Peering closer at the second floor table, I recognized him as Dr. Okono. He looked thinner, more emaciated than the spry and healthy man I saw from the video logs at the university. I turned from his gaze and looked back at the shades to avoid suspicion.

I put on a fake smile and nudged Vanessa to get her attention.

"Let's get a table, honey, this looks like fun," I said, pulling her to one of the three disc-shaped lifts. We walked to the platform and it whisked us up to the second level overlooking the bloody arena. We made our way through a dozen tables piled high with empty liquor bottles and dirtied food plates. The people at the tables wore expensive gowns, tailor-made suits, and tuxedos, all dressed up for the carnage created for their amusement.

"Ladies and gentlemen, are you ready for a team battle?" bellowed the disembodied voice of the arena announcer. As patrons stood up to yell their approval, I decided to make a move amidst the chaos. "Remember to get your wagers logged before the battle starts!"

We walked across the second floor platform and sat down onto empty chairs at Dr. Okono's table. At first, he failed to recognize Vanessa with her disguise. "Excuse me, but these seats are taken," he said. Then he peered closer. His eyes widened. A look of happiness flashed across his face that changed to concern. "Vanessa, what are you doing here?" he whispered. "You are in grave danger!" He looked behind him nervously and back down to the arena. A look of shame crossed his face. "They make me watch so that I can make improvements to their serum."

"We're going to get you out of here," Vanessa replied. She pointed down to the arena, pretending she was talking about a different conversation. "When the fight starts up again, I want you to follow us out of here."

"How--how did you know to contact me through my TauK Network?" he asked in a hushed voice. "And who is this?"

"I'm Vanessa's friend, Jonah. I'll be helping you as well. I was the one who replied to your message."

"But that's impossible," he gasped. He leaned closer to regard me, paying close attention to my eyes. He squinted, leaned a bit closer, and then and his mouth opened.

"Of course," he said. "The IRS gave you the newest serum. I can see it in your skin and the flecks in your eyes. But that serum was not ready for human trials--"

"Believe me, I didn't have much of a choice," I replied with a wry grin.

"And here we go with the next deathmatch!" boomed the announcer.

The crowd roared and jumped to their feet as a trio of human handlers guided four augmented shades into the arena.

"Get up, now," I urged. "Walk, don't run."

As Dr. Okono rose to leave, a large man emerged from a dark corner of the floor, grabbed the doctor by his shoulder, and pushed him back into the chair. The crimson display from his wrist-com brought Spenner's grim face into the light. A strange thought crossed my mind. How many people had the chance to grapple with their death a second time?

"Why such a hasty retreat?" said another voice behind Spenner. A well-groomed man dressed in a black suit walked to the table and took a seat. He raised his polished white shoes onto the table and leaned back. His black hair parted in the middle. Twin streaks of silver ran along both parts of his hair, the trademark style of Gabriel Charon. "Please, stay and enjoy dinner. I insist." More shapes shifted in the darkness around us. Six shades lumbered forward, forming a ring around the table.

"I'm curious. How did you discover us?" I asked.

"Money," Gabriel retorted, rubbing his thumb against his raised index finger. "It seems David Solomon and Titan Tech overlooked the talents of Dr. Evelyn Briggs far too long." He raised his hand, revealing his golden wrist-com studded with four knuckle-sized diamonds. With a flick of a finger, he caused a virtual projection to appear in the middle of the table.

"They're coming, Gabriel. Four of them, including Jonah. He's alive," whispered Evelyn. Her projected head turned around the table as the message repeated three times.

"Don't blame her too much." Gabriel urged. "You see, I also threatened to eject her parents into space and turn them into shades if she didn't help me. She made a sensible choice." When Evelyn's virtual projection faded, a pair of waitresses floated toward the table bearing four plates of food. They put plates down before Gabriel, Dr. Okono, Vanessa, and myself. The food on the plate looked exquisite, featuring a salad mixed with exotic fruits, and an ornately-prepared seafood dish.

"That's fugu," explained Gabriel. "If it's not prepared by a trained chef, the tetrodotoxin poison will kill you. Lucky for us, I moved the best chef in Japan to the Spire last month. Please, enjoy." Gabriel motioned for everyone to eat. Vanessa and I exchanged glances. To stall for time, I played along, and poked at the salad. Nothing looked dangerous, so I took a bite after Gabriel ate his first. I tasted kale, lettuce, blueberries, and ripened pomegranate. Vanessa took a bite of the salad as well.

"It's delicious. My compliments to the chef," I muttered.

"Now that you both have eaten from this world, you cannot leave," Gabriel said, grinning.

"What do you mean?"

"The vegetables in your salad were all grown at the Vitum hydroponic farm," explained Gabriel. "But the pomegranate you ate came from my personal garden, down here." He raised his fork, showing the juicy fruit impaled on his utensil. "Do you recall the myth of Persephone? Oh, you're not the literary one...perhaps your AI Sasha would enlighten us?" Gabriel motioned at a space next to Jonah and Spenner chuckled. I nodded and the distant whine of the v-cast generator heralded Sasha's virtual appearance.

"The story is commonly known as the Rape of Persephone," Sasha answered, materializing in her blue form next to me. "Hades, God of the Underworld, stole Persephone and kept her in his realm until Hermes, Messenger of the Gods, arrived to rescue her. However, Hades refused to let her go, citing that she ate the seeds of his underworld's fruit. Because of this trickery, Hades made Persephone return to his underworld for three months of the year. It is an ancient metaphoric mythology designed to explain the cyclical nature of the harvest."

"She is even more remarkable than your surveillance reports indicated, Colonel," Gabriel said to Spenner. Then he turned back to admire Sasha. "I understand why David Solomon is so eager to get his hands on your code. You're simply perfect. Well, we'll beat him to that patent too, won't we?"

"That would be a fitting ending to their story," Spenner agreed.

"No, you're describing a fairy tale," I retorted, holding back a rising rage. "We will be leaving, with Dr. Okono."

"No. I heard Dr. Okono has a new serum locked inside his brilliant head, one that allows shades to keep their minds intact. Sadly, I wasn't able to extract it in time for my father...so we had to make due." He gestured to the sixth shade behind him. I peered close and recognized the long face and close-cropped gray hair as belonging to Guy Charon, the former CEO of Goliath Corporation. Next to him, stood another shade, Guy Charon's old partner Mr. Grand. More of the disconnected puzzle pieces fit together in my mind. Gabriel used me, and others, like pawns to consolidate his take-over of the company. Given that Guy's corpse looked undamaged, I surmised Gabriel made the deaths of his father and Mr. Grand look natural, maybe a hard-to-detect poison to induce their strokes. It would not surprise me if Spenner himself performed the deed. It was a solid theory, but hard to prove. I looked into Gabriel's twinkling gray eyes, ignoring the veneer of charm and sophistication, and found no remorse, morality, or emotion reflected back. "It looks like the serum is now within you. So I don't think your escape is on the menu."

"Tonight's menu has been changed," replied Barnaby from behind me, aiming a pistol at Spenner. His shirt looked disheveled, no doubt a result of a struggle to acquire his weapon. Rose emerged behind him, then stood behind Vanessa. Unlike Barnaby, her dress looked unruffled, though another person's blood stained her knuckles. She pointed the wide barrel of a new grav-gun at Gabriel. "My team walks out of here, you surrender to me, and I'll make sure you're served your just desserts."

Spenner stepped forward, raising his wrist-com to strike. Gabriel smiled and held up his hand to restrain him.

"Jonah, you're right. Let's dispense with the stories," he said. "There is only one safe way out for you and Vanessa. Will you hear me out?"

"I'm listening," I replied.

"We all know what Dr. Okono discovered, and what that could mean for all businesses relying on shades. My partner Tomoe, for instance, just purchased a million shades for her daring new world project. Do you honestly think she will suspend that project and free all of those shades? No, they have a world to build! I've heard you have some familiarity with the project I'm speaking about?" Vanessa gave me a puzzled look and I held her hand under the table. "The solution is simple. Dr. Okono stays and is equipped with the best lab in the universe to duplicate his newest serum. Vanessa becomes my head of legal counsel. Then attorney-client privilege keeps our secret...and you, Jonah, best of all, can work with Tomoe as her head of technology, with Sasha safe at your side. We've been trying to recruit you since your Louisiana mission. Join us and I'll make your dreams come true." Gabriel grinned and looked to Barnaby and Rose.

"What about the agent and the Black Rose?" Spenner asked.

"I'm afraid Director Barnaby and Ms. Rose are loose ends," Gabriel replied, holding his gaze on them, and expressing an exaggerated frown. "I'm sure Lunar Security will side with us when they learn he went rogue, forced his way into my establishment, pummeled my staff, and threatened me." Gabriel lifted his hand to reveal his own grav-gun from under the table.

"Of course, Rose, we would be willing to give you a way out, as a professional courtesy," added Spenner. "If you agree to slay Barnaby in the arena below, you can walk out alive."

"C'est magnifique, monsieur Spenner!" praised Gabriel. "Yes, we shall have a sport of it. Rose, you're a one-woman-army. You would be the heavy favorite. I'd wager 5:1 odds."

"Go to hell," she shot back.

Then a gentle nudge grazed my back, like someone picking my pocket. I realized Barnaby managed to slide a pistol into my back pocket while still keeping his own gun trained on Gabriel. I let go of Vanessa and moved my hand ever-so-slowly behind me.

Everyone tensed while they waited for my response. During the time it took to reach for my gun, I considered Gabriel's offer. One year ago, maybe even three months ago, I would have accepted the deal to save Vanessa. Now, the burden of knowledge disrupted the scales of my morality. I faced the devil's offer to turn my back on the plight of the shades, bury that secret, and live a life of extravagant indifference. I looked to Vanessa to see if she offered any counsel on this decision. She nodded back to me as if to say that she would agree with my decision. The rational part of my brain warned me that in six months or less, Gabriel and his allies would consider us 'loose ends' too.

"After careful consideration, I'll have to decline your offer," I said. "Dr. Okono is a free man. We'll be leaving with him if he chooses." While I waited for Gabriel's inevitable, violent response, I cleared my head and focused on the TauK Network. This time the interface appeared when I first started to concentrate.

"Dr. Okono, I want you to dive away in three seconds," I thought. I wondered if he accessed the TauK Network like me or if he needed a device. I hoped he had an implant or an ear-receiver to receive messages.

"Three..." I counted to myself. Gabriel looked to Spenner, whose dour expression grew more sinister from the crimson light emanating from his wrist-com. My hand gripped the cold handle of the concealed gun.

"That's not the answer I was hoping for," Gabriel muttered. His free hand touched a gray streak of hair and curled it in his fingers. "Maybe we'll be giving my patrons a thrilling show after all?"

"Two..." I continued. This time, Dr. Okono flashed a look to me and blinked twice to tell me he understood. I saw the muscles on Gabriel's hand twitch and his index finger moved toward the trigger. Spenner's hand evoked the access console. I saw the crimson door to hell cracking open.

"Now!" I said to Okono, and he leapt from his chair. The table flipped over and everyone burst into action. With my right hand, I shoved Vanessa back toward Rose. With my other hand I whipped the gun from behind my back and fired first, launching a bullet straight at Gabriel's chest. Barnaby's gun unleashed his volley a tenth of a second later on a true course for Gabriel's left eye. Despite our quickness, Spenner proved to be faster. After my bullet left the chamber, he summoned his wisp. The nearby v-cast generator whined, and formed a body for the green-skinned creature in front of Gabriel. It howled when the bullets tore its virtual form in half, filling the air with embers of glittering proto-matter.

Rose reacted next, grabbing Vanessa and pulling her away from the fray. Gabriel returned fire at me and his bullet tore into my shoulder and exited through the muscle, sending a jolt of pain through my body. The ShadeOS interface appeared over my right eye, activating itself to repair the wound.

<<ShadeOS. Initiating deltoid muscle tissue repair>>
<<Serum levels at 93%>>

I surmised that the serum exhausted its energy levels when it needed to do major repairs. Self-healing, up to a point, but then I wondered what happened when the serum ever hit zero. Would I turn into a true shade?

"Spenner, eliminate them!" ordered Gabriel as he took cover behind the table. Already operating under that assumptive order, Spenner tapped his wrist-com and the air flared with a crimson ball of gaseous red light. The red shape took on a fog-like substance and blew into the mouths and noses of the silent guardians. Each of the shades trembled and let out a primal growl of pain. All of their leg and arm muscles bulged and the veins running along their neck and chest glowed with a brighter red and green bioluminescence. I realized with a growing sense of worry that Spenner turned them feral with one of his corruption viruses. We needed to neutralize him fast before he created more of them. Then a verdant light flashed and the wisp reformed next to Spenner.

"I have the wisp," Sasha whispered. She manifested right behind the green-skinned AI, and attacked it. The two once again locked hands and resumed their multi-level battle of dynamic code supremacy.

Rose joined the fray wielding twin stun-rods. I imagined she snatched those weapons from the twitching hands of a security guard who would be calling in sick for the next two weeks. She leapt over the table and struck down the first shade with a powerful combination of strikes to its head. As she followed through with the momentum of the attack, she spun to face Spenner. He smiled, bowed to Rose, and brandished his own customized weapon. It resembled a cruel medieval mace, with a red-sparking energy ball at the top. Undaunted, Rose swung her batons and Spenner blocked them both without much effort.

Then my view of their fight disappeared when three more shades charged at me with gnashing teeth and swinging fists. Crushing pain wracked my body when they battered me to the ground. The impact knocked my gun out of my hand and the air from my lungs. Consumed by a bloodlust, the frenzied creatures tore into me with sharp fangs and nails. Anger and desperation released raw adrenaline throughout my body, pushing me to retaliate with a flurry of blows. My fist smashed into the jaw of Mr. Grand before he could gnaw my right arm. With a hard kick, I snapped the second creature's leg. I knocked the third one back with a jab from my left fist and punched Mr. Grand again, shattering more bones. The damage slowed but did not stop any of them, though the punishment they inflicted on me started to take a measurable toll.

<<ShadeOS. Initiating multiple organ repairs of spleen, kidney>>

<<Serum levels at 68%>>

Then gunshots exploded next to me. Looking up through watery eyes, I saw the silhouette of an avenging angel. Vanessa held the pistol I dropped and emptied its full cartridge into the second shade's head. It whimpered once and crumpled next to me. Counting the shade Rose defeated earlier, I counted two down, four to go.

A quick somersault brought me to my feet in time to stop the third shade from striking Vanessa. Not particular about its prey, the thing switched its attention to me, burying its claws into my shoulders. It leaned in, opening its mouth to rip my neck with its jagged teeth. Fighting back, the serum expended more energy to augment my muscles. Endorphins coursed through my system, diminishing the searing pain in my shoulder. With a boost to my strength, I grabbed the creature's neck and squeezed. The first snapping noise sounded when it fractured my collarbone, followed by another crack when I broke its neck. After it slumped to the ground, I turned to face the next one. Mr. Grand rushed toward me, his grotesque jaw clinging to his busted mouth by dangling tendons. Embracing the fury stoked by the serum, I charged Mr. Grand and grappled with him. Vanessa looked on horrified by the ferocity of the melee, or maybe at the abandonment of my humanity. Then another shade ran at me with arms outstretched, and I grabbed that one with my free arm. Using Mr. Grand as a crude cudgel, I slammed his head into the skull of the other. This burst of power came with a cost to my energy reserves.

<<ShadeOS: Augmenting muscle issue strength>>

<<Serum levels at 38%>>

Across the table, Spenner's wild swings pushed Barnaby and Rose back. With Vanessa out of immediate danger, I jumped across the table to take on Spenner. The shade of Guy Charon spotted me and twirled to punch me. The blow cracked two ribs and caused a stomach bleed, forcing the ShadeOS to complain again about my dwindling power supply. The ex-CEO of Goliath Corporation raised both bony arms to finish me off. Another surge of adrenaline-fueled desperation stirred, granting me the power to kick the creature twice. The elder Charon fell to his knees. With one fluid motion, I grabbed his head, twisted hard, and ended his afterdeath service.

"No!" screamed Gabriel. "Father!"

Spenner spun hard with his mace, missing Rose on purpose but blindsiding me, his true target. The stunning end of his glowing mace smashed into my right temple and zapped me with enough lethal current to fry an elephant. This time, the ShadeOS alert appeared too large to ignore.

<<ShadeOS: WARNING! Initiating multiple systems repair>>

<<Serum levels at 17%>>

Double vision clouded my perception. A figure moved under the table near me. After blinking, my sight cleared enough to see Gabriel Charon lying near me and aiming his pistol at my head. Before he fired, Vanessa's red stiletto heel impaled his hand. She interrupted his pained shrieks with the butt end of her empty pistol. After knocking Gabriel out, she picked up his grav-gun. While she fired cover shots against the remaining shades, Barnaby, Rose, and Sasha all struggled against Spenner and his wisp.

"Get up, Jonah!" barked Barnaby. "We need you!"

Spenner's mace swung down and shattered one of Rose's stun sticks, creating a brief sparking electric storm from the weapon's broken shaft. He finished the attack by spinning and kicking Barnaby to the ground near me.

"If you can...hold him...I can take him out..." Barnaby gasped, rolling over to catch his breath. With a noticeable energy cost, my serum's healing factor kicked into overdrive to stabilize my wounds.

<<ShadeOS Repairs complete>>

<<WARNING. Serum levels at 11%>>

When the fog around my eyes cleared, I jumped to my feet, ran behind Spenner, and wrapped my arms around him. He elbowed me in the ribs and stomped on my foot. This attack smashed more of my bones, but I squeezed harder. A shade punched me in the back, crushing two vertebrae, but Rose bludgeoned the creature to distract its attention. Despite the searing agony along my spine, I held on tighter, eliciting a pained howl from Spenner.

"Colonel Colin Spenner, I hereby sentence you with high treason and war crimes," Barnaby rasped, cracking a blood-stained smile. While he limped forward, he traced a complex echelon across his wrist-com, causing its green color to shimmer bright. Realizing the danger, Spenner squirmed and flexed with strength that could break thick rope, but my anger and the serum's power made my arms like iron bonds.

"No...you...can't--" Spenner wheezed.

Barnaby's echelon program tapped into the nearby v-cast generator, summoning the virtual form of his emerald drake. Upon manifesting, it solidified and slithered around his arm and shoulder. Its green and crimson scales scintillated in the dim light. Then I realized the IRS designed it for one single purpose. It was a cleaner program, meant to devour the remnants of the Crimson Gate. Unmoved by Spenner's pleas, Barnaby unleashed his judgment.

"Your access is revoked."

The dragon leaped from Barnaby's shoulder and flew to its target. It landed on my arm, its talons gripping into my flesh for balance. Spenner struggled to break my grasp, frightened about what the dragon represented. With a ferocious roar, the drake extended its neck and opened its fanged jaw to swallow Spenner's right hand. I heard a sickening crunching noise followed by an ear-splitting scream of pain and rage. The drake's surgical strike amputated Spenner's tattooed hand, severing his bio-circuited connection to the Crimson Gate. I hoped this closed the last known access point to that trove of banned technology forever. The effort proved exhausting for Barnaby, who collapsed to his knees.

Cut off from its source code in Spenner's wrist-com, the wisp began to dissipate. With its dying action, it disengaged from Sasha and rushed to strike me. Its green claws scratched my face. At the same moment, Spenner struck me with his left hand, and broke my nose. The pain took me off guard, and he twisted loose. Free from my grasp, he sprinted toward the edge of the second floor, and jumped down toward the exit. The wisp tried to follow him but its form disintegrated with each footfall, leaving only glowing floating green ash behind its master. The ShadeOS activated again as it attempted to heal damage from the encounter.

<<ShadeOS. WARNING. Initiating multiple systems repair>>

<<Serum levels at 8%>>

Gabriel stirred, rubbing his head and rising with his hands up. Watching his once-trusted mercenary run away, he looked frightened.

"Tomoe!" he screamed. "Help me!"

In an instant, the empty space next to him shimmered with orange light. Tomoe Gozen manifested a translucent body, wearing her samurai armor and mask.

"You have become pitiful, Gabriel, and no longer an asset to me," Tomoe chided.

"But...our arrangement...you must aid me!"

"True, but our arrangement does not specify the type of aid. I will fulfill that obligation one last time. Goodbye, Mr. Charon." With that, Tomoe's hologram shimmered. Proto-matter particles released from the v-cast generator swarmed where she once stood and created a new pattern. When the lightshow dissipated, an eight-foot-tall, imposing knight resplendent in black armor manifested before us.

"Heinrich, you're a naughty boy for violating your parole," Barnaby said with a tsk-tsk.

The Hochmeister growled and hefted his massive staff, preparing to unleash a mighty lightning echelon spell. As sparks gathered around his weapon, Vanessa, Rose, and Sasha all unloaded a coordinated assault against him. Vanessa fired two shots at his helmet while Sasha and Rose pummeled him with kicks and punches. The quick damage proved too much for his pattern to sustain at once, and he exploded into a glittering cloud of proto-matter ash. The swift, almost comical demise brought a grin to my face. Gabriel had a much different reaction after seeing his last ally betray him. Like a blubbering child, he started to grovel.

"Please...please don't kill me!" he pleaded. "Sp-Spenner did all of this! He threatened my family, he said I had to go along with everything he said..." Plausible story, maybe, but my instincts told me Gabriel or Tomoe masterminded everything. Vanessa handed me the grav-gun, giving me the gavel to pass judgment. I fought the urge to put a bullet through his brain.

"You don't get off so easy," I answered. Barnaby and Rose approached, leveling weapons on Gabriel.

<<ShadeOS: MANDATE: Resume pursuit>>

<<Retire Colonel Spenner>>

My initial reaction was anger at the ShadeOS directive. That feeling disappeared when I realized the deed needed to be done. He would keep coming back for us until he completed his job. After all, his military training, his programming, compelled him.

"I've called the lunar police, they should be here soon," Barnaby said, clutching his injured side. "Jonah, this is your chance...get him before he slips away."

"Keep watch over her," I asked Rose. She nodded. Then I looked at Vanessa and held her hand. "I have to get him. I'm sorry, love, one more job to do."

"Go, I'll take care of Barnaby," she said touching my face with a brief caress. Then Vanessa picked up Spenner's mace. She moved next to Rose. They both held their weapons ready, standing guard over Barnaby. They looked like a deadly pair. Feeling confident they were safe, I bolted and jumped off the balcony, hitting the ground running without a stumble. After rushing through a crowd of people heading for the tunnel exit, Spenner's trail proved easy to find. I just followed the path of fallen patrons he had knocked down while escaping. With the serum still pushing my body to superhuman limits, I sprinted faster than ever before, gaining ground on him with each bounding step.

As I emerged from Club Purgatory, my eyes tried to adjust to the intense burst of light from the bustling uptown streets. At this hour, Nova Park Avenue flooded with gleaming allure. A long row of glowing signs, some virtual projections and other massive digital screens, all flashed enticements for their high-end restaurants, bars, and shopping plazas. The visual noise filled my eyes with dancing colored spots. I shook my head and wiped my eyes. A commotion at the far end of the promenade caught my attention. A group of incensed limousine drivers banded together to prevent Spenner from hijacking one of their hover vehicles. Lucky for them, he decided to give up on the car and spare their lives to run further away. I continued the chase as my quarry ran north. After a hundred yards, he turned right into a descending staircase.

Speeding up, I closed the gap between us, and followed him down into a public transport terminal. A crowd of travelers started to scream as he threw people aside. When I reached the platform, Spenner pried a closing canopy open, and ejected a crying woman from her pod. Then he entered the vehicle, and the door shut behind him. Seeing my gun, a young woman opened her pod's canopy and waved for me to take her spot.

"You're a police officer, right?" she asked while exiting. "He's a maniac, go after him please!"

When I jumped into her pod and revved up the pod's magnetic cushion, a crowd of travelers applauded my pursuit. With a quick jerk, the transport snapped onto the invisible magnetic rail, and my pod sped out of the station. Through my window, I saw a glimpse of commuters helping injured strangers caught in Spenner's violent wake.

CHAPTER 21
Atonement in D Major

*"If an injury has to be done to a man it should be
so severe that his vengeance need not be feared."*
- Excerpt from "The Prince", Niccolò Machiavelli

Unknown to all visitors and most moon residents, the Lunar Travel Authority concealed manual controls in each pod. Protected by a simple security layer, the controls appeared only for emergencies. After hacking into the system, two black, oval-shaped pads materialized before me. They stuck tight to my palms, granting visceral muscle control over the craft. A series of erratic, rapid twists from Spenner's vehicle told me that he assumed manual control as well. He shot forward like a bullet leaving a pistol's barrel, streaking by commuters locked into the slower moving lanes. My hands pushed forward, matching his speed and trajectory, sliding up alongside the slope of the tube-tunnel to avoid collisions. We blazed through the chute roads, spinning circular and ribbon-shaped paths around the traffic rush of slower pods. As we approached a two-way split, Spenner feinted toward the western tube. With a fraction of a second before the turn, he barrel-rolled upside down, twirling the pod, and landing inside the eastern tube.

"Holy--" I gasped, thrusting my hands and entire body to the right. I flipped the craft and drove inverted to stay on his tail. All air escaped from my lungs in that slow moment while my pod spun in the air. Physics and fortune granted their mercy, guiding me to a hard landing on the magnetic rail.

We raced across the Mare Frigoris at speeds three times the regulated limit. Spenner nudged a hapless passenger's pod ahead of him, sending it careening back to me in a dangerous tailspin. Surprised, I roared a scream as if the force of my voice might push the oncoming danger out of my way. A quarter-second before impact, my hands swept right and I flipped my craft to spin a full revolution around the pipe. With my left hand, I held my course and with the right hand accessed my wrist-com. I shifted my attention back and forth from driving and hacking the trafficnet. I sent an order to apply an emergency brake to the innocent woman spinning out of control. Her craft locked up and skidded to a stop. Inertia caused her head to hit the glass, but she lived. Undeterred, Spenner bumped more pods to slow me down, creating a minefield of spinning hazards. At my speed, it would be hard to avoid an accident.

"Save the others," I gasped. My hand pointed to a pair of pods about to smash into each other. Before I finished speaking, Sasha responded. She leapt into the guidance system of the nearest pod then leaping to the next, hacking at dizzying speeds, and steering innocents to a safer route. As we barreled past the chute transfer station at Enkidu Prime, Sasha's blue form flickered when she auto-connected to the local v-cast generator. My heart swelled with the love of a proud father, watching her jump to the imperiled pods, an angel stemming the loss of precious life. While she minimized casualties, I focused on the chase, coaxing more speed from my pod.

"This won't end well," rasped Spenner's voice through tiny speakers behind my head. I acknowledged Spenner's hacking of the communication system as an impressive feat, since he lost his primary hand and still managed to pilot his craft with expert precision. "There will just be pain, Jonah."

"On that point, we can agree," I shot back. My pod rocketed forward, and slipped along into an inverted position over Spenner's vehicle. Upside down, I looked down and saw him through his glass

canopy. A red-soaked tourniquet made from his torn shirt prevented his gory stump from bleeding out. His intact left hand made
swift gestures to reposition his craft away from me. However, I
countered each move with a precise adjustment. "I'm prepared, are
you?"

We raced parallel across a glassy expanse of gleaming black
basalt, switching positions within our cylindrical tunnel. From a
distant observer's view, we looked like two spinning magnets shot
through a long glass tube, our like but opposing natures bringing us
close and repelling us away.

As we approached another T-shaped junction, I maneuvered to
pass Spenner and force him into the chute's eastern pathway. A
moment before we reached the split, he pulled ahead with a burst
of speed and cut a hard left. With my vessel's nose aiming the other
way, I swung my hands fast to follow. The craft made the turn, but
it slammed into the chute upside down. The impact sent my pod
into a tumble. Spenner laughed through my speaker, and accelerated
toward a terminus station on the horizon.

My view twirled round-and-round until a jarring bounce
knocked the pod back onto the magnetic rail. Back on course and
resuming pursuit, I took a moment to evaluate any damage. A quick
diagnostic showed that all systems still functioned, but a miniscule
chip on the canopy's glass worsened into a growing hairline crack.
At its rate of expansion, I had three, maybe four minutes before the
integrity of the shield broke apart. Checking the moon roadway
map on the glass display, I weighed the good news and bad.

The good? No other chutes connected to the station ahead,
Terminus Bastion. Spenner chose a dead end. The bad? My pod's
guidance system estimated my arrival at five minutes. That last
minute would be excruciating. Either the canopy would hold, or a
suffocating death awaited in cold space. A calm came over me, and
somehow that worry ceased to bother me.

"Dead end for you," I taunted, channeling my fear back toward
him. "I'm coming."

"I wouldn't have it any other way," he hissed back.

The crack split into two lines with a disheartening *clink.* I held the vehicle steady, passing a straight expanse of charcoal-colored plains along the Mare Frigoris. Hundreds of shades, all connected to silvery tethers, moved along the moon's surface for their chute-paving duties. Another minute ticked by and the crack split off a third line. The other two lines forked upward, moving faster toward the top of the transparent canopy.

"I plotted the time remaining on the glass. Would you like to know?" Sasha asked.

"No. Yes. Wait, no, I really don't."

The cracked glass measured my remaining time like a lit oil-wick burning toward its inevitable end. A few miles ahead, Spenner slowed his craft to dock at the terminal. Given the damage to my craft, I knew I had to keep my speed up until the last moment, and risk a red-hot entry. The station's circular airlock seal split open to accept Spenner's pod, and then closed behind him.

"Structural integrity compromised. Breach imminent. Assume emergency positions," warned the onboard computer's mechanical voice.

"Strange. What position would increase any survival probabilities for that event?" Sasha inquired in her curious and comical tone.

"I think it's telling me to bend over and kiss my ass goodbye," I joked back. Sasha laughed, a sound I cherished, until the glass clinked again. The fracture now stretched all across the canopy. Twenty more seconds of holding my breath passed. When the station's outer door opened, I exhaled. We streaked inside, and I pushed the guidance control pads hard to slow down. Inside the airlock, the partial atmosphere allowed me to hear the screeching sound of our magnetic brakes igniting to control our entry. Before we struck the next gate, the secondary airlock parted to reveal the gleaming white interior of Terminus Bastion. We whizzed by a worrisome sign that proclaimed the station to be property of Goliath Corporation.

My pod started to rattle and shake, bouncing along the transparent chute as the backup speed dampeners activated. Hurricane-strength cushions of air rushed into the tube to slow the craft down further. Overwhelmed by my pod's inertia, the landing system shorted out with cascading explosions. Smashing through the landing bay supports, my vehicle skidded across the hangar's steel floor. Sparks flew under the pod as it screeched across a raised access ramp, launching it twirling in the air. Upside down, I held onto the side handles as the pod crashed into a series of control terminals, destroying the local v-cast generator array.

After my pod came to rest, I spotted Spenner running and taking cover behind the base of the bulky catapult-like sling-machine. I pulled my grav-gun, and fired two miracle longshots through the cracked glass. While I missed him by a wide margin, the canopy shattered, opening a quick exit. Then I jumped through the hole where the glass once shielded me. While reloading my gun, I ran past twenty-five shade workers carrying boxes, and dove behind the solid cover of a slingbox shipping container.

Fifty-foot-tall mountains of stacked containers, all filled with lunar ore, ringed the spacious warehouse. Since I saw no guards, I guessed the station operated unmanned, except for an occasional supervisor visit.

At the other side of the station, Spenner took cover behind the massive suborbital-sling. Its cocked and readied arm held a half-empty titanium container. As part of their work, the shades gathered minerals and filled the slingbox. Once the box became full, a foreman would materialize using the v-cast generator, set the appropriate coordinates, and launch the cargo with the catapult.

On the western end of the warehouse, another airlock opened, allowing a crowd of ore-bearing shades to shamble inside. Over one hundred workers walked toward the open slingbox to deliver their burdens. As the procession passed by me, I noticed that these shades appeared larger than average. Similar to Jebediah in Dr. Okono's lab, these unfortunate souls appeared altered by the serum-hack. All of their muscles bulged, and the veins along their bodies glowed with a yellowish-green bioluminescence. Then Spenner emerged from the cover of a rack of spare transport pods along the eastern side of the warehouse.

"We would have been a great team," he yelled across the space between us. "You're an asshole, but few partners kept up with me like you did. According to my intel, you would owe two and half years of service if you died right now. It's a good thing I'll be here to reap you, don't you think, Jonah?"

I answered with a gunshot that whisked by Spenner's left temple, almost matching the scar on his right temple. "I plan to outlive my debts," I growled back. "When this is over, there won't be enough of you to make a proper shade."

He sprinted across the open floor to hide behind a rusted lunar rover. The vehicle hovered four inches above the ground, suspended by a floating electro-magnetic service rack. The narrow gap from the floor to the undercarriage revealed Spenner's legs. I took the tough shot, unloading a whole clip of bullets. He dodged the volley, so I ducked back down to reload.

Sensing his opportunity, Spenner rushed toward my position. When I peeked over the lip of my cover, he had halved the distance between us. I steadied my gun at him a second before he fired his glowing rifle. Then the whole warehouse exploded with a piercing noise, one that I recognized from the mission in the Louisiana swamp. It was almost a mercy that his squealer rifle's attack burst my eardrums, replacing that awful screeching with a ringing sound. It took all of my strength to stay upright and hold onto my gun.

<<ShadeOS. Initiating repair of auditory function>>

<<WARNING. Serum levels at 5%>>

Knowing that he would follow up with another attack, I stood up and returned fire. With my equilibrium affected, my bullets missed and bounced off a metal canister. Protected behind cover,

Spenner spoke some words and pointed in my direction. With the squealer's damage still deafening me, I could not make out what he said. Then I felt the familiar feeling of the ShadeOS interface activating within my mind. A small inner sight display interface appeared over my eyes.

<<Tau Kappa Network activated. Authorization: Spenner.>>

<<Command: Kill the intruder...Kill the intruder...>>

How could Spenner have accessed the TauK Network? He must have deciphered Dr. Okono's research, or beat it out of him, but right now the how did not matter. I dared not take my hands from my gun to wipe the blood away. One of the three bullets I fired found its mark, and Spenner's left kneecap exploded with a shower of red.

As he fell, all of the shades in the warehouse, over two hundred workers, dropped their rock loads. They turned to me, their faces contorted with pure rage. The collective burning green glow from their veins lit the whole warehouse with an eerie light. Spenner's trap sprung all around me. He had lured me to a location filled with augmented feral shades, under his command, through his own secret access to the TauK Network.

Without my sense of hearing, it looked like the shades ran toward me in slow motion, but in fact they sprinted faster than the swiftest human. With only seconds before the first dozen shades tore me apart, I considered my options. My gun pinpointed the vital spot of the first shade in the advancing crowd. It would take one, maybe two bullets to drop it to the ground. However, the one hundred and ninety nine remaining shades presented a problem much greater than my skill with the grav-gun could overcome. A quick glance to the nearest operational travel pod, forty feet away, told me that the shades would intercept me before reaching half the distance. Helplessness gripped me and froze me in place. In desperation, my mind's inner sight looked to the TauK interface element hovering in my peripheral vision. The display filled with the sinusoidal waves of multiple dialogues, the hate-filled chatter from the shades intent on fulfilling their master's order. Instead of attacking or running, I focused all of my will. Angry utterances and guttural phrases filled the channel with their broken language. In that moment of trying to understand them, I heard Spenner's sinister transmission.

<<The intruder, Jonah...causes your pain...>>

The loud message echoed over the cries of the shades. Spenner took advantage of their suffering, and used their raw emotions against me with effective results. They understood that my death would be their salvation. That thought terrified me, and presented my only chance for survival. With my hands clenched, and my eyes rolled back into my head, I communed with the TauK Network. I opened my mind fully. No defenses, no mental barriers filtered the noise, chatter, emotion, and the pain of the shades. Even though my ears roared from the sonic damage of the squealer, in my mind I heard a vibrant musical chorus of melancholy and suffering from the shades. A tidal wave of desperation washed over me. All of them possessed a single-minded thought, that my death would deliver them from the personal Gehenna burning their souls.

"Spenner did this to you," I said inside my head. All of my willpower and intention focused on sending this message. I said it again in my mind, watching my retinal interface for any recognition that my communication worked.

With my eyes closed, my nose told me first that the shades reached me. Their musty stench filled my nostrils as five attackers leapt onto me. The first punched my face, while another clawed my left shoulder, leaving a deep bloody gash. My eyes opened, catching a glimpse of Spenner laughing while the shades knocked me to the floor and pummeled me with their long-nailed fists. The internal ShadeOS readout appeared to warn me about the plummeting energy levels. The serum worked overtime to heal the extensive damage, draining more precious energy reserves.

<<ShadeOS. DANGER. Serum levels at 3%>>

Dozens more of the shades caught up to me and started to pull my limbs in different directions. Given my penchant for hot dogs and soda, I always imagined my end as the mother-of-all-heart-attacks some time in my mid-60s, not drawn and quartered by a pack of feral shades on the worst lunar vacation imaginable. As the sinews in my legs stretched and popped, I gathered the resolve to keep living.

A shade tried to bite my right foot; instead it took a kick to its face. I twisted my body to escape the grasp of the three shades pinning me to the ground and jumped to my feet. Once more, I made an appeal into the TauK Network, this time pouring all of my desperate emotion into the message.

<<Your master causes your pain>>

<<Spenner causes your pain>>

I prepared myself for death, bracing for the moment that the shades flung my limbs to the four corners of the warehouse. I opened one eye first to peek at the scene and saw that the shades stopped their attack. Realizing I made a connection, I made a more compelling statement, a bold promise of salvation. I projected thoughts of rest, comfort, and an end of suffering. For the first time, I saw my thoughts manifest as new sine waves on the TauK Network.

<<Protect me and I will release you. I will end your pain.>>

That last message stirred the most dramatic effect among the shades. All of them stopped, looked at me, and then turned to run toward Spenner. My ears started to recover, since I heard their moans and cries mixed with scattered gunfire.

"No, no!" screamed Spenner, firing his pistol. His bullets knocked down six shades, allowing ten more to leap over their fallen brethren for the chance to kill him.

"Attack Jonah, not me!" he screamed with a shrill, frightened voice. Before the swarm overwhelmed him, he reached into his belt and tossed a cryo-grenade to the ground. It detonated and froze nine shades to the spot, giving him the chance to run toward the sling-machine. I raised my gun to try a shot, but too many shades blocked my aim.

Relying on his good arm, Spenner punched and kicked a smaller wave of shades in his way. With each one he knocked away, two more came at him. It was a battle pitting perfect fighting techniques against an unfocused, but unyielding horde. Each time he looked overwhelmed, he emerged from a pile and fought on. Despite my loathing for him, I had to acknowledge that he made one hell of a last stand. With too many of them chasing him now, Spenner retreated, running the fastest fifty-yard-dash I had ever seen. When I realized where he attempted to take cover, I grinned. It was time to trap the tiger.

With the shades no longer attacking me, I ran toward the operations booth that controlled the hulking sling-machine. At the same time, Spenner ran backwards into the only place that offered a defendable one-entrance position. Firing bullets with abandon, he back-pedaled into the interior of the nearby slingbox. He yelled at me, but the sounds of battle drowned out his curse. Then he disappeared into the container, with only the occasional bright flash of muzzle fire indicating he still lived. Over three dozen feral shades leapt, jumped, and crawled over each other to enter the box and resume their chase.

With a gesture, I activated the control panel inside the operations booth. A simple interface appeared with the option to close the canopy of the slingbox. With no hesitation, I pressed it, and watched the thick metal door rise up from the floor. Before the hatch closed, another eight shades squeezed into the narrowing gap.

When the slingbox door sealed, the control interface updated to request the destination. The previous launch setting showed a calculation that put the destination into a decaying sub-orbit bound for Terminus Noctus on the opposite side of the moon. I needed something more *remote*. With a wave of my hand, I dialed the launch angle to a seventy degree arc and set the sling's launch power to five hundred percent. The computer beeped, concerned that the trajectory pointed to deep space, and popped up a stern message to correct course.

<<WARNING!>>

<<This trajectory will send the cargo beyond the moon's orbit>>

<<Are you sure?>>

"Oh, I'm quite sure, thank you," I mumbled, bypassing the override. The sling pulled back its large metal arm and hurled the slingbox upward like a boy throwing a skipping stone into a black lake. I watched the container gain altitude and pass through the moon's orbit.

The remaining shades shambled and gathered around me. All malice and fury disappeared from their yellow eyes, even the glowing green veins covering their bodies dimmed. They came to collect the debt I promised them. They came for their freedom. I took a deep breath and rubbed my eyes and ears to collect myself. I holstered my gun and touched the shoulder of a nearby female shade. This gesture made me aware of a soft, wordless hum in the TauK Network. Unlike the melancholy music I heard before, the notes sounded like a hymn. The music did not evoke any negative or positive emotions, but the notes felt charged with apprehension and hope, possibly gratitude. No translation appeared before my eyes, though I understood the message. Then my retinal TauK display changed to show my serum power reservoir.

<<ShadeOS. WARNING. Repairing. System failure imminent>>

<<Serum levels at 0.92%>>

What would happen when all of my energy depleted? I thought about running toward the nearest travel-pod to seek help. I could come back for the shades later...though they could be rounded up and redeployed somewhere else. The old me would not have hesitated to flee without a care for these shades. Now I felt a kinship. I needed to fulfill my promise.

"You need to return to the Lunar Spire, sir, to seek aid," Sasha cautioned. "You are slipping away."

Feeling woozy, I steadied myself against the upturned, smoking travel-pod I piloted earlier.

"Soon," I whispered. I looked at the first one, a male shade that appeared to have died and reaped far too young. Acceptance and gratitude met my stare, erasing any doubt about leaving. Leaning against the control panel for balance, I loaded my gun, and set about the grisly business of repaying my debt, one by one, for all of them.

CHAPTER 22
The Alpha and Omega

"I wear this chain I forged in life...
I made it link by link, and yard by yard;
I girded it on my own free will,
and of my own free will I wore it."
- Excerpt from "A Christmas Carol",
Charles Dickens

Lucky to be alive needed to be a tattoo on my arm, I decided, after hearing it a tenth time in the last hour. I heard it most recently from a short nurse dressed in long white stockings and a red dress leaning over me. When I awoke, she offered a brief retelling of how my broken body reached the Lunar Spire Hospital. According to her, I managed to crawl into a travel-pod at Terminus Bastion, and arrived unconscious at Terminus Asechylus. A group of frightened tourists, alarmed by my gory appearance, had called emergency services.

Waking up, I blinked away the grayness fogging my vision. A raging storm of a headache thundered in my head. Strength gushed back into my limbs, a hot warmth seared my blood, like I received a transfusion of liquid fire. I glanced over to my right, cognizant that a taped needle pricked my arm, delivering the contents of the intravenous bag suspended over my head. I looked around my surroundings and realized the sterile white walls and medical equipment meant I made it to a hospital bed. Despite the dim lighting in the room, the fuzzy radioactive-like yellow glow from the medicine allowed me to read the writing on the bag itself:

Lazarus-440: Handle with care. Property of IRS
WARNING: Biohazard

"Doctor, your patient is awake," the nurse called out, summoning a crowd of unfamiliar and familiar faces. Dr. Okono, garbed in a clean white lab coat, entered first. A pair of male nurses trailed behind. They poured over the digital readouts from machines attached to my body. Then came the familiar face of Barnaby, wearing a new jet-black suit, silver-tinted sunglasses, and his usual stoic mask. Behind him shimmered the v-casting form of Erasmus. He glided across the room, his hands folded, and his face bearing an expression of relief. Vanessa entered next with a look of happiness and love. She approached, kissed my forehead, and held my hand.

"There is one final injection to administer," Dr. Okono said. "It's an immunosuppressant, a necessary precaution so he won't reject this serum treatment. It has to be in the neck. Jonah, this will only sting for a moment." He waited for approval. Barnaby looked to Erasmus, who nodded in consent, and Dr. Okono pulled forth a long syringe with a bluish-tinged fluid. He bent over my bed, drawing near to my head. The syringe pierced the flesh of my neck, just missing my carotid artery. Then Dr. Okono tapped his white wrist-com. I assumed he was monitoring my vitals. The TauK Network interface appeared, and I realized he sent me a private message.

<<I will settle my debt to you. Thank you, Jonah.>>

"All signs are stable," said the attending nurse, pointing to a holographic x-ray of my body, showing alternating updates on my circulatory, nervous, and endocrine systems.

"Better than stable, in fact. They're perfect," corrected Dr. Okono. "All signs of cellular degeneration are reversing. The serum is working."

Only visible to my eye, a different looking interface, tinged with a soft blue lettering, appeared with a welcome assessment of my health.

<<*JonahOS 1.0.* Serum levels at 100%>>

"Praise to Him. Thank you for your gift Dr. Okono," whispered Erasmus, invoking the sign of the cross with his hand. "How do you feel, my son?"

"Like I've been to hell and back," I responded, flexing my hands to increase circulation of my blood.

"An apt description," Erasmus agreed. "You have done a great service for your country and for many lost souls."

"Thank you," I muttered, still sore and feeling a pounding pain in my limbs, despite the doctor's upbeat appraisal of my condition.

"Speaking of souls," I asked, "what about Dr. Okono's research? What about the shades and the serum? What's going to happen?"

The room went dead silent. Everyone exchanged glances. Erasmus looked up, and Barnaby frowned.

"We convinced the Lunar Senate to stall Tomoe's rocket launches temporarily," Barnaby answered. "A summary of Okono's research is currently under review at our highest level of government. The corporations have hired their own teams of experts and lawyers. They have already attempted to discredit Okono--"

"Our brothers and sisters of the New Church are also evaluating the research," Erasmus interjected. "There are dissenters among us too, but I am confident truth will prevail. We will not support any further shade development if the research is verified. Which I suspect it will be."

"This is an extremely delicate situation." Barnaby added, "Before the IRS takes an official position, I'll need to deliver a full brief to the Deputy Chief. Then committees will form to order more reviews and referendums. This process...it will take time. Regardless of what Earth's decision is, the moon cities and the system colonies may invoke their autonomy. They will resist any changes to the status quo."

"And Gabriel?" I asked.

"We are pursuing charges against him. Goliath Corporation's Board of Directors has suspended him as CEO pending an inquiry. They are cooperating with the Lunar Senate, but as expected, they blame Spenner for the entire scheme. Gabriel will face sanctions, maybe, but putting him in prison will be...difficult. Especially with his family's veiled threats of secession."

"Most difficult indeed," Erasmus concurred.

"Which brings us back to you, Jonah," Barnaby said. "Your serum is different than the shades. Your body and soul are intact...but you will need more injections until your formula is perfected. If ever..."

Barnaby pushed an old-fashioned manila folder toward me. It spoke a volume that he still kept paper files in an age where a youth today would look at a sheet of paper and admire how thin the super-computer looked.

"That serum that's keeping you alive isn't cheap. And..." He paused for emphasis, opening the file to a spreadsheet highlighting itemized costs. It was a hefty bill for my hospital stay tacked onto an astronomical fee for the experimental serum coursing in my veins. "You owe your government. We need you to help us with a few more jobs to pay off your debt." Realizing that he sounded too gruff, even for Barnaby, his tough countenance softened. Then he sighed. "The truth is, you're one of the best. We need you, Jonah. The world needs you. Especially if we hope to make changes on Earth and on the moon..."

Ever uncomfortable with his counterpart's tough approach, Erasmus walked toward me with arms outstretched and a genuine look of empathy. "There are so many lost souls." His v-cast projected form flickered ever so slightly from the movement across the room. "Many of our trusting flock have been wrongfully sentenced to infinite service by the schemes of Gabriel and Ms. Gozen. These innocents...they must be set free. I know the work will be hazardous, but you will be well compensated. As for Vanessa, no matter what you decide, we would appreciate her counsel in the coming Reformation."

Barnaby and Erasmus continued to discuss details of their plans for me and how there would be big changes coming for both

Earth and space citizens. However, it became difficult to focus on them. Their voices quieted but their mouths continued to move. The entire room blurred around me. As they talked, Dr. Okono communicated with me through the private TauK Network.

"I injected you with an update to your serum," he said for my ears only. "The genetic coding in your serum is being re-programmed, so that Barnaby and Erasmus will not detect it. The first formula they administered to you was imperfect, requiring expensive, constant injections with progressively larger doses. Even with constant treatment, you would have died within two years. My new serum will correct those flaws. At this moment, the new injection I gave you is modifying your code to repair several critical bugs." It was difficult to put into words how receiving a software patch for my body felt, other than strange. Closing my eyes and focusing my mind, I responded using the TauK Network.

"Will I live?" I asked Dr. Okono, aware of how stupid that sounded only after the thoughts became words in the private network.

"You will die eventually, like all of us are meant to...but it will not be due to a defect in my new formula. God willing you will die of natural, old age. And when you do, my research, my damn cursed work, will die with you. Finally, this update also adds an important new feature improvement."

"What do you mean by 'feature'? I asked. Then another message flashed before my eyes.

<<ShadeOS. Execute removal program. Deleting ShadeOS>>

His final update to my ShadeOS was also the last. Dr. Okono removed my digital leash. He had set me free.

"The obedience algorithm, the ShadeOS, a core function in all serum formula...it was an integral part of your first treatment. However, at this moment, my update to your system is changing that. I give you a new Operating System. I give you back choice." When those words sunk in, I smiled. A sense of freedom and joy came over me.

"How can I repay you?"

"Live. Love. Choose. Help people as you see fit," he answered. "Barnaby wishes to compel you to do more work for the IRS. They will want to retire the shades whose timers had been extended for unlimited afterdeath. After that, maybe they'll want to save even more of them. One day, I hope all of the shades will find rest, so my name will not be stained forever. Perhaps their objectives will align with your desires...or not."

I nodded, taking a moment to grapple with Dr. Okono's message. Should it be my job to speed around space retiring overdue shades? Maybe as payback for a second chance at life, I needed to do more good? A rival thought encouraged me to abandon all responsibility and escape with Vanessa to the Lunar Spire. We could begin a new life.

"Whatever your decision, it will be the right one, and you will be free," Dr. Okono said with a warm smile. "I wanted to thank you for saving me and resurfacing the truth of my research. You can call me here if you ever need me again." A soft tap on my shoulder broke my concentration and the link to the TauK Network. Barnaby noticed my inattentive expression and looked irritated.

"Are you listening, Jonah?" Barnaby asked. "For a second there I thought you passed out on us. Now, where were we--"

"Perhaps we should let him sleep," Erasmus suggested. "He has endured so much. We can speak with him in the morning."

"You're right. Jonah, get some rest, and then set your affairs in order," Barnaby said, rubbing his wounded arm. "In a week, you and I will be heading to Mare Nubium. We suspect there's a group of expired shades in the new colony..." His voice was firm and forceful. It was the tone of an order from a master, one that anyone coded with the serum would need to obey.

I nodded, deciding not to divulge the change Dr. Okono made to my bio-chemistry. Tomorrow, I would walk out of the hospital room a free man. After a week, I would see if the serum's obedience protocol would activate and compel me to follow Barnaby's order.

After everyone left to let me sleep again, I realized I was late for my lunch date with Vanessa. Sasha was kind enough to hack a VIP table reservation tomorrow night at La Vie, the finest restaurant atop the Lunar Spire. With minimal effort, she made sure the bill would be sent to Barnaby. I was sure he would find a way to expense it...

CHAPTER 23
Epilogue

"Dawn, let the infant speak, let the child leap,
Sunrise, let the boy fly, let the mother cry.
Sunset, let the moonlight creep, let the father sleep,
Dusk, let that man come back to weep."
- Excerpt from "Unto Dusk And Other Poems", by Sasha

>> DATE: October 23rd, 2039. One month after Louisiana mission.
>> TIME: 10:52 PM.
>> LOCATION: Mons Ares settlement, Mars.

The red planet lived up to its name. Endless tracts of barren, rust-colored earth welcomed us while the slender deep-space shuttle descended. Unlike my last rocket trip, this time I enjoyed a comfortable paid seat like a typical passenger. Although the supply ship lacked first class luxury, I was able to enjoy the last of my smuggled beer and packaged dinner while the shuttle made a smooth landing onto the western hemisphere of Mars.

"To health and new adventures," Vanessa toasted. We both smiled and our glasses met, creating that pleasing clinking sound. It wasn't the top of the Lunar Spire like in my dreams, but it was close enough for me.

"I really appreciate that you came with me."

"Of course, Jonah," Vanessa replied with a warm smile. "I wouldn't let you face this alone. I'm here for you."

We departed the shuttle with a mixed group of prospectors, engineers, and star-struck pioneer colonists, all of them eager to create a new life on the next frontier. Unlike these passengers, I was not here for a new life, and I was not staying long.

At Mons Ares, the largest port on Mars, we walked beneath the domed town looking to hire a guide. The small town rested on a plateau, and consisted of a landing bay, a central defense tower, and a clutch of supply shops catering to the needs of settlers. Construction crews erected a steel barrier between the two sides of the nascent colony. Electronic displays suspended over the wall advised that shades were welcome on the west side, but not the east side. Perhaps these were signs of things to come? After a few inquiries, we found a miner who owned a ramble-rover capable of crossing the hard terrain of the Outer Boundary. Unlike the moon, Mars was years away from having an interconnected series of tubes and chutes.

"It'll cost twenty-five-hundred," said the guide in a gruff voice. I could barely see his thin lips through his thick salt and pepper beard. Fine red dust covered his once-white utility suit. "It'll take one day. You'll have to bring your own supplies...and I'm leaving in an hour. Mons Ares Control Tower is forecasting a big storm tomorrow. I don't want my ass twisting in an electric dust storm." His eyes narrowed while he waited to see if the terms were agreeable.

Two taps on my wrist-com transferred the money. Satisfied, he nodded and led us to his vehicle. Calling it a 'jalopy' would have been a kindness. Its dented, scarred chassis hinted at the treacherous terrain that vehicle had weathered. There were more patches than original tire showing on the wheels, micro-asteroid punctures covered the roof and hood, and the armored front bumper was bent from collisions with countless rocks.

"Will this even go five miles?" Vanessa whispered, smirking. I nodded and we entered the rover through a dented side hatch. With a grumbling roar, the fat-tired buggy lumbered down the winding mountain path out of Mons Ares. The jalopy lived up to its initial promise as the most uncomfortable ride imaginable. With its shock absorbers beyond repair long ago, Vanessa and I felt every bump along the grueling ride.

An hour into the trip, a video message from my mother flashed across my wrist-com. The news brought a wide smile to my face. The IRS agents had left her neighborhood. She thanked me for settling her bills. She concluded by saying she loved me, and that I needed to visit. Though I had a nagging doubt, Barnaby came through on his promise to clear her slate for my service. Now there was just one more matter to fix.

Every few miles, the onboard computer chirped our travel time estimates, reminding me of Sasha. She left my wrist-com ten days ago on her search to find the White Djinn. The evasion code we wrote together would keep her safe from the datanet's tracker hounds, I repeated to myself. We agreed to rendezvous in another week, and pool our talents if she had not found Oscar. To take my mind off worrying about her, I chatted with Vanessa about what we should do for our next vacation. Touching my wrist-com, she displayed a brochure for a tourism company specializing in off-world adventures. This one offered halo-jumps down the central, vertical chute of the Lunar Spire. I told her, with regrets, that I was retired from jumping out of buildings. We compromised on visiting Paris.

We watched the stars together for hours. The brother moons of Mars, Deimos and Phobos, perhaps curious about our journey, followed us as we scaled up and down red hills.

* * *

Swirls of glowing brown dust heralded the outer fringes of the coming storm. Pushing on, we drove to the next mining outpost on the furthest boundary of the settled territory. A rugged road, dug by the hands of a thousand shades, wove around the side of a massive rock outcropping and wound into a cave entrance. The rover's front lights illuminated the rough-hewn walls of the underground passage as we descended into the mine. A quarter-mile down, when the path slimmed too much, the guide stopped, and issued a stern warning.

"Yer' walkin' from here," he yelled over the echoing clatter of digging machines. "Get your business done in forty-five minutes. With or without you, I'm heading back to Mons Ares before that storm hits."

I gave a look to Vanessa, as if to say that I would be fine if she wanted to stay. She grabbed my hand, nodded, and followed me down to the last level of the cave. We passed another team of shades lifting large chunks of a black and gray ore.

At the bottom, we found our target. Standing in the middle of a pack of other diggers, I spied a tall shade in shabby, tattered utility clothes. Despite an emaciated form, his wide back and long arms hinted at the more muscular body he possessed during his former life. His massive hands ripped a chunk of sparkling rock from the wall without any apparent strain. I watched for several minutes, transfixed with this being before me. He worked with a dedicated purpose, doubling the output of all the others around him, a work ethic that afterdeath never quelled. My eyes focused on those large hands. I remembered them lifting me high in the air even when I was a teenager, supported by his strong back. When I was young, the gentleness of those strong hands comforted me with a touch to the shoulder after I had a bad day or the time I struck out at the plate during my team's playoff baseball game. Even in this sad state, my proud father showed the same drive that pushed him in life.

I went to him and whispered a private conversation. I uttered words for grief, words for love, words for peace, words for hope, and words for forgiveness. Then his servitude and pain ended with one bullet. I shed no tears for this mercy.

Vanessa and I walked out with plenty of time remaining to reach our guide. During the ride back, I considered my next move. I thought about helping the IRS full-time, saving shades cursed with infinite timers. Staring up to the sky, I considered David Solomon's offer for a job with Titan Tech. While thoughts of my future flitted through my mind, the dark pink surface of the Phobos moon skimmed near

Mars' surface. Deimos, twinkled further away, following its lunar brother. Those clockwork, celestial movements helped me forget my earthly concerns.

For now, I wanted to enjoy my freedom with Vanessa. Under this alien sky, I took her in my arms and kissed her the whole way back to Mons Ares, turning an uncomfortable trip back into a time of wonderful bliss. I felt like celebrating. I felt like living.

I had settled my debts.

THE END.

Acknowledgements

Many wonderful people supported me throughout the process of writing this book. In case I forgot someone, I offer a blanket THANK YOU to all my beta readers and friends who offered their time and sage advice.

Special thanks go to my parents who served as the first critics, editors, and fans. I could not have completed this book without you both. I love you. Also, I'd like to offer a heartfelt heap of appreciation to my dear friends, new and old. All of you spent time providing feedback, and it was invaluable. I'd like to thank the following people for their work, in no particular order than how they popped into my head: Elizabeth Dallaire, Richard Dallaire, Brendan Dallaire, Tricia Dallaire, Chris Whalen, Ron Lemen, Vanessa Lemen, Robert Mouck, Tommy Yune, John Nee, Jamey Scott, Scott Benefiel, Dan Gregoire, Farshid Almassizadeh, Renee Almassizadeh, Alex Bear, Chris Avellone, Mary DeMarle, Wilma Growney, Bill Growney, Ellen Long, Mark Long, David Costello, Dan Santat, Lars Liden, Dave Scarpitti, Jonathon Knight, Carlton Johnson, Kevin Hemmons, Kory Jones, Scott Faye, Gregory Ness, Frank Vitale, David Brin, Keith Kaisershot, Laura Crawford, Matt Weinhold, Steve Kim, Bryce Baker, Michael Rooney, Christina Pierce Rooney, Chris Allen, Kelly Jean Aker, TQ Jefferson, Jen Scarano, Mari Tokuda, Ed Byrne, Lee Borth, Tim Jones, Rafal Kania, Ross E. Lockhart, Joe Spencer, Matt Danzig, Michel Kripalani, and Matt McClure.

Of course, I would also like to thank you, the reader, for choosing my book. If you feel inclined, please visit me online to give your thoughts and reviews. I would love to hear from you!

About the Author

Eric Dallaire wrote his first book in 1995, the Strategy Guide for The Journeyman Project: Buried in Time for Prima Publishing. This led to a full time job at Presto Studios, a pioneer in the early CD-ROM adventure game genre. He became lead writer and designer of the acclaimed Journeyman Project adventure game series. Then Eric accepted the role of head writer for Activision, writing and producing Star Trek Hidden Evil and Away Team with Paramount Studios. Later, he formed his own mobile games studio and developed applications for Electronic Arts, Amazon, and other publishers. In 2005, he broke new ground with the Kindle, partnering with Amazon to create that platform's first interactive adventure novel. The sci-fi noir novel Dusk World became the first Kindle book to feature a nonlinear story with multiple endings based on reader choice. The digital novel rose to number 54 on the Kindle Top 100.

When he's not writing, Eric pursues the development of technologies to further educational causes. He co-founded TeachTown, a company with a mission to deliver online lessons and applied behavioral treatments for children with autism and special needs. He co-authored a study that showed TeachTown's intervention of behavioral science and game focused reward structure improved learning. More recently, he designed and produced Age of Learning's groundbreaking mobile application to teach English to Chinese students. If you'd like to read more about him, check out his site at www.ericdallaire.com for more updates.

About the Cover Artist

Ron Lemen is an illustrator, designer and instructor with an extensive client list. He lives in San Diego with his best friend and wife Vanessa who is also an amazing painter, designer and instructor. They are both whipped into shape by their pets Sadie and Zoe. They have their own school in Encinitas California.

www.revartacademy.com

He also teaches for:
Gnomon School
LAAFA
CGMA

To view more of his work, go to:
www.Lemenaid.blogspot.com

On Instagram: ronlemen, or you can follow his work on Facebook.

COMING SOON:

SHADES
CIVIL WAR

By Eric Dallaire

CPSIA information ca
Printed in the USA
LVOW07s235021081

451142LV00

5 181105